Praise for Adrenaline Rush

"This book grabbed my attention and didn't let go until I had read the whole thing. It takes you on a ride like no other. I felt totally connected with the characters."

Konstanz Silverbow–Author

"Twists and turns, non-stop action, and harrowing danger will keep you on the edge to the last page."

S. Tietjen–Reviewer

"Adrenaline Rush was fast moving and fun. Just when I thought I had it figured out, the plot took another unexpected turn and left me reeling"

J. Moore–Reviewer

"*Adrenaline Rush*–the next book in the Christy series–lives up to its title. From the very first chapter until the end, be prepared for an action-packed ride that will keep you guessing and leave you wanting more."

C. Anderson–Reviewer

"Christy is often at odds with her alias and the conflict between her and her assignment forces Christy to grow and stretch as a character. The villain of the novel is a raging madman so disturbing he could only be played by the likes of Sasha Baron Cohan."

S K Anderson–Author

"Combine a bizarre twist to the typical high school-type setting with a most colorful, yet nauseating villain, and this book can't help but live up to its name. I found the premise of Adrenaline Rush creative and intriguing.

I devoured the remainder of the book, experiencing multiple adrenaline rushes of my own."

Carolyn Frank–Author

"Christy's adventures have gotten better and better with each book, and *Adrenaline Rush* keeps this trend alive. With Christy older and wiser, she goes head-to-head with the most memorable villain yet while still delivering the action, adventure, and romance that have captured readers' hearts throughout the series."

Woiwode–Reviewer

"Well written, action packed thriller with just the right amount of romance. Clever plot twists to keep you on your seat. Loved it."

L. Sears–Reviewer

CINDY M. HOGAN

Other Books and Audio Books by Cindy M. Hogan

Watched
Protected
Created
Watched Trilogy
Gravediggers
Confessions of a 16-Year-Old Virgin Lips: First Kiss
Stolen Kiss
Rebound Kiss
Rejected Kiss

CINDY M. HOGAN

O'neal Publishing
Layton, UT

Adrenaline Rush

First Edition
Cover design by Novak Illustrations
Cover photography by Still Memories by Tomi
Cover model: Madeleine Coombs
Photographer: Karen Saffer
Edited by Charity West
Formatted by Heather Justesen

Layton, UT.

ISBN: 978-09851318-5-2

Library of Congress Control Number: 2013915131

Visit her at cindymhogan.com

Facebook page: Watched-the book

Twitter-Watched1

To those always seeking their next big thrill

Chapter 1

As I hurtled toward my destination at 500 miles an hour, I pulled out a notebook, placed it on the shiny mahogany table in front of me, and scribbled a quick to-do list. *Pick out an outfit. Get folders and notebooks. Switch into fourth period drama.* I chewed on the end of my pen. Oh yeah—just one more thing. *Get kidnapped.*

According to my pre-mission briefing, kidnappings were up in the States by five percent over the last five years. The significance of which didn't hit me until I found that the statistics for kidnappings had remained static for a good thirty years. The spike caught the attention of the FBI, and they put their best men on it. The problem? Right when they thought they'd discovered the pattern of the kidnappers, it seemed to change.

We hit some turbulence, and the force of it pulled me out of my reverie. I sucked in a deep breath, my hands resting on the soft leather side arms of my big comfortable seat as the Gulfstream jet jumped. I let the rollercoaster feeling wash over me like a wave, forcing myself to enjoy every last tingle. I only had this flight and a few hours tonight to assume my new thrill-seeking alias—the one that would lure the kidnappers and save the day before the pattern changed again. I might as well make the most of it.

There were four of us on board. I sat in a cluster of seats with Jeremy, my Division 57 handler. The two other agents I'd be working with, Agent Penrod and Agent Wood, sat in two similar chairs on the other side of the plane near the back. The smell of raspberries and cream still hung in the air from lunch.

I twisted the stud in my ear before brushing my hand through my long, inky-black hair. I couldn't wait to go back to being a blonde. Too bad my black hair was integral to the upcoming mission. I bit my lip and reminded myself that at least I'd been able to get rid of the lip ring and other piercings I'd had to wear for so long.

My eyes fell on Jeremy, the best protector ever, and I thought back to the first day we'd met. As a civilian, I'd just accidentally witnessed a horrific murder committed by terrorists, and he swooped in to protect me. He was serious about his job, too. He even took a bullet for me and then didn't hesitate to kill the terrorists who wanted me dead. I trusted him completely.

He set a file folder stamped Division 57 on the table sitting between us. He would be the one to protect me as I became the person the kidnappers would choose. I would be safe in the end. He smiled, and I tried to ignore the strong line of his jaw, his perfect nose, and his rumpled, light brown hair.

I grabbed for the file folder, reminding myself that he was my handler. The movement made me notice the faint tan line around my right ring finger. I squeezed my eyes shut, hoping it would help keep the stab of pain from my recent breakup with Rick from overcoming me. The hurt was still too raw to contemplate, but I couldn't help it. Sure, I hadn't met his stipulation of video chatting without fail every thirty days, but I was a spy in training, and while I'd missed one chat by a week, the last one had only been two days late. I had tried to comply, but if video chatting wasn't available wherever I was in the world, it wasn't available. End of story.

His words still cut me, though. *I can't handle it, Christy. If you can't keep a little promise like contacting me every thirty days, then this will never work. If, after I'm done with my training and you're still available, we'll talk then.* The look of hopelessness on his face on the screen was forever etched in my mind.

I rubbed the area on my finger where the promise ring he'd given me used to sit, and then quickly glanced at the papers in the file to distract myself. My photographic memory immediately filed their words, statistics, diagrams, maps, and the mission details away into a file in my brain named *Adrenaline Rush.*

I started to set the closed folder down, but I could feel eyes on me, so I opened it back up and then set it, open, on the table. My photographic memory was a major asset, but it wasn't something I liked to broadcast about myself. I made a point of appearing to study the material. I pointed to a paragraph on the first page and said, "So, the kidnapper takes eight kids—a girl and a boy that have red, blonde, black, and brown hair? From every school?"

"From the last three schools where they've abducted kids," Jeremy said. "The only commonalities between the kids seem to be their propensity for doing daredevil stunts and taking two of each, a girl and boy, with those basic hair colors."

I crinkled my nose. "It's like some sick twisted Noah's Ark tale." The group of eighteen-year-olds they wanted me to infiltrate was missing a key element: a black-haired girl.

"If there's only been three incidents, how did Division find a pattern?"

"All I know is that the kidnapper's MO apparently changes every six months to a year. Somehow, our computer guys were able to program some algorithms that pointed us to Roseburg High. The kidnapper is finally using a pattern we were able to find early enough to fight him. I think a lot of it was luck. I mean, at the last school he targeted, we identified two of the kids that were eventually kidnapped. Unfortunately, we didn't act fast enough that time."

"So, right now he's only taking complete sets of kids with particular hair colors?"

"Yes."

I would be the girl with black hair. The group I was supposed to infiltrate already had two people with the requisite hair colors except black. That, of course, meant that I would need to become a daredevil, too. I'd never been a thrill seeker, but would be now.

"It's crazy thinking Division was able to discover what school they were going to hit next. One day I need to learn more about computers and algorithms and all that stuff."

"I don't understand it all either but, it's not just the hardware that narrowed it down, it was the genius agents analyzing what the computers told them. Talia and Marcus are amazing. The FBI still hasn't figured it out. Which is probably good, because if they knew, they'd have to tell the public, and then the public would be paranoid and get in our way. This kidnapper is smart–and very hard to track."

"But now we'll get them." I smiled. The other two agents' eyes locked on me, and I could feel their skepticism. Anger grew inside me, red and hot. How dare they question my abilities? I swiveled in my leather seat, just slightly, and lifted my eyes to meet my soon-to-be fake parents' gazes, but they had already looked away.

Both shouted conservative by the way they looked. Agent Wood wore short, cropped, unstyled hair. His pants, pulled high, were cinched tight with a belt. His wire-rimmed glasses were pushed hard against his nose. Agent Penrod had big, frizzy hair, no makeup, and plain-styled clothes with pants all the way to her waist. There was no spark in their eyes. Instead, suspicion was etched there. Had years of spy work slowly scratched it in? I tried to convince myself it had nothing to do with me, but I knew it did.

I stayed twisted in my seat, facing the two agents, to dissuade them from staring or scrutinizing me. To them I was a freak, apparently. I perused the pages in the file again, pretending to study them, when in reality I was thinking about other things entirely. I wondered what it would be like to go back to high school now that I was a spy. I'd attended two high schools already, but never got the chance to graduate because terrorists had been hot on my trail, intent on murdering me. I guess it didn't matter if I graduated or not. But it would have been fun to be the valedictorian and speak at graduation.

Witness Protection hadn't been able to keep me safe back then. Only becoming a spy had. I smiled despite myself and chuckled a little. It blew my mind to think I was a spy. Would I be as good as Jeremy hoped I'd be? I wanted to be, that was for sure. I had to keep pushing the doubt away.

I turned the page in the file, pretending to examine it while, really, I was working on becoming Misha, my alias on this mission. I had to abandon safe and secure Christy and embrace wild, stunt-loving Misha. "Can't we just jump once we're close? This landing safely in an airplane on an ordinary tarmac is so completely boring. I've been sitting for six hours. Can't we do something fun?"

Jeremy picked up on my change in personality immediately and chuckled. "I don't think the parachute would hold all the weight of our gear. Nor could we hold it all."

"Have someone deliver it to us, then. I'm itching to fly." I shot at him, pleased with how naturally this personality was coming to me.

"Alright," he said, sending a shock wave of disbelief through me. "Good idea. I'm *itching* to fly, too."

I laughed. He didn't. He smirked at me, stood, and headed for the cockpit. My smile turned to a horror-filled frown. I tried to send it away and be carefree Misha, who would love the chance to jump, but I couldn't muster any excitement. After only a few minutes, he sauntered back to me.

"We can jump in about three hours," he said, grinning from ear to ear. "The pilot will fly low, letting us out in an area that is safe and flat."

"Are you serious?" It felt like my eyes might pop out of my head.

"Totally."

"I've never jumped before." I knew I'd broken cover already, letting scaredy-cat Christy in, but I couldn't stop myself. I was really scared. I twisted my palms together.

"There's a first time for everything, and I'm sure you'll be doing a lot of firsts on this mission. Where'd fearless Misha go, anyway?" He sat and started tapping a pencil on the pages in the file.

"Thanks, Jeremy," I beamed with exaggerated enthusiasm. "I'm so excited to jump!" A million worms seemed to be exploring my insides.

He laughed out loud. "Don't worry, I'll train you first. You'll love it."

My mind went to module 17.7 from the Bresen Academy: Parachuting Basics. I mentally flipped through the pages in my brain easily, and it calmed my fears a little bit, enough to let me overhear my new parents' whispers.

"If they failed with trained agents, what are they expecting to happen using a child?" Agent Wood was saying.

"She's supposed to be a prodigy in some way," Agent Penrod said.

"She must have connections somewhere, but I don't know why they'd send her on a suicide mission."

"It's not right to put us in the middle of it, either. I heard Henry set us up on this one as some kind of joke."

"He can be such a jerk. He's always wanted to see us fail. Not this time. We won't let her pull us down with her. That's for sure."

"We'll have to hold her hand the whole time."

I leaned across the table to Jeremy and whispered, "How can I work with a team that doesn't believe in me?"

My eyes darted from them to Jeremy and back.

"You didn't think it'd be easy to come out here as the youngest agent of Division 57, did you?"

"Maybe," I said, sulking a bit. "You know how stubbornly optimistic I am."

"To a fault, actually," he said, the grin returning to his face. "Despite that, you're going to have to prove yourself. Like it or not. However, I won't allow you to become reckless in the pursuit of acceptance."

"I'm never reckless."

He shook his head. "Yeah, never. Only when it comes to proving yourself. Seriously, this is your first real mission, and I intend on having you not only live through it, but be victorious."

I began to protest—I had been on missions at the Bresen Spy Academy, but he cut me off.

"I know you've been on 'exercises.' But in truth, your hand was being held while you did them. You're on your own, now. It's all up to you. You have to act as if there's no one to save you. You have to rely on you and you alone."

"What about my 'team'?" I asked, making quotation marks in the air as I said it. "And is there a blinking neon sign announcing to the world that I'm only eighteen?"

"They may not know exactly how old you are, it's not like they've seen your file, but everyone at Division knows you're the youngest agent, and they're all curious about you. They know Division wouldn't pick you up without knowing you're accomplished, but they're worried it won't translate into real-world spying.

"They're also skeptical that someone so young could be as accomplished as you are. I'm betting you can understand that. They don't want to fail because of your inexperience. Also, I'm thinking a bit of jealousy is raging within them. I'm sure it took them years to get their first high-level case, and here you are, going on your first real mission—and it's a high-level one. While it's important to use your team when you need them, I wouldn't completely rely on them. Count on yourself. You can, however, rely on me." He grinned a mischievous smile.

I snorted. I already knew that. He'd saved my hide several times already. I also knew the thing that separated me from them was my photographic memory. It gave me an edge in everything, including the spy world. I subconsciously rubbed my upper arm between my armpit and the crook in my arm, where two days ago, Division 57 had inserted a tracking device. I was glad it wasn't sore anymore.

Jeremy didn't miss it. "Just remember to activate that tracker in your arm for no longer than ten seconds, then deactivate it. It only takes a light tap. Either use your other hand to do it or press your entire upper arm against your ribs. When you've gotten the information we need, just tap it twice quickly, and we'll be on our way to extract you."

"No worries," I said. "I got it." I thought about this whole new level of incognito I'd attained. If I thought I didn't exist two years ago when the FBI erased me, I was way off the map now. It was my job not to exist. At least, not as a normal person.

"Why don't we practice your walk, talk, attitude, and—*jump*?" Jeremy said with a light hearted laugh.

"Okay," I said, trying to pretend I wasn't the least bit nervous about the jump anymore.

We practiced for a good hour before Jeremy said, "I'm going to call your agent parents over so we can discuss a few things before we jump."

A jolt went through me. I was really going to jump from an airplane.

Agent Wood and Agent Penrod came over and sat in the other two seats next to us.

"I'm assuming you've had time to go over your assignments," Jeremy said.

We all nodded. Agent Penrod crossed her leg and then pumped the one on top up and down, up and down, her lips pressed together. Agent Wood sat ramrod straight, his wire spectacles sitting loosely on his nose.

"Great," Jeremy said. "The basics, then. You are a cozy little family—the Robertses. Your mission, Agents Wood and Penrod, is to support Agent Hadden..."

My heart flipped hearing him call me Agent Hadden. It was thrilling.

Jeremy continued, "as her parents and help her as agents as she seeks to join a group of risk-takers at Roseburg High. Once included, she will make herself stand out in the group in hopes of being chosen as one of eight students to be kidnapped by the kidnapping ring. There are already nine in the target group, Madness, we discovered at the high school. They lack a black-haired girl. Christy will be that black-haired girl.

"We believe that once Christy is included in the group, the kidnappers will act quickly. Christy has a tracker inside her left arm that she can turn off and on to let us know her position without transmitting continuously and possibly giving herself up if she were ever wanded by some electronic device searching for trackers or wires."

"So," I said, "will all four of us meet regularly?"

"You," Jeremy said, "will fill Agent Wood and Agent Penrod in on a daily basis. They will then pass on any intel they got during the day from myself and Division. They will also be there to help you in whatever capacity you need. You will meet with me a minimum of once a week. Just remember that any communication must be sent over secure pathways or be coded. Make sure to use proper protocol when setting up meetings or communicating. Understand?"

"Yes," the three of us said in unison.

"Once kidnapped, Christy will let us know her position using the device in her arm. She will then uncover the reason these teens are being taken and press her locator again twice, indicating she is ready to be extracted. We will send a team to extract her and shut down the kidnapping ring.

"Any questions?"

The agents stared hard at me. I stared back. Inside, I was a mess, but I couldn't let them know that.

"Are you sure you're up for this?" Agent Penrod asked, skepticism in the crease of her brow.

"Of course," I said, pressing my lips tightly together to prevent them from quivering. While this scared the pants off me, I was ready.

"Nothing is ever as easy as it seems," she continued.

"I'm ready," I said with as firm a tone as possible and never taking my eyes off hers.

"You're out of line, Agent Penrod. Agent Hadden is a full agent and deserves respect. If you are having trouble recog-nizing this, I can get you reassigned."

Her face turned to stone. "No need."

I'm sure she was thinking that getting *reassigned* never looked good in your file.

"So, Mr. and Mrs. Roberts, we will meet you at the house. Misha is about to do her first daredevil act: skydiving."

The two of them smirked at me like they were sure I'd chicken out. Jeremy suited up and helped me do the same, but he seemed to be having trouble meeting my eyes.

"What is it?" I demanded in a whisper.

He whispered back, "You know, you don't have to do this. There are young-looking agents who could probably pull it off."

"Are you kidding me, Jeremy? You're not doubting me, too, are you?" I made sure the other agents were far enough away that they couldn't hear us. I couldn't believe he was suddenly telling me this. It made me nervous. He'd always believed in me before.

"No, no, no. That's not what I'm saying. I just don't want you to get hurt. What if something goes wrong when you're kidnapped, and I can't find you? Things happen all the time and even to very seasoned agents. In fact, it already did. The last mission to infiltrate this group was a major failure. It has nothing to do with my belief in you. Things just go wrong. You can back out now. No one would blame you."

"No way, Jeremy," I said. "I'm ready, and we're going to stop this kidnapping ring. We're unstoppable as a team, right?"

He shook his head but said, "Yes, but I want you to be ready for anything. I don't want you to think this will be easy. Anything could happen. Anything. Are you prepared for that?"

Part of me did want to bail, but a greater part of me wanted to succeed. "I am prepared. But, nothing will happen, Jeremy. Together we can do this and do it well. Please. I need you to believe in me."

"I do. I will support you and help keep you safe." The words were right, but he said it in a defeated way that didn't make me feel much better. I wondered how I could be successful on this mission when my team didn't trust me, my handler didn't trust me, and I didn't totally trust me. Once the plane slowed, Jeremy took me to the open hatch, my soon-to-be parents standing to the side, ready to close it after the jump. Then, without looking out or down, I jumped. I didn't hesitate. *Take that, doubters.*

Chapter 2

I forgot everything I'd read and that Jeremy had just taught me about skydiving. Terror gripped me for I don't know how long, but it couldn't have been more than thirty seconds. I had to pull the cord at one minute. All the organs in my body flew into my throat, and I couldn't breathe. My firmly shut eyes longed to open, but I couldn't do it.

Something grabbed my hand, bringing me back to myself. I opened my eyes. Jeremy was now reaching for my other hand. My eyes held his, and I refused to look anywhere but at him. I took a deep cleansing breath, concentrating on pushing the air out and in. The sensation of falling seemed to leave me as Jeremy smiled, and I found a smile to give him.

A bell rang in my ears, and an echo of Jeremy's voice reminded me that meant I needed to pull the cord within the next few seconds. Jeremy took my hand and put it on the cord. He winked and pushed away from me. Then he held up one finger. Then two, then three, and he nodded at me, pretending to pull his own cord, reminding me of what I needed to do. He nodded again, and I pulled. I don't know where I got the sense of mind to do it, but I did. The chute yanked me up higher in the sky, and I screeched with sudden delight.

I laughed out loud when the chute evened out and my descent slowed. It seemed I'd become a dandelion seed floating gently to the earth. I searched for Jeremy. He was a little bit above me and to the left, and it looked like he was laughing, too. What had started with sheer terror had turned into an extremely exciting moment. He motioned with his hands for me to look down.

When I did, the ground was coming up fast so I looked back at him. He used his hands to remind me to flare. Once I did, the parachute breaks jerked me up and at a slight angle. Right before I landed, it seemed the earth moved up to greet me instead of me it. I thought I might splatter, I was moving so fast. My feet hit hard, harder than I'd anticipated, and I sat, pushing my butt hard into the grass-covered earth. I laughed at myself as the chute floated to the ground next to me. I unhooked it. Jeremy landed only moments after and it seemed a graceful, easy landing. Totally not fair. After unhooking his chute, he made his way over to me and sat next to me.

"I thought I'd lost you there for a second." He looked me directly in the eyes.

I looked away. "I thought I'd lost me, too."

He started to laugh, and so did I. We both lay back and laughed and laughed for a good long while. He looked at his watch and said, "We better grab our chutes and get moving. Our extraction point is twenty minutes by foot, and they're expecting us in fifteen."

I sat up, grabbed his large, tan hand and said, "Thanks! That was the scariest thing I've ever done. And close to the best thing."

He stood up, still holding my hand and helped me stand. "Not for long." He winked. It was suddenly weird that I'd grabbed his hand, and I casually pulled it away even though a part of me wanted to never let go.

The next morning, I climbed out of my red Miata in the school parking lot thinking about how crazy it was to be putting myself right in the grasp of the kidnappers. I'd been taught my whole life to avoid this kind of people at all costs, and now I was running straight into their arms. I hopped on my longboard and casually glided down the sidewalk toward the school. I could feel the stares of the students at Roseburg High as I maneuvered carefully through the crowd, red cowboy boots in hand. I crossed my fingers that I wouldn't face plant and make a fool of myself. I needed this. Several of the kids in the daredevil group I was targeting loved to longboard.

Last night, as Jeremy taught me, we learned I wasn't that good at it, and I about gave up on the idea, but Jeremy insisted this would give me another point of contact with the group I needed to join. I figured if I bombed it, I could just tell people I got the board yesterday and was learning how to use it.

When I reached the main building, I grabbed the longboard and made my way up the steps in my yellow and red sundress with large red belt and huge brass buckle, red Vans, fake tattoo behind my ear, and fire engine red nail polish on my fingers and toes. I went for a sexy, flirty look that was sure to catch the guys' attention. The trick was in pulling off a cavalier attitude while remaining fun, friendly, and carefree. Excitement set in at the reality that I was about to forge a new path through my third high school. I sat on a bench just outside the main building and switched from the Vans to my red boots.

I'd never had to flirt before, so Jeremy and I had practiced as we'd hurried to the extraction point and for a short while at my new home. I felt like an idiot, but his response to my efforts made me feel confident. His nods, smiles, and laughter helped me feel beautiful, amazing, and carefree, as well as a bit guilty for letting him make me feel that way. I just had to remind myself that I was playing a part and it wasn't real.

As I walked to the office using the strut Jeremy and I had also worked on yesterday, boys whistled and cat called, and I knew I had made the splash I needed. I had less than a month to find the daredevils of the school, secure an invitation to join them, and have the kidnappers choose me as the black-haired adrenaline junkie of the group.

After checking in at the office, a senior ambassador showed me around the campus. We left the building we were in that housed the office, counselors, and the career center and made our way to the fine arts center. Not only did it have the theater in it, but also the cafeteria and fine arts classrooms. It was crawling with students who stared and whispered when they saw me. The senior ambassador showed me my locker, and after opening it, I dropped off my Vans. I carried a pen and notebook, nothing else.

Our next stop was the commons. It was packed with kids of all shapes and sizes, too. It surprised me that the population of Roseburg, 20,000, could support such a big high school. The library and media center sat under the roof of the commons and, of course, there was a gym.

The open, airiness of the campus was comforting. The ambassador left me at the door of my first class and gave me the school map to keep. She hadn't made an ounce of small talk. Once she walked away, I looked at the map and threw it into the nearest trashcan. One glance was all I needed to remember it, and it matched the one Division had given me.

My first class was English. I sat at the back of the class so that I could watch as everyone came in. I recognized two of the girls in Madness as they entered, Tarran and Mindy, both redheads. They made their way to the other side of the room by the windows. A few people smiled at me, and the girl sitting next to me said hello, but did nothing more to welcome me. After Mrs. Richardson called the class to order, she said, "Looks like we have a new student everyone. Misha, could you stand and introduce yourself?"

Heat rushed to my cheeks. I didn't expect this. I pushed the awkwardness of the moment to the side and stood. "I'm from Denver, Colorado, and I love doing wild stuff." I knew the second the words left my mouth that I'd regret them.

Several girls in the class snickered, and a few boys that sat near me whispered some inappropriate things to me. That had been a bust. Both Tarran and Mindy had been looking out of the window the whole time. I spent the rest of the class refusing all sorts of advances and sexual innuendo in notes from various boys in class.

Luckily, the science teacher, Mr. Edmondson, didn't feel the need to introduce me. I located two other guys from Madness: Tate and Camden, both blond. I was assigned to a group of two girls to work on a dissection. The only interesting thing that happened was listening to a boxy boy in the group next to us, who was apparently named Houston. He had crazy reddish black hair and seemed to enjoy everything about cutting up and examining the frog. That boy was nuts. He continuously talked about how cool it would have been to do this or that to a live frog. I tried to catch up with both Tate and Camden at the end of class, but their group had finished before ours and I just missed them.

My next class was drama, and I had to step up my game. I would approach at least one of the three adrenaline junkies in that class. If they wouldn't come to me, I would go to them.

There weren't any seats in the large, open room, so I made my way toward the edge of the makeshift stage where other kids were hanging out. I chose a spot nearest my three targets and casually pulled myself up onto the stage, letting my pencil slip from my hand. It rolled and softly bounced against the shoe of one of the boys, who had his back to me. He leaned to retrieve it, and as he handed it to me, I nearly gaped at his angular, strong jaw, tan skin, midnight black hair, and brilliant white teeth.

"Here ya go," he drawled. I just stared, tongue-tied. His picture hadn't done him justice.

He turned one corner of his mouth up in a smile and chuckled a little, then leaned against the stage next to me. I gave my head a quick jerk and reminded myself I was supposed to be confident, fun, and flirty, not awe-struck by the first hot guy I saw. He was the kind of beautiful that made you have to turn away and compose yourself before looking a second time.

I pulled it together, put the eraser of the pencil he'd just handed me between my teeth, and crossed my legs, making my light, flirty dress dance over them. I watched his eyes go from my red boots up to the hem of my flowery dress, just above my knee. His eyes finally rested on my face. I clicked the pencil between my teeth and smiled in thanks.

"So, you're the new girl I've been hearing so much about," he said, his husky, masculine voice falling hot on my ears. I'm sure he made all the girls fall all over themselves. What was it with my hormones lately?

"That depends on what you've heard," I said, turning my head to look at him straight on and biting hard on the pencil, hoping it would help me feel more courageous.

He threw his head back and laughed and then looked back at me. "Only that you were hot. The jury's still out on what you're all about. I'm Ian."

He raised his eyebrows as if he wanted my name, but the teacher, Mrs. Anderson, called the class to attention.

"Hello, hello, actors! Yes, I see some of you have met the intriguing Misha. A new actor is among us! Perhaps our next Desdemona or Elizabeth Proctor. It's exciting indeed, but I'll not excuse you for chattering away instead of preparing your minds and souls for the immersion into character. Remember: 'oftentimes excusing of a fault doth make the fault the worse by the excuse.' That's Shakespeare–King John–and you'd all do well to memorize it."

All eyes fell on me as Mrs. Anderson continued her monologue, and I allowed myself to look a bit embarrassed. I ducked my head and took the notebook and the pen to put them to good use by writing Ian a note.

Have you ever been sky-diving?

I slid the notebook, nice and slow, toward him. He pulled a pen from his pocket and wrote, *Of course,* before handing it back to me.

You know that feeling you get, right after you jump? The one that screams that you are dead or soon will be? That's what I'm all about. What are you all about?

I watched his eyes read the words I'd written and saw him clench his jaw and take a hard swallow before writing,

You'll just have to see.

The file indicated he was the most likely leader of Madness and probably the one recruiting for the kidnapper. It was easy to see why they came to this conclusion. I winked at him, just a nervous reaction, but he winked back. I felt ridiculous.

Mrs. Anderson's voice caught my attention again. "Today, actors, we will be honing our skill with acting out everyday tasks. Stage presence is communicated through our bodies, not our words! Everything must be completely natural and fluid." She waved her arms as if in a dance the entire time she spoke. She started handing out cards, each with a task or series of tasks on it, which we were to act out without using any words. "This isn't charades, people," she called out. "Make it real, make us *feel* your actions, *bring* us into your world."

I looked at my card. I had to act out getting out of bed and getting ready for school. Everyone was very thoughtful about the process and acted out the instructions step by step. I knew exactly what each person acted out. They were great. I was third to last and thought I might dodge the bullet and not have to act mine out because class was almost over, but there was time.

I took the stage, nervous butterflies fluttering in my stomach. I knew I had to play it cool. Misha lived boldly, and she would never back down from the chance to perform. I pushed down the butterflies and began my pantomime by batting at a pesky alarm. I acted out each aspect of getting ready, throwing in as much flair and personality as possible. I wasn't just getting ready for school. I was Misha getting ready for school. And Misha had personality in spades. Cort, the agent who had taught me the most about disguise and playing a part, would have been proud. As I finished, my classmates' applause was cut off by the bell indicating the end of class.

I took a bow, then hopped off the stage and quickly headed for the door. I wanted to see if Ian would pursue me. He didn't disappoint. About half way to the lunchroom, he caught up with me.

"I thought you wanted to get to know what kind of a guy I am." Ian leaned up against the wall of lockers and looked at me thoughtfully.

"Oh, sorry!" I said, my face heating up. I continued down the hall to the cafeteria. He followed me. "I do, it's just, when I get hungry, I kind of lose my brain." I kept walking, figuring he would continue to chase me because no girl in her right mind would ever walk away from him.

"We can't have that now, can we?" he said, taking my arm and leading me to the cafeteria. We headed for the turkey sandwich line. After I'd ordered, he ordered too, and, then paid for both our meals. Was he already recruiting me? I could only hope.

"You really didn't need to pay for me. I have money." He'd only met me an hour ago, and he was already being so nice. I guessed he wanted something from me. Why else would he be so chivalrous? He led me to a table with seven other kids, some with home lunches and others with food they'd bought at school. Everyone stopped talking and looked back and forth from Ian to me until he introduced me to everyone.

"These are my friends, Camden, Troy, Tate, Jensyn, Mindy, Abby, and Tarran."

Each said hi in turn, and I nodded.

"And I expect you to remember everyone's names," Ian nodded and chuckled.

Everyone else laughed. Of course, I did remember their names. I'd already seen pictures of them in Division 57's file, and I'd seen all of them in my first three classes.

"Misha, here," Ian said, as I sat at the round table, "likes to fall from the sky."

They all hollered out 'boorah' in apparent appreciation, and several either put up a hand for a high-five or gave me a fist to hit. I sat and tried to listen to everyone tell all at once about this time or that when something cool happened when they jumped. I paid close attention to what they said, looking for clues for anything to contradict my assumption that Ian was the group leader.

Jensyn had brown shoulder-length hair and a cute button nose. She had jumped in Brazil into some old ruins.

Abby was the blonde and had only tandem jumped. She'd been so unsteady, she caused her instructor to face plant it. She was vivacious, spontaneous, and fun and laughed along good-naturedly as the others teased her for falling.

Troy was lanky and sported black hair. He loved to ride motocross. He had jumped with his bike strapped to him and once he landed, he stood up and rode away.

Camden, one of the blond boys from science, kept to himself. Would the kidnappers choose Camden or Tate? Both were blond. I bit into my sandwich and noticed that there were four girls at the table, not including me, and four guys. Only one person was missing. The last guy finally came, grabbing a chair from another table and stuffing it under ours.

"Mrs. Woiwode's such a beast," he said, sitting down. "She made me clean up all the crap people had dropped on the floor all day, just because I was tardy to her class. My first time, too. I had no idea." His green eyes pounced on mine, and his liquid voice smothered me in chocolate. He ran his hand over his wild, yet somehow perfectly styled, light brown hair. "Well, who's this?" he asked, tilting his chin in my direction and looking me straight on for several agonizing seconds, before Ian answered.

"She's the new girl, Misha."

"Well, Misha," he said. "Welcome to Madness." He said it in a fun, flippant way. His eyes never left me the rest of the lunch hour, but no one bothered to tell me his name. It didn't matter, I already knew it. Dakota. I felt like a particularly great-looking bug that had caught the attention of a determined crow. I tried to ignore his continuous stare by listening to everyone talk about skydiving and all the cool places they'd like to go to jump. Relief filled me as the bell rang.

"What do you have now?" Ian said.

"Gym."

"Cool." He flicked a thumb at the green-eyed boy. "Dakota has gym right now, too. Don't cha, Dakota?"

"Yep!" He looked at me and then nodded his head toward the door like he wanted me to follow him.

My foot caught on the table leg as I tried to stand up, and I tripped. Ian grabbed me by the waist before I fell. My face must have created a new shade of red.

"Thanks," I said, keeping my head down and then grabbing his hand and giving it a squeeze to show him I was truly thankful even though I didn't look at him.

"No problem," he said. "We've all taken a spill because of those awful table legs at some point." I didn't know if he was telling me that just to make me feel better or if it was true. At the moment, I didn't care. I just appreciated his effort at making me feel less dumb. Dakota chuckled, and I felt my face fire up again as I followed him out into the hall. Dakota and Ian were by far the best looking guys in the group, and somehow I'd managed to get noticed by both in a very short amount of time.

It shocked me when Dakota grabbed my elbow and pulled me out the front doors of the school. I noticed his hand was a bit sweaty. Was he nervous? After letting go, he rifled through a bush and pulled out his longboard. "Hop on," he said.

"Alright!" I said as I hopped on the back of the longboard, trying to hide the prickly fear filling my chest. In the files, the profiler for Division had suggested I get together with Dakota. A relationship would solidify Misha's entrance into the group, and Dakota was supposedly the most compatible with Misha. They were right. He made my heart pound. He put his feet on the board next to mine and pulled my arm around his waist while he put his arm around my shoulders. If the board hadn't been under our feet, it would have looked like we were walking down a sidewalk, side by side. A tremor went up my spine.

"Put your other arm out," he said.

I obeyed, throwing my arm out to my side as he leaned toward the front of the board, sending us shooting down the steep sidewalk toward the gym.

He then pulled us to a sweet stop by grabbing onto the flagpole, sending us around and around.

I yelled out. At some point, he moved his arm from my shoulders and put it around my waist before pulling me off the board. It shot off into the bushes, leaving us standing, squished together near the pole. Nervous energy had me turning around to face him, thinking that he would remove his hands from my waist and take away the heat spreading through my gut. But he kept his arm around my waist as we walked, side by side up the steps. I giggled.

He then rushed forward to open the door to the gym for me. I gasped, letting my eyes go wide. "Why thank you, kind sir," I said with a curtsey. He gave an outrageously elaborate bow in return. Was he always so nice to girls? He made me feel special, and I liked it. Once inside the gym, he said, "That's your stop," and pointed to the door that read, *Girls*.

"Thanks," I said, smiling up at him.

"Any time." He pulled away, and I watched him walk to the boys' locker room. Before he entered, he looked back at me, smiled and waved me toward the girls' locker room.

I could still feel the heat from his arm around my waist as I pushed my way into the room. I hadn't expected to have such strong feelings for Dakota, especially not so quickly. I told myself to be professional and just do my job. Behind the door was your typical, run-of-the-mill locker room with girls changing into PE clothes and talking excitedly. Fruity smells of hairspray and deodorant filled the air.

I went straight for the coach's office, and she gave me the school uniform and my locker number with the combination to open the lock. The locker room was empty by the time I'd changed. I thought about the Vans in my locker in the commons, but since I didn't have any tennis shoes with me, I stuffed my feet back into my red, leather boots and clopped my way into the gym.

The students were doing jumping jacks, led by a student leader. I headed for the coach who directed me to the last row, fifth from the center on the girls' side. As I walked in that direction, the clomping of my boots finally caught her attention, and she called out, "Ms. Roberts, I'm sure you took gym in your last school, and I'm sure you were never allowed to wear such *interesting* footwear to class. Please follow me back into my office, and we'll see if we can't find something in the lost and found to accommodate those feet of yours."

Many in the class laughed. I took a bow before following her. I tried on several pairs of shoes and socks until I found ones that fit. It surprised me that someone had abandoned such a good pair of Adidas running shoes. The cute boots headed to the locker, and then I entered the gym.

I looked around for Dakota and spotted him in the middle of the guys' side of the gym. I watched his biceps bulge as everyone switched to pushups. I spotted him looking at me upside down at the height of the pushup, giving me a toothy grin. That's when I noticed I was the only one standing. I hurried to the floor and, since he was staring, I decided to show off a bit. In perfect form, I knocked the pushups out, catching up with the count of twenty push-ups before the leader even got to seventeen. I got up and grinned at him.

He sat and nodded at me. His approval felt good. I hoped this would help me hook up with him as quickly as possible.

The coach's voice rang out, "You'll be tested on the mile next week, so today I'll be timing you to see how you've improved from the first time. You'll need to improve your time if you want to get a passing grade next Friday."

Coach motioned to me as the student's filed out toward the track. "You're a bit behind, so we'll have to get you caught up with the other students. This will be your initial try, and you'll have until next Friday to improve your score."

I nodded and made my way out to the track, lining up with the other students to start the race. The coach blew her whistle, and we began running. At the start, I kept to the middle of the pack as I debated what my best plan would be to keep Dakota's interest in me. Then I felt a hand grab mine and quickly release it. Dakota ran past me, then turned and yelled back, "See ya at the finish line," a slight note of question, but mostly challenge, in his voice.

I would take his challenge. He was already at the first curve of the track when I took off and quickly caught up with him. Then I passed him, yelling over my shoulder, "Yeah! See ya at the finish line." Becoming a spy had done wonders for my physical body. It was a lean, powerful machine.

He was huffing by the time he caught up with me. I thought about speeding up a tad, just because I could, but a look behind us showed me just how far ahead of the rest of the class we were, and I slowed slightly. We finished together and lay on the grass, laughing.

"It'll be hard to improve on that, Ms. Roberts," Coach said, looking down on me. "You might have kept a slower pace and not gone full out until next Friday's test." She walked away.

I pretended to breathe hard and look tired, slugging Dakota and saying, "Thanks a lot!"

"Don't blame me, Speedy Gonzales," he said. "You're the one who set the pace."

"Well, you're the one who challenged me," I said. "I had to go for it." I sat up, still pretending to work hard to catch my breath and said, "Don't you love it?"

"Love what?" he said.

"The feeling you get after doing something thrilling, like running faster than you ever have?"

"Yes, I do," he said. "Yes, I do." He stared hard at me. I hoped he was thinking how great I'd be in his group. We watched the others trickle in. Several girls gave me the evil eye and then plopped down on the grass next to Dakota and flirted with him. I turned away, watching the walkers, the ones who didn't care if they failed gym, make their way to the end. When the bell rang, without looking at him, I moved toward the locker room.

When I came out, he was waiting for me.

"Your chariot awaits," he said, throwing his arm out for me to go out the door we'd entered before class.

He pushed me up the hill on the longboard back to the front of the school, and we ran inside to go to class.

Chapter 3

After school, I grabbed my longboard and Vans out of my locker and, after swapping my boots for the Vans, I skated to my red Miata. I threw the board in, and just as I was taking my seat, Ian opened the passenger door and sat inside.

"Any plans?" he asked.

"Whatcha have in mind?" I asked, and though my voice was completely casual, as though it was totally normal for hot guys to hop into my car unbidden, my heart was racing. The thrill of success bolted through me. I'd done something right. Ian was hot on my trail. Exactly what I needed. It appeared that I'd caught the attention of the most likely leader of Madness. If I found favor with him, I'd be in.

"We're going for a ride. Wanna come?" When he pointed his thumb toward the back window, I saw of group standing next to a Jeep, waiting for him. It looked like the same kids from lunch. Dakota stood next to the driver's door. They all watched us expectantly.

I was getting more and more convinced that Ian was the leader. He was the take charge kinda guy. The Division file had stated that the recruiter was most likely an older boy posing as a student and that he would run the show. Ian looked too old to still be in high school, *and* he'd been the one who spoke to me in drama class, *and* now he'd invited me to ride with them.

"Sure." I said. "Should we follow them?"

"Yep." His massive body looked comical in my tiny Miata. He raised his hand above his head and made a lasso movement with his arm. All the kids around the Jeep scattered, filling it and one other car. I put the little car in drive and followed them up into the hills near downtown, and we parked by a field full of horses.

"Horses?" I asked. "We're riding horses?"

"Ever ridden?"

"Nope," I said.

"This is gonna be fun," he said, getting out of the car and walking toward the others. "We have ourselves a virgin, guys."

I bowed. They all whooped and hollered, climbing up on the white fence and sitting on top. One of the girls sprang over with a rope in hand and walked toward the horses.

"Watch and learn," Ian said. "That's Jensyn."

I leaned on the fence. "Are they wild horses?"

"Sure are," he said.

I swallowed hard, not sure if I believed him. I would have to pay attention and pretend to be awed, not scared, just in case.

I watched Jensyn, her brown, shoulder length hair bounced as she twirled the rope above her head and let it fly once within about fifteen feet of the horse's black, shiny head. Once the rope was around its neck, she pulled gently on the rope, cinching it tightly around the horse's neck. She then rubbed the horse's nose, grabbed ahold of his mane, took a few quick steps, and pulled herself up, throwing one leg over its tall back. She kept one hand in its mane and one holding the rope as it took off running. She screamed out.

I was suddenly glad I'd worn tiny shorts under my little skirt. Camden and Troy were next, and they did the same thing with ease. It was kind of funny seeing Camden and Troy together. They looked nothing alike, one boxy, the other lanky.

Movies had made wild horses look much harder to rope. Did they just overdo it in the movies, or were these horses tamer than Ian had led me to believe? I felt a rope being pressed into my hand. Dakota stood next to me grinning.

"About ready?" he asked.

"Maybe after the next few go," I said, still feeling completely unsure.

"Watch the next two, and then we'll be up."

"We'll?" I wasn't going to have to do this alone?

"I'll be in there with you since it's your first time." He leaned in closer. "I tied your rope for you," he whispered into my ear, his breath tickling my neck.

"Thanks," I said, relieved, but trying not to show it.

I watched both Ian and Mindy rope and mount their horses, then Dakota gave me the run-down of the parts of the rope. "You want to hold the tail in your left hand because you're right handed." He showed me with his rope, and I did the same. "Hold your other hand right outside the honda, next to the circle of rope. The space between the tail and the honda should be about shoulder length apart. You want your circle to be almost as tall as you are, and when you swing it, do it level above your head, just like Ian and Mindy did. Got it?"

"I think so," I said, visualizing myself doing it and gripping the rope tightly. I hoped that if I failed, I would at least look cool doing it.

"You'll be just fine." He sprang over the fence, and I climbed it, jumped down, and followed him to a palomino. The palomino shook his head at us as we neared.

"Whose place is this?" I asked.

"Some rancher who loves us riding his horses here before he breaks them." He grinned from ear to ear and winked at me. We obviously weren't supposed to be here. I felt bad about hijacking someone else's animals without permission, but this was my job. I'd have to get over it.

"Alright. Go for it."

I whipped the rope in a big circle over my head and then threw it like I'd seen the others do. At least I attempted to. I missed. I tried again and again. The horse moved from side to side with each attempt, but didn't run away. I thought it curious that it didn't just run away. I tried again. My throw was way too short. I said a little prayer in my mind and tried a few dozen more times with Dakota giving me little hints here and there. Finally, I moved close enough that I could almost smell the horse's breath, or at least feel it, and tossed the rope. By some miracle, it took.

I walked carefully toward the horse, my hand outstretched, surprised that he let me stroke his nose. I grabbed ahold of his mane and threw myself up, my leg easily clearing his back. I almost overshot and had to pull myself back up. He didn't run away like all the others. He stayed still.

"What the..." I said, looking at Dakota.

Everyone started laughing. And I suddenly got it. I was the virgin so they gave me the tamest horse of all. The truth was, they were all tame. I raised my hands in the air and shook my head, yelling out, "You guys are jerks, but I like it. You got me. You got me." I figured it'd be best if I laughed along.

Camden said, "I like this girl."

In the meantime, Dakota roped his horse. He grabbed my rope from me and let the horses run with us. That's when I held on to the horse's mane for dear life.

"Keep your eyes on the path in front of you," Dakota yelled out. "Never look down at your horse, it will make you dizzy."

I obeyed. We ran and walked through the woods, taking the occasional break, across acres and acres of land and around a huge lake, until it was almost dark. I felt free–wild, even. I thought I could ride forever, but I was exhausted when we made it back to the main field. I brought both my legs over to one side of the horse and started to jump down. Ian hurried over and caught me. It turned out to be a good thing. My legs were like jelly, like after riding a Harley all day. He carried me to the fence and then handed me over to Dakota.

My heart pounded. I pulled my head into Dakota's shoulder, his arms holding me tight. I heard him take a deep breath of my hair before setting me down. Was he feeling the same connection between us that I was feeling? Moments later, my legs gathered their strength. He didn't let go of me. If anything, he held tighter.

"How can you still smell so good after a two hour ride?"

A nervous laugh escaped me, and I pulled away. "I always smell sweet," I said. "I never sweat, either." I laughed.

"That, I believe," he said seriously and after a pause, added. "I'm so glad you fit in with us."

I grinned. Was I in?

Driving down the hill, I thought I saw a familiar face in a parked car. The man was reading a newspaper. It was Jeremy. What was he doing here? I smiled.

I followed Dakota's Jeep to Abby's Pizza, Ian in the seat next to me. We laughed about Abby's parents naming the restaurant after her. Hunger suddenly gripped me. We ate ourselves silly on some of the best pizza I'd ever eaten. When we were done, we used the self-serve ice cream machine to fill a bunch of balloons full of ice cream. Then we went outside and played a balloon toss game, throwing the balloons across the street to our partners. We were all a sticky mess by the time the balloons were gone.

When I got home, I met my agent parents in the office to tell them what was going on. "Can you believe I got into the group my first day?" I figured they would congratulate me and start really believing in me now. Instead, I got a lecture.

"Look, Misha," Agent Penrod said. "What you did today was reckless. You didn't call and you didn't activate your tracker. If you want to make this seem real to the kidnappers and Madness, you're going to have to call us and ask if you can do things before you do them. This is amateur stuff here. Good grief." She was so like my mom.

"She's right, Misha," Agent Wood said. "I was worried about your ability to see this mission through, and it looks like my worry was justified. What if the kidnappers had decided to snatch you while horseback riding? We would have no clue what had happened to you. Nothing like this had better ever happen again."

They were right. I needed to be better. But, they didn't need to treat me like a little child. "Sorry guys. You're right. I should have let you know what was going on, and I should have activated the tracker."

Agent Wood clenched his teeth as he listened to my apology.

I saw Agent Penrod smirk, but it was gone as quickly as it'd appeared.

"I'm really sorry," I repeated. "It won't happen again." I hurried to my room. No point in hanging out with the two of them any longer than I had to. When I walked into my room, I noticed a note from Jeremy. My heart flipped, and I wondered why. After reading the note, I figured it was just because someone recognized my good work. Despite what my agent parents had said, I rocked it today.

Congratulations on nailing it today. Great work. Looks like you got in on your first try.

I looked at the note one more time. In my mind, I saw Jeremy in that car behind that newspaper, and I smiled. Just like in DC, he would protect me at all costs. I couldn't ask for a better handler.

Chapter 4

The next day, I was so saddle sore, I didn't even dare try to longboard up to the school from where I parked. Instead, I hobbled up. Several other members of Madness walked just like me. Throughout the day, it became more and more clear that Ian called all the shots with this group. They all looked to him as their leader. When ideas were bounced around, Ian always had the final say.

After school, I jumped into my car and rolled the window down. I was about to drive away when Ian's fingers grabbed the door and he leaned in.

"Wanna come over for dinner tonight? My parents are out of town," he said.

Right, no parents. That's because he lives by himself and is twenty-five and a recruiter for a kidnapper.

"Sure," I said. It was kind of scary to think about being alone with Ian in his house, but I'd do anything to get on the right side of the leader of the group and be one of the eight chosen to be kidnapped. We *had* to figure out what was going on, and what had happened to the other kidnapped kids. Besides, I could handle myself.

I made sure to fill Agent Wood and Agent Penrod in on my plans, and they gave me some unsolicited advice about what information to get out of Ian and how to do it. I listened patiently, biting my tongue. I knew they just wanted to help me.

I arrived at seven, and followed Ian into his massive kitchen. He had made spaghetti with meatballs. It smelled rich and meaty. No way he was a high school senior.

"I hope you like spaghetti," he said. "It's a specialty of mine."

"I love it. It smells amazing. I had no idea you were a chef. I figured we'd be eating pizza."

He chuckled. "Actually, spaghetti with meatballs is the only thing I can make." He ladled two big meatballs with sauce over a bowl of spaghetti and handed it to me.

"You seriously made this by yourself?"

"Seriously, so you better love it. I'm kinda protective of this recipe–it's my grandfather's." He made himself a bowl, too, before opening the oven and pulling out two crispy pieces of garlic toast and placing one on my bowl and one on his. After pulling out two forks from a nearby drawer, he led me out onto the patio where we sat at a table covered with an umbrella. The sun was low, about to set, and the reddish ball peeked through the thick trees surrounding his property.

"This is amazing," I said after swallowing my first bite.

"Thanks," he said.

We chatted aimlessly as we ate. My skin prickled with goose bumps when the sun went down.

"You cold?" he asked, looking at my hands running up and down my arms.

"Just a bit," I said.

"I'll be right back." He went inside and brought out a couple of blankets. We moseyed out to the garden area and sat on loungers, and I wrapped up in one of the blankets he handed me. We looked up at the stars. "So, tell me about where you came from," he said.

While my cover told me some specific things about Misha's past, I was charged with coming up with a lot of the unimportant things. I'd fill my team in on what I'd come up with later. I had to be flexible in order to be the person I thought others wanted at that moment. I'd anticipated this question and had come up with a lot of fun things to tell him about.

"I hated leaving all my friends in Colorado," I said, hoping to get things on a personal level. "But the worst was leaving my cat and dog. They were really my older sister's, and she said she couldn't handle having them so far away from her. She and her husband moved into a new apartment that allowed pets right before we moved. I was so mad at her. I'd been taking care of them for the last two years since she got married. She only came to see them about twice a week, and she never cleaned up after them."

"I don't have any siblings, so I don't know what that would be like. I can't imagine fighting with my brother or sister. I think I'd be so glad to have one, like we'd always have awesome times together."

"If only it could be so easy. Sisters can be a huge pain." I told him a few funny stories about the dog and cat and then my sister. I drew on my experiences from my real family in Montana. I was hoping to get him to talk about his personal life and get him to give me a hint as to his real age so I could confirm he was the recruiter for the kidnappers and not just a student caught up in this mess unawares. He didn't take the bait, which made me think he really was the recruiter–trained not to talk about personal stuff. I changed tactics to a more direct approach.

"It sucks—moving senior year, you know? But I've decided to look at it as a rockin' adventure." I grinned at him and added, "Especially now I've found you guys. I can't wait to find more awesome things to do in Oregon. Turns out this state might not be so bad after all." I paused, then turned the conversation to Ian. "What about you? Are you from here?"

"I was born in Portland and moved here when I was ten."

"Oregon is your home, then?"

"Yep. I plan on dying here, too." He shifted on the lounger and looked at me. "Where're you planning to go to college?"

"Not sure. I was thinking I'd go to Colorado State. I might still end up there. I haven't decided yet." I pulled the blanket up tight around my neck."

"You should consider University of Oregon. We're all hoping to go there."

I assumed he meant members of Madness. "I'll look into it."

"So, why don't you have a girlfriend?" I asked, curiosity getting the better of me.

"I don't like being tied down. Girlfriends can get in the way. Only Troy has a girlfriend right now. She goes to a different school."

"None of the girls have boyfriends?" I knew he'd know I was asking about the girls in Madness.

"Not right now. It's hard to keep a girlfriend or boyfriend outside the group. It's hard to make them understand the relationship we have with each other. They all end up getting too jealous. The drama isn't worth it. We date, we just don't stick with one person. Dakota dates more than any of us. While I have the occasional girl ask me out, Dakota is bombarded with girls asking him to go out."

Great. I had to get involved with the ladies' man. This might not be as easy as it looked.

"Have any of you ever dated each other?"

"Sure. I dated Abby and Tarran for a while, but once the heat died down, we decided to move on. There've been a few other hookups, but they never seem to stand the test of time. In the end, I think we're too much like a family to have romantic feelings for each other."

He considered them his family, and he was planning to have them kidnapped? That didn't sit right with me.

After that, the conversation died down. I'd never heard such loud chirping of crickets. At nine, he said, "I hate to kick you out, but I promised my parents that if I invited anyone over, I'd send them home at nine. It's nine."

I was a bit shocked. Had I done or said something wrong? Why would he follow his parent's rules if he didn't have any? Or was he bored? He stood up and held out his hand for me to take. I sighed loudly and took it. I kept waiting for him to make a move on me, but he never did. He was a complete gentleman. He hugged me hard at my car door and then opened it for me. I sat inside, still a bit shocked.

"I didn't do anything wrong, did I?" I figured the direct approach would serve me well in this situation.

"Of course not. I think you're the perfect addition to our group."

I don't know why I thought he'd be interested in me. He was looking at me as someone to send to the chopping block, nothing more. Could he really be working for the kidnappers? "Great. I think you guys are a lot of fun, too."

Once home, I told my agent parents what I'd told Ian about my life, and that Ian was the definite leader, and that I was in.

"Don't be so hasty in your judgment," Agent Wood said.

Agent Penrod took a step toward me. "It's important you get to know all of the members of Madness a bit better before you pass that judgment. Remember," she cooed, rubbing her hand down my arm, a patronizing look on her face, "Division wants you to focus on Dakota and Ian, but it could be anyone."

I tried not to show how upset I was at how they were treating me. I didn't want to rock the boat. I'd let them baby me, for now. My actions from now on would show them I didn't need their coddling.

The next day, Tarran, the redheaded girl in the group, invited me over to her house. After a quick call to my agent parents, which I ended hastily when Agent Penrod tried to baby me, I drove over. Apparently, every other Thursday the girls and guys split and had a contest to see who could come up with their next big thrill. All the girls were there.

We crowded around Tarran's computer screen to watch YouTube videos and news reports on risky behavior.

"We always start off," Tarran said, "with three or four new skater videos to remind ourselves that skater tricks suck. Besides, they're hilarious." We laughed and screamed at those videos and then moved on to ones that could spark ideas for our next few adventures. After about an hour, our initial list had five things we thought would be fun.

Jensyn ordered some Chinese food and everyone that could pitched in to pay for it. Tarran made up the difference.

While we waited, we chose our top two activities to present to the boys. Once that was done and we were chowing on the Chinese food, Mindy started to spill her guts.

"If my dad rips on my mom one more time, I'm going to make him a batch of brownies with extra strength Metamucil. I hate the fact they're divorcing, but I'm starting to see why it might be best. They hate each other. I have no idea why they got married in the first place. My mom's doing the best she can. If he were married to someone like him, he'd end up behaving the same way she does."

"Down with terrible husbands and fathers," Jensyn said, raising her heavily caffeinated drink in the air. When all the others grabbed their cans and raised them up to meet Jensyn's, I hastily did, too. The clanking of the can was somehow satisfying.

Abby pulled Mindy into a hug, and Mindy started to cry. The rest of the girls crowded around her.

"It'll all be okay," Tarran said.

"Don't worry, you've always got us," Jensyn said.

"It'll all work out," Abby said. "You'll see."

At that point, they all started to cry. They really were like a family.

I also discovered that most of the kids in the group, with the exception of Ian and Mindy, all grew up in different states and within the last few years had moved here.

On the way home, I thought about everything I had learned. I wasn't sure what it all meant—was it important that most of the group were out-of-staters? What were the kidnappers after? I maneuvered the car mechanically, focused on my thoughts, until a bright light coming from the middle of the street shined up at me in a quick spurt.

Startled, I jerked the car to the side, barely missing hitting the light. I almost hit the curb, but stopped just before. I gripped the steering wheel, breathing hard, then slammed my door open and jumped out of the car. My eyes swept the road, searching for the source of the light.

That's when I saw her—a girl sitting on top of a metal safety rail on the side of the road. She held a flashlight in her hand, and she was staring right at me. Her red hair flamed in the dim light from a street lamp above her. She laughed, flipped the flashlight from one hand to the other, the light dancing around in the night sky, and then took off.

My instinct was to chase after her, but I stopped myself. It wasn't a part of my mission, and I needed to stay focused. I could have killed that girl, and she was laughing. Her face was permanently etched in my mind.

I didn't bother telling my agent parents about my almost accident when I got back. I gave them a quick run-down of what I'd learned and hurried to bed.

The next morning, I knew I'd done something wrong when Dakota met me on the stairs to the school and looking me over said, "Roberts, what's up with the pink?"

"Huh?" I said.

"It's game day, and Madness loves game day." I couldn't help but notice his orange T-shirt with the outline of the head of an Indian, apparently the school's mascot. I hadn't pegged them for the 'school spirit' type, but concluded it must be the small town atmosphere that made even Madness love school sports.

"Well, if someone had told me, I would have been prepared." I raised my eyebrows at him.

"Don't you listen to the announcements?"

"Very funny," I said. "No one hears those."

"No worries," he said. "I've got you covered."

"You do?"

"Yep," he said. "I just sent Tarran to the save the day. She'll be here before you know it." And she was. He must have been watching me from the time I pulled up with my car and then seeing my clothes, had sent her, without a thought, to go buy me a game-day T-shirt. I admit it, I swooned a bit.

I yanked the orange shirt over the pink one I already had on. It clashed harshly with my plaid skirt and pink Converse, but I didn't care. It had been a nice gesture. There was an excitement in the air I'd never experienced in all my high school career. Nothing got done in any class, even English. No one had anything but football on their mind.

I did my duty when I got home, telling my faux parents about my day and what would be happening that night. They peppered me with questions and had me rolling my eyes only a few minutes into the conversation.

I switched my pink converse with black ones before Dakota picked me up. We got to the tailgate party about an hour before the game started. I discovered it was the community's life, too. The parking lot was full of trucks with their backs down and grills cooking hot dogs and hamburgers.

"This is nuts," I said.

"What?"

"All these people. I've never seen so many people so excited about a high school football game."

"I know, and if we don't get here early, we don't get the seats we like. Camden and Jensyn should already be inside, saving our spots." He looked me over. "Nice," he said. I looked down at my black converse and brushed my hands over the front of my short black pleated skirt. I'd cut the orange shirt he'd given me up all the seams. Then I'd cut some horizontal strips on each seam and tied them together so that the shirt fit more snuggly.

He pulled on one of the ties at the shoulder of the orange shirt.

"I hope you don't mind me cutting it up," I said. I didn't want to offend him since he'd bought the shirt.

"I'm sure you'll start a trend with it," he said, letting go of the tie and grabbing my hand. My first instinct was to move my hand out of his even though it felt nice, but I had to force myself to stay in character. He led me to the booth to buy tickets. "But it looks like I'm going to have to come to the rescue again."

"What are you talking about?" I said, looking down at my outfit as we stopped in the line.

"Once the sun goes down, you're going to freeze." He chuckled.

He talked to the girl inside the ticket booth, and I pulled out some money to give him. He pushed it away and paid for me. I bit my lip, thinking about how much I was impressed with this guy. He would make a girl very happy one day. I had to pretend to be that girl.

People packed the stands in some areas. In others, seats were marked by stray sweatshirts, blankets, or portable stadium seats. The racetrack circling the field was teeming with bodies walking around it. Dakota pulled me over to a stand selling T-shirts and sweatshirts and bought me a school sweatshirt, again refusing the money I tried to put in his hand. "It's my treat." Money didn't seem to be an issue for him. Was his family loaded? They must be, because normal teens didn't have a lot of cash on them. It was already starting to get chilly, and I happily slipped the sweatshirt over my newly cut shirt. He pulled me to him, putting his hand on my waist. Our sides bumped together.

That's when I saw her, the girl I'd almost hit in the road last night. I turned to Dakota and said, "Who's that girl?"

"That's Frankie," he said. "Stay away from her. She's bad news."

"Really?" I said. "I saw her last night."

"You did?" he said. "I thought you were with female Madness last night."

"I was," I said. "But as I was driving home, I saw this light flash in the middle of the road, and I swerved out of the way. When I got out of the car, I saw that girl running away, laughing. She had a flashlight in her hand. I could have killed her."

"She's constantly doing stuff like that. She doesn't care much if she lives or dies getting her rush. Just stay away from her and you won't get hurt."

I looked behind me, catching a glimpse of her before she slipped into the crowd. Did she do this stuff alone or were others there, hiding in the darkness?

Chapter 5

Dakota pulled me into a huge bear hug. I could feel his heat radiate through my hoodie, and I felt safe. A strange sensation under the circumstances. I pulled back slightly and smiled up at him. He grinned at me, and his eyes dilated. He liked me, for real. I tucked my head back into his chest to prevent the kiss I could see forming in his mind.

Roseburg won without much effort. The other team seemed to lie down and die and, even though it was twenty-eight to nothing, we stayed until the bitter end. All ten of us in Madness sat together in a clump over three rows.

"You ready for a wild ride tonight?" Dakota asked.

"I guess," I said, wondering what he meant by that. Were we going to ride horses in the dark? Maybe bucking broncos? He did say wild.

"You'll love it," he said. "You like to get wet, right?"

Hmm. No horses then. I assumed that meant we would be swimming. I should have known better. "I love to swim."

"Good." He laughed.

We swung by my house, and I put on my swimsuit and dressed in some sweats and a T-shirt. As I pulled the sweatshirt over my head, I noticed it smelled faintly of

Dakota. In spite of myself, I took a deep whiff. I grabbed a big bag, stuffing a towel, spandex shorts, and all my bathroom stuff into it. I flung it over my shoulder before heading back to the Jeep.

I hollered out to the house that we were going swimming and left.

"Where are we going?" I asked once back with Dakota.

"You'll see." He turned the music up, and we sang along. We pulled up behind Ian's car on the side of the road just outside of town. Dakota jumped out and ran to my side, opening the door for me. He didn't let me out, however. Before I could jump down, he moved close, pressing his body to mine. His hands went to my hips and then he said, "Just in case we die, I want to die with your kiss on my lips."

It was a line, but I'd take it. I needed to strengthen my connection with this group. My job was to become his girlfriend, and I guessed I'd accomplished that. I needed to take advantage of the situation. I couldn't back down. My lip quivered as he moved slowly in. *You are not Christy, you are Misha, and Misha is starting to feel things for Dakota, so make it real.* I was surprised when Jeremy's face flashed before my eyes, and my heartbeat quickened. Dakota's lips, warm and soft, met mine and a zing passed through me. He pulled me closer still. His breath was minty, and he smelled like guy, through and through. My heart pounded. I wanted to kick myself for having a physical reaction to Dakota's kiss. I wanted to be professional, playing a part without having it affect me. I wanted it to feel like nothing, but it didn't. It felt great.

A loud smack had me pulling quickly away from him. Troy had smacked the front of the Jeep with his palm. "Time to float, man. There'll be plenty of time for that after the run."

Dakota smiled a crooked smile, and then slowly opened his eyes. He had kept them shut after I'd pulled away. Wow! He was a real Casanova. He smiled really big, and then helped me out of the car.

I tried to convince myself this was a dream, that it wasn't really happening. But it was. He pulled me close to him again and gave me a sweet kiss. Then he stripped down to his shorts and water shoes. I didn't move to change.

"You'll want to take those off so you don't freeze when we get wet on the river—and you *will* get wet."

We were running the Umpqua River in rafts. In the dark. This seemed just as dangerous as Frankie's stunt.

"Abby is meeting us at the end of the run with our clothes and towels—she doesn't like getting cold—then we'll meet the rest of the seniors at the bonfire at Charlie's," Dakota said.

"Everyone knows everyone here, don't they?" I said.

"Yes, we do."

I slipped out of my clothes and felt naked even though my suit was a one piece and all the other girls' were bikinis. It did endear me to Dakota even more when he turned away as I started to undress. I handed him my clothes and bag, and he ran them over to a big SUV. Abby drove away. I quickly activated the tracker in my arm to let Division and my agent parents know where I was. The chill in the air gave me goose bumps, and I shivered. Right then, Dakota pulled me close and walked with his arm around me to the river and the waiting raft. It shocked me when I saw it. They had made it glow-in-the-dark. Ingenious. He picked me up, carried me through the water, and set me gently in the puffy raft. The air smelled of rubber and paint. Ian handed me a life jacket, and I quickly put it on.

I looked at everyone. All there except Abby. They really did do everything together. It surprised me that no one but Ian had asked me about my past. It was always about the here and now. At least so far.

Dakota untied the rope holding the raft where it was and hurried and jumped in. Water splashed on me, making me shake. At first the boat glided gently through the water. With the dense trees covering the river it was really dark, and the first rapid hit me by surprise. The fear was gut wrenching. The trees and shadows made it even scarier. I could hear Ian calling to the others, telling them when to use their oars, and I felt like we were trying to get out of a twister. I wasn't prepared for the huge dips and swells. The water that splashed on me made my teeth chatter.

Ian cried out, "Whoa!" The raft seemed to be trying to climb into the sky. I grabbed a handhold and held on for dear life. The raft tossed and turned and lunged and dove until finally everyone was screaming. We took one last swell, and we all flew into the water.

It was so cold it took my breath away and hurt my skin. Rocks banged into my legs and branches whipped at me before I came to the surface. I gasped for air, bobbing up and down in the water. All I could think about was the fact that I hadn't held onto the boat like Dakota had told me to do. How would I find the raft, now?

I heard a voice call me, and I whipped around to see the glowing raft with what looked like the shadows of two bodies in it. I tried to call out, but I got dragged under for twenty seconds or so. Coming back up out of the water, I coughed and sputtered. I was finally able to call out. "I'm here." Then I went under again, bobbing up and down, up and down. The next time I came up, a light shone right in my eyes, and hands grabbed me and dragged me to the raft. As I was being lifted in, I heard shouts of excitement and fun. I thought I would die, I was so waterlogged, but I couldn't show it. Once I hit the floor of the raft, I forced myself to squeal. Then I felt lips on mine.

"That was awesome, wasn't it!" Dakota said.

"Definitely," I said, sitting up and letting him help me back onto the puffy side of the raft. Once I had it straddled, I looked out ahead into the darkness and prayed for all I was worth that the raft wouldn't tip over again. It did, one more time, but right before the nice calm section of river where Abby waited for us. I think I only went under once that time.

Conversations swirled around me as I slogged my way to shore. "That rocked." "That was the best spill ever." "Good thing we made the raft glow. In this darkness, I never would have found it." "I love that feeling that you just might not make it." "I wish we could run it one more time."

Just as I climbed out, Dakota barreled into me, sending the both of us back into the freezing cold river. When I came up, I tried to gasp and sputter as lady-like as I could. At least the water wasn't too deep, and I could stand. My teeth clacked together as I came up out of the water.

"I'm so glad you came!" he said, kissing my forehead and then my cheeks and my nose.

"Me, too," I lied. He pressed his forehead on mine and then kissed me soundly. I shivered violently.

The sound of the car's horn had him picking me up, still kissing me, and carrying me to the shore. After setting me down, he grabbed my cozy towel and wrapped me up in it. He wrapped himself up in his own, too, and we climbed into the SUV.

"Get a room," Jensyn said, laughing.

"Seriously," Abby said with humor. Abby peeled out and drove us to our cars up the road. It wasn't that far. I thought we'd been in forever, but it'd only been an hour. Crazy. I shivered and Dakota pulled me close. I stopped shivering immediately.

Once back at the Jeep, I shimmied out of my swimsuit on the far side of the Jeep when Dakota's and everyone's backs were turned. I pulled out the spandex shorts from my bag and slid them on. I pulled the sweats and T-shirt on, then yanked the sweatshirt back on. I ran the brush through my hair a few times, trying to create tousled look before the car started to move. I used his mirror to fix my face.

The bonfire was raging when we arrived, and I gave my tracker a quick pulse. Charlie, the star quarterback, lived in Glide, about twenty minutes from Roseburg, out in a remote part of the town. I think every star was visible that night, there was almost no black in the sky. Big logs and rocks surrounded the fire, and there appeared to be a lake to the far right of us, though I couldn't see it well in the dark. It looked like at least one hundred kids had shown up. Most had a beer in their hands. When we walked by the cooler, everyone in my group grabbed one out, so I did too. I just wouldn't drink it. I'd abracadabra it away.

I wondered if adrenaline junkies used alcohol to wind down. I hoped they didn't do drugs to heighten their experiences.

I quickly discovered they did use alcohol to wind down. I let the fire warm me as I sat next to Dakota on a huge log. I pretended to drink the beer while we roasted hot dogs. Dakota disappeared for a few minutes and then returned with s'mores fixings. He made the best s'mores. Somehow he got the chocolate to melt. My chocolate never melted. Slowly but surely, the group divided into pairs.

Dakota rubbed my nose with his, and we laughed and talked about our families, friends, and past. It was comfortable being with him. He pulled me close and kissed me. It didn't taste like he'd been drinking the beer that sat on the ground next to him. Was he doing what I was doing: faking it? At the same time I had the thought, he asked, "Don't you like the beer?" I stared at him in shock. I'd been discovered. My kiss had given me away just as his had. Then he whispered in my ear, "Me neither." I felt a gush of relief until he continued and said, "I prefer something else."

Drugs flew across my mind. My hand went immediately to my hoodie pocket, where I kept the pill Division 57 had given me to counteract the effects of drugs. I felt for the anti-drug pill. It was there. Was I about to take my first drug? Maybe I could magic it away instead. He grabbed a few blankets from the Jeep and led me away from the crowd. What I had thought was a lake was actually a river. He spread the blanket out under the stars and near the river. I noticed several other couples wrapped up along the bank, also. They definitely weren't star-gazing. I hoped that wasn't the thing he preferred, either. I wouldn't go there. I had to come up with a plan to get out of it, if it went there. Fear sent a shock wave through me.

It scared me that a part of me wanted to make out with him, to see what it was like, but part of me was holding back. I wasn't sure I was ready to get close to someone again, even if it was just pretend.

I knew part of my mission was to get Dakota to be my boyfriend, but was it necessary to be so intimate with him? My heart pounded in anticipation and dread. He sat down on the blanket, inviting me with his smile to sit next to him. He took something out of his pocket, I figured it was some type of drug, and stuck it in his mouth. He handed me some, too. It felt like a candy-coated piece of gum. It was gum, wasn't it? I had to ask to be sure.

"Of course it's gum. What did you think it was?"

I wanted to recover quickly, so I said, "Do I have bad breath, or what?"

He chuckled. "No, I just like to have a strong piece of peppermint gum when I'm outside. It helps keep the bugs away."

"It does not," I said.

"Does too," he said. "Try it."

I listened to that inner voice that told me to believe him. This was gum, not a drug. He chewed for a minute, and he lay back. I did, too. He pulled the other blanket over us, tucked his hands behind his head and looked up at the stars, quietly chewing his gum. Was this what he preferred? Within minutes, his chewing slowed, and he fell asleep. This was how he relaxed? I loved him for it. The chill from the river made me slide closer to him. I rested my head on his arms. Soon, my breathing matched his, and I was fast asleep.

Dakota woke me at about three o'clock and said he'd take me home. Other kids were fast asleep in mounds all about the property. I wondered if their parents knew what they were doing and where they were or if they even cared. Did kids still lie to their parents or did parents just let them do what they wanted here? My real parents would have freaked if I'd stayed out past curfew, which was ten, and they never let me have sleepovers. Never. I'm sure that much hadn't changed.

He seemed nervous, fidgety, on the way home. Our conversation was forced, so unlike how it had been the past four days: natural, spontaneous, and fun. Once we pulled up to my house, I was a bit anxious to get out and leave the awkwardness behind. Tomorrow would be back to normal, I told myself. As I pulled on the lever to open the door, his hand fell on my arm and he squeezed.

"Hold on. I want to tell you something."

I let my hand drop from the door handle and turned to him. What was he about to say? Was he already breaking up with me? Had I done something wrong?

"I don't want you to freak out on me when I tell you what I'm about to say, but I have to say it, so I guess I'll live with the consequences." He took a deep breath, then continued. "I've never fallen so fast," he said, taking my hand, "for a girl, I mean, ever."

I smiled at him, feeling pressure to say the same thing back to him. I would have thought his profession of love for me after so short of a time would have made me conclude he was needy, but I cared deeply for him already, too. Luckily he started to talk again.

"I know we've only known each other for less than a week, but I feel this connection with you."

He felt that connection because I had engineered everything to make it so. I dressed in a way to attract him. I went along with his group's crazy stunts. I said all the things an adrenaline junkie would want to hear. I lied. And I made it obvious I wasn't going anywhere, no matter how wild he was. Guilt hit me hard. Crap. But–he was my mark. I couldn't let feelings of guilt rule me. I pushed the guilt away. This is a job.

"I hope you don't think I'm weird that I chew peppermint gum under the stars to wind down. I've never shared that with anyone. Come to think of it, I've never *wanted* to share that with anyone. I'm just so comfortable with you. I feel like I could tell you anything, show you anything, and you wouldn't judge me or turn on me."

He was right about that. He was a means to an end. He helped me fit into the group that would be kidnapped. I hated that it made my heart hurt. I hoped I'd be better able to control my emotions on this mission than the last one, where I had to befriend the daughter of a terrorist so that Division 57 could bring him down. I had allowed myself to get too close to her. I truly counted her as one of my best friends, ever. And here I was, getting too close to a boy this time. Would I ever be able to control my heart?

"You're right about that," I said. "I never would."

He kissed me, told me to stay put and then ran around the car and helped me out.

Deep inside, I knew he spoke the truth. I made a promise to myself right then–when we were all kidnapped, I'd make sure to keep Dakota safe. He was the real deal, something special. He, and all the other kids, were counting on me—even if they didn't know it. I had to push away all the feelings I had for him and focus. I had a mission to complete, and my heart could not overrule my head.

I woke at ten the next morning. My parents came into the kitchen while I ate breakfast. I briefed them on all that happened, leaving out the kiss with Dakota. When Agent Wood started to lecture me about boys and the birds and the bees, I had to put my foot down.

"Look guys," I said. "I know you see me as a child, but I have been through more than you know and truth be told, I could take both of you in a fight without much effort. I am a spy for Division 57 because I am good at what I do. Do I need to take you on to prove that to you?"

They both looked at me with wide eyes.

"We're supposed to work together." I stood up. "I'll let you know if I need advice or help."

"You have to see this from our perspective," Agent Wood said. "If seasoned agents couldn't do it, why do you think you have a chance? How old are you? Sixteen?"

So they didn't know how old I was after all. "First of all, it doesn't matter how old I am. The only thing that matters is that Division believes in me. I *can* do this. You'll see. And I do know what I'm doing. Have some faith."

Neither spoke. They only looked at me.

I turned and left the room. Those two were really something. I wanted to scream. Before I debriefed them each day, I would let them know if I needed any advice, not only to remind them of this conversation, but also to get them thinking while I was talking.

Chapter 6

The next morning, I got a text from Ian. The texts for Madness always came from Ian. I let my now silent agent parents know I was heading to the mall to get stuff for the upcoming dance at school. I wasn't sure why the Madness kids wanted me to go shopping; no one had invited me to the dance yet. I got ready anyway and met them at the big department store at one end of the mall. Pricey. None of them seemed to notice. We went to the men's department first, and the five guys tried on several different suits. They all looked quite hot in them. We laughed a lot at some of the extreme coats and pants Camden chose.

"Who are you going with, Mindy?" I asked.

"No one. We all go together. Sorry, we should have told you," she said.

"Oh," I said, feeling quite the relief. I didn't want to feel any pressure to find a date, and I certainly didn't want to run into whomever Dakota had asked. Talk about awkward. Now that I knew he hadn't asked anyone, the trip to the mall became interesting and fun.

After the boys had found their outfits and some of the girls had found their dresses, we headed for Chic-Fil-A to get the best chicken sandwich in the world. I couldn't help but notice that Ian kept looking over at a table at the other end of the food court.

Frankie and some other kids sat at the table. Their heads were close in to the center of the table like they were discussing something serious.

Dakota knocked my arm with his and pointing toward Frankie's table, he said, "I'm sure they're about to either pull off a great heist or hurt a lot of people."

"I didn't realize there was a group of them."

"Yep. They call themselves the Avengers. They avenge boredom with their acts of pure stupidity." He shook his head as they disbanded and threw their trash away.

Abby slapped Dakota's arm and said, "Come with me. I'm desperate to find that perfect dress." He looked at me, and I said, "Go! Help away." Why was he asking my permission? I didn't want to get on anyone's bad side in this group. No jealousy allowed.

I watched them go, my eyes finding Frankie again. She walked into an electronics store across the way. She interested me. That stunt she pulled the other night–it was as though she was actively courting death, not just risking it in the pursuit of a good time. And now I found there was a group of them. I'd counted six. Ian grabbed my garbage and threw it away before saying, "Let's go. I've got to get some new headphones. Mine cut out all the time."

"Alright," I said, grabbing my bag.

While Ian and I headed for the electronics store, the others split up, going in different directions.

Before we even got to the headphone section, Ian got sidetracked with the games lining the walls. I watched

Frankie. She also looked at the games but already had some expensive cables in her hand.

"You ever played this?" Ian said, pointing to a game in front of him.

"Never," I said.

"This one is super fun," he said. "We can all play at one time."

"Cool," I said and felt someone bump into me. I turned to see Frankie there.

"Sorry about that," she said. "I tripped."

"No problem." I smiled at her. Her alert eyes caught me off guard. She didn't smile back; instead, she headed for the door, empty-handed. What had she done with her stuff?

Ian moved on to the headphones, and I headed for the wireless speakers near the exit. I heard a *psst*. I looked in the direction of the sound. Frankie was standing just outside the entryway, her back to me.

"Did you say something?" I asked, looking at the speakers and pretending like I wasn't talking to her so I didn't look like a fool when I found out she hadn't been talking to me.

"Come here," she said, still looking away. "Hurry."

I did, why wouldn't I? The second I passed through the security sensors, they rang out, I would have stepped back in, but I felt Frankie's hand on my bag, and I jerked it away. "Stow something in my bag?" I asked.

"Just give it to me, quick, and you'll be off the hook. They'll have no proof you took anything, and I'll get away." We both talked a mile a minute. Time seemed suspended somehow. I could see the manager of the electronic store looking at me, starting to move in my direction. Frankie's eager hands were begging for the loot.

"You'll go to jail," she said. "Do you want to go to jail? Just hand it over. He can't see me from where he is. There's a blind spot behind this wall, I've done this a thousand times."

My heart burned and pounded. I could see the manager moving in. Ten feet. Seven feet. I had to decide.

Frankie finally turned to me, eyes wide. "You've lost your window. Enjoy juvie." She started to run, and I did the dumbest thing ever, I followed.

"Don't follow me," she yelled.

"You better show me a way out or you'll regret this," I shot back.

I looked over my shoulder for a split second at the electronics store. The manager was on the phone, customers and others were gawking at us, and Ian's mouth was curved into a smile.

"I never regret anything," she said and sped up. I had no problem keeping up with her. Mall security was descending on us from all four spokes of the mall walkway. I had no idea how we were going to get out of this. What was I thinking? Why hadn't I just jumped back into the store and told the manager about Frankie? Because my heart burned and I felt a *voice* tell me to. That was the tale-tell sign that I was doing the right thing. I pressed my arm into my side, hoping to activate my tracker and let my parents know I was in trouble.

I was only eight the first time I felt that feeling and recognized it for what it was. I had been swinging with my best friend on her amazing twenty-foot high wooden swing set. We each sat on a flat wooden seat. Two thick pieces of rope were knotted on the bottom of the seat that then twisted its way up into the beam above us. We pumped and pumped our legs until we'd get even with the beam holding us up and scream and yell with delight as our stomachs dropped.

That particular day, I felt this feeling in my heart, maybe my soul, that told me to get off the swing. In truth, it was more than a feeling. A voice spoke to me to get off. The voice was accompanied by a burning in my chest like when you are so thirsty on a cold day and those first few sips seem to spread out and fill your chest with warmth.

The third time I felt the voice, I put my feet down again and again to stop my swinging. The moment I stood, the thick, flat board of the seat broke in half. I stood there shaking. From then on, I learned to recognize and listen to the voice and feeling. The more I listened and heeded the feeling, the more often the promptings would come. I quickly discovered that the feeling didn't only protect me from physical danger, but also emotional and moral. It even directed me for little things like answers on tests or where to find something. In the end, I discovered that if I followed the feeling, good things would happen, when I didn't, bad things did.

The feeling right now told me Frankie was important. I must need her for something on this mission. The manager probably wouldn't have believed me if I'd stepped back into the store. I hoped I wouldn't end up in juvie. She was running straight for the elevators, the stairs were all the way the other direction, and the elevator light showed it was on the first level. We were on the third.

We would be caught.

I was about to stop and give myself up, when Frankie jumped up on the tall handrail, took a few adept steps near the elevator and then caught hold of a pipe that went from the ceiling on the third floor all the way down to the main level. I couldn't hesitate. I slid my jacket on, knowing it would tear my hands and arms up to slide down that pole without some protection and without losing a second, I hoisted myself over the railing, grabbed the pole, using my converse for some traction, and let my arms, wrapped tightly around the pole, slide down it.

My feet hit hard into the tiled floor, jarring my knees, and I quickly spotted Frankie, heading for a large department store not far from where I stood. I high-tailed it in her direction and caught up with her, just as she entered the empty loading dock.

"You still here?" she said.

"Yep. Now get me out of here," I said.

"Your wish is my command," she said, barreling through a side door that sent sirens wailing.

"This was your exit plan?" I shouted.

"They don't have guards in the loading dock area after one. You'll be fine if you're fast. This is the fun part."

She ran full speed across the open parking lot. If it had been me, I would have found a car, picked the lock, and slid into the driver's seat so that I looked like I was just leaving the mall or just arriving. I would have blended in. Not this girl, she wanted to be noticed, to be chased. I saw a police car turn into the parking lot as we ran into a nearby apartment complex. Even in the great shape I was in, I started huffing. It was all that adrenaline.

She zigzagged through the buildings, and I heard the wail of the police siren coming our way. We got to a garbage bin, and she pulled herself up with little effort. I followed. She walked on the top of the metal sides like a tight rope walker and. once at the back of the container, she jumped over the fence and into a backyard. I did the same, but I scooted along the ledge on my butt, not my feet. From there, we walked down the street like we belonged and then climbed into a van idling on the corner. I pressed my tracker again.

Seven pairs of eyes stared at me as the van door closed. The driver turned and took off. He had been the only one missing from the mall powwow.

"Who's this, Frankie?" A boy with purple hair asked.

"A stowaway," she said, shrugging her shoulders.

"What does that mean?" A platinum blonde girl asked, swearing colorfully.

"She wanted to come along. I figured if she could keep up, I'd let her. Obviously, she kept up." She looked at me with a sort of awe.

"We can't have stowaways, Frankie," said a large, muscled boy–I realized with a bit of a start that it was Houston, the frog torturer from my science class.

"Why not? She did *Henry*." All eyes darted to me. Who was Henry? And what did I do to him?

"No way," the purple-haired boy said.

"Yes way," she said. "And she stuck the landing."

"You ever done that before, stowaway?" Houston asked.

I shook my head, figuring they were talking about the pole I'd slid down. "No, but it rocked. You should have seen the looks on the cops' faces when she jumped. What I wouldn't have paid to have that on camera."

No one spoke at first, and then the purple-haired boy said, "We'll have to see if we can arrange that." He smiled, then said, "What's your name?"

"Misha."

"Well, Misha, welcome to the Avengers. I hope you're tougher than you look, because we do all kinds of heart-stopping stunts."

They all started yelling, stomping their feet and hands and bouncing. I joined them, looking around at each face in the group, and I realized something. Sitting all around me were seven kids, each had colored their hair in some crazy color. No one had any normal colored hair. This couldn't be the group I was looking for. Their hair color wasn't right. Unfortunately, my gut told me otherwise. It told me this was the group I was looking for. My gut had never led me astray before. Why would it now?

Chapter 7

I felt my phone vibrate and pulled it out. Ian had called about ten times. I looked at my phone again and then spoke to the Avengers, "Hey Guys, any way you could drop me off at the bank across the street from the mall? My friends are picking me up there." I'd text Ian to come get me after they dropped me off.

"You mean Madness, right?" Frankie said. "They suck. I ran with them for a while but they wouldn't *allow* me to do certain things. Stick with us. You've got what it takes to take it to the next level."

"I'll think about that," I said. "But first, I need to explain what just happened to them or they'll freak out. They're very protective."

"We need your cell number, then," the platinum blonde girl, Maddie, said. I gave it to them. Maddie was the only one who put it in her phone. Did she act like their secretary or something?

"You won't have to worry about that with us," the purple-headed boy said. "We let you do your own thing. I'm Duncan, by the way."

"We're here, and I'm Lunden," the driver said, pulling up to the bank. His hair was brown with streaks of green.

"Thanks, guys," I said, getting ready to get out. Then I remembered the stuff Frankie had put in my bag. I reached in and pulled it out, "I almost forgot, here you go." I handed them to Frankie, and she pushed them back to me.

"You're the one that lifted those. They're yours," she said.

I pushed them back to her. "No really, I wouldn't know what to do with them. I give them to you." Then I jumped from the car. "Thanks!" I'd reimburse the store for the items.

"Rock climbing the Callahans on Monday. Join us?" Duncan said.

"Sure," I said, waving goodbye.

My mind reeled. Why did I have this pull toward the group of kids that didn't fit the profile as well as the other? Did Division know about this other group? Had they already discounted them, and I was spinning my wheels giving them a moment's thought? I'd ask Penrod and Wood and see what they had to say. If nothing, which I believed to be the case, I would ask Jeremy. I would have to be a part of both groups until I could figure everything out. But how would I know?

I texted Ian. He came and picked me up. "Where's everyone?" I asked, noticing he was the only one in the car.

"I told everyone your mom picked you up. If Dakota found out you were with the Avengers on my watch, he'd kill me."

I let that sink in, thinking of the feeling I had running from the cops. It was pure adrenaline that pushed me to jump to that pole—Henry, they called it. Flying from that railing was so scary, yet completely thrilling.

"What were you thinking?" he said. "You can't hang with them if Dakota is anywhere near. If you must do some truly death defying things, do it on the down-low and make sure he never finds out. I didn't peg you for a true adrenaline junkie. You look too sweet. You lack the edge those Avengers have."

Why was he giving me hints about how to do things with the Avengers? Why hadn't he told me to stay away from them like Dakota? It struck me as odd. "Are you saying that because I don't have a wild color of hair?"

"No. I'm usually good at assessing personalities. I always make dinner for prospective Madness members and can tell who would fit and who wouldn't. You didn't give me the vibe of someone turning to the dark side of thrill seeking."

"Dark side?" I turned the stud in my ear.

"Those kids have a death wish. They don't seem to be able to see the difference between what gives you a rush and what kills. They like the stuff that kills, maims, or gets them arrested. Is that what you want? You want to end up in jail or dead?"

It was like he really wanted to know. He seemed to be measuring me, seeing if I'd fit with the Avengers. A few things struck me at that moment. He had been staring at the Avengers in the courtyard at the mall and then, right after Frankie went into the electronics store, he had taken me there. He'd said he wanted new earphones, but then he'd gone to the video section where Frankie had been. It wasn't until Frankie left that he went for the earphones. Had he set me up? Was he testing me to see if I had what it took to be a part of the Avengers? Could he be the recruiter for that group, too? My mind debated for a quick second before answering him. How should I play this? If Ian is the recruiter for the Avengers, did this mean he was also the recruiter for the kidnappers? If he was, did they want the group of kids that felt the rush, but were mostly smart about it, or did they want the kids that held no regard for themselves and only sought the biggest rush? Did the kidnappers want hard-core or soft-core adrenaline junkies?

"I don't know why I did it," I said. "Frankie put that stuff in my bag so she could steal it. She gets a rush from it. I wanted to experience that too. To steal, right in front of everybody and get away with it? That rocked." I grinned big. It had been a thrill to be chased like that, even though I knew stealing was wrong. "Have you ever been chased? Man, that was the best."

He shook his head. "They're crazy, Misha. Really, you should stay away from them. They're trouble. There's a reason Dakota is so against them. You've got to return that stuff."

"I can't. I gave the stuff to Frankie." Was he going to try and dissuade me now? Was he testing me further, to see if I would shy away from them?

It was obvious he was the leader of Madness. Was his active leadership in Madness a way for him to separate himself from the group that would be chosen or was that a group he sent all the exclusions to? I felt like Frankie's group would be chosen by the kidnappers. Someone looking for groups of eight with specific hair color had to be mad. He would want recruits that were like him or at least close to his craziness. Right? But this second group didn't meet the hair requirements to be kidnapped. Madness had to be the right group. A dark, angry feeling filled me. I needed to feel peace.

I needed to talk this out with someone. I was all messed up. "Ian, they're just people who want to experience everything. What's wrong with that?"

He kept shaking his head. "Look, Misha. You're old enough to choose for yourself. But, I'm telling you to stay away from them, and Dakota would tell you the same if he were here. You better not ever let him know you were just with them. He'd freak."

"You're right, Ian. I am old enough to choose for myself, and neither you nor Dakota can tell me what I can and can't do."

He held up his hands in surrender. "Just be careful, girl. You're playing with fire. Make sure when Dakota finds out, and he will, to tell him I told you to stay away from them." He pulled out of the lot and headed toward my house.

He was telling me to be careful and not let Dakota know. "Maybe I like fire," I said, just loud enough for him to hear.

He chuckled.

When we got to my house he said, "I'm sorry for lecturing. I want you to stay safe. Even after such a short time, I can tell Dakota would be lost without you, and he's my best friend."

I looked at Ian and smiled. "Apology accepted, but I can take care of myself." I bounded out of the car and into the house so he wouldn't see the shame on my face. I shut the door and leaned back on it, taking a deep breath. My phone vibrated.

Is everything ok? It was Dakota.

Everything's fine. Chores. ☹ I texted back.

That sucks. Come when done.

Can't. Grounded. I wrote. I needed some time to figure some stuff out. I also had to meet with Jeremy to talk this all out.

Tomorrow? He wrote.

Sure.

Then I texted Jeremy, as per our protocol, and set up a meet. I told my parents about what had happened while I waited for my five o'clock meet with Jeremy. They were totally paying attention and interest seemed to spark in their eyes when they realized there might be another group.

"A second daredevil group?" Agent Penrod said.

"There is one hitch," I said. "They don't seem to meet the hair requirements. They all have brightly dyed hair—red, blue, and purple."

Agent Wood sighed, throwing his hands in the air and leaning back in his seat. "Didn't you read the file? The kidnapper hasn't taken a group of kids that didn't follow the hair pattern."

"Yeah but my gut—"

Agent Wood laughed. "You're not old enough or experienced enough to even think you can interpret what your *gut* feels. Forget about them. Do you have anything of substance for us today?"

I stood up and put all my weight on one foot, irritation claiming me. "I'm telling you the Avengers group needs to be looked into. It won't hurt you to check each person out."

Wood rolled his eyes. Penrod looked at me sympathetically.

"Whatever," I said and left the room. "Just look into them."

I met Jeremy at the abandoned warehouse outside of town later that evening. The sight of him gave me a lot of comfort. I knew he would help me.

"There are two groups that fit what we're looking for. Two, Jeremy. Actually, one doesn't match exactly, but my instincts tell me they're the real group. My mind tells me they can't be. Which group are the bad guys targeting, and how can I be sure?" I went through my reasoning for thinking it was the more dangerous of the two groups, and he thought my reasons were sound.

"I'll check the files," Jeremy said, "and see if there appears to be a pattern with the types of risks the kids have taken. I'll call the information specialists and have them sift through the information again, adding in the possibility of two groups. I've been looking into Ian and Dakota, and it appears that Dakota is the stronger contender for the recruiter. He–"

"That can't be right," I said. Jeremy's face flushed. "It couldn't be Dakota. Ian practically admitted to me he's the leader of Madness. The things he said about the Avengers, they all lead me to believe he leads both. He just doesn't want to be directly linked to the Avengers for some reason."

"Are you sure you're not letting your feelings for Dakota get in the way of your good judgment?" He tapped his pen on a metal railing next to us like he was irritated about something. "The holes in his history worry me. Ian doesn't seem to have any holes."

"I'm sure," I said. "Ian's separation from the hard core group swayed me. He wouldn't want to be directly associated with the group that got kidnapped. He wouldn't want the kidnapping to be traced back to him. He's not adamantly against them like Dakota is. And I don't have feelings for Dakota." I felt a blush creep onto my face despite the fact that what I was saying was true. I wasn't sure why I felt embarrassed that Jeremy thought I had real feelings. I guess I just wanted him to believe I was professional–a real spy.

"Despite your surety, Christy," Jeremy said. "I'm going to keep digging. Now, we have some work to do." He pulled out some papers and had me look them over so they would be forever in my brain. The papers had information about the rock climb I would be making Monday. He also brought equipment, and we practiced climbing in the warehouse. I would be meeting him here early in the morning tomorrow, and he would take me to the Callahan Mountains to practice. When he asked what Penrod and Wood had said, I told him the truth.

"I'll talk to them. I worried this might happen. They aren't the most progressive of agents." He rubbed his hand through his hair. "But, they are good at what they do. Really good. The best in a lot of ways."

"No, you can't," I said, grabbing his arm. "I have to solve this problem on my own. I can't have them thinking I run to you with my problems. It will only reinforce their biased opinion about my youth. I'll just have to be that much better to rise above their subtle sabotage."

"You're probably right, but they should be updating you on any intel they receive. Have they told you anything?"

"Yes."

"I'll send them an email and ask what your input was on the information I sent. Maybe that will force them to start up a dialogue with you again and treat you like the agent you are."

"Good idea."

"As for the Avengers and Madness, go ahead and play both teams until I can get a lock on which one it most likely is. We should be able to narrow it down. At least I hope we can do it in the time we have."

"All right. I'll do my best to figure it out, too."

Chapter 8

With a sore and tired body, I went to bed, knowing I'd need all my strength to go climbing with Jeremy at four a.m.

Something knocked at my window. I jerked my head to look at the clock. Had I somehow slept in and missed my meeting with Jeremy? No. It was only one a.m. I cautiously walked to the window, ready for anything. Frankie stared at me, her face all goofy-looking. I covered my mouth so I wouldn't laugh out loud. I pushed my window open, and she climbed in.

"We're going tagging. Wanna come?"

"Tagging? As in spray painting?" I said.

"Uh, yeah," she laughed. "Don't tell me you've never been."

"Guilty as charged," I said, grinning big, hoping it took away from the apparent geekiness I displayed.

"We'll show you how it's done," she said. "Wear black and hurry." She climbed out of the window, and I pulled the curtain shut so I could change.

Of course, we couldn't just tag the sound walls along the freeway or someone's private property. We had to break into the city government offices. We parked several blocks away and walked over. Anna, the blue-haired girl, had disabled the alarm system in about five minutes. She yelled, "Three minutes and counting." She had explained on the way over that once she turned off the alarm, a secondary alarm would alert the authorities. It took them four minutes to respond. That gave us three to get all the tagging done. I watched as they created pretty cool paintings of wildlife in those three minutes. I got nothing done. I stood and stared, amazed, wondering how much money I should send the city to clean up this mess. Of course, I pressed my tracker.

"Time!" Anna yelled and everyone took off toward the door we'd entered. As per the plan, we were all to split up and meet at the van in ten minutes. I heard sirens and took off. When I turned on the block where the van was, I couldn't help but notice the police car parked behind it. I turned back around and walked to the next street down. My phone vibrated. The text read,

Old Woolworth Building

I mentally pulled up the city map of Roseburg and headed over. Once we were all there, Lunden hotwired a car, and we piled on top of each other and took off. Maddie drove.

"That was great!" Houston shouted, running his fingers through his longish red and black hair.

"Perfect timing, dude," Payden said, and he knocked knuckles with Houston.

"Thanks," Houston said. "Let's go to my house. I drew up the plans for next week's raid on mall security–to get Frankie and Misha's tapes. I thought we better go over it and see if any of you find any flaws in my thinking and also divvy up the jobs."

"What about your dad?" Lunden said.

"He'll be snoring his happy, completely wasted snore by now." I noticed several in the group looked wary.

"We could do it at my house," Payden offered.

"No need, he'll be out, you'll see."

"He'd better be," Duncan said. "My knee's still hating it from the last time he went after us with that baseball bat."

"He will be," Houston said, nodding his head. "My dad won't even know we're there. I can't wait to see the footage of Frankie and Misha from yesterday."

They made all kinds of excited noises as they agreed with him.

Houston's house stood on the corner, only the city streetlight giving it any light. The front yard was dirt with a smattering of weeds. An old car on blocks sat in the middle of it where I'm sure grass once grew. Shutters hung askew and paint peeled in curls all over the house. If I hadn't known he lived here, I would have pegged it for abandoned. We entered like thieves through the back door and slinked into his bedroom, every one of us having to pass his father who snored like a freight train. Once in his room, Houston pulled out a laptop from between his mattresses.

We all gathered around as he talked about the plan.

"I don't know why we hadn't thought about getting this footage before," Maddie said, pushing her platinum blonde hair behind her ear.

"We just needed Misha to open our eyes," Duncan said.

Frankie high-fived me.

Houston had used a complicated design program to map out the mall in 3D and even had all of them, looking eerily like themselves, in the design doing the various tasks he thought they should do.

I couldn't help myself and said, "Dang, Houston, that's amazing. You should be an architect."

Lunden said, "That's what we've been telling him. Once we saw his amazing drawings in art, we *found*," he coughed, "him this program, and he's mastered it."

"I'm going to design bridges, buildings, whole towns when I graduate from college," Houston said, beaming as much as a muscle-head could beam.

This was incredible. This group had found Houston and given him hope, direction. I looked at all their faces as Houston began describing their jobs to them. I now saw them differently. They were freaking cool. They had very likely saved Houston from becoming some career criminal. Sure, he was doing crap now, but as an adult, he could rock it. This group supported each other as Dakota's did, just in a different way that wasn't readily apparent.

"Maybe I'll be a safe designer," he threw out there.

Anna was quick to say, "Hey, that's my department."

"You're the safe cracker, not the safe creator," Lunden said.

"You're right, I'm no good with design, but give me any safe and I'll crack it."

"That's right," Duncan said. "You'll have your own company testing people's safes and alarm systems."

"And I'll be one rich chick."

They all swore colorfully as if money and the accumulation of it were the whole reason to live.

As they talked about their assignments in retrieving the tapes, I realized they all had important talents to offer the group. These lost kids weren't lost at all. What could I add?

"I think it all sounds great except for the part that I'm not included," I interrupted.

"What if you were a lookout?" Duncan asked. "You want to be a second lookout? We can always use a second."

"I think I like that idea. I could be the lookout that lures the officer away should he return unexpectedly." I changed my voice to a sassy one and said, "I could wear a short, little skirt, a flirty top, some nice wedge heels, and shiny cherry flavored lip gloss." I laughed and they did, too.

"Alright," Duncan said. "Now you have the perfect job. Just change your lip gloss flavor to strawberry and you'll even have me drooling."

"I'm starving!" Payden said.

"We can't eat here," Houston said. "We ain't got anything anyway."

"I've got forty bucks in my pocket," I said. "How about Denny's?"

"Awesome," Payden said. "Breakfast on the newbie. Can't beat that."

We drove to where we'd left the van. I guessed the officer hadn't been able to find anything wrong with it and just left it there. Anna hopped in and followed us back to Woolworths where we put the stolen car back where we'd found it. I left some change I had in my pocket on the floorboard to pay for the gas we'd used.

"The owner will never even know," Maddie said, grinning from ear to ear.

Once at the restaurant, I once again tapped my tracker. Breakfast was filled with normal teen chatter about how parents were so lame and old boyfriends or girlfriends were jerks. I'd never spoken nasty about my parents, but I joined in happily, referencing my agent parents. Frankie was the only one who abstained from talking about hers.

"You're not in the parent-hating crowd?" I whispered to her.

"Nah. It's only my mom and me, and she works really hard to keep us afloat. She wants the best for me, just doesn't have the time to give it to me. With two full-time jobs we barely see each other."

"What does she do?"

"She's a bartender."

"That's hard work, I bet."

"Yeah! She comes home totally wasted," Frankie said. "But I don't blame her. She has a hard life."

"You gonna tell Misha about your mom's second job?" Lunden asked.

"Not necessary, Lunden," Frankie spat. "Thanks a lot."

"You don't have to tell me if you don't want to," I said. "It doesn't bother me." I didn't want to hear about anything else sensational that night.

She sighed. "It's okay, I'll tell you. I just can't stand Lunden's big mouth." She slugged him, and it wasn't a playful slug. It was hard. He grabbed her hand and kissed it.

"Sorry hon," he said. Then he laughed.

These guys were like brothers and sisters. It was pretty great. I was suddenly really glad these kids had found each other. Who cared if they were doing dangerous things? They had each other. They valued each other.

She never did tell me about her mom. We got pulled into Duncan's story about spelunking the first time.

During his tale, he must've thrown in ten different compliments about kids in the group. That's when it hit me: he was the one who made this group work. He was the one who led the encouragement. The perfect leader.

It shocked me when they dropped Houston off at his house, and they all blew him a kiss. He blew one back.

"I hate dropping him off there," Duncan said. "I wish he'd come live with me. It'd be nice to have someone to talk to."

I guess Duncan's parents were absentee parents. It further shocked me when they did the blowing-the-kiss thing each time we dropped someone off, including me. They truly cared about each other. They were strength to each other.

By the time they dropped me off, it was almost four in the morning. Jeremy would be here soon to take me rock climbing.

When he did come, I sprawled out on the back seat of Jeremy's car and slept the whole way to the Callahan Mountains. We drove to the section of the mountains called the Turtles. He woke me with a soft brush of his hand on my cheek. He was so handsome. He stepped back as I sat up. I wondered if I had morning breath and pulled out a stick of gum before getting out of the car.

He taught me how to climb the gorgeous sandstone mountain while he belayed, holding the safety ropes firmly while I climbed. I only climbed half of the 1500 feet, but I could see how fatigue might play a huge roll in my success or failure tomorrow. He then started me on free soloing. Talk about difficult. My arms shook more often than I cared to admit, and I only climbed about 100 feet. Jeremy made me take the ropes to get back down.

"You don't have to do this, Christy. It's so dangerous. You can't infiltrate the kidnapping ring if you're dead." He saw the look of determination on my face and sighed. "At least, if they give you a choice, go up attached." He grabbed my arm and rubbed his thumb over my skin. "You have nothing to prove, and I won't be here to guide you. Can you trust these kids to teach you well?"

"No worries," I said. "I don't want to die. I'll be as safe and careful as I can be."

"I had Toni, our electronics guru, make this lip balm to help protect you. If it's within fifty feet of you when you activate your tracking beacon, it will protect the signal, effectively making it undetectable to anyone but us. That way, you won't have to pulse it, you'll be able to send a sustained signal. Still, you won't want to let it send longer than about a minute just to be sure, but Toni outdid herself on this one. Keep it with you from now on.

"Whichever group it is they will be kidnapping, now that you've appeared on the scene, I'm sure it will happen soon. I don't know how you fit in with the Avengers besides being number eight, but we need to be alert from now on. I have to have you safe and be sure I can find you when the kidnappers take you."

Hearing him say it that way really drove the fact that I was about to be kidnapped by some crazy person, and I had no idea what they did with the teens they took. What if we were to be used as sacrifices, or for torture, or for experimentation? What if I never had the chance to activate the tracker in the first place?

He gathered me into a hug, and I thought I felt him kiss my hair, but I must have been mistaken.

"Be careful, watchful," he said.

"I will," I said.

When he pulled back, he sighed. "I guess that's all I can ask. Let's get this over with."

On the drive home, I took the opportunity to ask Jeremy about himself.

"So, how old are you anyway?"

He looked at me briefly and smiled. "How old do you think I am?"

"When I first met you in DC, I thought you were about twenty-one."

"That's right. I'm twenty-one."

I slugged him. "No you're not. You couldn't be. You've been doing this for a while."

"You're only eighteen and you work for Division 57. Why not me, too?" He raised his eyebrows at me. "You think you're special or something?" He chuckled.

I laughed, too. "Give it up, *ordinary guy*. What's your age?"

"I take offense to that," he said, trying to keep a straight face. Then he busted up a bit, pushing a rush of air through his nose and smiling. "You really want to know?"

"I wouldn't have asked if I didn't."

"I'm twenty-five."

"Oh, man, you're practically an old man."

For a mere second, I thought I saw sadness pass through him, but then it was gone just as fast as it flashed by.

"Yep," he said. "Could you hand me my spectacles, young chic-a-dee, I can't seem to see the road." He swerved dangerously close to the edge of the road and then wove in and out of the two lanes of highway.

I screeched. "Okay. Okay. I take it back. You're a quarter of a century *young.*"

"You better remember that," he said, smiling and straightening his driving.

He took me to lunch in a town on the way home. Dakota texted me a few times, but I ignored him. After lunch, we drove back to my house. I slept the whole way. At home, I took a shower, and only then did I text Dakota back. I picked up the lip balm Jeremy had given me and noticed in the fine print it said, *Believe in you! Ltd.*

Code, of course.

I giggled, putting the lip balm up to my lips and closing my eyes. With Jeremy protecting me, I wouldn't have to worry about staying safe.

I got a text from Frankie,

No rock tomorrow. Next Mon. Surf the rails Wed.

I hated to admit it, but I was glad. I was pooped. I went to bed early, and I got up late, my body aching. I was in great shape, but rock climbing used muscles I don't think I'd ever used before. I took a few ibuprofen with my breakfast and it eased the ache. I let Agent Wood and Agent Penrod know about my plans for the day, and they actually seemed interested and didn't talk down to me. What had caused the change?

After school, Madness got together to create a video for drama class. We acted out a modern day *Tristan and Isolde.* Ian was Tristan, and Abby was Isolde. They'd made up the modern twist on the play a while ago, but did a few clever things to add a part for me. They'd gone all out with costumes and props. Camden was the camera man/director. Troy would be editing it the next day, and we'd have a movie night Wednesday to view it. I'd never done anything like that before.

Dakota coached me a bit before I made my cameo appearance. He was a great director. I had no doubt the final product would be extraordinary. He was kind and forgiving when people made mistakes. There was no way he was working for the bad guys. Dakota wanted me to stay afterward, but I told him I wasn't feeling well. I had to start distancing myself from him now that I thought he probably wasn't a part of the group getting kidnapped.

Much to my relief, neither group did anything together on Tuesday. I pretended not to feel well the whole day at school so that Dakota wouldn't push doing something together after school. While he cuddled me a bit, he didn't kiss anything but my forehead, and when hugging me at my car after school, he told me to rest and get better.

There was no time for rest. I met with Jeremy in the abandoned warehouse for a few hours to learn about rail surfing and work a little bit on climbing again. I claimed exhaustion at nine, and he spread a blanket out on the floor, set a flashlight in the middle of it, and pulled out two take-out boxes and two bottled waters and sat them next to each other.

"Dinner?" I asked.

"Not exactly," he said, and raised his eyebrows. The scruff on his face made him look extra enticing. "Why don't you open the box and see."

I did. Inside was a Belgian waffle. A real one. Not like the fake, fluffy ones we had in the U.S. We're talking an authentic, rich, dense, luscious waffle.

"Oh no, you didn't!" I squealed with delight as I sat in front of it.

"Oh yes, I did," he said, sitting next to me and then opening his box and digging in. He could be so thoughtful. I hadn't had one of these since leaving Belgium and the spy school. Jeremy and I had gone out to a couple of international restaurants while I was at Division 57 headquarters, and I always ordered one if it was available.

I closed my eyes to enjoy the crispy crunchy outside and rich, dense inside more fully. I could feel chocolate sticking to my lips and didn't even care if he saw it there. I was in heaven—I'd clean up when I was done. When I opened my eyes, his lips were covered in chocolate, too. We laughed and playfully bumped our shoulders together. He gave me his last bite, popping it into my open mouth. Something about the way he did it caused goose bumps to rise on my neck. We were so close. He smelled fantastic, and I had this sudden desire to touch his arm. I resisted and began cleaning up. Despite my sudden chocolate high, after we'd cleaned up, I was totally ready to go home and sleep.

The next day after dinner, I went to Troy's house to watch the video we'd made. Dakota hadn't arrived yet, so I plopped down in the middle of Mindy and Tarran. Troy had done a great job of editing. He even made me look good. He had one of those cool, old-fashioned popcorn poppers and a soda fountain. He ordered pizza from Abby's, and we pigged out on junk watching and rewatching the video. Dakota was a good hour late. I waved at him and smiled when he walked in, but made no move to go to him. We laughed so hard a few times, tears rolled from our eyes. My gut ached from both the junk food and the laughter. We wrapped it up about ten. Dakota walked me to my car and hugged me tight.

"Why were you late?" I asked.

"My dad needed me to do a few things for him."

"You didn't miss much, anyway."

"I missed sitting with you, so I missed a lot." He looked me in the eye and then kissed me. He knew just what to say. I wished he didn't.

Chapter 9

Back home, around midnight, my phone vibrated, and then I heard a knock on my window. It was Frankie letting me know the Avengers were there to get me. No one had told me what time or where to meet for the rail surfing, so I had guessed they just forgot about me. It felt good that they hadn't.

She climbed into my room with a bag in her hand. "Here are some clothes for you to wear." She handed the bag to me. "I hope they fit."

The tags were still attached when I pulled them out.

"How much do I owe you?" I asked.

She laughed quietly. "You think I bought those things? Are you crazy? Did you see how expensive they were?" She laughed again.

I shook my head and started to dress. I made a mental note to send money to the store Frankie had lifted the clothes from.

The clothes were black and form fitting. The socks and shoes were rubbery, gummy even. I could see them easily sticking to slick surfaces. The gloves had the same stuff on them. I felt I could grip anything with what I had on. I didn't put the mask on. I figured I'd wait until we got there.

Once I climbed out the window and closed it, I made a sound like a bear roaring and chased Frankie to the car.

"You're such a dork, Misha," she said, climbing into the van.

"I know," I said. "Every time I try to reign it in, it gets worse." I followed her. "So, I just let myself be."

Duncan gave me a little tutorial on rail surfing as we drove. "We need to jump on the train while it's still in the yard. It only goes about ten miles an hour in the yard. Even a newbie can jump on a train traveling at ten miles an hour."

"Okay," I said. "I'm a fast runner anyway.

"It'll be easy, really," he said. "The trick is getting on the train without being seen. Typically there aren't any workers around that time of night, but we have to make sure. The train only has one conductor, too. We'll be jumping on cars at the back of the train, so he'll have no idea we're even there. At this time of night in the darkness, he'll never see us."

"Convenient."

"Indeed. Once on the train, we'll hunker down until the train gets up to its maximum speed, which on this train, on this track, is fifty miles per hour. It's a respectable speed for a beginner. Once at speed, we'll climb to the top of the train and then stand."

"Cool."

"We all usually take our own car, but Frankie will double up with you until she feels you have the hang of it. At that point, she'll move to the car in front of you."

After that, Duncan told me pretty much the same general things Jeremy had said. The train would not be smooth, but rock from side to side. A wide stance and rubbery shoes ensured a stable ride. I would start out crouched and on the balls of my feet then slowly rise up like a surfer in water. That I understood. I'd lived in Florida, and surfing had been a favorite activity of my friends there.

Duncan informed me that they would be tricking it, but that I shouldn't try to trick it. Apparently, they didn't only stand when on top of the cars, but they did tricks on the car top. They'd been practicing for years.

"It might look easy," Duncan said. "But it isn't. Depending on how you do tonight, we'll teach you some tricks before we go again, okay?"

"Okay," I said. I couldn't imagine doing tricks on a moving train anyway. Jeremy hadn't told me about doing tricks. I wondered if he knew about kids doing that.

"In all honesty," Duncan said. "Fifty miles per hour isn't that fast. You shouldn't have a problem staying upright."

"You should try riding a passenger train in Germany," Payden said. "I about got myself killed surfing there. Those babies go over 125 miles an hour."

"Yeah!" Lunden said. "And don't even think about trying the TGV in France, that baby goes about 250 mph. You'd need to be anchored down for sure."

We each had a set time and place assigned to us to jump on the train. Houston was taking his turn to drive and meet us up at the pickup location about fifty miles away. I was in third position, a place they thought would be safest. We were pretty much guaranteed not to be seen for three reasons. Number one, the train was long and we'd be at the end of it, and two, there were only five workers in the yard tonight. Three, we were boarding on a straightaway, and it was dark.

This made it almost impossible for the conductor or agent to see us.

The train yard was big and scary. I pressed my tracker. Shadows hung all around and the smell of grease, metal, and rotten wood filled my nostrils. The longer I looked around the yard, searching for workers, the more it seemed there were a lot of people about, causing shadows to jump out at me. I had to force myself to stay put until it was time. The screech of the train moving hit loud on my ears. I was hidden at about the halfway mark.

Frankie was hidden about fifteen feet behind me, and I was to follow her lead. When she ran, I was supposed to run. Air brakes and clanking filled my ears as the train pulled out. I watched for Frankie. She darted to the car right beside her and jogged at the same speed as the train until she grabbed a handrail and pulled herself up onto the first of three stairs that led to a landing at the back of the car.

As soon as she jumped aboard, I left my hiding spot and easily jogged at the same speed as the train. When I hit a steady rhythm, I grabbed the same rail Frankie had and pulled myself onto the step. She was huddled against a metal door in the middle of the landing. I sat next to her, and we waited for the train to leave the yard and pick up speed. It didn't take long. It felt weird thinking I was breaking so many rules. My nerves were on edge.

Climbing on the top wasn't as easy as it appeared. The rocking of the cars made it difficult. The ladder was on the side of the car, not the back, and the rungs were rough and dug into my hands. Frankie was there to guide and encourage me the whole way.

Once on top, she went in front of me and showed me how to get safely into standing position several times. My stomach clenched as I followed her lead. It wasn't as hard as I thought it would be, and I relaxed a bit. The difficult part was staying standing. Frankie made it look easy. The rocking of the car was completely unpredictable, and I lost my balance several times, ducking each time into a crouch so I wouldn't fall off the train. After about ten minutes, Frankie climbed down and made her way to the car in front of the one I was on.

She had no trouble balancing. Once in the middle of the car, she bent over and did a handstand. She stayed up for a count of ten. Pretty amazing. She rocked to the side a couple of times, and I thought she'd tumble off, but she never did. Then she did several cartwheels as well as somersaults. Crazy.

I looked around me, enjoying the feeling of freedom that coursed through me. Life for me had been restricted, plain, and rule-driven until my trip to DC, where everything changed. Now I was a rule breaker, and it felt great to be Misha. Christy, that little bit of the real me that I clung to for my own sanity while using an alias, on the other hand, screamed for me to get down and be safe.

I found it exhilarating to let the wind slide over my face and body and tug at my clothes. I thought bugs would be slapping me, but they didn't. The person who really surprised me was Payden. He was an amazing tumbler and would do back tucks, layouts, and fulls, a front flip with a 360 in the air, all on top of the train car behind us. I could do those things, but not on a moving train.

Getting off the train was the hard part. Duncan, on the car in front of us, signaled we needed to get ready to de-board.

I hunched down and scooted my way to the back of the car to get down. I didn't trust myself to move standing up. I climbed down the ladder and shuffled to the edge of the car, waiting to feel the train slow for the curve where we were supposed to jump. It was easy to feel the train brake. I saw both Duncan and Frankie jump and roll. I didn't even give myself a chance to think. I just jumped and rolled. It hurt. The ground was hard and rocky.

They didn't wait until we reached the car, a good fifty yards from the tracks, to start celebrating. They danced around and talked about the success or failure of this trick or that, stopping to demonstrate as we made our way to the car. Houston sat outside the van, a cooler by his feet that he opened as we got close. They all grabbed a beer from inside.

"Go ahead," Houston said, noticing my hesitation.

"That's okay," I said. "I'll drive back. I owe you guys that much."

He nodded and grabbed his own beer. Twenty minutes later, we were on the road.

School was pretty routine every other day that week. Every one of my seven classes had at least one person from one of the two daredevil groups I was a part of in it, so I stayed in close touch with both. Dakota met me in front of the school every day, and I sat with Madness for lunch every day. I tried to slowly move away from Dakota, waiting to text him back, getting to school right before classes started so we had no time together, and making sure I had other things to do in my free time.

We longboarded to and from gym class, and he met me at my locker after school. The girls of Roseburg High seemed to hate me. I had taken one of its most eligible members off the market. I got told I wasn't good enough, that I wasn't pretty enough, and got called all sorts of unsavory names. It was lucky that I was constantly with people from the two groups, or I may have found myself in some pretty messy situations.

Once, I opened my locker just as Dakota arrived. Several notes lay on the floor of the locker. Dakota picked them up.

"You can just throw those away," I said, a casual tone in my voice. "They're just fan mail."

"Fan mail?" he said, opening one written on red paper.

I chuckled. He didn't. After reading the first one, he opened one on yellow paper. "What is this crap?"

"I told you, fan mail."

"Who would do this? I'm gonna find out and–"

"It's no big deal, Dakota," I said. "Honestly it doesn't bother me. It's kinda funny actually. To think–"

"There's nothing funny about this. They're threatening you." His eyes were wide, and his mouth was pressed into a hard line.

"They don't mean it. You should see the bathrooms."

The girls' bathrooms and locker rooms had derogatory statements about me all over.

"What?" he said, moving down the hall toward the nearest girls' bathroom. By the time I caught up with him, he was reading all the comments on the stall doors. Many were about me. He'd gone in the girls' bathroom for me. A thrill moved through my body.

"Dakota, it's okay," I said, moving toward him. He walked passed me to the paper towel dispenser and pulled a bunch of towels out, then wetted them in the sink. He scrubbed furiously on the first door.

"That won't wash anything away."

He kicked the door. "What's wrong with people? This isn't right. I'm going to see to it that it stops."

"You think this is bad?" I said, grabbing his head and leading him out into the hallway. "This is nothing. There was this girl at my old school–Katie Lee. Now *she* was a real piece of work. She bullied me from the second I got into high school. It wasn't pretty."

He pulled me to the side of the hallway and stopped. "I can't do anything about how people treated you in Colorado, but I intend to make this stop right here, right now. And I need you to understand that you shouldn't put up with it. It's not right. No one has the right to say these things about anyone. They are all lies. Do you understand this, Misha? You don't deserve this. You should demand better treatment."

It was hard not let an overwhelming love spread through me for Dakota at that moment. He was on fire and amazing. He was protecting my honor. He was my knight in shining armor. I pulled him to me and kissed him hard until a teacher broke us apart. I wasn't even embarrassed we'd been caught. This guy was the real deal.

He went and complained to the office and then found the janitor and asked him to get rid of the garbage on the walls. My hero. He or someone from Madness kept an eye on my locker as much as possible, and the notes stopped coming before the end of the week.

Agent Wood and Agent Penrod told me several little updates from Division and even laughed with me when I told them about my fan mail. I was making progress. Slowly but surely. I wondered if I had time to get them to fully trust me before I was kidnapped. I was surprised it was taking so long.

***

I was supposed to be meeting the Avengers at the mall on Thursday to retrieve the tapes of our heist. So, when I woke up, I met with my agent parents to see if they could help me with some problems I could see with the heist.

"I'll be with the Avengers at the mall after school. We're breaking into mall security and the risk of getting arrested is high. They like to be chased, so they're cutting it close. Too close in my opinion. They've discovered response time is five minutes. We need seven to be in the clear. I need you to give us that extra two minutes. I can't get kidnapped if I'm jammed up. Could you help me out?"

Penrod's eyes narrowed slightly, then returned to normal and she unpressed her lips. trying to hide some agitation.

Wood took a step back and put his hands on his hips. "When did you plan this little heist? A little warning would have been nice."

"Sorry, I should have told you sooner." Great, now I would be back in the little kid corner. "Could you please help me out?"

"We'll try," Agent Penrod said, letting her eyes flash. "There are other things we needed to be doing, though."

Once we were all in position, Payden created our diversion. He was dressed all in purple and black spandex and began tumbling his way around. He began in the food court. People whistled and cat called and because he was so good, they also clapped and begged him for more. Sure enough, the security guards came rushing out of their office, and Anna went to work on the locks. She had to disable the electronic security and open the door with a lock picking kit. She was fast. I watched from the end of the hallway, hoping I wouldn't have to use my womanly wiles against the two security goons.

Anna was in and out of the office in five minutes flat. The guards should have been making their way back, having received information that someone was breaking into their office, but the guards were nowhere in sight. It was funny to watch the three others in the hall with me wait around, hoping someone would come and chase them.

We all just walked out of the mall, no one on our tails. The whole adventure had been a letdown for the Avengers. No one even got close to catching them. Thank you, Agent Wood and Agent Penrod.

School let out early on Friday so that everyone could travel to Eugene for the football game. I liked this school. Excused absences for football games? That rocked. Madness caravanned there in three cars. I rode shotgun with Dakota. I couldn't figure a way to get out of it. Tarran and Troy sat in the back seat. I loved the way my hair blew in the wind when we drove with the top off.

Madness all sat together in the bleachers, and I happened to be on the end. At half-time, someone tapped my shoulder from behind me. It was Frankie.

"We're blowing this joint, Misha. There's this awesome half-pipe about a mile from here. Want to go check it out with us?"

Before I could respond, Dakota stood and turned to Frankie. "Get out of here, Frankie. Misha's with me."

"She can choose for herself," Frankie said. "You don't own her."

"I told you to leave, Frankie," Dakota said, his teeth clenched together.

That's when I saw Duncan, Payden, and Houston making their way up the bleachers. This wouldn't be good. The rest of Madness must have clued into what was happening because the guys all stood up. I stood up when the Avengers were only ten feet from us and put my arms out as if to hold the two groups apart. "Look guys," I said. "Like Frankie said, I can choose for myself and tonight, I want to stay here with Dakota. Thanks for the invite Frankie, but I'm going to pass."

"Whatever, Misha," she said, turning to go.

I thought Dakota would watch them until they disappeared. Instead, he trained his eyes on me, a look of complete disbelief on his face. "You're going to pass? Have you hung out with them before or something? They acted like they know you."

"Let's sit down, Dakota," I said. "Everyone's staring." And they were. I sat, and the rest of Madness, excluding Dakota, followed my lead. Dakota continued to stare hard at me and finally sat after what seemed like forever.

He took my hand from my lap and said, "Please tell me you haven't been hanging out with those goons."

I had the perfect lie. "Of course not," I said, my insides trembling. "I know them from my classes at school, Dakota. They seem nice enough, especially Frankie. What do you have against them?" My throat constricted. That was a total lie.

He rubbed the top of my hand, looking down into my lap and then back up into my eyes. "Trust me on this one.

They're no good. Stay as far away from them as you can." The fire in his green eyes slowly melted away as he pleaded with me. "Please. Promise me you won't ever hang out with them." He squeezed my hand.

While I knew I most definitely would be hanging out with them, I couldn't let Dakota know that. He hated them. I'd no idea how much until now. "I promise," I said, a hole seeming to open up in my heart with the lie.

He grabbed me into a hug. "Thank you, Misha. I just want you to be safe. Those idiots put their lives in serious danger every day. Thank you for trusting me." He pulled away, and our eyes met. He smiled, and so did I. When his lips met mine, the requisite fireworks exploded in my gut, and the Avengers were a distant memory.

That time the Roseburg Indians won by a field goal. It was a nail-biter.

On Saturday, the drama department was holding a music festival fundraiser to get a new sound system. We had to be there at six in the morning to set up. My assignment was with foods, and Dakota wasn't happy about it. He was with the theater department.

"I'll go ask Ms. Anderson if she'll let you switch to theater. I'm sure she won't mind."

"It's okay, Dakota, really," I said. "I don't mind working with the food. It will be fun."

"I have no doubt about that," he said. "I just don't want you working with the partner they've assigned you to."

My partner was Houston. Yesterday Dakota had made it crystal clear that I wasn't to hang out with anyone from the Avengers, and Houston was an Avenger. Dakota quickly stalked up to Mrs. Anderson who was talking to Duncan. This could be bad.

"Could you move Misha over to the theater detail, Mrs. Anderson, we could really use her inside." I wondered how long his diplomacy would hold out.

"I don't think so," Duncan chimed in. "We need her with the foods, both Tasha and Millie haven't shown up yet, and they probably won't."

"Could we talk privately?" he asked Mrs. Anderson, his eyes ripping through Duncan.

"I'm sorry, Dakota, but Duncan needs her. You'll have to make do without her."

"But–," Dakota said.

"No buts, Dakota," Mrs. Anderson said. "My word is final." She turned to talk to Duncan, and I saw Dakota narrow his eyes at him. He kicked at the ground and then turned to me. "Sorry," he said. "You're going to have to work with those idiot Avengers." He pulled me to the side. "Don't let them fill your head with nonsense. They are crazy, every one of them."

"Dakota, thank you for looking out for me, but I feel I'm a good judge of character. I can figure it out." It was hard to keep the bite out of my words.

His phone beeped.

"Crap," he said. "I've got to go. Just don't talk to anyone."

I gave him an irritated look before turning and going to the food volunteer area.

I quickly found out what a big deal this was. There were twenty kids working the foods area of the festival. I would be rotating around each of the six booths throughout the day, starting in the cotton candy booth with Houston and ending with snow cones.

Houston was interesting to work with. The food and games required tickets. When certain kids came up and held out a ticket or two for the item they wanted, Houston would whisper to me to give them extra, citing reasons like they were poor, his mom is mean, her dad doesn't even pay any attention to her. He would also give substandard product to certain people that he had an obvious contempt for. How could Dakota judge him so harshly? I also learned more about the kids in the Avengers, including the fact that Frankie's dad was in an accident when she was five and lost his hearing. He'd gotten involved with several groups for deaf people and three years later, left Frankie and her mom for a beautiful deaf woman.

Duncan was the student leader in charge of all the food booths. He had amazing organizational skills and was efficient and effective. It was interesting to see him lead outside the daredevil group. He was responsible, and didn't take any chances. It was like he was a different person. Another Avenger Dakota had no clue about. He was great.

There was also the games section with blow up slides, bouncy castles, and obstacle courses as well as a go-fish booth and ponies to ride.

Most of Madness and only Frankie from the Avengers were working in the theater. They would be doing improv, mini plays, and one-act shows. At only three bucks apiece it was a bargain. Dakota was in charge of that part of the fundraiser. He made sure the right people were in the right places at the right times. He was able to sneak out a few times to say hello and kiss me while giving scathing looks to every Avenger around me. I would have to educate him about how great the Avengers were.

I had no doubt they earned enough money for the lighting system plus some. There was nonstop business the whole eight hours we worked. I was bushed and thought everyone else would be, too, but I was wrong.

The Avengers had other plans. We broke into the cage that contained the driver's ed. cars and took them on a joyride up the canyon. We built a fire, and they drank beer. I discovered all kinds of interesting information. The Avengers were started by Duncan and Anna. They found each other in juvie. Then they siphoned off several members of Madness who wanted a bit more of an edge to their activities. Maybe that's why Dakota didn't like them. They had taken several members away from his beloved group.

Lunden said, "Yeah, Duncan could go to juvie every day and it wouldn't matter. His parents would get him out."

"At least your parents pay attention to you," Duncan said.

"I'd rather they leave me alone, like your parents."

"It's not fun being left completely alone. Besides, they expect me to be perfect."

"You are perfect. You can't fool anyone anymore. No one would ever believe you're a part of our group."

"That's not true. My hair is purple if you hadn't noticed."

"You just need some bling on your skin man."

"You know that's not happening."

"You got any ink, Misha?"

"Maybe. That's for me to know and you not to." I felt like being smart.

"Actually," Frankie said, "She has ink behind her ear. I've seen it."

I'd almost forgotten about the small bird tattoo Division had given me.

"Do you have it anywhere else?"

"You'll never know."

"Ooh! Challenge!"

Once the fire died down, I drove everyone back to the school. Neither of my agent parents were at the house. Had they been out observing me and just hadn't come back yet?

Chapter 10

I met Jeremy for a short meeting late at night. He filled me in on what he'd found out about Dakota. It matched what Dakota had told me about himself. It made me feel good that Jeremy might be leaning toward Ian as the leader, too.

"Dakota's not out of the woods yet, Misha. I have a couple of guys still digging, seeing if they can discredit the things we uncovered on the first round of discovery. We're hoping to have all the info by tomorrow. Did Agent Wood replace your tracker?"

"No. Why would he do that?"

"Didn't they tell you yours was acting up? Sometimes it works and sometimes it doesn't. We got the memo from headquarters earlier today."

"Maybe they didn't get the memo. They were gone when I got back from joyriding."

"Regardless, I want that replaced tomorrow. No excuses."

"All right." Certainly they would have told me had they known. Where were they anyway?

I planned on telling Dakota that I couldn't meet with him on Sunday, but he showed up at my house with brunch, so we spent a few hours watching old movies. I had still been in bed when he arrived and didn't get the chance to confront my agent parents about where they'd been and get them to replace my tracker.

Dakota told me about recruiting Tarran and Mindy to Madness.

"So, you were just wanting to hook up with the girls?" I said.

"Truth be told, you're not the first, but I hope you will be the last." He grabbed my hand and kissed me.

A sweet thrill ran up my spine. My plan on distancing myself from him was not going well. I thought I might need to be a bit mean. Could I be? I had to be. "How can you be sure? We've only known each other for two weeks."

"Are you mocking me?"

"I don't know. Maybe."

"Stop it," he said in a seductive voice. "It doesn't become you." He kissed me.

Nothing would work on this guy without me having to be downright mean. He was too determined.

After he left, I walked into my agent parents' office to tell them about my defective tracker and to remind them about the plan for tomorrow and not to expect me until late. They could replace it then. I stopped short when I saw them huddled together in front of the fax machine whispering.

"Did we get a fax?" I asked, remembering that Jeremy said he would be sending some information.

They turned around slowly and both said, "No," a bit too quickly. While they hadn't done anything obvious to make me believe they were keeping something from me, after they turned around, they seemed a touch too stiff. As if they noticed I had noticed, they both relaxed.

"Are you sure?" I said, moving in their direction. They moved away from the fax machine and let me by. There was no paper in there. Out of the corner of my eye, I saw Agent Wood put a piece of paper in the basket on the desk.

"We're sure."

"Whatever," I said, pretending not to care. I would look at that fax when I got home after school. I didn't have time for this. Even if they destroyed it, I had learned at headquarters how to retrieve a copy. Why were they keeping things from me now? We were supposed to be a team.

"We did get an email from Jeremy, however," Agent Wood said. "Your tracker isn't working properly, and we need to replace it. And Jeremy had to go out of town to meet with one of his detectives. He won't be back until tomorrow. He said to be safe on the climb and use ropes."

"We'll be there, watching," Agent Penrod said.

I had a sudden attack of anger. "Did Jeremy tell you to come or something?" I tried to say it in a way that showed curiosity, nothing else. I don't know why it got me upset that they would be watching. I never felt this way when Jeremy was there protecting me.

"He did. He doesn't want you to go anywhere alone again. He thinks your kidnapping is imminent."

The way he said it got my back up.

"And you don't?" I didn't like people to question Jeremy.

They exchanged a glance.

"We think he's barking up the wrong tree," Agent Wood said. "We were in California looking up birth certificates."

"What?"

"Dakota was not born in California."

Before I could protest, Agent Penrod said, "He's the one, we know it."

"You two don't know anything. He couldn't be it."

"You can't let your hormones get in the way of this mission. We are not going to fail simply because you choose not to see the truth through your sex-crazed teen haze." Agent Wood scowled at me.

I had to resist the urge to stomp away. I balled my fists instead and held my ground. "If I was letting my feelings for Dakota get in the way, I wouldn't have been spending the last week distancing myself from him now would I? I want to complete this mission just as much as you do. In fact, I will complete it and you'll see, the kidnappers will not be taking Madness. It's the Avengers they are targeting. I just know it."

"We've been tracking Dakota, Christy, and he disappears for long periods of time." Agent Penrod raised her eyebrows at me.

"He's been at school every day, you guys, what are you talking about?"

"Where was he, for example, the afternoon you guys watched your play, Tristan and Isolde? He arrived an hour late and we'd been unable to track him since school let out." Agent Woods blurted. He had such a mean tone to his voice.

"I don't know." I shook my head.

"We don't know either. Ian, on the other hand, has been completely traceable."

"You need to listen to reason." Agent Penrod said.

"Jeremy is with his informant right now. He's been doing some other checking on Dakota and Ian. What do you bet he'll come back telling us it is Dakota?" Agent Wood smirked.

My head was swimming. Dakota was no kidnapper. He was too kind, too attentive, too raw. "I guess we'll just have to wait to hear his report, now won't we?"

We stared at each other.

"Believe me, you guys, I want to succeed more than anything, but I need you two to believe in me. My age truly has nothing to do with my ability. I can do this. Please, trust me."

"It's our job to keep you safe and be your support on this mission. Inherent in that charge is to watch for danger and misdirection. We feel you are going down the wrong path, and we are facing you, adult to adult, and telling you that you are going down the wrong path." Agent Penrod looked at me like I was her own teen daughter, and she desperately wanted to keep me from making a bad decision.

I pressed my lips together. I knew they were wrong, but my intuition wasn't going to cut it with these guys. How could I make them understand what I knew in my gut?

"Would you at least humor us until Jeremy gets back? We'd really like you to go hang out with Madness tonight." Agent Penrod was at least trying to be nice.

I huffed.

"It's not like you have anything else to do." Agent Wood sneered.

I took in a deep breath, holding my tongue. I could be mature about that. I could humor them until Jeremy got back. What would it hurt? "Alright, but you guys owe me a steak dinner at a super nice restaurant when he comes back saying Dakota is in the clear."

"Sounds good," Agent Penrod said, smiling, eager to have me on board.

Agent Wood rolled his eyes.

"What about my tracker?"

"We'll do it in the morning. Now, go. You're going to miss them." Agent Wood's voice was hard. "You'll need tennis shoes. They're long boarding tonight."

I nodded and left to get shoes on. I wasn't scared about not having a perfectly functional tracker, because I knew it wasn't Madness the kidnappers wanted. It was the Avengers.

I pulled up to Camden's house and put my head on the steering wheel. I'd told Dakota I didn't feel up to long boarding tonight. I really needed space from him. My agent parents had been right about my budding feelings for Dakota. It was hard to resist a guy like him. If I wasn't on a mission and just a normal girl, I'd have fallen hard and fast. I'd never admit that to Penrod and Wood, though. I did need to get my hormones in check.

Someone knocked on my window and startled me. Jensyn. Right behind her, Tarran and Mindy came flouncing up, followed by Troy, Tate, and Dakota. I couldn't stop the stutter in my chest at seeing him.

While we took turns driving, two of us would hold onto the car bumper and ride our longboards. While it was dangerous, I couldn't help think that if the Avengers were to do the same activity, they would have secretly grabbed a hold of cars at stop signs or lights instead of having the controlled environment Madness had created. Which did I like better? Only weeks ago, my answer would have been different for sure.

Dakota's warm arms around me reassured me that he was good. As I drove home, I tried to imagine him as the kidnapper or the recruiter, and I couldn't make it fit no matter how hard I tried. I couldn't wait to get word from Jeremy that he was completely cleared. My mind would not settle the whole way home.

I was emotionally and physically exhausted as my head hit the pillow. I would report to Wood and Penrod in the morning.

I woke late and scrambled to get ready for the day. My head throbbed. I grabbed all the things I needed for school and the rock climb with the Avengers and stuffed them into my backpack and a duffle bag. I grabbed a protein bar and a bottled juice on my way out the door. I called out, "See ya, guys," as I went out the door.

As I pulled down the drive, Agent Penrod ran out the front door. I stopped and rolled the window down. "We need to put that new tracker in your arm."

"Shoot. I'm already late. How long will it take?"

"A good twenty minutes."

I sighed. "How about we do it at lunch, then."

"I guess that will work."

I smiled and pushed the button to roll the window up but remembered the lip balm Jeremy had given me and told me to keep with me at all times. Would it matter if I didn't have it since my tracker wasn't working? I let go of the button and called out to Penrod, but she'd just shut the front door.

I didn't dare drive away without it. I put the car in park and ran up the walk. After snagging the lip balm, I headed for the front door. Hearing Agent Wood say my name, I paused and moved silently, toward the voice. I waited, just outside the kitchen door, listening to the conversation. It was ridiculous that I had to sneak to get the truth out of them.

"I'm totally worried she's going to get hurt in all this." She sighed loudly.

"You're worried about her? You need to be worried about us and what will happen when she blows this because she's wrong about this whole thing and won't listen. She's acting like a spoiled child."

What was I wrong about? Maybe Dakota was the recruiter and Ian knew nothing about it. Could Madness be the real target? Was I being pigheaded? What had the fax said? Did it say something that proved Madness was the target? No. Wood would have rubbed it in my face if he had anything else that was concrete. I did want to see that fax, though. When I came home after school, I'd check the fax and adjust accordingly. If I didn't have to go rock climbing, I wouldn't. Even though I'd tried to dissuade Dakota, he was still hot on my trail and it would be easy to fall right back in with him. I was flexible. After all, I was a spy.

"If nothing else, this will teach her not to be so brash and maybe even humble her a bit so she can learn something from the masters." Agent Wood chuckled.

"They should have had a seasoned agent who looks young do this. She's just a child. It's just too important. Since they didn't, we need to help her, but not the way you've been going about it. You're pushing her away. We need her to trust us."

"You heard Agent McGinnis on the plane. She is a full agent and must be treated like one."

I heard movement and slipped quickly back out the door and into the car. I drove slowly down the driveway, hoping they wouldn't hear. When I was alone with my thoughts, my eyes burned with tears, and I questioned my involvement. If I couldn't even force them to show me what they were hiding or show them how great of an agent I was, what was I doing here? I was a chicken, through and through. I shouldn't be on this mission. They were right.

A few minutes later, I was mad again. Why did I let them get to me? I was determined to show them up. I was not arrogant and unteachable. I would have to get into that office and read that fax before the climb.

I would take a look at the fax at lunch when I got the new tracker inserted.

Unfortunately, I didn't get the chance. Frankie got me right after third period, before lunch, and had me head out to the parking lot with my climbing gear. We drove straight there.

I pressed on my tracker and just in case the tracker hadn't transmitted, I texted Agent Penrod to tell her I was on my way to the climb. They wouldn't like it, but they'd have to hurry to catch up to us.

Five of the eight of us free soloed, without the aid of ropes, but not me. I admitted I wasn't experienced, so they hooked me up. Lunden would free climb after both Anna and I made it to the top. Anna was the newest member to the group besides me. She had long, blue, full hair. All her features were small: small nose, mouth, eyes, and ears. She reminded me of a long-haired mouse. She even had a high-pitched voice that sometimes put my teeth on edge, but I was happy to follow her up the cliff.

Once near the top, I lost my grip and called out for Anna to give me a hand. She must not have heard me because she never came. I slipped, but the rope caught me thanks to Lunden, who was about two-hundred feet below me, belaying.

He hollered up, "You okay?"

I hung there and called down, "Fine. I lost my grip." I worked hard, grunting to get vertical enough to get a handhold. Where was Anna? I called to her but got no response. I was on my own. I finally found a crevice I could slide my hand in. Then I swung my leg to the wall and searched for the right foothold. I only found one, but it was a good one. I pushed up hard, and one hand was able to grab the top of the cliff. I put my other foot where my hand had been and pushed up, flopping onto the top of the mountain with a thud. I rolled over onto my back, panting and cursing Anna. Not only Anna, the others, too. Those free-soloing had passed us up in a hurry. Then I heard Lunden call out, and I remembered I needed to unhook him in order for him to be able to free-solo the rest of the way up.

"Unhooking now," I yelled down.

"Unhooking now," he yelled up, following rock-climbing protocol. I pulled on the rope until I had it all at the top. I looked over the edge and saw him climbing fast.

I rolled over onto my back trying to rid myself of angry feelings before I went to find the rest of the crew. A puff of something foul blew into my face right as I tried to stand. I saw two pairs of hands grab my arms. It was the last thing I remembered.

When I woke up, I was in a large helicopter, tied up and gagged next to a knocked out Lunden. I had a raging headache, and the air smelled of antiseptic. The other six of our group were awake, but in the same situation I was: gagged and bound. We had been kidnapped. I'd chosen the right group. There was no going back now.

Chapter 11

My mission had truly begun. I shoved my arm hard into my side to activate the tracker again, praying it would activate. I chided myself for not getting it replaced this morning. How could I have been so dumb? Then I remembered that my agent parents had planned on following me. They probably had a lock on our position already. They had probably witnessed me getting kidnapped. I could feel the chapstick digging into my leg, but I couldn't get to it, so I pushed and pushed my arm into my side, hoping it would transmit one of the times I pressed it.

I tried to free my hands, but they were bound tightly with hard plastic bands. My feet were bound too. Two guards sat nearby, watching us. My arm felt sore. It hadn't felt that way since the day after they'd implanted the tracker. Maybe it had to do with the defect in the tracker. I tried to get a look at it, but couldn't. It was comforting, nonetheless, to know that either way Division had a trace on me; my agent parents had seen me get kidnapped and were keeping track of me, and Jeremy was most likely tracking me somehow, too.

I had no idea how long I'd been out. I looked around at the Avengers. Their faces showed shock and disbelief. It surprised me how calm I felt. I guess knowing this was all part of the plan made me a bit numb to the horror of it all. I wished I could tell the other Avengers that someone was watching out for all of us, that we had a connection on the other side.

I'd been in a helicopter like this before, in Spain. It had been a military helicopter. This couldn't be a military helicopter, could it? I tried to see out, to watch for landmarks to help me know where I was, but I couldn't: there were no windows low enough for me to look out. I shifted, trying to take the pressure off my backside. It was a long flight.

Finally, the helicopter touched down, and the force of the landing slammed our bound bodies into each other. Before we had a chance to even try to untangle ourselves, our captors rushed into the hold. They swiftly cut our feet restraints and pushed us out of the chopper while the blades were still turning, the wind beating us around. They led us through a door and down several flights of stairs.

We were met by a row of girls and boys in black uniforms with crazy colored hair: blue, green, magenta, orange, turquoise, pink, a weird brown, and a reddish black. They stood at attention until a tall, large man in white with natural-looking brown hair said, "At ease." Then they assumed a relaxed posture. The first boy in the row, who couldn't have been older than twenty, called out Houston's name.

"Follow me," he barked.

Were they creating some kind of youth army here? Houston looked at all of us and then followed orders. I bet he was aching to wrestle the boy to the floor. Each person in black called out another name from our group, and they disappeared down the hallway to our right. I was the second to last to be called. The girl who called my name had reddish black, shoulder length hair that was straight as a board. Her face was kind. Her lips turned up naturally in the corners.

She led me into a room that looked like a small dorm, with a twin bed, perfectly made, a desk, a lamp, and a small rug on the tile floor. Not much more would fit.

"Where am I? Who are you?" I stared hard at her.

She opened a door to my left, giving no response. It was a closet. She pulled out a bright yellow jumpsuit. She cut my plastic wristbands and then said, "Please dress yourself." She turned to the side slightly so that she wasn't looking at me straight on as I undressed. I slipped the lip balm into my hand as I took off my shorts. I snuck a quick peek at my arm. What was going on? It was red and inflamed.

If I'd have wanted to, I could have easily taken her right then, but I could still find more information for Division while I waited for them to come get us. I found a white shift inside the jumpsuit when I unzipped it. I slid that on first and then put the jumpsuit on, slipping the lip balm under the bed Houdini style. After I zipped the jumpsuit up, the girl turned to me and said, "Does it feel like it fits? It looks like it does." Her voice was friendly, not commanding.

"Yes," I said, rubbing my hands down my front and thighs.

She didn't speak to me after that until her pager or watch or something vibrated. She brought me into the hall at that point. The man in white had us line up in the same order we were called when we arrived and then marched us into a room that looked like a hair salon. It was non-threatening enough. Were we going to get a makeover?

We each stood in front of a salon chair with our guides. Two men in colorful scrubs walked up to Houston and started putting something around his neck. Houston threw a punch that was swiftly and easily blocked by one of the men. The other man grabbed his arm and twisted it behind his back. Houston called out, obviously in pain.

Several in the group looked away, the rest stared on with morbid curiosity. The one that had blocked the punch put a thin metal collar on Houston that buzzed when hooked together. This was not good. It must be what they would use to control us. Each of us got a collar, and no one else put up a fight.

The men in white had us sit in the cushiony salon chairs next to us. Our guides wrapped a smock around each of us and the sound of hair clippers filled the air.

"No way!" Duncan screamed out and Frankie, sitting next to me, kicked the girl who was about to cut her hair and yelled, "You can't do that."

The moment their words were out, screams of agony filled the air. Both grabbed at their necks as their screams turned to gurgling sounds like they were choking. Out of pure instinct, I took a step toward them and cried out, but my guide put her hand on my arm, her thin fingers pressing hard into my arm, holding me in place, and shook her head almost imperceptibly. Was she protecting me? The looks on the faces of the other five Avengers were of pure terror. Both Maddie and Anna touched the wires at their necks, eyes wide.

The choking sounds stopped, replaced by shocked heaving breaths as Duncan and Frankie leaned over their knees and gulped air. Their guides firmly pushed them into upright positions and then into the chairs. Frankie's face was white, Duncan's more of a pale green, and neither fought as their hair was sheared from their heads.

In the end, the boys' hair had been cut to about a quarter inch and the girls' to about half an inch. I'd have to go back to spiking it, and I'd just grown it out how I liked it. Both Anna's and Maddie's faces were streaked with tears. They were losing their beautiful, long locks. Maybe I should give the signal to come and get us. Nothing good could be going on here and Division could figure out what it was all about after saving us. Really, all they needed to know was the location of this place. I pushed my arm hard into my ribs, twice, ignoring the shooting pain in my arm. Since it wasn't working consistently, I would do it as many times as I could. My arm ached from the pressure. Something was definitely wrong with my tracker. Hopefully, Jeremy and the crew would be on their way soon. This had to stop.

Our guides colored our hair a bright yellow to match our jumpsuits. I thought our hair color was important to whoever ran this place. Why was he changing it now? Apparently, even the little information Division 57 had had was irrelevant.

The room was so quiet; I could hear everyone's breathing.

All of our jewelry was removed, and our faces were made up like a clown's. They even put a yellow foamy nose on each of us as well as a big yellow clown wig. If we hadn't been different heights and weights, we would have looked identical. I was starting to freak out. What if Division didn't save us before something terrible happened? I tried to calm myself with the reminder that it was Jeremy looking after me, and he'd never let me down.

The guys in white moved us and our guides to some big metal doors at the back of the room. I could hear muffled voices coming from behind them, but they weren't loud enough for me to hear what was being said.

The guide in front pushed the doors open, and she marched through, Anna alongside her. One by one, we marched in with our escorts and stood in a line in the center of a large room or a field or something. Bright lights were trained on us, and it was impossible to figure out where we were. The silence in the room ended when a booming voice said, "Welcome to the Circus of Feats."

The room erupted in loud claps and shouting.

Chapter 12

I tried to look past the lights to see who was clapping and shouting, but it made my eyes water. Looking down the row of us, I could see both Payden's and Maddie's hands were trembling. Lunden and Duncan had theirs clasped tightly in front of them. Frankie and Houston, however, made fists at their sides. With all the clown makeup, it was hard to tell what they were feeling, but I knew most were scared, a few angry.

"You all know how I love a good clown," the voice said. "Today we have eight new clowns for our selection."

Starting with Anna and ending with Frankie, the commentator introduced each of us by name. As the introductions took place, the lights moved to spotlight whomever he talked about, and I was able to see more of the room and who clapped and shouted.

A couple hundred people dressed in bright, rainbow colors as well as black and white, encircled us, sitting in stands just like at a real circus. I couldn't see the commentator. The lights seemed to be coming from one central point that may have been concealing him.

"Those who complete the Circus of Feats today," the speaker said, his voice echoing all around us, "will eat dinner with me in my private dining hall and will be selected. Those who don't will suffer a less than ideal fate. Beware." A lion roared. It sounded completely real and close. Would those who didn't finish be thrown to the lions? I shuddered.

"The first feat?" The voice continued. "Water picking."

A girl dressed up like a circus performer, complete with a top hat with a long ribbon tail, high heels, tights, and a black sequined body suit, pulled a covering away from a huge, glass tank of water. Inside were two sets of large chains and manacles with big locks that hung from the top piece of glass. The lights dimmed, and all around us, curved TV screens popped to life, all depicting clowns trying to free themselves from the locks in the tank. Some were successful and others struggled and then went lifeless, eyes staring out at us.

I knew that Anna was the resident lock-picker and had been teaching the rest of the Avengers the skill, but could they all do it? I wished I had five minutes to teach them. But who was I kidding? Even if I could teach them the rudimentaries, being put upside down in water would make a beginner freak out and forget everything. What if they didn't know how to hold their breath and not inhale water? Could I even do it? I wondered how many of us wouldn't make it past this feat.

Next to me, Frankie whined, a sad, high-pitched whine. I shifted my body next to hers, trying to give her comfort. The rest of the group had looks of complete terror on their faces. I pressed my arm hard into my side, twice. Where was Division? I pushed on my tracker, over and over. This was complete madness, and Division had to get us out of here. The pressure stung my arm. For good measure, I repeated the process several times.

"Yes," he continued, his deep, playful voice grating on my nerves. "All good clowns must have a handle on the ability to pick locks. It is a fundamental. Of course fundamentals can be boring, so I added water. Water can be very exciting, and it is one of the four elements. We all love a thrill, don't we? I'm sure you'll all find that this gets your blood rushing."

Anna's guide brought her over to the tank. She glanced at us with wide eyes several times. Her guide handed her something. For a moment, I wondered if it was a key. Then I scoffed at the idea. Perhaps bobby pins or something like it? I looked at the screens still playing the scenes from other clowns either succeeding or failing to open the locks, hoping to figure out what those who succeeded were doing.

The guide had Anna climb stairs to a little deck area. She lay down, and the girl secured her ankles to the top piece of glass from the tank. She didn't resist. Who would after what we saw happen to Frankie and Duncan? My own collar chaffed at my neck, a physical reminder not to get out of line.

A crane-like machine hooked Anna by the ankles and lifted her high in the air. The machine lurched awkwardly, swinging her around until she was just above the tank, her clown wig already brushing the water.

The audience went silent.

Then the crane dropped her into the tank, the water splashing upward as her body plunged downward. Immediately, I saw her go to work, pulling her body up and grabbing the lock with one hand. Watching her, I realized it would take strong core muscles to pull the body up, too. This task was looking harder and harder to complete.

A huge clock hung near the tank and counted the time. It had been fifteen seconds. She needed to have that first lock undone already, but she didn't. Panic rose in me, as my eyes darted between the clock and my friend. Twenty seconds. Anna's hands worked feverishly in the water, and she freed one leg. It dropped down.

Could she hold her breath long enough to do the second one?

She struggled in the water, then with a sudden jerk, her other leg fell and she pushed her head out of the water, gasping for breath. I looked at the clock, forty-five seconds. That was a long time to be struggling upside down under water. Miraculously, when she stood up on the platform the wig and makeup remained, just as they were before she got dunked. The wig may have even stood taller now. They took her behind the platform, probably to let her change.

I watched Houston make his way up to the tank. He looked petrified. I didn't blame him. Then, Anna yelled out, "Sweet spot left." We heard a scuffle behind the platform and a stifled yell. Anna probably just saved all of us. Not needing the time to search for the sweet spot would make this task doable by even a novice picker—if the water didn't get to him first. It sounded like she'd been punished, however.

They tied Houston's legs and lifted him up. Just as he hit the water, he raised up, grabbing his legs to steady himself. In twenty seconds the first cuff was off. He must be a novice, I realized, or he would have done it quicker. The next one only took him fifteen. I took heart. Maybe we would all make it through this. Anna emerged from behind the platform, black duct tape over her mouth with big white "X's" across it. At least she had dry clothes on.

When it was my turn, I walked up the steps, taking deep calming breaths. I lay down. My shoulder blades dug into the hard, uncomfortable platform. I said a prayer in my heart over and over, *Please let me live to help these people. Please.* The hook swung above me and as it lowered, I breathed deeply, willing extra air to fill me. My guide handed me two bobby pins. I only needed one. The bright lights made it hard for me to keep my eyes open, so I kept them closed, breathing deeper still.

Fear gripped me as I plunged into the water, holding my legs as Houston had, clutching the bobby pin for dear life. It saved me vital seconds. I went left as I picked and the lock popped free. The other was also a lefty, and I made quick work of getting it open. A gush of relief filled me when my head popped out of the water. I took a quick, deep breath and was fine. The clock read fifteen seconds.

I followed my guide down the steps once I was out. She took me behind the platform and looked over my face and wig, making sure they were all in order. She had me change out of the wet coveralls and shift. Then I pulled on new ones, nice and dry. After a few small touch-ups to my hair and makeup, she brought me back to stand in line with the others on the far right of the circus arena.

I pushed on my tracking device several times. Where was Jeremy? How long would it take before they got here? I hoped no one would die before then. I kicked at the dirt, it was real and pretty solid. Only a slight puff of air swirled about us after I kicked at it. Were we in an enclosed space? Outside? A makeshift shelter? I looked up and noticed the striped fabric above us and the huge pole in the middle of the tent, and it hit me—we were in a real circus tent set up just for this event. The man who'd kidnapped us must truly be mad.

"That was aaaamazing," the kidnapper said. "Unfortunately, we couldn't really assess the quality of the last seven clowns due to Miss Anna's outburst. But, as they say, *the show must go on*. Every self-respecting risk taker must know how to handle fire, the second element we will conquer today. We don't want to be getting burned, now do we? Should we see if they can handle the heat?"

The crowd roared.

From flaps in the tent top, six fire rings sailed down, stopping at different heights. Six girls dressed as circus hands pushed small trampolines of various heights out on the floor, and three others brought out puffy pads, blown up big to give a soft landing to someone sailing through the highest rings.

I looked at the ring nearest the ground and noticed that only a small core in the center was fire free, and then I looked at the highest ring, the trampoline next to it and the landing pad. That must have been twenty feet off the ground. How was it possible? I reached up and touched the massive clown wig and realized even it wasn't small enough to fit through the eye of the fire. This was suicide. The videos that played all around us showed one clown after the other catching on fire. Not many made it without either dying or sustaining serious burns.

This time, they started with me. I wished it had been Payden. I'm sure he would have made this look easy. With all the cool tumbling he could do, I bet he'd be amazing at this. I could have tried to copy him. I was led to the shortest ring. It looked like I could just hop through it, but I took my time to think it over. My best chance of making it without catching on fire would be to jump through, head first, arms outstretched and then summersault my way out of it, but could it be done at this low height? Could I tuck and roll without burning? I would be the guinea pig. Try as I might, I couldn't come up with a better solution.

A countdown started, "Ten, nine, eight, seven." I didn't want to imagine what they would do to me if I didn't jump by the time the countdown got to one. I had to land far enough away from the ring that my feet, when they came through, wouldn't catch on the ring. In order to do that, I had to aim for the area just below the top of the fiery circle. I figured my hair would catch on fire, but I could always stamp that out rolling on the ground or if worse came to worse, I could use my hands to pat it out.

Just as the countdown reached one, I sprang. I made it through but as my hands hit the floor, my feet clipped the top of the ring. Fearing the worst, I rolled around on the ground to put out any fire that may have caught. I patted at my hair, but it hadn't lit. I had felt the ultra hot heat as I sailed through. I should have lit on fire–my feet hit the ring. I could feel the burn on the tops of my feet

My guide led me to the next highest hoop, and I didn't waste time thinking it through. I would use the same technique. It had worked once, and I'd try it again. I didn't shoot quite as high, but almost. The countdown hadn't even started. I felt the burn, hot on my hands, neck, and feet as I flew through the hoop. I rolled again, just to be sure I wasn't on fire. The third and the fourth rings were difficult, but in a way, easier than the first two because they were higher off the ground, and it was easier to tuck and roll after going through them. The final two were a different story. I would have to bounce just right and go through the ring at the correct angle and then flip my feet up as I descended. I'd then have to flip in the air or I'd break my neck on the landing, puffy landing pad or not.

I was not so lucky. I didn't bounce just right, and I didn't go through the ring at just the right angle. My head hit the top of the ring, and I heard and felt the wig catch on fire. Pure momentum sent me the rest of the way through, my feet grabbing the bottom of the ring, stopping my upward flight and plunging me down. I tucked, hoping I wasn't dead. I landed on my head and upper back and my legs crashed over my head.

Amazingly, I wasn't hurt, at least not by the fall. Once I bounced back up, I felt heat on my head. With my arms, I swatted at the fire that was melting my wig, trying to avoid burning my unprotected hands. I rolled on the pad, too, hoping to put out any other fires that may have started. I didn't feel any more heat on my head and figured I'd extinguished the fire. That was close. My heart pounded hard against my ribs. I still had to do one more ring.

I prayed as I bounced, trying to get a feel for the bounciness of this trampoline. I should have done the same thing on the last one, maybe then I'd still have my clown hair and not have burn welts on my feet. The pain seared through me as I jumped, but I persisted, pushing hard, then soft, feeling for the best bounce to take me to the right height.

The countdown was already at five, and I still wasn't completely satisfied I would be safe, but I'd run out of time. Besides, I wanted to take every second I could to give Division more time to arrive. Every time I bounced, I hit my arms into the tracker, making sure Jeremy knew how urgent this was. I kept the prayer in my heart and pushed off the trampoline at what I hoped was the right angle. The melted cap seemed to heat up as I soared through, but I didn't hit the ring. I cried out as fire licked the burns on my ankles and feet, but I'd made it.

I flew forward out of the ring, letting myself flatten out a bit before tucking and flipping slowly in the air before hitting the pad flat on my back. When I bounced back up, I rolled around, but was sure I hadn't lit that time. It was as perfect a jump as I could muster.

My guide led me back to the side of the tent to watch the others.

Lunden was next, and fear gripped me. I kept praying and praying that everyone would make it. Where was Jeremy? I watched, terrified, as Lunden barely made it through each hoop. Then, on the second to last ring, his jump went askew and his body crashed into the side of the ring. His whole body lit up like a light bulb. I couldn't stand to watch; I had to look away. I almost fainted from the smell. I grabbed Frankie's hand, and we supported each other. What would they do with him? Was he alive? Several people came out and carried him away after swatting out the flames. Would he be fed to the lions? My whole body stiffened and I thought I would wretch, but somehow held it back thinking about Jeremy—I knew he'd come for me, for us. He'd get us out of here. I had to be strong and make it through, and do what I could to help the others.

The Avengers were down one man. I had to support Frankie, whose knees gave out as soon as Lunden caught fire. Her body shook as she attempted to hold back the tears coursing down her cheeks. My chest heaved, and I concentrated hard not to give in to my panic. Frankie's whole body was convulsing now. I couldn't look at her, or I'd lose it even more. My training had not prepared me for this.

Were we here for nothing more than the madman's sick pleasure? Did the audience love this, too? *Where was Jeremy?*

The rest of the crew made it through all the hoops, but no one came out unscathed. The amount and severity of the burns were the only differentiating factors. Everyone slumped a bit in line, so I tried to stand up straight to give my friends courage, and to show these crazy people they would not get the better of me. If it was my time to die, I would do it with my head held high. Once I straightened, it seemed Frankie, next to me, did too. Fire lit inside me now. I would make it through this. I would see this man punished.

"Oh, shoot, there's only seven of you left," the commentator said. "We lost one. Never fear. We will continue without him to bigger and better things. Let's tackle height, should we? A great clown is willing to go to unknown heights to be the best clown he can be. Let's see how these clowns do with conquering the element of air as they walk."

Someone dropped a ladder rope from the ceiling, and another person ran over and fastened it to the floor. I followed the rungs with my eyes up to a small platform that looked just big enough for two people to stand on, if they stood very close together. There was a rope strung a good fifteen yards across the middle of the tent. It must have been thirty feet up. Another small platform hung at the opposite end and a wooden walkway jutted out from it, leading to a real ladder near that side of the tent.

A bunch of people in black rolled in huge sections of tall fencing that curved inward at the top, and others moved the landing pads underneath the rope. What were they creating with the fencing? They hooked the fence sections together and then clicked the rollers on the bottoms of the fencing sections up, out of the way, making the fence stationary. They attached it to the floor with some fasteners. Bars lowered from the ceiling covering the area above the fence but leaving a section open near the tight rope so that a person could stand and fall without hitting the fencing.

I heard a roar above me and looked up to the screens. A tiger chased a clown to the fence. As the clown climbed, the tiger ripped at his legs and then followed. The clown's jumpsuit was ripped to shreds, and judging by the amount of blood dripping below the shreds, so were his legs. His screams pierced the air, and my whole body quaked as the tiger climbed up after him and pulled him to the ground. Some of the clowns did make it across the rope and even others made it through openings high up in the fence that were big enough for a human to climb through, but not a big tiger. Still, I wasn't comforted.

"By the way," the voice said, "in case you fall, I am giving you a second chance. If you can make it through one of four openings in the fence before Sarah gets to you, I'll let you continue with the circus today. But, if I were you, I'd conquer the air by making it across. Sarah will be sad, but she'll live."

It was Frankie's turn to be first. I felt a surge of hope. If anyone could stay on the rope, it was Frankie. She was a monkey. She'd introduced me to Henry and walking on ledges.

By the time she reached the top, her arms and legs were shaking. It's not easy to climb a wobbly rope ladder thirty feet into the air. She shook out her arms and legs once on the platform. She breathed deeply, several times, her chest moving in and out, in and out. The timer started. *Ten*. She shook her arms. *Nine*. She shook her legs. *Eight*. She breathed deeply. *Seven.* She breathed again. *Six.* She put her arms out. *Five*. She put one foot on the fat rope. *Four*. She placed the other foot on the rope. She gained her balance and looked toward the other platform, never at her feet, moving one foot after the other. She checked her balance once or twice, but made it across.

The six of us remaining seemed to let out a collective breath. She'd made it seem easy. I was certain it wasn't. I replayed the routine she'd gone through before starting across. I would mimic her. I hoped the others would too.

Payden was next. He fell about halfway across but caught the rope when he fell. He pulled his legs up and shimmied across. It must have killed the burns on his legs to do it, but his will to live was strong.

Houston made it across without much effort, too, but he went as slow as a snail.

Duncan fell a quarter of the way across, grabbed the rope, but screamed out and fell. I'm sure he couldn't stand the pain of his burned hands and let go. He bounced high on the pad. After looking to see where Sarah was, he scrambled to the other side of the tall blown-up pad and made it up the fence and through an opening.

Maddie was next to fall. In her haste to get to the fence, she forgot to look for the tiger, and Sarah got her. I had to not only close my eyes, but turn completely away. My stomach roiled at the screaming, roaring, and tearing. I puked and puked again. I wasn't the only one. I couldn't seem to find my happy place with Jeremy or my prayers.

Anna fell next, but it was no shock that she escaped. The tiger did scratch one of her legs, though.

I was last, and I fell too, but was able to catch the rope. It cut grooves into my hands by the time I made it to the platform on the other side. The red, inflamed sores on both hands burned and pinched. I wanted to kill Division. Where were they?

"Down to six, are we? It's pretty impressive that six of you remain. By this time, we are usually down to four, but this is no usual group, is it?"

There couldn't be much more, could there? I'd noticed we'd seemed to be doing something that involved the elements. We'd already done, air, fire, and water. There was only one element left: earth. What had he thought up for earth?

"The Bible says we come from dust and will return to dust when we die," the voice boomed out, confirming my suspicions. "To celebrate the fact that your bodies came from earth and will one day return to the earth, you will fight another from the earth. The choice is yours."

It bothered me that he was using the Bible to back up his demented actions. A curtain behind us opened. Six fighters stood in front of us. A male boxer. A male wrestler. A woman karate master. A woman dressed up in a special forces uniform. A male cage fighter. A male knight.

"Which type of dust would you like to fight? Oh, I have a little twist at the end of the fight I think you'll all really enjoy," the commentator said. I was so sore, I couldn't imagine fighting any one of these men or women. Each of the three tasks we'd already done had sapped the strength out of us. I didn't want to fight anyone.

Houston got first pick.

He did well against the wrestler. The man seemed listless, except for a few times when he seemed to get it together enough to pull Houston close and speak in his ear. He did this several times. Why would he do that? Houston brought him down after about five minutes. Maybe he was better than I thought. Then a skinny girl dressed to the hilt brought out a pillow with a knife on it. She placed it before Houston.

"Time to finish the job," the announcer said.

Houston's body slumped slightly. His head was bowed down, his chin resting on his chest.

Now I heard the man yell out. "Please, please. My family. They need me."

The timer started. *Ten.* What would he do? Certainly he wouldn't kill the man. *Nine. Eight.* Why doesn't he just let go of the man and stand up? *Seven. Six.* I moved forward slightly, wanting to grab him into a hug and tell him it would be okay. He didn't have to murder anyone. *Five.* In a sudden blur of movement, Houston grabbed the knife and then thrust it into the man's heart. Blood spurted all over. I gasped and looked away. Houston had done it. He had murdered someone. It was a horrible, senseless killing. Houston rolled to his side, sobs wracked his frame until his guide picked him up and forced him back in line. The kidnapper had to be stopped. Rage boiled within me, but at the same time, fear niggled at me, twisting up my insides. I would also have to choose.

My name was called next. I made my choice: the karate master. As I made my way to the karate mat, I tried to figure out what each of these challenges told him about us. What kind of people did the nutty announcer want in this place? He obviously wanted someone who could fight, but why wasn't winning enough? Why the twist at the end? Why the dagger?

I was a master at karate, and I doubted any of the others in the Avengers were. They wouldn't stand a chance against the woman this crazy man had standing there. She also seemed a bit slow, off her game, although we were fighting on a very advanced level for about five minutes. Then she got the right move in and brought me to the floor and whispered in my ear, "Please. I have cancer. The chemo makes me weak. I will beat the cancer. I must beat you."

I pushed her away. A ploy? Why was she whispering to me? I got her several times, and she slowed significantly, until I made a mistake and she brought me down again and whispered, "Please, let me win. My family. I must save my family."

Had this madman taken the family members of these fighters and would kill them if the fighters didn't try to win? She had me firm on the ground. I thought of giving in. It would be the charitable thing to do. The first fighter must have said the same types of things to Houston. They must be here under duress. I couldn't be responsible for her death. I wasn't afraid of death. But I hadn't come here by myself or for myself. The others who'd been kidnapped—I was responsible for them: they were my mission.

Then it hit me. The madman wanted soldiers that showed no mercy. The woman I held captive deserved my mercy, but I couldn't give it to her. I had to complete my mission. If I didn't, there was no hope of me saving the several hundred kids here. I would have to take one life to save the many. Could I?

Then the countdown started. She must have been given the knife. If I let her kill me, the commentator would still be able to hurt people. I had to stop him. I had no choice. I would have to kill her so that I could stop him. I had to keep the bigger picture before me.

I saw the knife in her hands and knew it would be plunged into my chest in about three seconds. I found the strength to free my arms and grab her wrists. I twisted her onto her back and in one swift movement, grabbed the knife from her and plunged it into her chest. It was nothing like I'd imagined it. It felt almost like the knife didn't even go in her body. Sort of like when I'd attacked someone with a knife suit on. There was no resistance, but there was plenty of blood. She lay there unmoving. The only way I could make this the right decision was to save everyone here. I would find a way. I must find a way.

I quickly stood and walked away, not able to face what I had done. My chest burned with the rightness of my decision, but at the moment, it didn't help the anguish I felt at killing an innocent person. I hoped her family would be spared. I would survive so that I could beat this man at his own game.

I know the others fought, but I couldn't seem to focus on anything anymore. I looked, but didn't see what was right in front of me.

At some point, my guide led me to the middle of the floor and had me climb up some stairs. I stopped at the top. The bright lights shining down on me hurt my eyes. I covered them. My guide was immediately by my side.

"Here, you need to put your hand like this," she whispered urgently, demonstrating that I should to put my pinky and the two next fingers out straight, while tucking in my thumb and pointer finger under my palm and place it on top of my heart. She helped me do it. I couldn't seem to work my fingers.

I looked down, letting my eyes adjust. Frankie, Houston, and Duncan stood on the platform a level below me. I was on a box, one level higher than everyone else. They all stared up at me. Frankie's eyes were swollen with tears. Duncan looked at his feet, Houston looked a bit triumphant. They had all killed their opponents. Had it been the right thing to do? I'm sure they felt they had to preserve themselves. Would they be able to live with themselves now?

I looked around for Payden and Anna. They were not there. They were gone forever. Deep hurt spread throughout my body as I heard a type of anthem play. I let my hand drop from my chest. Only slight pain from my burns registered.

Determination filled me. I set my jaw. I would stop this madman.

Chapter 13

Once the anthem finished playing, the crowd roared, and we were escorted back to our rooms by our guides. Mine instructed me to shower. I did but only used cold water. My burns couldn't take any heat. My head whirled. I sorted through all the information I'd ever read, intentionally or unintentionally, about crazy madmen and the psychology around them. The kidnapper must have an endgame.

What did those tests he did today show? What were his motivations behind them? I brought up an article in my mind about this very thing, and I remembered something interesting. He wanted to see if we would be merciful. Did he want us to be merciful or not? He was cruel, and the people he employed showed no emotion with the circus feats. They were heartless. We won if we killed. No, he was looking for those of us who were not merciful, but why? Were we going to be his soldiers? The documents in my mind highlighted the most likely psychological profile this kidnapper would be looking for if he were creating assassins. If so, they would be strong willed, yet easily influenced, have no compassion, love an intellectual thrill, need an ego boost, and be able to conquer fear.

When I got out, my guide handed me a shift to put on and she tended to my wounds, putting ointment on them and dressing them. She then put me in a bright yellow jumpsuit and painted my lips yellow. At least this time I didn't get a nose, wig, or clown makeup. I wanted to sleep. Instead, I would be going to a dinner with the enemy while I plotted his demise.

The magnificent oval dining hall screamed with wild, garish color. I felt like I'd walked into a demented rainbow. The walls were bright yellow and purple. The floor was a fluorescent green. The wooden, oval table and the chairs around it were hot pink, except for one. It sat at one of the top ends of the oval and looked like a king's throne. It was gold. I wondered if it was solid gold. Could it be real? The plates on the table were a dark blue and the flatware, silver. We had goblets made of red, colored glass. Our napkins were orange. The colors didn't blend, and they hurt my eyes. Videos of today's triumphs were playing on screens high above us. I refused to watch them.

A man entered the room, dressed like a servant from long ago, and said, "His Majesty, King Sterling." I felt a sudden desire to laugh at the absurdity of it all, but was able to stifle it by closing my eyes and pressing my lips together. I desperately wanted to see this man. The man I would take down. So, I slowly opened my eyes. I watched the tall, comical man stand next to his chair of gold. He wore a black, pin-striped suit with a bright orange shirt, an orange tie, and orange socks. His hair was also bright orange and stood a good four inches out from his head. It looked like spokes sticking out.

The man who had announced Sterling proceeded to undress him. I looked away. What in the heck was going on? After a few minutes, the man spoke again. "Your King."

I was afraid to look, but knew I'd be punished if I didn't. He stood next to his throne still, but he now wore only the tie and a pair of boxer shorts. They were white with orange hearts on them. His face was painted white with orange triangles above his eyebrows and below his bottom lip. He obviously had a color fetish. His eyes were accented with a thick line of black paint. He looked wickedly cruel. His mouth was somehow familiar, and it raised goose bumps on my arms thinking about it.

He took a seat after someone blew a horn, like the announcement of the arrival of a true king in medieval times.

"King. King. That is so formal. I would rather you all call me Sterling, instead. Please enjoy the movie while you eat," he said. "I certainly will." He had this odd twitch in his right eye. It happened every time he ended a sentence. It was quick and almost imperceptible, but I was only four seats away from him and saw it.

Our meals rose out of the table and a movie projected all around us: *Sniper Serenade*. It appeared to be a Hollywood movie, but I'd never seen anything so brutal before. I tried to avoid the movie, but discovered that if I didn't look up every so often, I would get a low grade shock from my collar. Duncan, Frankie, and Houston seemed to be having the same problem because they would pull at their collars every now and then and shift in their seats. I couldn't help but notice that Houston seemed to watch more than any of us. No one ate much.

It was obvious Sterling was trying to acculturate in a hurry. He wanted us to change our views so that what we had seen as bad or unacceptable our whole lives was suddenly good.

When the movie ended, he stood up and had two servants dress him back into his suit. Our dishes and remaining food disappeared back into the table. Then he turned around and addressed us.

"Welcome, new selections. I'm so excited to have you here as a part of this exclusive program. You were chosen because of your impressive skills and willingness to do what it takes. You will be directly involved in helping eliminate this world of those who oppress us through media and other means." He started to pace and then moved down the side of the table where I sat.

"What is truly interesting about the four of you, is that there are *four* of you. The maximum number of selections one group has provided us has been three, until now." He was standing directly behind me. "I'd been watching your group for a good, long while, but you were missing a key element." I felt his hands press on the top of my chair. "You were missing a cute little blonde-haired girl. Lucky for you, this little beauty showed up." He spun my chair around, and I looked up into his scary face. A shiver raced down my spine. "Yes, you were nothing without this one, here. A blonde-haired goddess to be sure." He pinched both my cheeks, hard. I would bruise. How did he know I was naturally blonde? Did he know who I was in real life? Had I somehow broken cover?

"You will find there is no greater thrill than the mental preparation and the physical execution of a well-thought-out kill. You will be doing rigorous, death defying stunts on a daily basis to prepare you for your tasks. You will find that many of these stunts will be played out in your mind, however."

On the screens all around the room, pictures of people who had died recently flashed across the screen. I recognized most of them from the news. Cheri the Chameleon, a popular wrestler, died of an overdose of steroids. Jeff Monroe, an actor who played edgy roles, died during the filming of one of his movies. I watched as a politician who was secretly involved with terrorists died on his knees, hands tied behind his back and blindfolded, obviously savagely beaten at the hands of men who looked like terrorists. A TV personality, Sinclair Scott, died of an overdose. He had been known for his love of drugs. One actor, Jason McNeal 'fell' from a balcony in front of all his fans. A judge died when a huge gavel at a local courthouse fell on his head. Others I didn't recognize also died in horrible, strange ways. Sterling narrated it with gusto. He had orchestrated all the deaths? Most were done in some poetic way, but were never determined to be foul play.

Was his plan to really use us as elite assassins? Were all of those kids in the circus tent assassins? I shuddered.

Had Division 57 ever received my signals? Or was I alone like Jeremy had told me I would be? It had only been one day, but the most horrible day ever. I thought Division would be here by now.

He finished his narration and then added, "Yes, you will help rid the world of smut, indecision, lawlessness, and greed. I will judge and announce sentence accordingly. You will carry out the sentence."

My whole body felt weak and strong at the same time. I didn't want to do what I had to do. I wanted to run back to the safety of Bresen Academy. But I also knew that if I didn't find a way to stop him, Sterling would continue kidnapping and killing innocents to carry out his vigilante justice. I had to stop this man, and I would.

At the end of his speech, he led us outside. It was dark, but a huge bonfire raged in front of us, casting ugly shadows everywhere. The smell of burning wood brought back memories of camping as a child. I tried to hold onto those happy moments.

"Now for the induction ceremony," Sterling said.

I noticed a small stage set up in front of the fire.

"Please, head up onto the stage." As we climbed, I saw that we weren't alone. In the background were a bunch of kids. The same kids from inside the circus tent? They started shouting a chant, "A world without smut. A world without indecision. A world without lawlessness. A world without greed." They repeated the chant over and over again. Sterling held up his arms and the crowd silenced.

"We welcome our new selections today. They have proved their worth in the Circus of Feats and will not fail us." He turned to the four of us. "We pledge to give you all the skills necessary to be a valuable asset to the team. You, therefore, pledge your undying loyalty to me and our cause.

"Please, make the salute, and place your hand over your heart."

We did. My stomach churned.

"Repeat after me, I pledge my faithfulness to Sterling and the cause."

We repeated when he paused. A cold sweat hit me.

"To rid the world of smut, indecision, lawlessness, and greed."

My throat caught, hearing my friends say the words. Houston was especially fervent. He seemed to eat this all up. What was up with that?

"My loyalty will never falter, and my allegiance is to all who help further our cause for justice for this world."

We finished and the crowd cheered. I was taking in everything around us, thinking of escape.

"Can you hear all the voices of those that support you and will protect you at any cost? We are a family and will be fierce about our loyalty to you. You must be fierce about your loyalty to us." His voice carried a sure warning.

"Now we will finish the ceremony. Please step down and surround the pit of coals." He pointed to our left to a large pit filled with glowing red and white coals. We surrounded the pit. I couldn't help but notice the thick black sticks jutting out from it. They had wooden handles. My eyes followed the shaft into the fire.

Brands. Cattle brands.

Sterling pulled one out of the fire and held up the glowing brand into the air. It was one big box tipped so that one corner pointed up. Each corner bore a small triangle. I recognized them as the Greek symbols for the elements. Fire was a triangle with a dot in the middle, the triangle pointing up. Air and water were triangles that pointed down, only air had a horizontal line through it. Earth's triangle pointed up and had a horizontal line through it.

"As the final act of your allegiance," Sterling said, "you will brand each other with the symbols of the elements that you overcame today. You have overcome the world today. Be proud."

Frankie inhaled deeply. I felt my knees give ever so slightly. Sterling placed the brand back into the fire, and my stomach knotted realizing how many people surrounded us. All these people supported Sterling? It couldn't be true. There had to be dissenters.

The four people who had helped us stepped forward and put their right hands out to us, palms up. On the inside of their upper arm, in the same spot where the doctor had inserted my tracking device, was the brand. Would this hurt the tracking device? Was the device even working? Such a tender area of skin. I could feel the fear emanating from both Frankie and Duncan. This would hurt like crazy.

I prayed for strength for what I must do. I had to lead. I held out my arm to Frankie. She looked at me and gave an almost imperceptible shake of her head. I stared her straight in the eye and nodded several times. I looked at the brands in the fire and nodded again. Slowly, she grabbed one. Fear coursed through me.

I said, "Do it quick, but firm. I don't want to have to go through it twice." I glanced at my arm. Not only was it red and inflamed, it looked like there was a small cut at the very spot Division's tracker had been inserted in my arm. Had they found the tracker and removed it? No, I had felt it there as I pushed on it, over and over trying to get them to find me. Maybe all the pushing was pushing it right out of my skin.

She nodded, tears streaming down her cheeks. One helper steadied my arm. Another stood behind me, holding me at my waist. The brand shook from Frankie's trembling hands. A helper came and held them steady. The brand hit my arm. The most horrible, terrible pain rushed through me as it sizzled on my skin. I had learned techniques to ignore pain, but this was beyond pain. I couldn't see. I heard myself scream, and all feeling ceased.

Chapter 14

When I woke, I was in bed, and I was hot. Too hot. The room spun when I tried to sit, so I stayed put. Everything looked a little strange, and I closed my eyes to stop the nausea from overtaking me. I went in and out of sleep. Hot and cold. Night and day. I couldn't figure out where I was or who the people were that populated my nightmares.

The room filled with light, and my world stopped spinning and stretching. I sat up slowly and noticed an IV in my right wrist. The lightness turned to dark as terrible memories filled me. I screamed out for Jeremy, and two women rushed into my room. Where was he? Why hadn't he stormed the castle yet? He always had before.

"You're all right, dear," the first woman said in a tiny, mousy voice. "You're safe in your room. You got a terrible infection that caused a white-hot fever. We didn't know if you'd make it."

"We're so glad you did," the second woman said. She smiled sweetly. She reminded me of the picture I had at home of Old Mother Hubbard, kind and loving.

I lifted my hands up to my face to wipe away an errant strand of hair, but both my hands were wrapped in white gauze. My eyes, wide as saucers, must have alarmed the women.

"We put antibacterial cream on your cuts and wrapped them. We did the same with your burns, with the addition of a great burn cream developed in Sterling's labs. We cleaned and changed them both days."

"Wait!" I said. "How long have I been out?"

"Two days."

I sat up. "Two days?"

"Lay back down," she said. "And yes, two days."

I pulsed into frantic mode. "What happened in that time?"

"Just the same things that happen every day." The first woman looked at my IV and checked my bandages on my arm and feet.

"What happens every day?"

"Tomorrow you'll be given your training schedule, and you'll figure out how it all works. It's quite easy and straightforward. I think you'll like it here."

Were these women here under duress or were they willing members of this crazy group? They were too sweet to be a part of this. I watched their arms as they worked, but never got a clear shot of the area under their arms. It stung when they changed the dressings on my brand. The red incision I'd seen on my arm just before it got branded, filled my mind.

"What time is it?"

They pointed to a digital clock on the wall behind me. It read 7:00.

"How long am I going to have to be hooked up to this?" I said, pointing to the IV.

"Now that your fever has broken and you're awake, I'd say the doctor will probably release you tomorrow, but don't quote me on that. He has a mind of his own."

I had to get out of here and fast. I wondered how much they knew.

"My friends. The three that were with me. Are they alright?"

"I'm assuming so," one woman said. "You're the only one we've been nursing since the selection."

I sighed, relief engulfing me.

"Let's get you to the bathroom and get you a shower."

I was shocked at my feet and arm. They still stung and burned, but I thought I'd have huge blisters. I didn't. It felt great to get clean. I pumped the women for answers, but got little. Their knowledge seemed quite limited.

"How come I'm not in an infirmary?"

"Everyone here recuperates in their rooms after the doctor fixes you up in his office."

I wished I'd been awake to see that office. He had to keep files on a computer. Maybe that computer had access to the Internet.

After finishing their work, they left. I sat in the room stewing, wishing I'd seen more so that I could plot or plan something to topple this kingdom. I had nothing. Obviously, my locator hadn't worked, or Jeremy would be here already. Maybe he came and couldn't find me? Impossible. My thoughts raced and reeled. I slept a lot and prayed a lot. I ate broth and crackers four separate times.

I took the time to sort through all the information in my brain's files on mad men, cults, zealots, and assassins, trying to get a better sense of whom I was up against. Most of it scared me silly. How could I overcome a brilliant madman? Would I have to become brilliant and demented? I never thought I'd wish I'd studied more madmen.

I woke the next morning to whispered voices. The two nurses who had helped me yesterday were back. I smelled rubbing alcohol.

"Oh dear," one said. "I think we've woken her up."

"We'd have had to wake her in ten minutes anyway," the other said. "What's ten minutes?"

They helped me to the restroom and freshened me up for the doc who came in a little later to check on me. I couldn't believe I could walk. That burn cream must really have been great, and the cuts on my hands were almost completely healed.

The doctor looked so ordinary, so *normal*: short cropped hair, wire rim glasses, and pale, smooth skin. He had a gentle, calm demeanor. Like the nurses, it seemed wrong for him to be involved in this. He spoke softly, asking me about all my different injuries. I sugar coated my answers so that he would free me. I needed to find a way out of here and a way to sink Sterling.

He seemed to want to keep me from getting off of my sick bed. "Are you sure?" he said. "I think you might need a few more days, don't you? I can have them send you real food, you won't starve." He didn't seem to understand my desire to get out, and quick. Maybe he knew what awaited me and wanted to spare me.

Finally, after a thorough exam, he said he'd release me the next morning. I used the time to plot and scheme about escape plans, going through all kinds of interesting scenarios that had no foundation whatsoever. It kept my mind occupied, though, and I needed that. I hardly slept the whole day. A good sign that I was truly getting better. By the time the doctor took the IV out the next day at four-thirty in the morning, I felt a million times better than I had waking up from the fever two days ago.

My guide came in and brought me breakfast and fresh clothes at five. That's when I noticed a neck collar just like mine around her neck. She was a prisoner, too. I dressed while she looked the other direction. I was glad the jumpsuits weren't form fitting. It hurt to slide my branded arm into the sleeve, but I pretended it didn't bother me, so that she couldn't report I was in any pain.

She had me make my bed and then sit on it. She handed me a sheet of paper. My schedule. I took a mental snapshot of it, but then kept looking at it, pretending to read over it. Instead, I was digesting the names of the classes: Natural Poisons, Guns, Chemicals, The Hunt, Disguise Thyself, A Poetic Ending, Run for Your Life, and Fighting the Right Way. I felt sweat trickle down my back, and I had to wipe my forehead to stop the sweat from dripping into my eyes.

Eight to nine hours of classes. Full days. I'd have to get creative to find the time to work on getting out of here. The schedule was not straight forward, either. The hands-on classes were two hours each and had a rotating schedule of four a day. Monday, Wednesday, and Friday we did bookwork. Tuesday, Thursday, and Saturday we did hands-on stuff. Even a nutter like Sterling recognized the need to have one day as a day of rest if he wanted us in top form. It felt right that he'd chosen Sunday as the day of rest. I would start today, Saturday.

"You are to memorize your schedule this morning. You will have to turn it in to me before you go to class. There are severe penalties for not being where you're supposed to be at the right times. Do you need me to help you memorize it? It's so important."

"What's your name?" I asked.

"I'm Zoey," she said, folding her hands together in front of her.

"Do you love it here?" I asked. I hoped I could get her talking.

"I do love it here," she said, no conviction in her voice.

"Have you already completed an assassination?" A part of me wanted her to say yes, but I didn't want her to tell me that, either.

"Oh no," she said, stiffening. "I was caught by my mark while attempting it, but Sterling rescued me and is giving me a second chance because I show so much promise."

"Am I part of your second chance?" I asked, taking a step closer to her. My heart pounded.

She blinked her eyes hard in assent, but said, "Now that's just silly." She stepped away from me. I guessed we were being monitored. Since she didn't just nod, I figured there must be video and audio surveillance in the room. I played along.

"Maybe I *would* like you to help me memorize my schedule." I said, wanting a chance to get some info out of her if I could.

She sat next to me on the bed, and she coached me a bit on memorization. I played dumb. After about half an hour, I said, "Okay! I think I may have it. Can I use your pen?" She had a pen in her front pocket.

"Sure," she said, handing it to me.

I turned the schedule over and said, "Let me see if I can write it out."

I said one thing and wrote another.

Is there any way out of here? Has anyone ever escaped? What are Sterling's weaknesses?

Her eyes grew to the size of quarters when she read my three questions. She moved her eyes from side to side, which I figured meant she couldn't say. I continued to write.

Please tell me. I will help you get out of here.

She said, "Wait, that's not right, is it?" She took my schedule from me and turned it over, pretending to look for something specific. "That's what I thought. Instead of Natural Poisons at ten, you actually have Chemicals, and Disguise Thyself is at four." She wrote,

There's no way out. He has no weaknesses. Forget it.

I said, "I can't believe I missed that. I'm usually very good at this kind of stuff."

I wrote,

There has to be. I will find it and get you out of here. You'll see.

She gave me a weak smile. She couldn't even hope. "Even the best of us goof up sometimes. Give them to me out loud, one more time."

I did.

"That was perfect. I think you're set." She took the schedule from me and said. "I'll send this to the incinerator. You don't need it anymore."

"Thanks for your help," I said.

"That's what I'm here for. If you need anything, just push this button on the side of your nightstand." She pushed the bedspread away and showed me three buttons, one yellow, one red, and one green. "I'm yellow. If you're in trouble, push red, and don't ever push green. That's your direct link to Sterling. See you at breakfast."

I laced up the boots she'd set on the floor by me. "Okay," I said, excited about finally getting out of the room. "Wait, I don't know where I'm going."

"Right," she said, blushing. "You've never been there or anywhere. Let's go. I'll show you the way. Oh, and your neckband is programmed to let you into the areas you're supposed to go to, no others. It's kinda nice not having to walk around with keycards. It's all automatic. You'll love it."

"Great," I said, touching the strong wire that sat at the base of my neck, and I wondered what kind of crazy twists Sterling would add to my daily life here, wherever *here* was.

Chapter 15

While walking down the hall, I kicked myself for not using the paper to ask Zoey where we were. I had no idea what state or country we were in. I'd have to find a way to ask her. Before I'd fallen asleep, it had occurred to me that my best bet of being able to study Sterling would be to stand out. One characteristic of intelligent mad men, according to papers I'd studied at the spy academy, was that smart crazy people were attracted to people just like them.

The only drawback to my plan was that while madmen were attracted to other smart, crazies, they tended to react in one of two different ways to prodigies like themselves. Either they buddied up with the kindred soul–or they saw them as a threat and got rid of them. It would be a dangerous gamble; I wasn't sure which reaction he would have, but it was my best chance to get face time with him. It was my only workable plan at the moment, so I would work it. I thought about it on and off the rest of the day.

"This training facility is laid out like a wagon wheel," Zoey said once we got to our first intersection. The mess hall is in the center of it all. From there, the spokes lead to classrooms and dorm rooms. Classroom halls are bright green, and as you can see here, dorm room halls are red."

I noticed the bright red paint on the walls of the hall we walked down. That was easy enough to remember. It smelled like strawberries, too.

"Where were we that first night I got here?"

"We were in the circus tent. It's at the end of the green hallway with the elephants painted on the walls."

"And Sterling's dining room?"

"That's down the red hall with forks and knives on the walls."

"Is his house attached to it?"

She changed the subject, which I figured meant that was off limits. "Wasn't it cool how your food came up out of the table?"

"It was," I said.

"That's only the beginning. Just wait until you see all the amazing things Sterling has provided us here. We are in the Garden of Eden. No one wants for anything." As she said those things, her nose was scrunched. She didn't believe the things she was telling me. She had to say those things.

"I bet," I said. "But I sure could use a cute skirt and my cowboy boots about right now. I feel about as attractive as a slug." I ran my hand over my newly cut yellow hair.

She laughed and said, "We don't want anyone to feel inferior to anyone else, so everyone dresses the same. We all wear jumpsuits and get our haircut. It's like a new birth.

"Each new selection of kids is dressed in one color. Your color, obviously, is yellow. You will remain in that color until you become an accomplished assassin. Then you will wear white. The color of purity. I can't wait until I can wear white." She rolled her eyes at me, and I had to stifle a laugh with a loud coughing fit. We made it to the mess hall. It had taken us almost the full ten minutes. This facility was very large.

I wanted to ask her about the hair thing. Why did he break the rules when he grabbed the Avengers, who didn't have a boy and a girl with each of the four natural colors? And if his MO was consistent with the color thing all along, why did he just cut it and color it a color he wanted it to be? I couldn't ask though. She might not know what I was talking about, and it might tip her off that I'm not just any old teenager.

"I almost forgot," I said. "Where was that bonfire?"

"Oh, that's the induction section. You get there by going to the green hall with fire on the walls."

"Not hard to remember."

"Nope. Listen Misha, it's super important that you are on time to all your classes and you work hard. Don't be sloppy doing anything. Sterling only accepts your best work. If you shine, he gives you special favors."

I intended to get those special favors. I saw the doors to the mess hall close and heard a click, like someone had locked them. She nodded at me. "It's best just to be early wherever you go here. Now you can go eat. Sit where you'd like. I have to sit with the Blackies." She looked down at her black outfit and swept her hands from her shoulders to her hips, emphasizing the black color of her jumpsuit. "You can sit wherever you want, though, except at the Blackies' tables." Had everyone at the Blackies' tables botched their missions?

She headed off. I looked around. The mess hall provided a relaxed, fun atmosphere to eat in. Odd. Were we in jail or not? Music blared from a jukebox in one corner, and several kids were playing some shoot'em up video game. Kids laughed and joked around. Every shade of the rainbow, including white and black filled the space. Those who wore the same colors seemed to clump together. That's when I spotted my group's shade of yellow.

Frankie and Duncan sat alone at a table in the middle of the room. I looked for Houston. He shone like a star in the middle of a group of Whities. He was a bit too excited about this assassin thing. He obviously knew Whities were the successful assassins. It seemed he wanted to be just like them. He talked animatedly using his arms and hands.

I hurried through the line of gourmet foods. Zoey hadn't been kidding. I could eat anything I wanted here, and it all looked fantastic. I filled my plate, my stomach grumbling like an upset child. The broth they'd fed me over the last few days had been used up a long time ago. It shocked me that we would be so well fed. I had assumed that madmen starved their victims.

I sat next to Frankie. Her eyes went big, and then she threw her arms around me. "Misha! I thought you were dead. Oh, I'm so glad you're here. This place is crazy." I hugged her back. It took her a whole minute to let me go. "Where've you been?"

"I was really sick with an infection," I said. "But the doc thinks I'm safe now."

"Good," she said. "Houston has gone totally military on us. He is completely enamored with this place and Sterling. It creeps me out. I've got to get out of here."

I moved my finger up to my lips, exaggerating the movement so that she would recognize it for what it was.

"You think–"

"I think we ought to eat up before our food gets cold," I said.

"Oh," she said, holding onto the 'O' for much too long. But at least she'd gotten the hint. "What's your schedule?"

I rattled it off to her.

"It's the same as mine," she said. "Yay! I hated being alone."

"Don't Houston and Duncan have the same schedule as you?" I looked at Duncan.

"Yes," she said, "but I meant I hated being the only girl. Duncan's been great!" She looked at him and smiled and then whispered in my ear that he hadn't spoken a word since that first night. I guessed she didn't want him to hear. Now I looked at him. He'd come around. He'd have to.

"How's it going Duncan?"

He didn't even acknowledge me.

"Do you like your guide?"

Nothing.

"He's a jerk, is he?"

He didn't even move; he was totally catatonic.

"What's he doing that's so jerky?" I hoped I could trick him into talking, but he said nothing and just continued to eat.

This must be a truly traumatizing experience for him on so many levels. First off, he'd watched his friends die. Second, he had almost died several times himself, and third, he'd had to kill someone. On top of all of that, he had always gotten what he wanted at home, and no one was ever around to tell him what to do. Now he was being monitored 24-7, and he was told exactly what to do and when to do it.

I scanned the room for signs of cameras. I knew they were there, but where? I couldn't find any. Some kids turned the jukebox up loud, which made the kids playing video games turn up the sound system. Was this a free zone where Sterling didn't listen in?

I needed to get info about this place, so I would ask Frankie and Duncan about what had been happening the last four days. I wasn't going to let Duncan off the hook. This had been traumatizing for us all, and I needed their help.

"What's been going on, you guys?" I addressed them both, speaking just loud enough for the two of them to hear.

"I started classes on Wednesday with Duncan. We had to wait until the doc cleared us. Whatever the stuff is the doc and our nurses used on us, it makes us heal quickly."

"Duncan, what's going on with your legs?"

Nothing.

"Do you still feel a lot of pain?" I asked.

Again, nothing.

"What are classes like?"

"Really serious," Frankie said. "Everyone works really hard. They do really hard stuff. I don't know if I can do it."

I turned to Duncan. He didn't say anything.

"Look Duncan, if we're going to have a chance at getting us all out of here, I need you on board. You were the leader of the Avengers. You are the one that made the group work. I need you to lead us out of here. For you to do that, you need to talk to us."

"There's no way out," he whispered. "We're going to die here."

"That's no way for a leader to talk," I said. "Especially you, Duncan. You are the most optimistic and creative person I know. It's time to step up. We are going to find a way."

"Look, Misha," Duncan spat. "I've been looking the past two days. There are no holes in the security of this place that I've been able to find." He grabbed the wire around his neck. "This, as well as other things, makes it impossible."

"Tell me everything, Duncan, and Frankie, as he talks, think about other things you've noticed. Like, have you seen anything you might steal that would give us an advantage?"

Frankie nodded, and Duncan gave me the rundown of what he'd seen and experienced. He'd noticed a hierarchy. It appeared that the Whities were at the top of the food chain. I'm sure he'd been wondering how he could get into that group. Born leaders are always looking for a way to lead.

The way he told it, this place was more secure than a military base. There had to be weaknesses. I would find them.

We had two hours of poisons class today. We followed the frog-painted walls in one of the lime-smelling, green halls to a huge lab. It was the most amazing lab I'd ever seen. There were probably one hundred stations surrounded by long tables, and the walls were lined with machines and cabinets. Many kids were already busy at their lab stations. I stuck with Frankie and Duncan and went to their station. Houston soon followed. I raised my eyebrows at him, and he rolled his eyes at me.

"Let's get busy," he said. "I need to hurry through all the experiments so I can move on. Besides, I can't wait to see what happens to the frogs." He laughed an evil laugh. I had a flashback to my very first day at Roseburg High—Houston had seemed eager to injure small creatures even back then.

That's when I saw them, the frogs, jumping around in a container on the table. Were we dissecting frogs? I had hated doing it in Mr. Edmondson's class, and I would hate it here, too. I guessed Houston was being forced to stay with us. He'd rather be in a different group.

Duncan brought some vials marked *Poison #490*. Frankie got out the equipment we needed.

"I'm glad you found your group," a man said.

I turned to see who spoke.

"I'm Mr. Kine," he said, taking my arm with his hand and pulling me away from the lab station so he could talk to me alone. "I'm the poisons instructor. Since everyone has different levels of knowledge, we do a lot of general lessons together, but most are done as group study, and I supervise and help when needed. Don't hesitate to ask if you have any questions. Your group is starting with basic natural poisons.

"Here is your computer tablet. It contains all the information you need about your classes. As you finish a lesson satisfactorily, it will automatically take you to the next one. If you'd like to get caught up, feel free. Otherwise, you can sit back and watch what effect the poisons the students made yesterday have on your subjects, the frogs." He wore a smile on his lips and his eyes smiled, too. I smiled back. Could he be trusted, or was he in league with Sterling?

"Am I allowed to go as fast as I'd like, or must I remain with my group?" I asked.

"It is advised that you stay with your group, but if we see that you are more advanced than they, we would consider moving you to another group during poisons class."

"It's just that I'm great with chemistry, and I'm a pretty fast reader. I'd rather not be bored." I wanted him to think I was advanced, but I wanted to keep my photographic memory to myself.

"Understood," he said. "But you also need to remember what you've learned. You will be given comprehensive tests every two weeks. Why don't you go read up on what we've learned so far and catch the end of the experiment?"

"Okay," I said. I made my way over to some tables around the outside of the room he'd pointed to, and I turned the tablet on. The information was quite technical and caught my attention right away. I had to hold myself back from rushing through all the pages and then sorting them in my mind. Instead, I took the snapshot and then perused the page for several minutes before going on to the next one. I really learned a lot. Yesterday's lesson taught about ten different poisonous plants and how to use them. The part that made me sick to my stomach was at the end of the lesson, where it described how several of the poisons had been used to create a poetic ending to several people's lives. I went back to lesson number one on poisons and quickly passed the lesson for today.

I couldn't help myself. I went on to the next lesson that popped up and then the next. There were points where I wanted to quit reading because it was so disturbing, but at the same time, I needed this information to move on, to show Sterling I was special and he should pay attention to me. Before I knew it, class was over and the bell rang for us to move on to our next classes. I realized a bit too late that I'd finished twenty lessons and was ready for the two-week comprehensive test. Had Mr. Kine watched me? Did he have any idea how far I'd gotten? Did I want him to know? Would it give me away? I slipped the tablet in my front jumpsuit pocket.

I stayed behind to wait for Frankie who was still putting supplies away, while Duncan and Houston hurried out. I thought about Zoey's advice to get everywhere early. With only ten minutes between classes, I should have left, but I figured Frankie needed me. She looked torn up again. After putting away the last of the supplies, she whispered in my ear, "I don't know how much longer I can take this. What those poisons did to those frogs..."

I casually put my finger up to my lips to remind her that someone was most likely listening and watching. I'm glad I didn't have to see the poisons do their stuff to the frogs. Reading about it was bad enough.

She looked at her feet. So, with my hand hanging by my side, in what I thought was her sight line, I used sign language, just the letters, to send her a message. Since her dad was deaf, I figured she must know sign language. *Courage now. Escape later.*

She jerked her head up and then looked back down. I signed the same message, slowly. She smiled at me. The first time I'd seen her do that here.

Chapter 16

The air was thick with humidity when we walked outside. That ruled out about half of the states in the U.S. as the location for this place. If we even were in the U.S. I took note of the trees, the bushes, the grass, anything that might give me a clue to where we were. We passed the bonfire area and walked a good fifteen minutes before we reached the rifle range. I didn't panic about being late because a lot of kids were walking a little bit in front of us in no real hurry. I memorized every last detail, analyzing it, looking for a way to escape. Two twenty-foot high cement walls surrounded the whole place, and the wire fence in front of the one closest us was electrified. Big signs were posted on it warning us not to get too close.

Could those walls surround the entire compound? I couldn't see the end of the property to know. I thought of the Berlin wall. It was possible. A wide strip of green grass lay before the fence and looked very tempting until I saw the guard towers. Men with machine guns stood at the ready. The set up echoed that of a prison or a concentration camp. The great escapes I'd read and learned about populated my mind, the methods behind their escapes taking center stage.

We were positioned at the first station. A tan, thin Blackie came and handed each of us a rifle. It felt heavy, awkward in my hands. I'd used a handgun back at Division, but never a high-powered rifle. Its black barrel gleamed in the sun. Sweat dripped down my spine. The humidity was killer.

I wanted to be a great shooter. Maybe I could become a good enough sniper that I could take out all three guards in the towers surrounding us. Then I'd just climb over the cement walls. Sun glinted off the glass in front of the guards. I'd bet money it was bulletproof glass. I could see intermittent holes in the glass. I'd have to be really good to get the bullet through one of those holes and into the guard.

The Blackie gave us a short lesson on gun safety, explaining that we should always treat every gun like it's loaded and that we should always point a weapon down, or down range. We then went over how to load the rifle. After putting on ear protection, we were instructed to lie prone with the gun directly in front of us, our legs spread out a bit wider than shoulder width for stability.

A man with salt and pepper hair barked out instructions after that. We all had beanbags to support the stock of the gun. We pressed the butt of the gun between our shoulder blade and neck groove.

We practiced squeezing the beanbag and flattening it to get the target in the crosshairs.

Once we had the target in the crosshairs, with constant even pressure, we were to pull on the trigger. I pressed the butt hard into my shoulder, hoping the kick wouldn't be too bad. I practiced with my finger away from the trigger first a few times and then tried to imitate the movement on the actual trigger. Bang. It shocked me how loud it was. The kick hurt but only a little bit. We were a good hundred yards from the target, so I couldn't tell where I'd hit it.

Frankie had never shot any kind of gun, and the kick really hurt her shoulder. From then on, she also pushed it hard into her shoulder.

Even though it was really difficult to hit the targets, shaped like cutouts of people, it turned out to be kinda fun. For about the next ten shots, I jerked the gun, missing the target completely.

"Roberts," the man with salt and pepper hair said. "You're anticipating the shot. Give the trigger a nice, even, constant pressure, and you'll get your shot back. You want to be surprised by the shot, not anticipate it."

I was not a natural marksman, however, and had to really concentrate not to force the shot. The instructor shot for us multiple times and physically helped each of us several times. Frankie was pretty good at it and was a fast learner. The boys seemed to be having fun, especially Houston. It was nice to continue to hear sounds come from Duncan's mouth.

I also took everything in about the area and the instructors. There were three that I could make out, each taking care of a third of the range. They never left their posts and were either helping someone in their group with something or watching individuals in their group fire. The same grassy strip, electrified fence, and cement walls were in the distance. I couldn't see the end of them. Forest filled the area that hadn't been cleared for the shooting range.

The bell rang for us to clean our guns. The Blackie instructor once again came and demonstrated for us. Frankie and I were the last ones to leave once again.

"Don't worry, you'll get just as fast as they are with some practice," our instructor said. The man with the salt and pepper hair sent a message to our chemicals instructor that we would be late. I noticed the guards in the towers had turned their bodies out toward the perimeter of the area instead of on us.

Frankie and I got to the chemicals class as fast as we could. We opened the doors to an enormous lab and found about one hundred kids already hard at work at one of about fifty lab stations. A man, who I figured must be the teacher, roamed about the room. I pulled up the class syllabus on my tablet. This was advanced chemistry wrapped in wickedness. Everything we worked on had to do with delivering nasty chemicals in the most effective ways. I thought about a man I'd targeted on a test mission a while back who'd used animals as his delivery method. I wondered if that would come up. I wondered if Sterling knew Dr. Ramirez. Wouldn't that be a coincidence?

We focused on airborne delivery for the lesson today and used different methods to put the chemicals in the air, killing off many frogs in glass containers and sealed rooms. It was horrible to watch them die. The really bad ones were when they bubbled and burst, but it was all bad. I didn't know if I could take this violence and cruelty day after day.

Lunch was just as good as breakfast had been. There were tons of choices, and everything tasted delicious. It was nice to have a full hour to relax and eat. I ran into Zoey in the line for food.

"After our next class, we get free time until ten p.m. on Sunday." Her eyes lit up like this was the time she loved.

Our last class was on fighting. We walked to the large gym. The hall leading there had silhouettes of men and women in fighting stances stenciled on the walls. We were working on different techniques to kill using our bare hands. Basically, it all required a huge amount of strength. The temple, the summit of the nose, which I'd had experience with, the area between the upper lip and the bottom of the nose, the Adam's apple, and testicles all required maximum force to cause death.

An attacker could also hit the front side of the jaw, whipping the head back and causing the neck to break or hit the small of the back, snapping the spine. We worked on life-like dummies. Near the end of class, we also learned the classic move they show on TV a lot where the attacker grabs the mouth and the back of the skull and twists the head with a sudden, violent jerk.

Out of nowhere, Sterling showed up in his pinstriped black suit. Instead of orange hair and accents, fluorescent blue attacked us all. He walked straight up to me and people stopped what they were doing to watch and listen.

"How's it going today, Misha?" he asked.

I stiffened. He remembered my name. This was exactly what I wanted, to have him take notice of me, but I just stood and stared, a deep cold starting in my feet. His eyes were so dark, soulless. "Good, thanks," I finally answered.

"Show me the temple kill."

I turned to the dummy and demonstrated it, my heart hammering in my chest and my breathing erratic.

"How about the summit kill?"

I did that too, slowly gaining control of my racing heart.

"Pretty good," he said. "Let's move on to breaking the dummy's back."

I did. I was able to breathe normally now.

"And can you snap his neck?"

I did that move, calmly, in complete control.

"Fabulous, Misha. Just fabulous. Now I'd like you to do the skull jerk on me."

I turned and looked at him in a sharp, fast movement. My heart sped up and my breathing turned quick and shallow. This was the moment I had been waiting for, and I didn't even have to wait long. My heart sang. I wanted to shout out, Yahoo! He was giving himself to me to kill. I could accommodate him. But of course, it couldn't be that easy. He was up to something. I readied myself in fighting stance.

Several things happened at once but in slow motion. I noticed about ten men, around the area but nowhere close, that hadn't been there before. They all held rifles trained on me. I also saw the crowd that had formed around us. Their eyes and stance told me to beware. They loved this man. How had he inspired love? Was it Stockholm syndrome? Were these kids so neglected at home that they adored him? Did they believe that this was a far better world for them than what they had had before? He had given them a sense of purpose, of belonging. They felt safe and protected, and all their needs were provided for. I stepped back, relaxing.

No, I couldn't kill him. He was too beloved. Sure there were some eyes egging me on, begging me to do it, to just kill him. But I knew if I did, I would die, too, and then one of

Sterling's lackeys would take over for him. No, killing him now would accomplish only my death. I would have to wait. I would have to sneak out and bring reinforcements with me. These kids would need serious psychological help after what Sterling put them through. They may never be the same. My chest burned, and I knew I'd come to the correct conclusion. I would spare him now because they loved him. I took a second step back.

It had been less than half a minute, but Sterling had caught my hesitation. "Why did you hesitate?" His smile was broad. He had done this to teach me. To teach me that they loved him and would kill for him, that I had no choice but to bend my will to him. I couldn't believe he was asking me this in front of everyone. What if our conversation hadn't ended in his favor? He must know he would win, or he wouldn't be challenging me here.

Something in my head told me to be honest, so I was. "I realized these people love you. They're loyal to you. And if I were to kill you, I would accomplish nothing. Your legacy would live on, and I would be dead. I'm incapable of taking on a hundred of your supporters or your snipers." I stared right into his eyes, showing my hatred of him.

He chuckled. "I knew you were special the moment I got the call that you were being tracked by someone other than me. I knew you'd understand why I gave you the opportunity to do your heart's desire."

It took all my concentration not to grab at my arm where Division 57 had put my tracker. That would give me away for sure. No, I had to pretend I didn't know about the tracker. I didn't dare look away. He knew about it and still kept me alive? Why? I let shock and terror enter my eyes. "What are you talking about?" I cried. "I'm not being tracked." I made my eyes scrunch together, adding confusion to my look.

He raised his eyebrows. "You claim not to have known?"

"I don't know what you're talking about." I let anger enter.

"When my men retrieved you and you were unconscious, they inserted a tracker in your upper arm in the area you now have your brand."

"What? I have a tracker in my arm? What are you saying?" I was trying to act as if I was on the verge of hysteria. I pulled my arm up and looked at my brand. It was still tender, but I poked at it anyway. I wondered if my infection came from their little 'surgery.'

"When our tracker failed to work once inserted, they figured it was a dud tracker and made an incision to retrieve it. And guess what they found, not one tracker, but two. Somehow their signals shorted each other out. They fried each other. That made things a bit more interesting, you see. It made it so that we couldn't figure out who it was that had been tracking you before us. So, be a good girl and spill the beans."

He wanted to make an example of me, here in front of everyone. He wanted to root out a traitor while everyone looked on. Is this what had happened to the other agents from Division who had failed? Had Sterling discovered their treachery and killed them?

"You know what I think?" I said. "I think you're a liar. No one was tracking me. Why would anyone track me?" I was freaking out inside. My Division 57 tracker had been removed, and now I was being tracked by Sterling. All my hopes for intermittent signals were lost. How would I ever get away? Jeremy definitely had no idea where I was. They had removed Division's tracker on the helicopter. I couldn't hope for Jeremy to find me now. His words on the jet came back to me. *What if something goes wrong when you're kidnapped, and I can't find you? Things happen all the time and even to very seasoned agents. It has nothing to do with my belief in you. Things just go wrong.* Things had gone wrong, and I was completely and totally alone.

"That is the question isn't it?" He tilted his head to the side and stared hard at me.

I tried to look confused, angry, and scared all at once. It helped that I was already angry and scared. All I could hope for was that he would think someone had put the tracker in me without my knowledge.

"Well, no matter," he said. "You're clean now, and your tracker is working just fine." He smiled a maniacal smile. "One day you will confide in me because you will discover that I have your best interests in mind. Together we all make a difference."

A loud chant arose from those around us. The chant they had recited when we were inducted into this group. "A world without smut. A world without indecision. A world without lawlessness. A world without greed." His brainwashing had been very effective with these kids.

"I expect great things from you," Sterling said. "I'm sure you won't disappoint." He was so direct. So out there. I knew why he wanted to do this to me in front of everyone, but why did he want his soldiers to witness it? Was he trying to make them wary of me? I would need to be bold with him. He waved me into a copse of trees, away from the crowd. The instructors told everyone to get back to work. Why did he now want me alone?

I tried not to freak out, or think that he was leading me away to murder me without witnesses. I knew that was irrational. He thought I was interesting and wanted me to stay around. I had to open and close my hands repeatedly to get rid of some of my nervous energy as I followed him. Once we were out of earshot of the others, he said, "I know it's frightening; you're not sure whom to trust. One thing's for certain. I will not hurt you."

He wouldn't, but one of his lackeys would. And there was that collar.

"I'm here to help you achieve your potential while giving you the greatest adrenaline rush you've ever experienced. I'm here to make your life full. You were chosen because you have great physical strength, you're a quick thinker, and you're creative. Only the best are chosen for this program. You should feel honored to be here. I can't wait to see what you accomplish. I see great things in your future."

Fire licked my throat, and I wanted to protest, but I held it in.

"That was pretty impressive back there. Most kids would have let their anger overtake them because they don't understand what's going on. You demonstrated great control, and control of anger in this profession is as important as air is to life. When I look for the elite, I have to weed out those who don't quite fit. You survived the weeding process. Four of you from the eight. That is phenomenal, really.

Congratulations, you are one of the elite. Houston appears to be a natural. He never questions anything and always does his best. Beyond his best. But does he have control? Only time will tell."

I could imagine Houston puffing up and standing a bit taller had he been here to accept the praise.

"Frankie, on the other hand, is going to take a while to come around. She is the simmering type, while Houston is a constant hard-boil. I'm not sure about Duncan, yet. I don't think he's sure either. He's somewhere in between those two."

"Why are you telling me all this?" I spat.

"I observed you in the lab today," he continued, ignoring my question.

I had to pretend that my insides weren't quaking right now.

"I could see that I could count on you to be one of my best soldiers. I saw how quickly you absorbed the information. Yes, we are fighting a war, and we will conquer. I think we should work together for the good of the people. Stop viewing me as your enemy. Together we can conquer faster."

Was he trying to appeal to my desire for power?

"So, are you ready for some friendly sparring?" He smiled and waggled his eyebrows.

I raised mine.

"I haven't had a good opponent in a while. Let's see if you can take me. We won't truly hurt each other."

"I don't think I could stop in time, sir."

"Good, honest answer," he said. "You have my attention, Misha."

We sat in silence for an awkward minute with him looking me over. He moved closer and put his hand on my upper arm. I wanted to grab him, throw him to the ground, and break his neck.

"I think we could be good friends if you'd open your mind and see the big picture. In fact, why don't you come Monday morning for breakfast, six sharp, and we'll discuss it? I'll convince you that we are here to make the world a better place."

He patted my arm before removing his hand. It made me feel like throwing up. Acid burned in my throat.

"I'm just not into the whole, let's-kill-everybody-because-they're-bad idea. I don't kill, period."

"On the contrary, my dear, you already have."

The face of the karate master from the circus tent appeared vividly in my mind. Everything about her was seared into my memory, especially the sound of her voice as she'd pled for mercy. She'd said she'd had chemo, that she had a family. The horror of what I'd had to do washed over me. But I'd had to do it–if I hadn't, not only would I have been killed, but I would have let Sterling continue his reign of terror unchecked. It was his fault that woman had died. Still, the memory of the knife in my hand, and the blood seeping out, sent a shiver of revulsion and shame through me.

"No!" I growled, low and angry. "You did that. You killed that woman!"

"Yes, it was very realistic wasn't it?" Sterling continued.

"Realistic–what–?" I stammered. What was he saying?

"Well, after all, we did go to great effort to make it appear so. I'm sure it even felt real to you, didn't it? Hmm, yes. But the fighters were wearing body suits that were triggered when the knife, a stage prop, hit the suit," he grinned wickedly, clearly taking pleasure in the diabolical nature of his ruse. "You see, when the blade hit your opponent's body, it retracted. At the same time, a needle protruded. The needle does two things, it punctures the knife suit, and it immobilizes the victim. Oh, and for the selections, blood seeps from the handle of the prop knife. Very convincing, very realistic."

His words washed over me like an ocean wave, and I gasped for air, trying to make sense of what he was telling me.

"You mean–she's alive?" I whispered, barely daring to hope he could be telling the truth. "But *why*? Why would you do that? You kidnapped those people! You took them away from their families, all for what? Some game, to make us believe we were *murdering* innocent people?"

"They may have appeared innocent to you, but the reality is that they were the worst of offenders. I am merciful. I gave them a reprieve," he paused, looking me over, as if deciding what would be the best way to explain it to me. As if any explanation could sway my opinion of him. "Someone as intelligent as you–I'm sure you've heard of trial by battle? The accused are given the chance to prove their purity through combat. A test, to see if their repentance is complete. If the good Lord felt they had paid their dues, they would be victorious. A few were, weren't they? The others? Guilty as charged, and now they can receive just punishment."

"But what about my friends?"

"They're fine, just fine. Well, all but one. He's still fighting for his life. My vote is on him."

My eyes must have been the size of golf balls. "Is Lunden alive, then? Did you not feed him to the lions?" I asked.

He chuckled. "No, no. None of your friends received such a fate. We will put them to good use. They are very much alive."

I gaped. Was he lying to me? Was it possible they were all alive and well somewhere? The thought made my heart race with wild hope. Maybe I could still save them.

"I'm a bit disappointed you hadn't already figured that out, Misha. So ready to believe what your eyes tell you. That makes me wonder, though, what kind of a person do you think I am?"

"A mad one."

"Good answer. Sometimes I do see myself as mad. I guess there's one thing I can count on from you, and that's honesty, no matter how brutal it seems."

What was he doing talking about brutality?

"Understand, though" he said. "All the kills we do are necessary. Justice demands it."

"And what if I don't want to murder people? I don't want to be the judge."

"You're not the judge. I am. You execute the orders of the judge. You get it, execute? Sometimes I crack myself up. You'll see, you'll come around. Go back to your fighting. Become the best and don't settle for less." Then he walked away, turning back only to say, "Monday. Breakfast. 6:00. My dining hall. Follow the forks and the knives." He threw his head back and laughed.

Chapter 17

I didn't know what to think. I went back and was both mad and pleased. Mad that my tracker was gone and happy that Sterling seemed to be enamored with me. Pleased also that my friends were alive, and I hadn't killed that woman with cancer. None of us had killed anyone. Mad that he had tricked us like that.

My plan was working, Sterling wanted me to work with him, but how could I escape when my tracker was gone and Sterling's tracker was inside me? I'd have to find a way to remove it before I got out of here. Ian popped into my head, and I wondered if I'd ever see him here. He probably didn't dare show his face. Not after what he'd done. Or was he truly heartless and watched us all on monitors, laughing at us like Sterling?

After class, Frankie whispered with a ton of agitation about what had happened with Sterling the whole way back to the lunchroom.

"Way to go. Bring attention to all of us." She swore colorfully. "He's going to make our lives miserable."

"No, he isn't." I said. "He said he's impressed with me."

"Why you?" Houston said, coming up behind me. "Why are you the one he's impressed with?"

"I don't know," I said.

"I brought down six people in fighting class in under three minutes, and Sterling didn't notice because you stole the limelight."

"Houston, I don't want any kind of limelight. You go ahead and take it. Grab it. Own it. Run with it. Go ahead and murder as many people as you want, because I won't." I knew I was being harsh but I couldn't help myself.

"Then you're just stupid," he scoffed.

"Then don't think of me as a threat then. Go and be the best assassin you can be. Just leave me be."

"Well, maybe one day I'll get the okay to take you out. What then?" He smirked.

"I don't know why you'd wanna do that."

"'Cause this is the best thing that's ever happened to me. I love this place. I totally belong here. I'll never go back to my dad, never. Maybe I'll get approval to assassinate him."

"Don't say that, Houston. I can see that you feel like you belong, but don't go after your dad. Everybody sees that you'll have an itty bitty learning curve and be an amazing assassin. So just let your dad be, and let me be. Let me *not* be an assassin." Deep down I felt truly bad for him. His home life had been so terrible, he saw Sterling as an angel, delivering him from evil.

Some guys came up from behind us and enticed Houston away from us, screaming and shouting about how rocking tonight was going to be.

Frankie was still next to me. "I just hate that you have a target on your back."

"Don't say that. I don't believe it, and you shouldn't either." Is that why Sterling did his little stunt in front of all those people? Did he want me to have a target on my back?

"Did you notice that everyone was staring at you? They're still staring at you. You are a target."

"Well, if that's true, then I'm going to use this to my best advantage." I didn't know what that would be, but I hoped to figure it out.

"I'm sure you will," she said, shaking her head.

I looked down at my tablet.

Reminder! Tonight: dance after dinner and tomorrow a circus.

Mess hall open 24 hours a day.

No curfew.

"Are you kidding me?" I said to Frankie. "He rules our every move for almost five and a half days a week and then he lets everyone go free for a day and a half? That just doesn't make any sense at all."

"I don't care why he's doing it," she said. "I'm just glad he is."

Her words answered my question. He did this because the kids would love him for it.

Frankie and I walked into the mess hall and saw Zoey pacing and wringing her hands in front of the table I had sat at for breakfast and lunch. What was up with her? She spotted me when I was only about ten feet away and sprang forward.

"What have you done?" she said, grabbing my arm and leading me to the side of the room. Frankie followed.

"What's going on, Zoey?" Frankie asked.

"Do you have a death wish?" Zoey asked me.

"Not you, too. You know I don't have a death wish. I want to live and help save everyone." I stared hard at her.

"Just an FYI," Zoey whispered, "the last person Sterling challenged like that was dead two weeks later."

I raised my eyebrows. I guessed he was the type of madman who killed his equals. No buddies for him. I could be in trouble, but it didn't feel like it. I pointed to my ear to remind her he was listening.

"He only listens in your room, not out here." She ran her fingers through her hair. Frankie shifted from one leg to the other. "He sees everything, but doesn't hear everything outside your room. I told you to stand out, sure. But this?"

"He was the one who came after me. I don't want to challenge him or be an assassin. What did you want me to do?" I was ecstatic that he only listened to us in our rooms. This gave me more hope of escape.

"Lay down and play dead, that's what." She threw her arms out to the side. Frankie leaned on the wall.

I whispered, "It didn't feel right to do that. I had to do what my gut was telling me to do and that was to play him hard. Besides, he likes me." I felt the burning again, the voice, almost a whisper, telling me I was on the right track.

"Well, now you're going to have to pick it up. You're going to have to play the game and play it really hard or he'll know you're holding back. He *will* hold you accountable. He's a harsh judge, if you haven't noticed."

"I'm sorry." I said, looking at her black jumpsuit. "I'm sorry you have to be a servant because of him. I will do everything in my power to get us all out of here." I reached out and brushed her arm.

"That's the thing, Misha, you have no power here." She pulled away from my touch. "He has it all. He has all the love, the support. He has everything. You. Me. We have exactly nothing."

"Stop!" I said, louder than I'd intended. "Don't say that. It's not true. It's what he wants you to believe. You don't have to believe that. We can have all of that. All of it. So let's go for it."

"I hope you know what you're doing, because he certainly does. What did he say to you when he pulled you to the side?"

"He wants to have breakfast with me on Monday."

"Oh, man. You be careful. Tread lightly."

Frankie's attention had left us. She now watched a group of boys playing some shoot 'em up video game. She wasn't so boy crazy back in Oregon. What had gotten into her?

"I'll just continue with what I've been doing. I'll remain honest."

"I don't know if it'll serve you well." Zoey took a small step away from me.

"Well, it's gonna have to, because that's all I've got. I have to be honest." Ironic, but that was another lie. I knew I'd never be able to tell the truth here. I thought of all of all the lies I'd told since getting on this mission and felt momentary guilt. I had to be honest on my terms now. Terms that pushed the greater good.

"Please, for me, if you won't do it for yourself," she said, taking a step toward me and grabbing both my wrists. "Go full force." She looked so serious, so desperate.

I reached out and hugged her. "Don't worry about me. I'll be okay, really."

It shocked me to see tears on her cheeks when she pulled back and walked away. She thought I was dead. I could see it in her eyes. How many of her friends had she seen die here? I didn't want to hurt her more by putting myself in harm's way again. But, I had to do what I felt was right. Good things followed me when I chose to listen to my heart. I hoped Zoey wouldn't suffer in the meantime.

At our table, I pulled Frankie and Duncan in close and told them what Sterling had told me about Lunden, Maddie, Payden, and Anna, that they were alive. As if the spell had lifted from Duncan, he said, "Are you serious? They're alive? Even the people we fought?" A wave of complete and total relief washed over Duncan. He took deep, cleansing breaths, staring intently at me.

"Yes!" I said. "They're alive and well. Except maybe Lunden. I think he's still recovering. There was poison and blood in those knives Sterling gave us. It was all staged."

Duncan stood up, raised his arms and his head to the ceiling and called out, "Hallelujah!"

Duncan must have been unable to deal with the fact he'd killed a man. Now that his guilt was lifted, he'd found his voice. Maybe he would now become leader material again.

Right after that our table suddenly became the interesting table. A bunch of Whities and Blackies came over. They came to see me. Maybe Sterling had wanted everyone to look up to me. They wanted to know what Sterling had said to me. I had attained celebrity status. I told them it was between him and me and not to worry about it.

A Whitie came up and said, "What spell did you place on Sterling and will you teach it to me?"

"No spell," I said.

"Well, I think he's in love with you." The boy chuckled.

"Hardly." I tugged at his white sleeve and said, "What was your kill?" I didn't want to know, but I needed allies.

"You want to see it?" he said, totally excited. I watched his name, Seth, flash across the screen of his tablet before he pulled the video up.

"You recorded it?" I asked.

"Sterling records them all. Check this out."

It's terrible to watch anyone die.

Seth's mark was an evangelist preacher who promised people healings and blessings when they donated to his church. The healings were bogus—staged by his own family members. People with real illnesses and disabilities sent him their money, sometimes their entire life savings, and got nothing in return. On his show he pledged he would dedicate all donations to further his ministry of healing. In private, he piled the money in stacks around him as he bought yachts, luxury houses, and cars. None of the money went to help anyone but himself.

The man was in love with his money. Seth had used that love of money to create the poetic end for the preacher. The preacher always made a ritual of opening letters in his office, pulling out the money and running any donation higher than ten dollars over his lips and taking a big whiff. When he did this to the bills Seth sent, he seemed fine, moving on to several other bills when suddenly, his lips and nose began to blister and pop. Boils and lesions appeared on his face, neck, and hands. He started screaming as they all popped and festered. He died in less than five minutes.

Seth was laughing and pointing, making fun of the man in his agony. I had to choke back the bile in the back of my throat and disappear into my happy place, reminding myself that this kid was brainwashed. Before he met Sterling, he'd most likely been a normal boy.

"That rocked," I said to him, trying to force enthusiasm on my face. "I can't wait until I get my chance."

"It'll come soon enough, Roberts. You're obviously one of his favorites. It won't be long." He stood up and went to join the kids playing the video games.

After dinner, I wasn't ready to go to the dance, so I went outside to explore, instead. Frankie and Duncan were excited to go to the dance and left to get ready. My spidey senses had been raging all day. Danger. Danger. Of course there was danger. This whole place was laced with danger.

I was getting to the point where I was ignoring them. I wished I'd been able to sense Sterling arriving during my fight class through all my noisy feelings, but I hadn't. I headed for a forested area and thought I noticed a heightened sense of warning, but couldn't be sure. I looked around and tried to discover what might be causing it. I couldn't see or hear anything, so I continued on my path deeper into a wooded area to the left of the building. I had to push on a lot of branches to make my way through. I would have to start listening to my spidey senses a bit differently. This would be a good test.

Finally, I emerged into a small, open space where several trees had been cut down, and it looked like someone had made a fire pit in the center. Smoke swirled out of it. I walked right up to the hole and stared down into it. Red and white coals flickered. At that moment, someone grabbed me from behind, his big hands and arms lifting me up into the air and then slamming me to the ground next to the fire pit. I didn't have a chance to react. Dust billowed around my face and body, and I coughed hard once I'd caught my breath. I guess I *had* felt a heightened sense of warning.

"You," the strong boy said, forcing his knee into my back. "Who are you, why are you here in our meeting place, and what is it that makes you so special that Sterling would honor you?"

Sterling had hardly honored me. I took a deep breath, trying to get enough air to answer my attacker, but ended up coughing my guts out as more dust flew in. He pulled me up by my arms, wrenching them behind me. I had to totally hold back and not fight them. A group of about twenty kids filtered out of the woods and into the clearing. None really looked familiar, but I'd only been here a few days. One thing I did notice was that they all wore white jumpsuits. All were successful assassins. They made a circle around me. The person holding me let go. I brushed my hair away from my face and used my sleeve to wipe away the dirt from my lips and eyes.

"I'll ask you one more time," the boy said, "who are you, why are you here, and why is Sterling paying special attention to you?"

The boy had reddish hair, bulging muscles, and a thick, red five o'clock shadow. He stood a good foot and a half taller than me. I vaguely remembered seeing a tuft of reddish hair at the shooting range. I think he was in the advanced group of snipers.

"My name is Misha," I said, spitting out dirt after I said it. "I was just exploring the grounds. I didn't know this was your special spot, and I don't know why Sterling has taken an interest in me." In my mind I was thinking of how I could take them all out if necessary.

Several in the circle snickered.

"Who are *you*?" I asked.

"We're a group of Whities dedicated to protecting Sterling and this cause." Immediately after he said it, the group chanted the chant and stomped their feet.

"We'll be watching you, Misha. One misstep from you and you can kiss your life here goodbye."

I wanted to laugh. That's all I wanted. He was referring to my death, but I thought it would be interesting if they actually knew a way out.

"Well, I won't be misstepping," I said. "How can I help?"

They all laughed. "You," the naturally red-haired guy said, "can't help at this point. You have to be a Whitie to join us." He pulled at the jumpsuit he wore.

"Alrighty then, should I stay away from here from now on?"

"Yes! No non-Whities allowed."

"I'll be sure to steer clear, then. Sorry to interrupt. May I leave?" I figured if I pretended to be humble, I'd get out of there unscathed.

"Sure. Remember, we're watching."

I waved goodbye and pushed my way back out of the forest. I had to learn to fine-tune my spidey senses to feel imminent danger when danger hung all around me. I had to learn to filter, if that was possible.

Once inside the building, I ran into Zoey.

"Misha," she said, grabbing my arm, "Where have you been?" She trailed off, looking around her like she didn't want anyone to hear us, and then started again. "What happened to you?" She pulled me to the side of the hallway to let some other kids pass. She scrutinized my face and then my injuries. It felt good to have someone care.

"Nothing really. I ran into a group of Whities that have taken on the security of Sterling."

"Oh, them," she said, eyes wide. "Stay away from them. Their bite is *way* more impressive than their bark. They are dangerous." She looked at my scraped up elbows and forehead and led me back to my room. "Looks like you got off easy." The door opened for her when she tried the knob.

"Hold on," I said. "You have access to my room?"

"Of course," she said. "I'm your helper. All helpers need 24-7 access to the one they are helping. I'm responsible for you." A put-off look crossed her face.

"It surprised me, is all," I said, feeling very annoyed and trespassed even though I really liked her.

She went straight into my bathroom, wet a towel down and gently washed my scrapes. "Well, this simply won't do. You've got to shower and get all this dust off you. You're a mess."

I followed orders. After I showered, I made a point of looking for the incision they'd used to insert my tracker. Even though it was still tender, I poked around until I felt the small, hard tracker, and then took note of the position of the small incision on the still tender brand. It would be easiest to remove the tracker from the same spot it had been inserted—when I was ready.

When I came out, she was digging under the bed. I took a deep breath, feeling my eyes turn the size of lemons. The lip balm from Jeremy. How had I forgotten about it? I should have moved it to a safer place. Before I could protest and tell her I'd get the first aid kit, she'd pulled it out and set it on the bed. I sighed with relief and sat down so she could goo me up.

"How have you been able to stay tender and kind living here?" I asked.

That seemed to take her aback, but she answered in a whisper. "I pretend I'm someone else while I have to do all the awful stuff. I tuck that person away when I don't."

She acted–just like I did.

Only once Zoey was sure I'd been completely patched up did we head for the dance. I saw a bunch of kids writing things down on pieces of paper and sticking them into a box. I walked over. "What is this?" I asked.

A girl with curly orange hair chimed in. "It's the weekend suggestion box. You can suggest activities and events for the weekends. Sterling really tries to accommodate all our wishes." She smiled brightly. "I hope he picks mine."

We turned to go into the lunchroom that had been transformed into a dance hall. Sterling must do this to help further foster loyalty and love. He truly made them forget their old lives by giving them things they'd never get at home. I remembered hearing about Houston's dad chasing the Avengers out of his house with a baseball bat when he was drunk and the poor conditions under which Frankie lived, never seeing her mom and having an absent dad. This place might start looking good to kids like them once the initial shock of it wore down.

Sterling was a master at making everyone feel included from the second they walked into the Circus of Feats. He called them elite, amazing, and rare while pushing and pushing and telling them they could do it. He was slowly making the normal world look abnormal.

I didn't want to dance, but I needed to discover who my potential allies and enemies were. I knew some of the Whities were contenders for enemies already. What about the rest of them? Once inside, it seemed that everyone wanted to get close to me because I had been close to Sterling. I knew all of these people were contenders for my enemies and wouldn't be subversive.

Frankie flirted her way into a group of boys and girls that danced every song. She looked like she was in heaven. It was looking less and less like I'd be able to center her attention on escaping. Zoey had disappeared. By midnight, I realized I was in the wrong place to find Sterling's detractors. I began to walk off the floor, but was met by a short boy with a goatee and slicked black Dracula hair.

"Whoa! Whoa!" he said. "You're not leaving this dance floor without dancing with me first, right?" He batted his eyelashes at me and grinned.

"You know that's a girl's move, right?" I said.

"I was trying to win your heart with laughter. Go ahead now, laugh." He laughed hysterically and then said, "Please, dance with me?" He was nervous as all get-out.

"Fine, but just once."

"Great." He turned and gave a thumbs-up to a group of guys who had been sitting in a dark corner all night long. He was their hero right now. I rolled my eyes.

I spotted Zoey, and we locked stares. She knew I needed help and when the song ended, she came to my aide.

"Goodnight," I said to the boy, who never told me his name, and hurried off.

Zoey acted as a bouncer, telling guys as they approached that I was bushed and had to go to bed. Once headed down my hall, she stopped me. "Aren't you the superstar?"

"I don't want to be the superstar."

"Well, you are now." Zoey had a way of pointing out the obvious. She moved closer and then whispered in my ear, "I've been busy finding some people you want to know."

"Ah Zoey, I can't—"

"You'll *want* to meet with them. They're rebels." She moved back and waggled her eyebrows.

"Fabulous. Have I told you lately that I think you're amazing?" I said, wanting to give her a big kiss. "Where could we possibly meet, though?"

"Out by the bonfire. Go sit and start to roast some marshmallows. Someone will join you."

I did just that, and only moments later a boy with crooked teeth and messy brown hair sat next to me. "You are one of many," he said. "I don't know if you remember me, but I was to your left when Sterling came to challenge you."

"I remember you," I said, his face popping up in my mind. "You were with all those crazy kids backing Sterling."

"Yep," he said. "You never would have guessed I was a subversive, right?"

"Right." I looked at him thoughtfully.

"We are thinking about letting you join our group, but I need to see that you are who Zoey claims you to be."

"Who does she claim I am?" I ate the perfectly browned marshmallow off my stick.

"She says you're the one who will put all the info together and get us out of here." He put a marshmallow on a stick and put it over some coals. "I need a little proof, of course."

"What kind of proof?"

"I need you to show us you've got what it takes to subvert Sterling without being obvious about it."

"Okay."

"Zoey told me you're having breakfast with Sterling on Monday. He always eats with a gold fork. Steal it and bring it to me."

"Is that all?" I asked.

He nodded, rose, and began walking away.

"Wait!" I called out. "What's your name?"

He didn't even slow his step, but turned his head slightly in my direction to say, "Adam." Soon he was out of sight.

I needed to talk to Frankie about stealing techniques. She was the master, after all.

As I walked back inside, I saw some kids walking off, away from the building. I stopped and sat on a bench, away from the fire to observe where these kids were headed. There didn't seem to be a specific direction. Some were alone, others were in pairs, while still others were in larger groups. They talked in quiet whispers and didn't seem to notice me. Even though I was tired, I couldn't stop thinking about these kids and where they might be going.

I followed a group of three girls who quietly whispered amongst themselves as they left the pathway and moved into the woods. Silent as a mouse, I followed them. They weren't truly trying to be quiet, so whatever they were going to do must not be so terrible. Maybe I'd followed the wrong group of kids. I almost turned back because I was so tired, but something made me keep on. The terrain started to go up and they slowed down. Darn it. Only minutes later, I couldn't hear them anymore. I sped up. I couldn't see them anywhere. I searched the area. Where had they gone? It was too dark to track footprints, so I veered to the right on the little rocky hill. Feeling along the surface, I found a crevice. Could they have gone in there? I put my ear up to the opening and thought I heard shuffling. That was good enough for me.

I turned sideways and slipped inside. After going straight for about twenty hesitant steps, I ran into a wall. My claustrophobia gripped me. I took several deep breaths before I started back. Then I heard a clatter and discovered the tunnel continued in a sharp switchback. I wished I had my go bag or at the very least a flashlight. I looked that direction and could see faint light on a surface at what must be the end of another switchback.

I followed the light until I hit the wall where the light shone. I could see that in another five steps in another switchback, I would enter a cave of sorts. I walked the five steps and peeked around the corner. There were eight people in there, two of whom were sitting behind a crude wooden desk and sitting on wooden stools. The cavern was not huge, but the eight people were not cramped together, either. On the desk were two lanterns. Where had they found those? Did Sterling have emergency kits anywhere in the buildings? That was the only reason I could think of to have lanterns, for emergencies. Maybe the two people behind the desk had found an emergency storage room or something. Maybe there was something in there that would help me escape.

The girls I had followed in were writing on something. After they set the pencil down, the girls received two small packages from the girl and boy at the desk. Interesting. What could be in those packages? The girls headed toward me. I figured there must only be one way in and one way out, and I was blocking the way. I scurried out and hid in the bushes. I followed them as they trudged away to another part of the forest. The sat and opened the packages.

Soon after that, they were smoking. It wasn't your everyday cigarette, either. It was marijuana. I stifled a laugh. There were drug dealers here. What would Sterling say if he knew? He wasn't as in control as he thought. I'd seen three groups now that operated right under Sterling's nose: the protect-Sterling-Whitie group, the rebels, and the drug dealers. I suspected there were even more subcultures here. I'd thought this place would be more militaristic and that such groups wouldn't, couldn't exist. I had been wrong.

As I headed back to my room, I decided to discover all the sub-culture groups I could over the next little while. Maybe a few could help with my quest.

Chapter 18

I dreamt about Jeremy once I'd fallen asleep. It was intense. He finally found me and rescued me. He held me close and whispered that he loved me. Even in my dream it was as if I felt his breath on my ear and his hot touch on my arm. I woke wondering where that had come from.

Only two other girls were in the mess hall when I arrived. After having the chef on duty create me a breakfast crepe with bananas and strawberries, I went and sat by them. They took one look at me, eyes wide with fright, and moved to another table. What did they have to be afraid of? Had Sterling made them afraid or had people been talking about me, making me scarier than I was? I had to make friends, allies with as many people as I could as fast as I could. This wasn't going to be easy.

Once done with breakfast, I went exploring. All the doors I tried seemed to be open except Sterling's dining area and the classrooms. Through one of the classroom windows, I did catch a glimpse of some kids working on something, but when I tried the knob, it was locked. They all looked my way, but didn't move toward the door. I waved at them, trying to get them to open the door. I smiled big and everything. They simply stared at me until I finally walked away. How had they opened that door? Had a teacher opened it for them? Sterling? Or had they figured a way? I'd have to find out.

I found the cave I'd gone in last night. It was quite the clever hiding place, the opening was not obvious in the daylight, either. I went back into my room. Since it was Sunday, I pulled up the scriptures in my mind and *read* for an hour or so. I prayed that I'd make the right decisions and that I'd know when something was right. I prayed God would lead me to the people I needed to meet to save everyone as well as to the information that would free us as soon as possible.

Someone knocked on my door, and I stood up to go open it. It was Frankie. "You want to go to the circus with me?"

"Sure," I said, following her out into the hall and then down the green, lime-smelling hall with the elephants on it that led to the circus tent. I wasn't planning on going to the circus. There were too many bad memories associated with that place– it was the tent where we'd lost half of the Avengers. But I didn't want to leave Frankie alone and I needed to talk to her about stealing the fork. We whispered about it all the way to the tent.

I gasped when I entered the tent. It looked just how I'd imagined a real circus, not Sterling's jaded Circus of Feats. Clowns were juggling and playing when we arrived. People in black walked around with cotton candy, popcorn, hot dogs, and sodas. No money required. The real performance was supposed to begin in twenty minutes. I was awestruck when it did. The performers even pulled people from the audience to do fun tricks with them. The performers were outstanding and the animals extremely well trained. In the end, groups of twenty got to go check out the animals and talk to the performers.

I nudged the boy sitting next to me while we waited our turn to go down to the circus floor. "Does Sterling fly all these people in? How does he get the animals here?"

He chuckled. "Actually, the animals and people live in another section of the grounds. The performers are Blackies. They get to dress up during performances."

"They're Blackies?"

"Every one."

"Sterling is really good about finding jobs for the kids who fail the selection or class work or even their missions. Everyone has something to contribute, he always says. I love how he always thinks of others."

"Sounds like he's good at that." A hot rock dropped hard in my gut. Could one of the Avengers be in this circus crew? Sterling said they were alive.

"Yep," he said, standing up to go down to the circus floor. Frankie and I followed him.

"Did you hear that?" I whispered to Frankie.

"Hear what?" she said, her eyes looking far off to the left of us.

I glanced over and saw some of the boys in the group Frankie had hung out with last night. She must like one of them. "Maddie, Payden, Anna, and Lunden could be Blackies in this circus. Keep your eyes peeled."

"Uh, huh," she muttered, still looking at the group of boys.

"Focus, Frankie. They could be here. Don't you want to see them with your own eyes? They're your family, right? And just think if we could get to use Anna's unique talents with locks to help us get out of here."

"Sorry," she said. "You're right." She scanned the area as we descended the steps. I did, too, but there was no sign of any of them. Maybe it was too early. Maybe they were still in training. I kept my eyes peeled as I touched all the different animals. I'd never touched an elephant or tiger. It was pretty darn cool.

With no luck in finding the lost Avengers, we headed out for lunch. We met Zoey, who was eating with a bunch of Blackies.

"Zoey," I said. "The circus was made up of all Blackies?"

"Yes." She got up and moved to the side of the room.

"Why not you? Do you get to choose what you do?" I asked.

"Oh, no. He assigns you a job. The only reason I'm here is because he thinks I have promise."

"Hey guys," Frankie said, "Do you mind if I go say hi to some of my new friends?"

"No," I said, but she'd already begun walking away. I shook my head, knowing she was a lost cause. I turned back to Zoey. "You probably don't want to talk about it, but what happened? On your mission, I mean."

She shook her head. "I was known for my stealth, so Sterling assigned me to assassinate a CIA operative who was getting too close to Sterling's operation. I was supposed to use my talent to draw him out. But, he was stealthier than I. Never underestimate your opponent. Or become cocky."

It was a good reminder to stay humble. "I was thinking about the other four kids that came with us. Do you think they could've been a part of the circus today?"

"Probably not. If they were hurt during the Circus of Feats, they'd still be recovering, and even if they weren't, they'll go through conditioning before they are put in a group. The men in charge of the periphery groups are very choosy. If Sterling hadn't stepped in on my behalf, I'd have been a grounds keeper. They had classified me as one. Can you believe that?"

I laughed a little. "No. I can't."

"I'm worried about what Sterling has in store for you. Make sure you stay at the top of your class. I hope you're as smart as I think you are."

I ignored that, and instead asked, "When did you find out about your mission?"

"About one week before it was supposed to go down. It was simple. Others spend weeks and weeks planning and revising and all that."

"Hmm." That wasn't very much time to get the info to Jeremy.

"Sometimes he permanently disables his targets. He does that when death isn't the worst thing for a person."

"What does that mean?"

"Oh, he'll amputate a runner's legs, mess up a movie star's face. Stuff like that. He takes away what they love most, what they live for."

"How does he choose the people he targets?"

"There's a lot of conjecture, but no one really knows. Some say people hire him. Some say he comes up with them all on his own. I guess we'll never know."

I would find out.

I remembered the group of kids I'd seen in the locked classroom and described them to Zoey. She knew immediately who I was talking about.

"Oh, we call them the scholars. But I don't know how they got in that room–it should have been impossible."

Interesting, I thought. *An impossible skill like that could come in handy.*

I noticed a group of girls and guys sharing a table. The girls folded their sleeves and pant legs in a particular way. They styled their hair in a specific way. From the way they held themselves, as if the world revolved around them, you could tell these would equate with the popular kids back home. The cheerleaders and the jocks. The boys muscles pressed hard against their jumpsuits. They flirted incessantly and talked about sports and competitions.

I realized that this place was like a mini high school and probably had every clique in the book.

I also realized that everyone had different lengths of hair. It seemed that Sterling didn't require anyone to keep his hair short after the first time it was cut. That would help me discover who had been here the longest. Of course, with guys, many opted to keep their hair short. They would be harder to track. If I could find someone with longish hair who belonged to some sort of a rebel group, maybe I could elicit their help in my escape.

After lunch, we headed for the sports area. We played volleyball on a coed team. Frankie had been bit hard by the love bug and couldn't hit a darn thing. She spent more time staring at the boy next to her than anything else. At least I now knew who she was after.

A movie was playing in the theater that night, a movie that'd been in theaters six months ago, *Quick Death*. No one here seemed to know that, though. It was all new to them. I never would have gone to see it at home. Violence wasn't my thing. Everything at this compound seemed to be here to either condition us to think killing was a normal part of life or make us feel like we couldn't live without Sterling. We watched the movie. Well, sort of. I was really thinking about other things while I pretended to watch. We headed back to our rooms at about ten because at ten-thirty, everything would be locked up and our free reign would end. School started early tomorrow.

"Zoey," I said as we walked down the hall to our rooms, "I followed some kids into a cave last night. Kids were doing drugs, marijuana."

"Yeah, the dynamic duo heads that up. Christopher and Kalinda. They're chemical whizzes and created a drug that isn't addictive, but gives you a great high. They have the gardeners grow their weed and they dry it and package it. Kids sign up to do their chores for them in exchange for the drugs. The dynamic duo probably doesn't have to do any work for ten years already."

"Doesn't Sterling know about them?"

"Who knows? If he does, he doesn't stop them. You'll find all kinds of weird cliques and groups here."

I thought about the kids in the classroom and the Whitie group I'd run into.

"There's even a group that calls themselves the tunnelers. You know what they do?"

"No, what?" Frankie and I said at the same time.

"They dig tunnels. They dig and dig and dig, trying to find a way out. I know for a fact that Sterling knows about them. He even goes and checks on their progress. The tunnelers say they're helping Sterling by attempting to find security risks."

"Interesting," I said. He was probably actually gauging their success and assessing the likelihood anyone could escape by digging. I wondered if they'd helped the drug dealers dig their cave or if it was naturally occurring. "This place is just huge—I can't get over the massiveness of this compound."

"I heard planes aren't allowed to fly over this area. And no radio transmissions are allowed. I don't know why, or if it's even true, but I bet it is," Zoey said.

If that were true, Sterling would have to have some amazing connections. "You've never heard or seen a plane while inside or outside?"

"Never."

Not good. I'd watched a special on a public TV station about a radio quiet zone in West Virginia that allowed a huge telescope to hear things that would normally be too quiet to hear. No cell phones, Internet, or radios were allowed in a very huge area, 13,000 square miles. People actually chose to live there and loved the silence. The NIOC and the NSA also collected sensitive intelligence data for the government from that zone, but there wasn't anywhere else like it I'd ever heard about. Maybe kids here were getting information they'd heard about that zone, and it got all jumbled up and confused as they tried to figure out where this compound was.

Zoey thought for a second, then said, "But I have seen Sterling with a cell, so that couldn't be exactly right."

"How long have you been here?" I cocked my head to the side and waited for Zoey to answer.

"Three years."

I tried not to show the horror I felt at her having been here that long. "That's a long time," I finally said.

"Yes it is." She lowered her voice even more. "And it's time I got out of here."

Chapter 19

Monday arrived. I woke earlier than usual, a few minutes to five. After getting ready, I went to Sterling's dining hall fighting to maintain my nerves. The door opened automatically for me as I neared it. I touched my neckband. It was a brilliant device. I needed to find someone who could remove it. Sterling wasn't in the room, yet, but arrived only seconds after I did. He went through the same ritual of stripping out of his suit before sitting to eat. Bizarre. His color today was bright red.

"Please sit," he said. "I think you'll enjoy this breakfast."

"Are you going to poison me?"

"Oh, no. That wouldn't be very poetic, would it? If you'd like, we could switch plates."

Now he was playing with my mind. I took a few bites of the chocolate chip pancakes. I had to admit, they were perfect. Sterling ate with gusto, and I noticed his gold fork. I'd have to try to steal it if I wanted to win Adam's trust. I wondered if I'd get the opportunity today.

Finally, I'd had enough of eating in silence. I decided to start right in with my questions. Maybe since I'd been forthright with him, he'd return the favor. "Why eighteen-year-olds? We're really only children."

"Exactly. You are old enough and still young enough."

"Why not just advertise and get people who want this life? Really want it."

"I believe," Sterling said, "that sometimes people need some guidance to go in the right direction. In truth, there is something here for everyone. For some, being an assassin is the right thing, but for others, assassination is not their thing, and they join a different part of the necessary elements of this place. Or they join groups, such as our grounds crew, tech crew, something better suited for them. Everyone wants to help the cause once they understand it."

He was such a narcissist.

"All of the people here came from high schools?"

"Let's not talk about dreary business. Let's talk about you. I, of course, did my due diligence and had someone retrieve your files from the school. I think you've had quite the interesting life. You've moved around so much, never let roots grow anywhere."

"I loved moving. The adventure of it was great, and I've always enjoyed meeting new people and making friends." I figured an adrenaline junkie would love the unknown associated with moving. It was bound to be an adventure.

He pulled out pictures of me with Madness and the Avengers at Roseburg High. Some were in the lunchroom, others outside the school or at school functions. I noticed Ian wasn't in any of them. Had he taken them?

"You took pictures of me?" What had he seen?

"Of course I didn't. I had someone do it. It's not easy picking the most amazing eight students from a school. Pictures are critical. Color tells so much about a person."

I wanted him to continue talking about color and why he'd chosen the Avengers and not Madness. "I looked so cute in that outfit." I pretended to muse and wish I had that outfit on right then. "But I really loved my hair." I wanted him to tell me the deal with the hair. I had to let him say it without asking directly or I'd give myself away.

"Indeed you did," he said. "Would you rather wear the jumpsuit or my outfit?" He ran his hands down his muscular, tall, yet aging body.

I swallowed a bit of throw-up that rushed into my mouth. "While your outfit is fun," I managed to choke out, "I'd rather wear the jumpsuit. But what I'd really like to do is wear what I'd like to wear. Keep my hair the color I like it." I dug into the eggs on my plate, mashing them up in some ketchup before taking a bite, pretending we were just chatting.

"Hair," he said.

He'd taken the bait.

"It tells us so much about a person, doesn't it?" He ran his fingers through his hair, which was slicked back, showing his widow's peak. "I like to have a rainbow of hair color fly into this compound for each selection. Do you realize, I go through great pains to always ensure I have a rainbow? I don't take just anybody in, like I said. I make sure I have a girl and a boy with each natural hair color. You were one of the blondies from your selection."

My eyes widened. He picked from natural hair color, not the dyed color.

"Lunden was the other blondie. Let's hope he continues to heal. I have a special love of blondies. But you know, by doing this, I can guarantee I will have representatives from all the natural hair colors when the selections make it to purification. It's quite the marvelous sight to see all the Whities together in a gathering. It is like the story of Noah's Ark. The selections come in twos to this compound and with my help they can become purified. Just as the earth was purified by water, those who complete their missions become pure. The rainbow in their case comes from their natural hair color. It's beautiful really."

I wanted to say that four hair colors didn't a rainbow make, but I was sure this madman would try to make me believe it.

He turned pensive and then said, "You have your own style. I like that. So, let's talk shop now. Let's see if you can keep up with my amazing mind."

My left eye twitched at the same time his did. I hoped he didn't notice.

"I'm going to tell you about my latest assassinations. I want you to get in the spirit of things before we work on the one I'm hoping to prepare you for."

I nodded and pressed my lips together, bracing my elbows on my knees.

"Last Tuesday we had to take out a talk show host. I couldn't allow him to fill the airwaves with his smut any longer. He tried to make deviant behavior acceptable. He put people on his show who would, without exception, fight, scream, and divulge intimate, private information. He gave these people their ten minutes of fame and destroyed them instead of giving them hope."

I could think of several such TV hosts. Why had he chosen the one he did?

"So, I put some of my men on it, and we dug up some of his juiciest secrets. We called him into his own studio on the day everyone was off. We tied him to one of the chairs his guests always sat in and trained the camera on him. Marty, a great actor here, acted as the TV host and forced him to confess to all his own deviant behavior and then talk about his most intimate secrets in front of the people they involved. At least he thought they were those people. In reality, they were actors, dressed up exactly like them. They sat in the front row of audience seats, so he never got a good look.

"In the end, they beat him to death, throwing chairs, shoes, and whatever else they could get their hands on at him. We, of course, did not include the portion of the tape where the actors beat the man, but the rest, we put up on YouTube and sent it to several sensational magazines. It was a beautifully poetic death." He paused, obviously waiting for me to say something.

I said the first thing that came to my mind. "I can see you put a lot of thought into your assassinations, but I still don't know if I agree."

"Thank you for recognizing that. This next assassination was prepared just as thoughtfully as the other."

I didn't know if I wanted to hear.

"There was this certain senator who couldn't seem to make up his mind on gun control. A friend of mine contacted me with the problem and asked me to take action. I'm not a political man, Misha, but he was my friend, and I told him I'd look into it. If I deemed this senator was violating our mission statement, I'd have to take action. Lo and behold, he was actually violating two of the four. Not only was he being indecisive, he was also being greedy.

"While he wouldn't allow guns in his home, he voted three times to end several gun control laws. Then, he voted three times to strengthen them. Why? Greed. Cold hard cash. He was being paid under the table by lobbyists to vote one way or the other. As you can see, he had to go. My friend was right to tell me about it."

That answered my question from yesterday. Some of these assassinations were indeed initiated by people other than Sterling.

His phone rang, and he answered it. "Yes," he said. Then he paused for about a minute, listening. "Marvelous. I'm so glad it went without a hitch. How's the video?" Another pause. "Send it over now, could you?"

"Misha, you are one lucky girl. You are about to watch an assassination that occurred minutes ago. Fresh and perfect."

"Yay," I said, trying to be enthusiastic, but failing miserably. At least I'd get out of the gory details of the senator's death.

He opened a drawer in the table and punched some buttons. The screens above us lit up, and the assassination filled the screen.

A guy was sitting, watching TV in his living room. He wore a jacket with a skull and crossbones on the front right corner. His head was shaved, and a large tattoo of skull and crossbones was on his forehead. Above it, I could just make out the words, *The Skulls*.

A voice echoed through the room, "Bones. Bones?"

The man stood up, grabbed a gun from the side table and said, "Who's there?" He cocked the gun and spun around in a circle.

"No one's there, but we're here."

"Who's here?" Bones asked, the gun in his hand shaking slightly.

"You think it's alright to kill innocent people and then get off on a technicality?"

"It's time for you to stand trial for your crimes." The sound of air escaping something inflated, like a raft or blow-up bed, filled my ears. The man fell on his face. The video cut out. When it came back on, Bones was in a witness seat in a real courtroom. How had Sterling managed that?

There was a judge, a prosecutor, and an audience, but no defense attorney. The prosecutor laid out his many crimes, and the judge handed down the verdict of guilty on all charges. Then the sentence was announced, death by hanging.

Then they shot both of his feet, his knees, and his hands, before hanging him from the courtroom rafters–all things he liked to do to his victims. I felt weak after watching it. Completely sick in my soul. It was so twisted, demented. He wanted me to think the same way. I didn't know if I could.

Sterling clapped and clapped after the video ended. "So completely beautiful. We cannot stand back and let injustices like that happen, now can we?"

"I don't know, yet."

"You're still not convinced? All the good ones are hard to convince. I know you'll come around. And once you do, you will be the best."

"I don't understand why you would say that. You know nothing about me."

"I'm a good judge of character, Misha. I see beyond what others see. Let's keep meeting, shall we? I think I'd like to keep a close eye on your progress. We'll have breakfast together every Monday."

It wasn't an invitation, and it seemed he didn't expect a response from me.

There was a good two-minute awkward pause. My tablet beeped, telling me it was time to head for class.

"What I want to know is," Sterling said, "what would you do in the following circumstance?" He stared right at me. His eyes intense.

"Sir," I said, interrupting him, hoping he wouldn't make me stay and miss class. "It's time for me to get to class. My alarm just went off."

"Class?" He seemed to look off into nowhere.

"You know, sir, the classes that will make me an amazing assassin?" What was wrong with him?

"Oh, yeah, class. An assassin..." He trailed off, still looking off to my left not focusing.

"I'll see you next Monday then," I said, standing and heading out the door. He didn't respond, so I hurried out, not wanting to be late to class.

Things had gone well, I thought. I'd been subjected to Sterling's mad thinking, and his behavior at the end had been even more bizarre than I'd seen. But I knew all this was bringing me closer to my end goal.

Plus, I reminded myself cheerfully, *regular Monday meetings with Sterling means more chances to steal his fork and get in good with the subversives.*

Since it was Monday, I had class work. The classes were sure to be informative. It was taxing to pretend to go through the information slowly. I was still going much faster than anyone else, but only a tenth the speed I normally would. I couldn't tip my hand, however. My true abilities would have to remain hidden.

At lunch I noticed a group of kids sitting at a table, laughing and pointing at something I couldn't quite see. I made my way over, casually, to check out what they were doing. They were drawing anime and comics on some brown paper. It looked like the paper from the dispensers in the bathrooms. I wondered where they got the pencils and colors for their work.

From my momentary glances, the pictures looked amazing. They'd found a way to continue to do what they loved right under Sterling's nose. A piece of happiness in this crazy place. They were subversive in their own right, but I couldn't figure out a use for their talent in my escape at this point. I would try to befriend them, however.

I circled around a few other tables and then walked right up to them and said, "Great pictures. How'd you find pencils? I'd love to draw on good old fashioned paper."

They all threw their arms out, attempting to cover their work. I'd already seen it, and they couldn't hide it from me. A superhero was blasting Sterling in one of them.

I blinked my eyes several times and then said, "What's the big deal?"

"You better not tell Sterling what you saw," a boy with blue hair said.

"Why would I do that?"

"We know you had breakfast with him this morning. You're his nark."

"I did have breakfast with him this morning," I said, wondering how they knew. "But I'm not his nark. I don't even like him. What kind of powers does the superhero you've chosen to save us have?" I sat down on a seat and leaned in, hoping they'd open up. "It seems to me, he'd have to be pretty ingenious to beat this guy."

The guy hiding the picture with the superhero pushed it my way and started telling me how he was Electroman and defeated Sterling with electricity. Maybe they would be a good source of unique information. Getting rid of power to this compound would go far in hurting Sterling.

They had made their own colors using plants from the gardens. It was super cool. It was one example of a need causing ingenuity. They'd teamed up with the people they called the chemists and the gardeners to make them. A complete social structure had arisen right under Sterling's nose. Maybe if we all banded together we could find a way to beat Sterling. I would have to find all the other groups. He couldn't know about it and let it happen could he?

I didn't find any other groups the rest of the week, and I spent the weekend running around the compound and making notes in my mind about the layout and security of this place.

It seemed impenetrable, but it couldn't be. I'd find the weakness.

Whenever I wasn't out doing surveillance, I hung out with Zoey, Frankie, and Duncan. We'd go outside or in the mess hall and talk about how crazy everything here was. I thought it interesting that Zoey was the only Blackie from our selection who hung out with us. The others only did the minimum and didn't even try to befriend Frankie, Duncan, or Houston. She was the exception.

The next Monday I met with Sterling again. He didn't bring up anything he needed help with. He just tried to bring me around to his way of thinking. He asked me to think of the politician who wanted to tax us to death. The bully at the school. The bully at work. The polluters. Rapists. Murderers.

Abusers. Parents who locked their children in closets, ruining them. The terrorists targeting certain races or countries. He made sure I knew he took care of these people. He felt it his duty to rid the earth of them. He wanted me to catch the spirit of his goodness. He showed me lots and lots of videos. Videos of people who had done very bad things and even admitted it and yet were free on technicalities or were never caught.

I'd decided we had to be in the U.S. All the footage was in English and in our courthouses.

"The way we operate, everyone receives justice," he said. "He who is guilty is just that—guilty. He will receive quick punishment." He then flipped through five video stories about some of his latest kills. I didn't even feel queasy anymore. I learned to look but think of other things so that I really didn't *see*.

"I can see you're considering what I'm saying. Let the seed grow. You'll find that I'm right. We satisfy the demands of justice."

I'd finished off my orange juice and wheat toast. It wasn't that I didn't agree with him. Certainly, guilty people should be punished. However, we were not the judge, jury, and executioners. The justice system had flaws and needed to be overhauled, but this was not the way to do it. Unfortunately, the justice system was made up of human beings, and human beings made mistakes. That would never change.

Somehow there needed to be a way to increase its accuracy. The people needed to rise up and force the changes to up the efficiency so that the truly guilty got punished and the innocent went free.

"It will be fun to see you become a believer. I'll bring you along as slowly as I need to. You'll see, and we will be a force to be reckoned with. Of course you could choose not to be with me, but that would be tantamount to suicide. Give it a chance."

I told him I would. It was a lie.

Leaving Sterling's dining room that morning, I found a path that led out to a beautiful garden I hadn't noticed before. Several gazebos were sprinkled about, and the place was alive with all kinds of flowers and shrubbery. A few girls and boys were sitting on the benches. I wondered if they were spouting poetry or talking about endangered plant and animal species. A few girls and boys holding hands wove their way on the path that wound through the garden. I walked to the end, and I found I could either double back or go out. I chose out. I ran into the wide strip of grass next to the electrified fence and cement wall. I turned away from it and explored other sections of the grounds.

When I reached a boundary, it looked the same. I took note of the location of the tower and the guard in it. I'd found eighteen towers and thirty-two guards so far.

That night, Zoey, Frankie, Duncan, and I ran into the tunnelers. Their workplace wasn't exactly secret. They worked out in the open. They laughed loudly as they worked, pulling out dirt from their ever-growing tunnel to create a mountain nearby.

"They tunnel until they get to the boundary," Zoey said. "And then one of them goes and tells Sterling. He comes and congratulates them on a job well done. A week or so later, they find a new spot to dig. This is the third I've seen them work on."

So it took about a year to complete one of their tunnels. That was a very long time. I would not be using the tunnelers' main dig for a possibility of escape. Maybe I could recruit several to dig a secret tunnel, one that started closer to the cement walls. It would have to be in the forested areas somewhere. But would it be worth it?

My next meeting with Sterling, he wore bright yellow accents, and breakfast was egg and bacon quiche. He took his time getting down to business, finishing everything on his plate first.

"Like I started to tell you another time you were here, I would like to know what you'd do in the following circumstance. It has come to my attention–through that same friend I mentioned before–that the President of the United States has been taking bribes from a pharmaceutical company, called Harward Pharmaceutical, throughout his career. He has been hiding the money as campaign funding. In return, he has been making sure laws and rulings go their way. You know, he tampers with the FDA findings and pressures judges to rule in their favor.

"Why would he do this, you ask yourself. The reasons are many. Like I told you before, I don't like to get involved in politics, but when my friend brought this to my attention, I studied it out, watching show after show highlight everything about it. I sent in detectives to enlighten me on the finer points that were hard to understand. You know, Misha, if you dig deep enough, you will most assuredly find the motive behind the action.

"The President has not waffled on his decision to take these bribes. It seemed he did not go against our indecision mantra. However, he has helped get FDA approval for drugs that cause major problems in people who take them, and he has helped Harward Pharmaceutical conduct illegal human testing from a building in DC. What's more, the company hides its illegal testing behind the façade of a hospital, and the President actively participates in hiding this facility. Many people suffer at their hands. They promise their subjects good compensation for their drug trials, but if you end up deaf, blind, or dead, the money means little.

"This flies in the face of justice for those who need help. Completely lawless. But, his actions also show intense greed. He doesn't think about all those people who are unknowingly taking drugs that could kill them or hurt them in some way. He just wants to have full campaign coffers. Don't you think?"

"Sure. He wants to remain president. But won't all of that be lost once the truth comes to light?"

"In politics, it's always a crapshoot, so I can't answer that. But, we must act."

Why couldn't politicians just be honest? "Can't you just put whatever it is he's hiding from the people out there for everyone to see? You'd be exposing him and–"

"Oh, but that wouldn't be quite as fun as coming up with an amazing poetic death, now would it?" He smiled like a Cheshire cat. "How might we go about giving him a poetic death?"

"I'll need more information before I can hope to help you."

"Good answer. Knowledge is power in these things." He pushed a button and a picture of the President of the U.S., Benton Hillsdale, popped up on the screen. "I don't like how this man looks. He has no color. His hair is gray. His eyes are gray and his skin...what color is that, Misha? Gray again?"

I didn't answer.

"Yes. Yes. We must rid this land of gray." He stared thoughtfully at the screen.

He was off his rocker.

Then he went off on a rant about how there wasn't enough color in the world today.

My tablet buzzed. I needed to head for class. "Sir," I said. "I've got to get to class."

"Yes, yes," he said absentmindedly, still staring at the screen but waving me out with one hand.

I left feeling a bit overwhelmed. Why did he want me to brainstorm poetic ways to kill a president? I wondered if Sterling had had this same little powwow with the guy he'd killed a while ago, the one Zoey told me about. Or was this a new tactic for him? It seemed he only planned on killing me if I crossed him. I couldn't make it easy, but I couldn't make it too hard, either. My change of heart had to seem real. Little by little I'd let him think he'd convinced me.

I was amazed at how much I'd learned over the last several weeks. Even though everything was twisted in a way to enable it to be used for evil, I thought it could all be turned around to be used for good. I also searched and searched for things that would help me get out and save all these kids. I wouldn't allow myself to be pessimistic.

While sitting in class on Friday, I came up with a way to kill the president. I wanted to tell Sterling, so I went to his dining room at dinner. I tried the door, and it opened. A bit shocked, I looked around. No one was near, so I went inside. I heard his voice and someone else's through a crack in the door he'd used to enter the room both times I'd been in there.

The voice was familiar. I thought about eavesdropping, but I couldn't quite make out any words. Then I saw the gold fork next to Sterling's plate that had been set for his dinner. I needed that fork to gain the trust of the subversives.

I didn't want to get any closer than I already was. How would I explain the fact that I was so deep into his dining area without his permission? The fork seemed to gleam in the light, and I had to chance it. It had been two weeks since Adam had challenged me to get it. I probably wouldn't get a better chance. I moved quickly, silently, and grabbed the fork just as I heard Sterling say, "Just get it done!" to the person he was talking to. I shoved the fork in my pants pocket and hurried back to the door I'd entered through. I turned and called out, "Hello?" as if I'd just arrived.

I heard some shuffling behind Sterling's door, and then Sterling called out, "Be right there." I heard urgent whispers, and then he opened the door fully and walked in.

"Was I expecting you?" he said, looking around the room.

"No, sir," I said.

"Then how did you get in here?" I could hear the worry etched in his voice.

"I just tried the knob and it opened. I could hear you talking to someone and didn't want to surprise you, so I called out."

He looked at the door and at my neckband, then said, "No matter. What is it?"

I don't think I was supposed to be able to walk right in. "I think I figured out how to orchestrate the president's poetic death."

He raised his eyebrows. "Take a seat. I'll order dinner. You talk." He pulled out the drawer under the table and typed furiously for a minute.

"I think you'll like this," I said. "What if we told one of the president's advisors that we knew about the hospital where they do illegal testing and that we would be leaking the information to the press in one week's time?"

"Why would we do that?"

"Hear me out. It would give him a week to 'fix' the hospital in question so that he can use it to his benefit. Of course, he'd only be repairing the obvious things and with only a week, he won't be able to do a good job of it."

"I'm waiting for the punch line..." He scowled at me. The man came and undressed him as I talked.

"Patience," I said, smiling broadly. "When we release it to the press, he'll set up a big press conference to tell the world his accusers are off their rockers and that while he supports pharmaceutical companies, he's never condoned illegal human testing. He'll also contend that the hospital clinic was exactly that, a hospital clinic.

"Meanwhile, we will get poison that transfers through touch on the podium and microphone he will be using for the press conference. We'll have 'reporters' set up to ask the president if he'd ever go there and push him on it.

"He'll be forced to say he would go there. About this same time, the drug we put on the podium and microphone will start taking effect. It will, of course, be one of the drugs from one of the companies he accepts bribes from. He'll announce to the world that he would indeed go to that clinic and in fact, he was feeling a little under the weather and would go there after the press conference to get checked out. He'll have to do it to save face.

"They will try to get his personal physician in, but we will have made it impossible for him to come in. His backup physician will be called and allowed to come.

"His advisors and security will try to tell them they can't do it, but he'll be so bent on not looking the fool, he'll give them an hour to make it secure for him, but he'll tell them he would be going."

There was a dramatic pause.

"I must say," Sterling cooed, "that's a great plan. How did you come up with it?"

"It popped into my head in class today." A smug smile danced across my face.

His eyes pierced mine. Our dinners lifted out of the table. He reached for his fork, but found nothing. He looked around, punched something into his keyboard and waited, staring at me while I dug in.

The man who'd undressed him hurried in. "Sir?"

"Where is my gold fork? I can't *eat* without my gold fork."

The servant looked at the empty spot on the table and said, "I put it there myself before your dinner." He searched all around King Sterling's throne, even under the table. It was not there.

I tried not to feel guilty. The servant would definitely be punished. "I will go back into the kitchen and find it, sir."

"See that you do. And hurry up! I'm starving."

I kept eating while Sterling repeated my plan back to me. I corrected him when necessary. Five minutes later, a defeated servant reentered the room. His head hung as he whispered,

"The fork is nowhere to be found, sir. I take full responsibility for its loss."

Sterling growled. "Then you will sit here and feed me with my golden spoon and knife. See how well you do."

Was he kidding? Bring him a different fork for goodness sake.

The servant quickly pulled up a chair and fed him. I guess he wasn't kidding.

It was disgusting to see a perfectly able man be fed by someone. It ruined my appetite.

Once finished with dinner, I said, "Well, goodnight. I need to study up on chemicals. It's not an easy subject."

"No, it isn't, is it?"

I shook my head as I walked to the door.

"Misha, next time you need to contact me at a time other than our scheduled visits, do so over your tablet."

He had me punch in his address and test it. It worked.

"We'll need to start meeting twice a week soon in order to get all the finer details of the assassination hammered out. Why don't we start meeting on Fridays for breakfast, too? Next week will be our first Friday."

"Okay," I said and left, knowing this was a turning point. I was plotting to kill the President of the United States.

Chapter 20

That night I dreamt of Dakota. He told me to walk across a ravine, but there wasn't a bridge. He told me to trust him. There was an invisible bridge that would carry me across. After much persuading, I took the step and fell to my death.

I woke up in a heart-pounding sweat—I lurched out of bed and stumbled to the bathroom to splash cold water on my face. My hands shook, and I had to grip the edge of the sink for support.

Get it together, I thought. I took a deep breath and banished the dream from my mind. I had work to do. I went back to my bedroom and immediately sent a coded message to Adam, the subversive leader.

That day we had hands-on training and it included Chemicals, The Hunt, Disguise Thyself, and Run for Your Life. I made a point of talking to as many kids as I could and congratulating the ones that did well. I wanted to appear nice, approachable, like a team player. When I returned to my room after classes, I saw I had gotten tons of messages from kids I had befriended that day. I scanned through them quickly, then found the one I'd hoped for: a coded response from Adam.

He wanted to meet out in the English garden by the fountain at eight. I was to bring Zoey and Frankie.

I enlisted Zoey easily, but Frankie had plans with her boyfriend and didn't want to come. I begged, reminding her of how I'd gone to the circus with her and she relented, but brought Xavier with her. I hoped Xavier wouldn't make Adam abandon the plan. When we got there, Adam and four others were already there.

"Hey guys," he said. "You want to play hide-n-seek with us? We needed a few more players."

"Sure," I said. "You guys okay with that?" I asked the three I'd come with.

They all shrugged their shoulders like they didn't care either way.

After explaining the rules, Adam said he'd be 'It' first. He winked at me. Everyone scattered, and he closed his eyes and counted. I pretended to go hide, but then came back and sat down in an obvious place for him to find me. He opened his eyes and, seeing my hiding place, walked directly to me. He said nothing, but held out his hand expectantly. I fished the fork out of my pocket and handed it to him, glad to be rid of it.

His eyes sparkled in the moonlight.

He walked away and said, "You're in."

Nothing changed the next few days, and I was antsy to know what benefits being *in* with the subversives afforded me.

That weekend, I met Adam by the bonfire again.

"Normally, we'd make you jump through a few more hoops to join, but Zoey's vouching for you, and since she's your helper, she knows more than anyone else about you. We trust her judgment."

"How many of you are there?" I asked.

"More than you'd think," he said. "I can't give you details, it's too dangerous. We've been gathering information for almost two years now, but we've been unable to use the information to secure an escape. We need fresh eyes, a fresh take on things. Are you willing to enter our secret covenant to bring Sterling and this place down?"

"Yes," I said. I had no problem with that.

"We will pass information to you so you can help us out. We only use our tablets to set up meets. No sensitive information is ever passed through messaging, coded or not."

That was a good decision, considering the code he'd used to set up this meet was ridiculously easy.

He was telling me this with humor in his voice like he was saying a joke, when suddenly, he said. "Time for you to laugh for the cameras. We can't be too serious, it's the weekend."

I laughed, and he did too. Now that I knew what we were doing, I relaxed and pretended for the cameras, too.

"How can I get you out? I can't even save myself," I said, trying not to choke up at voicing the concern.

"We believe we have all the information you need. You just need to make sense of it." He smiled at me reassuringly. "We've devised a system of note delivery within our group. Everyone has assignments. Anyway, you need to memorize more code a girl named Jenny will be giving you in a minute. Now you have to memorize the drop locations."

He went over them all, and I remembered them easily.

"The code will come by way of your tablet, of course. There are a few words you have to know in order to communicate with us." He went over the rules. I recited them back to him.

"Jenny will finish your training. I'm headed off to bed."

After he left, Jenny came over with hotdogs. We laughed and chatted for a minute, keeping up appearances, and then she quizzed me on what I'd learned from Adam.

"We'll trickle the information out to you. We can't give it all to you at once because we don't know how you will respond to Sterling's conditioning. Expect your first drop to be in two weeks."

We both laughed for the cameras, but I didn't feel like laughing. "Two weeks? I'm ready for it now."

"You're getting the code now," she said, a light tone to her voice. "Two weeks. Remember, patience is a virtue. Kramer, our secret weapon, has been working on getting us into the computer systems but has been unsuccessful so far. We believe in him just as we believe in you. You're here to find what we've missed. We've been watching you in class. You're amazing, probably a genius. I feel it, just like Zoey does."

A tremor went down my spine. "Where are we, Jenny?" I asked. If I knew that one thing, I could free us.

At first, she looked at me like I was crazy then understanding dawned and she said, "Oh, we don't really know. Some say western Tennessee, others say Alabama. It's all conjecture, though. We inventoried leaves from all the different plants as well as how often it rained and how hot it got. Who knows? It's humid enough to be either of those.

"As far as the information drops go," she said. "We all rotate through them. That way no one is seen with anyone too often. We keep ourselves pretty separate."

We laughed and talked about something else for a minute.

"We only meet in person when it's totally natural, like now, or completely necessary." She then explained the code to me. It was pretty complicated with certain words and letters meaning something totally different than normal, but I created pictures in my mind to help me remember.

"You've got it," she said after about an hour. "Remember, you can't fudge on the code. It has to be 100% accurate or we don't act. I'm sure you can understand why."

"It could be someone trying out code in order to find us. Yep. Safety is our top concern. We don't want to lose you, like we lost the last guy."

"What guy?" Was she talking about the guy Zoey had referred to?

"A guy we thought would lead us to freedom but ended up dead instead. Be super careful, Misha. No mistakes."

"No mistakes," I said.

"You'll know who members of the resistance are by our handshake. We fold our pinkies in and wiggle them three times when we shake hands. Like this," she said. She took my hand and shook it. I could feel her pinky wiggle, one, two, three times. "Make sure they only do it three times. Well, see ya later," she said, taking off.

Sterling and I made a lot of progress on planning the death of the president during our breakfast chats over the next month since we were meeting on both Mondays and Fridays. It didn't seem real, though. It seemed more like a game. I'd discover a solution, and he'd come up with a potential problem. The demise of the president was taking form.

On our last Friday of the month, we tackled the problem of the president's personal physician. We decided we'd drug the president's personal physician *and* his backup physician to make them unavailable to the president. It was the easiest solution. We discussed possibilities about causing a blackout of all the hospitals around except the target one. Sterling brought up the fact that he wanted me to brainstorm ways of making sure there was plenty of coverage on TV, cell phones, cameras, and all other personal and professional devices. It would need to be spontaneous coverage with cell phones, iPads, personal cameras, as well as the professionals all snapping pictures and recording video.

He wanted me to open my mind. Nothing was off the table. He informed me he had access to the president's schedule, too.

At one point, Sterling said, "It seems like we've always been together, doesn't it?" He was looking at me, but it felt like he was looking past me, his eyes were completely unfocused. Then he focused again, and his evil eyes really looked at me.

"This plan of yours makes me feel like you could be the queen. That's what this organization needs, a queen. We could open a whole new facility, and you could be the queen of it. Yes. Yes. That sounds right." He spaced off again. "You know, kings and queens aren't born, they're made. I will show you how. I want you to think of everything that could go wrong with your plan and the solution to each thing."

I intended to. My plan couldn't have gone any better. It had been a little over two months, and he was totally ready to give me my own facility.

"If kings aren't born, but made, what made you the king?"

"That's easy. I realized as I was watching TV how this society had turned to garbage. So many people were watching silly, uncolorful people do silly things on TV and then emulating them. Idolizing them. I decided to start with media and get rid of the worst offenders first. I studied the people and their habits and made sure all my kills were needed, helpful, and justified. That meant that a few of the people I thought needed to be assassinated weren't the ones that truly needed to be. Someone else was pulling the strings. So, I adjusted and got the right people.

"You can't just go around killing people willy-nilly. I got better and better as time went on. In fact, I got so good, people started contacting me with their problems. I realized the smut, indecision, lawlessness, and greed extended beyond the media. While I still use media to discover a lot of it, it is prevalent everywhere. I had to broaden my approach. When I did, I became king. I am the final say when it comes to those four things. People count on me to weed that garbage out of society. It is expected of me. As time goes on, the wickedness seems to continue to grow. There is definite room for a queen. You and I over all my facilities. Oh the things we will accomplish together." He looked me square in the eye, and I had to bury my feelings of disgust and allow a touch of admiration to enter my eyes. The most difficult thing I'd ever done.

Had he said *institutions*? There was more than one?

The first piece of information I got from the subversives was the guard's shift schedule. It rotated every day. It was an odd/even three-day switch up. Odd and even days had the same things, but every three days it was a different schedule. This was very useful information. Sterling and his teachers reminded us continuously about how great it was to have the guard towers to protect us from the evil world outside. Did everyone believe that crap? I wondered when the next Circus of Feats would be occurring. I thought it might open up some information I could use to get us out of here.

I wondered if I'd ever really get out of here. The security around the place seemed impenetrable, and the information the resistance fed me was so little, that it would take a year to even get it all. I would not be here a year. They were so conservative on this drop, it about killed me. I wanted more. If only they'd give it all to me. I couldn't wait on them. I had to act now. Besides, I was slowly losing Duncan and Frankie.

I also had to really start pushing the idea that I was getting closer to embracing all that Sterling taught. At our meetings I started peppering him with questions like, how do I know they're all guilty? Why do they deserve to die? Can I choose which people to go after? Can I choose who I think is guilty and who isn't? And when he'd answer, I'd murmur things under my breath that would give the impression he was getting through to me.

While I was getting good at faking it, Houston embraced it fully. Frankie started saying thing that showed me she was falling into Sterling's trap. And Duncan agreed with some of the crazy *Sterlingisms* I would talk about with other kids. I would do my best to bring them back from his conditioning each time I was with them. Memories of our previous activities together and sweet moments like serving the community at the drama fundraiser worked really well to remind them that Sterling was an evil kidnapper and nothing more.

One thing that was fun was to see Frankie get a boyfriend. Actually, she got several boyfriends in a short amount of time. Instead of comforting her about home, my job was now to be a shoulder for her to cry on when a guy said or did the wrong thing. It was nice to have a break from her whining about home, but that connection with home was quickly being severed and that was not good.

More and more, it was Zoey and me by ourselves. Cross words were often spoken with Duncan, but he wasn't a lost cause. He'd also found a girl that he was interested in and tended to hang out with her.

I emailed Sterling one Friday evening that I had figured something awesome out. I couldn't believe it had taken me almost three months to figure it out. When I tried the dining room door, it opened, so I went in, thinking he'd gotten my message. He was once again talking to someone in the room to the side of the dining room with the door open. I wished I knew what was behind that door. Was the person he was talking to a new client, a recruiter? This time I could hear clearly what was being said.

"Why are you giving me excuses?" Sterling said. "Just get it done."

"I don't understand," a familiar voice said. "Why can't we just take a break? You have plenty."

I couldn't breathe. I knew that voice. I knew the spicy scent that wafted into the room. I started to back up.

"Are you needing a break from our quest, our calling?" Sterling said.

Shallow, fast breaths rocked my body, and my head started to spin. I gasped for a deep breath. It was too loud. I had to see with my own two eyes. I had to confirm it. I felt his kisses on my lips. His sweet words of love and trust. I moved toward the door behind which the conversation was coming. I felt a presence behind me, but I didn't care, I had to see. Could it be? Only a few more feet. Something hit me hard on the back of my head. As I fell, Sterling pushed his door open, and my fears were confirmed. Next to Sterling stood Dakota.

Chapter 21

I was in the doctor's office. I tried to sit up and my vision swam, so I lay back down. My head pounded, and I reached up, feeling a large goose egg on the back of my head. I heard someone breathing and turned to see Dakota sitting in a cushiony chair staring at me. Before I could say anything. He pressed a button on a pen he had in his pocket.

"We only have a minute and a half to speak freely."

"You!" I spat. "If I could move, I'd break your neck." Was that a jammer he had?

"I told you to stay away from the Avengers. Why didn't you listen to me?" His face lined with worry.

"Maybe because you told me to." I gave him a dirty look. "Did you send us here? Did you pick us to be tortured?"

"No. I never told him to take you. Look. I don't have time to argue with you. It's super important that you pretend we only know each other through Madness. You can't tell anyone we were together. You would be in extreme danger if you did."

"So, you're telling me what to do again?"

"Please. Sterling won't kill you if finds out we've kissed, he will maim you, making you pay for the rest of your life."

"Pay for what?"

"He doesn't want me to be distracted, and he has a very strict rule that I not get involved with the selections at all. He doesn't want me to have a soft spot for anyone here. It's a smart policy, really, 'cause the second he took you, my mind immediately started working on a way to save you."

"And you came up dry?" I forced myself to stay mad.

"I did. Sterling is more powerful than you'll ever know. Once you're in his organization, you're in or you're dead."

"Why do you work for him?" I leaned forward.

"It's complicated." He slouched in his chair.

"Why didn't you tell him we were together? Then he wouldn't have taken me. Instead you let him take me."

"No."

"None of this would have happened if you'd been honest with him. It's almost been three months and you show up now? What the heck!"

"Number one, I did not tell him to take you. One of my colleagues told him he saw a blonde-haired girl surfing the trains with the group. That was all he needed. He'd waited a long time for the group to be complete. He didn't consult with me. He just snatched you guys. And number two, I've only been here twice since you were taken and the first time was only for a couple of hours. I have to follow orders."

I started to object, but he held up his hand and said, "Stop! I need you to listen to me. Please, don't acknowledge me or give me a second glance. We must be as good as strangers here."

"But we're not."

"I know and I want to help you, but now's not the time. I have to protect you."

The penlight went out.

"You're awake," he said, as if we hadn't been talking already. "I'll get the doctor." He left the room. Would he come back? What if I never saw him again? I had been stupid. I should have used the time to get him to help me, not be angry and yell.

The doc came in without Dakota.

"Let me look at those baby blues," he said. He used a small flashlight to check my dilation. "No concussion," he said. "But you've got a nice goose egg that will be tender for some time." He turned, opened a drawer, and pulled out a hand-held mirror. He angled it so that I could see my bump. It was a big one. In the center was a dark blue circle. It would have a black bruise even when the swelling went down.

"You fainted?" he said. "Tell me what happened. I just ran your blood work and it looks fine."

"I'm not sure," I said. I guess I'd play along with the lie Sterling had told the doc. "I smelled something spicy, and I suddenly felt weak. My knees came out from under me." I still couldn't believe Dakota was the recruiter. The betrayal hung around my neck like an anchor, and I started to sink into the depths of the sea.

"Do you know if you were locking your knees, then?"

"I guess I could have been. Honestly, I don't know." Darkness swirled around me.

"Well, we'll chalk it up to that, then. Watch those knees young lady." He patted my shoulder and smiled.

"I will."

"All your other tests look fine. Healthy as a horse. You're free to go."

"Thanks," I said, hopping down. I felt invisible water fill my lungs, and I gasped for air. Dakota was the recruiter. Then I spotted the doc's computer in the corner of the room. I pretended to sway. The doc caught me.

"Maybe you should lie back down for a little bit longer."

"Okay," I said, lying back. He made sure I was comfortable, and then he left the room. Once I heard the door click shut, I carefully made my way to the bathroom to the left of the room, casually taking note of the one camera in the room. It seemed to be trained on the table I'd been lying on and the door to the room. I hoped it couldn't see me sneak along the wall by the bathroom and behind the computer. I pretended to go into the bathroom, but passed it and continued to the computer. After clicking the computer on, I was pleased to find that my medical chart was up and that the computer was hooked up to the Internet. With lightning speed, I pulled up another tab, set up a false email account and typed a coded message to Jeremy using a very difficult code I'd seen in one of my Division manuals.

I gave him all the info I knew about the area and that the head of the place was Sterling and Dakota was the recruiter. I heard the click of the exit door. I hit send, closed the email tab and put the screen to sleep. I then slid along the wall to the bathroom and grabbed the door, acting like I'd just come out.

"You feeling better already?" the doc asked.

"I think so," I said. "I just needed to go to the bathroom."

"Would you like someone to help you to your room?"

"I think I've got it. I'll go slowly." I smiled, using biofeedback to slow my heart, and made my way past him to the exit door. "Thanks for your help."

I tried to make my way to my room, but the adrenaline I'd used to send that email was gone, and I had to stop and brace myself on the wall, lean over and take deep breaths to be able to go further. *Dakota was the recruiter.* How could it be? Once I made it to my room, I closed the door and after pressing my back up against it, I slid to the floor, my knees coming up to my chest. I wept bitter tears of betrayal.

Chapter 22

I woke up, screaming his name, "Dakota!" My back ached from falling asleep scrunched up by the door. My muscles ached as I stood. I let hot water pelt me in the shower for a good half-hour and when I couldn't take it anymore, I got out.

When I walked back into my room, my towel snug about me, Zoey was sitting on my bed, eyes looking concerned. "Do you want to talk about it?" she said.

When I didn't say anything and only stared at her, she said, "I came by to get you last night, and I heard you crying, I didn't mean to intrude, I..." She let that hang out there.

I relaxed and pulled on all the strength I could muster and said, "I just had a bad evening, that's all. Sorry you had to hear it."

"You know, you can tell me anything."

"I know," I said, tugging on my towel. "It was just a bad day." It bugged me knowing that Sterling had seen it all on his monitors.

"Alright then, let's make this afternoon better then. What do you say?"

Her smile was infectious and even though I wanted to stay in my room and wallow in self-pity, I said, "Sounds great.

Now, get out of here so I can get ready. I'll meet you in the mess hall."

She stood up and left, pausing only to give me a hug.

I ate a ton of breakfast: crepes with lemon and raspberry sauce. I was glad it was hands-on training today. If it hadn't been, I probably wouldn't have gotten anything done. There was no way I could get away with that in these trainings. I was forced to participate.

Because it was Saturday, after dinner we played water games on the playing field. It was nice to let loose for a while and escape. My head started to ache after about two hours of the fun, so I went to my room to sleep it off. I definitely didn't want it to turn into a migraine. I wondered if getting my hair colored bright yellow again had anything to do with it. I took heart that it was a good two inches long now.

Surprisingly, Zoey had to wake me up in the morning. It was already ten. She grabbed Frankie and Duncan while I finished getting ready, and we left to watch motocross racing at a track we had to be shuttled to. It was exactly what I needed to do to forget about Dakota. We had to walk to the baseball field and then a safari-type, bus-like vehicle drove us to the track. I looked all around trying to find a chink in the compound's armor as we drove, but there really wasn't anything to see. We drove on a path through a densely forested and hilly area. This place seemed to have no end, no boundary. I noticed a few kids bail out into the forest after we'd been driving about ten minutes. I noticed a bush with big, round black berries next to two trees close together and figured I'd jump off at that same spot on our way back to see what was up.

It was pretty fun to see the motocross riders perform. Frankie took off with her newest crush and they sat, glued together, kissing, hugging, and acting silly the whole show. I wondered when she'd come crying to me about something he said or did. I wished I could tell her about Dakota. I shut my eyes thinking of the effect his betrayal had on me.

We sat in a strategic position for Zoey to be able to look at, but not interact, with James. He was a shy, modestly attractive Whitie, and Zoey had had a crush on him for over six months. I doubted she would ever actually talk to him. It would take a miracle.

Zoey, Duncan, and I grabbed burgers, fries, and drinks from the food stand when we got hungry and walked around the area chatting and laughing about the stunts the riders had pulled. I wanted to go check out that place in the forest where I'd seen those kids bail on the ride over before it got dark, so when they started back to the track, I said, "I'm going to head back, I'm feeling a bit dusted and noised out."

"No way, Misha!" Duncan said. "You've got to stay so you can try out the bikes. You'll love it."

"It's tempting," I said, and it was, "but I'm getting a headache, and I don't want it to turn into a migraine."

"Well, I'll come with you, then," Zoey said. I could tell she really didn't want to.

"No you won't," I said, walking away backwards. "I forbid it. Go ride the bikes. Someone's gotta give me a blow by blow." That way she could also spend more time staring at the boy she adored and maybe even see him ride.

She brightened. "Are you sure?" She tilted her head to the side. What she was really asking was if I was going to go back and cry my heart out again.

"Definitely! But watch out for lover-girl there." I indicated Frankie. I grinned and then turned to run and catch the shuttle that was pulling away from the stop.

I sat backwards on the shuttle, hoping I'd recognize the spot I needed to find. When I saw the bright red bush and two trees close by it where the others had jumped, I jumped off. It was nothing like jumping from a train. The shuttle moved so slowly, I just hopped off and walked away. I found what I thought was a trail and followed it in stealth mode. It wasn't long before I heard voices. About seven kids sang and worked in an area cleared of trees. They were weeding, planting, and watering a garden of all kinds of things like beets, carrots, tomatoes, and corn.

I noticed right off that they were happy. They laughed, told jokes, and sang interesting songs I'd never heard before. They'd found their little piece of heaven in this terrible place. I thought about them helping the artists with their colors and wondered how I might have them help with an escape. I wondered if they grew anything poisonous. While I needed to find a different kind of subversive, these gardeners were still subversives, and I bet if push came to shove, they would help me.

I moved away from the path and found a tree to sit against, and I listened to them. It relaxed me, and brought me home to working in my parents' garden every Saturday in the summer. It was an activity I thoroughly enjoyed. I even loved canning what we grew, especially tomatoes and strawberry jam.

At some point, I dozed off. I woke when my head bobbed. Dakota sat next to me. In an I-just-woke-up panic, I scooted away from him. He put his finger to his lips and pointed to the gardeners who were still hard at work. He stood, and waved for me to follow him. I'm not sure why, but I did. Once we were far enough away from them and they couldn't hear or see us, he turned and grabbed me into a hug. I resisted at first, but when I heard him sobbing, I relaxed and let him cry.

Once he stopped, he said, "I'm sorry. I'm so sorry that you're here."

Anger still burned in my chest. I couldn't stop it from entering our conversation even though I needed to win him over to my side.

"I thought you were back home, looking for me," I said, "worrying about me, mourning me. I thought you were frantic and here you are, the one who sent me here."

"I already told you," Dakota said. "I didn't know you were the blonde girl they said joined the group—you had black hair. I didn't even know it *was* you. The day after they took you, when I discovered you were gone along with all the others from the Avengers, I thought I might break into a thousand pieces."

I could see he was telling the truth, but I wanted to hurt him like he'd hurt me.

"You should have trusted me and told me what was going on instead of professing your love for me that night. This is your fault."

I watched the hurt in his eyes turn to anger. "Yeah, right," he said. "'By the way, Misha, I help someone kidnap eighteen-year-olds. We're about to abduct the Avengers. So stay away from them.' I don't think so. You should have just listened to me."

He had a point, but still, I was mad. "How can you be a part of this?"

"I didn't have a choice." He shifted his weight to his other foot.

"We all have choices."

"I don't."

"You do." I tilted my head to the side.

"No. I don't. If Sterling knew that I was here, right now with you, he would make your life more than miserable. I made sure he would be busy right now and not be on the hunt for you."

"What are you talking about?"

"If he knew something was between us–"

"You keep saying that. What does that mean?"

"He can't know."

"But there is something between us. You can tell him, and he'll release me."

"Not on your life. Not now, anyway. Not now that you're his favorite. That he sees you as his star."

"I've been trying to get on his good side so I can bolt."

"And you're doing a great job. I have no doubt you'll find a way one day to get out of here. I mean, you counsel with him." He shook his head.

Was jealousy lacing his words? "Not because I want to, but because I have to. If you would tell him to free me, this would be over."

"No, he has strict fraternizing rules. Why couldn't you have simply worked under him, not with him? You could have been a normal soldier, out of his line of sight. Then maybe I would have had a chance to help you. Instead, you meet with him? You've made yourself untouchable. I can't help you as much as I want to."

Was my plan backfiring on me? Should I have laid low like he said? "Why do you work for this evil man? Quit. Or at least tell someone about what he's doing. You are free out there and could tell someone."

"I can't quit. There are things in play here that you don't understand. I can't tell a soul."

"You could find a way. Whatever he's holding over you, you can find a way around it. I believe in you." I had a sudden thought. A ray of hope. "Take a letter to my parents so they know I'm alive."

"There's no way. It's too dangerous for you. If Sterling found out, he *would* kill me and you. I'll try to protect you while you're here, but I'm stuck, just like you. I was so mad at you that you didn't listen to me and stay away from the Avengers. I thought I might go mad with grief. I want to help you so bad. But—it's just not possible.

His shoulders hunched, and I could tell he was about to lose it again. I felt bad for him. I think he really believed he had no choice.

I sighed and gave his hand a squeeze. I wasn't going to give up on this, but I sensed it was wrong to push it tonight. We stood in silence, holding hands, until my tablet chimed, alerting me that the last shuttle from the motocross stadium was leaving.

"I'd better go," I said and began walking back toward the path.

"Wait," Dakota pulled me back toward him. "I have to leave–day after tomorrow."

"Off to find new assassins, then?" I said cuttingly. "Well, have a good time. Try not to fall in love with any of *them*. It might make your life difficult."

"Stop, Misha. It's not like that," he said, his voice soft and sincere. "You're the only one I care about. I want to help you, there's just nothing I can do." He paused, as if unsure if he should continue. "Will you meet me again tomorrow?"

It seemed as though his entire world hung on my answer.

I hesitated, then finally nodded.

Once in my room that night, I wrote a letter to give to Dakota to take. I was betting on getting him to agree to take it. He'd said it was impossible, but I knew he could find a way. I was sure of it, because I knew something about him. He loved me.

Chapter 23

My third chore day came around. I worked in the laundry all day. It was terribly hot and humid work. At seven-thirty, I made my way out to the baseball field. Dakota held a bundle of blankets in his arms, hugged tight to his chest as if protecting himself. It made him seem so helpless, my heart softened toward him. I was still angry from yesterday, but I pushed those feelings down. I knew I had to let my affection for him come to the forefront. I needed him, and I needed him to see that. I had to let myself be vulnerable, too.

I spoke first, letting some softness into my voice. "I knew you were trouble from the moment I saw you." I laughed quietly to let him know I meant it fondly.

He lifted a hand to my cheek. "You're the one who's trouble."

I leaned my head a little into his hand.

"Remember that time we rafted the river? I never told you this, but that thing with the peppermint gum... it completely won my heart."

"Really? The gum? Not my good looks, not my amazing feats of bravery–gum?"

"Amazing feats? Hardly!" I teased. I pushed him a little, and he dropped the blanket. I helped him spread it out on the ground, and we sat down. I played with a stray thread for a moment, then I looked him straight in the eye. "No, it was the gum. While everyone was off getting drunk, you chewed peppermint gum in the darkness, and fell asleep on a blanket. It told me something about you that no *amazing feat of bravery* ever could."

"And what was that?"

"It told me you were someone I could love."

He looked down, and I was surprised to see shame on his face.

"You shouldn't..." he choked on the words. I held my hand to his lips and shook my head, moving closer to him and leaning my forehead against his. My fingers slowly dropped from his mouth, and I replaced them with my own lips. I kissed him long and deeply, and I could feel him relax as I gave him this expression of trust.

I pulled away and sighed, "Do you have to leave tomorrow?"

"Yes, I don't have a choice. I'll be back in about three weeks."

"Dakota," I said, reaching into the pocket of my jumpsuit and pulling out my letter. I put it into his hand. "I'm their only child. Please take it to them."

"I can't." He tried to hand it back to me. I pushed his hand away.

"They must be worried sick." I let tears pool in my eyes.

"And they won't be, knowing you're here?" he scoffed.

"I didn't tell them where I was. I lied. Here, read it."

He opened the paper and started reading it out loud.

Mom and Dad,

I love you. I'm sorry I left without telling you, but I couldn't take the chance you'd try and stop me. I ran away with a great guy, so you don't need to worry about me. I love him. We are great together. I need some time and space. I will come home eventually if you just let me be and stop looking for me. I love you and miss you. Please don't worry. I'm happy and safe. Your loving daughter,

Misha

In the letter I had coded, Dakota is the recruiter, huge compound in the south, humidity, assassins, extreme danger.

"I want them to have hope." My voice caught.

He grabbed me into a hug.

"Please. Get word to them." I said into his chest through my partially fake tears. "So that they won't mourn me anymore."

"I want to, but it would put you in too much danger."

"I can protect myself. Besides, you're smart. You can find a way to get it to them without endangering you or me. I know it." I pushed back from him and let him see my tear-stained face. I needed him to see my emotion again. He brushed my tears away.

"It's too risky."

"No. No. Unacceptable. I know you can do it. I won't take that letter back."

He was shaking his head. I was nodding mine.

He started to argue, then something in his pocket beeped. He pulled out a phone. He had a phone? Zoey had been right. This wasn't a no-radio-transmission zone. I had to get my hands on that phone. He read the text and then said, "Look, I just—I don't think I can do it."

I had to push. I let some of the anger back into my voice. "You find a way!"

"Can't we just be together and enjoy each other right now? I leave tomorrow."

"It's kinda hard doing that here with your boss watching."

"Well, he can't see or hear us now. Let's enjoy the moment." He kissed me gently, and I tried to figure out a way to get my hands on his phone. I thought if I waited long enough, he would fall asleep. He never did and the way he was holding me, it was impossible to even try. I would get it next time. I didn't dare risk a move that he might detect. He would never trust me again. Patience. Patience.

When I finally went back to my room, Dakota still possessed the letter I'd written to Jeremy.

It would be a long three weeks wondering if Dakota delivered the letter. I didn't sit idly waiting, though. Instead I continued exploring the compound. One day, I ran into a group of boys and girls laughing in the woods. I stole closer to them and noticed they were looking at something propped on a tree. A few steps closer and I could see they were watching TV on someone's tablet. They had figured out how to get TV? No way. If they could do that, maybe they could get Internet.

"Hi guys," I said, moving in and taking a seat before they could react. A boy with magenta hair reached for the tablet they were using to broadcast TV. "It's okay," I said. "Please don't take it down. I haven't watched TV in over three months, and I'm dying to."

Suspicious eyes fell on me.

"Please!" I whined.

"Aren't you Sterling's right-hand girl?" a girl with white hair asked.

"I don't know what you mean by that, but if you're asking if I'll tell Sterling about you guys, the answer is no. I want to watch TV just as much as the rest of you."

"It's back on," a girl with puke green hair said.

The group fell silent and watched the show. It was fun watching TV with everyone. At the end, I asked, "Why do you only have it on one tablet? Is there a way I can get it on mine?"

"It's expensive, and the guys that do it won't do it for everyone."

"Expensive? What do you mean?" I frowned.

"All ten of us had to take several weeks of the guys' chores in order to get TV on this one tablet. We all shared in the cost."

"Can I share in the cost, too, then?" I asked. "I'd love to watch with you." The commerce of this place was interesting. Goods and services cost labor. I understood how valuable that could be now that I'd spent three long days doing chores.

"We'll discuss it after you leave. If everyone's okay with it, we'll get in touch with you the next time we watch."

"Oh," I said, standing to leave. "Thanks for considering it. Please. Please let me." I put my hands together like I was praying as I walked away.

Someone, or several someones, here were very tech savvy. I needed to find these people and get the Internet.

As I blasted through all my classes, I kept telling myself I was making myself a better spy by gaining all the knowledge the classes gave me. That idea, thoughts of Jeremy, and weekends were my only escape.

My six meetings with Sterling while Dakota was gone were interesting to say the least. He demonstrated such erratic behavior. He took me into the room where I'd seen Dakota and had me sit in the middle of what he called the four elements: a lit candle, a jar of earth, a jar of water, and a fan. Then we watched ten different TV shows. He asked the elements to guide him to the person he was supposed to banish from the earth next. He was a psycho. I was glad when we only did it three times in a row.

The last three meetings, we worked on the president's assassination. We discussed power outages, blocking cell reception, blocking off streets, and cutting power to generators. I spent my time between meetings trying to figure out a way to save the president. There was no way I was going to actually kill him.

Since I was so far ahead with my studies in chemicals, I volunteered to help the other advanced students in conducting special research with the chemicals instructor.

Frankie got a new boyfriend and so did Zoey. Frankie had a secret talk with the Whitie, James, and got him to take Zoey out. They double dated. I didn't especially like either one of the guys, so instead of being the fifth wheel, I got Duncan to help me search the compound for anything that might help in an escape. I found that he was easier to keep on board if I involved him in important tasks. We found seven generators and figured there were probably more elsewhere. Duncan wanted to believe I could pull together a great escape, but his faith was faltering, and I had to re-talk him into the idea every time we got together.

I got several things from the subversives, including a delivery schedule for linens and cleaning supplies, food and clothing, and lab materials. They were all flown in. If only there were cars—they were much easier to hijack. I also learned the location of the compound that housed all the Blackies that weren't on campus on a regular basis.

Sterling and I discussed the drugs we were going to use. They would have to be slow acting, taking about two hours to take full effect. Sterling would assign a team to discover which of the drugs the research facility had been illegally testing would be the best. They wouldn't have a chance to fly or take the president anywhere because without speedy medical attention, he would die. Besides, there wasn't a landing pad at the hospital.

It shocked me when Dakota sent me a message to meet him just past the outdoor volleyball and basketball courts. It had already been three more weeks? I started to really reckon time with his visits. It had already been four months. Unbelievable. I ran to him when I saw him. I had to make him believe I cared for him the same way he cared for me. He cradled me under a big maple tree. It was devoid of leaves, and the air was cold. He smelled good and I inhaled deeply.

"Three weeks is too long. I could hardly stand it." He sighed and planted a kiss on my forehead.

"I know," I whispered into his chest. I put my pointer fingers into the very top edges of his jeans pockets, hoping to get him used to feeling me touch around his pockets so I would have a better chance of getting his phone. I wanted to ask about the letter and if he delivered it, but thought I'd wait until we'd been together a little while at least. Since it was comforting to have him here, it wasn't difficult to make him think that his presence was the greatest thing ever and the letter didn't matter.

He held my hand, stroking the back of it with his thumb. He told me about what he'd been doing the past three weeks. He'd moved on to a new high school and was just scouting out the kids.

"Which high school?" I said.

"I can't tell you that."

"Why not? Who could I possibly tell?"

"It's not that..."

"Never mind. I get it." I was trying to keep things happy and interesting. I had to control my temper. "How often do you bring in selections?"

"About once a year."

"But there are so many people here."

"Yep. I'm not the only one recruiting."

"If there are other recruiters, why won't Sterling let you stop?"

"It's complicated. You have no idea."

"Clue me in then. Why is a great guy like you doing the dirty work of a deranged man?"

He shook his head slowly back and forth. His face was red with either embarrassment or anger, I couldn't tell.

"You just don't understand," he whispered and looked at his feet.

"Make me understand!" I spat through my teeth.

"He's my father," he whispered. "My father." He stared at me, hard faced, his eyes swimming.

My hand flew up to my mouth. I didn't know what to say. He rocked back and forth from one foot to the other, his face angled down now.

"Sterling's my father," he whispered to his shoes.

Christy would never have done it, but Misha pulled him into a hug. Not only because she wanted to comfort him, but because she could use his desire for her as a way to get out and stop his dad. He moved his face across mine and kissed me hard, our tears mingling, wetting our faces.

"Since I'm his son, he thinks I should be just as excited about this whole thing as he is. He wants to cleanse the world like God did with the flood. I think he loves the power, really."

"You can pretend until you get me out of here. We could disappear together."

"I don't know that we will ever be free of him," he said. "He's too smart."

"I think we could be," I said. "We're smart, too. I know you'll find a way."

We sat in comfortable silence for several moments. Then he let another bomb fall.

"I got the letter to your parents."

I scooted away from him. "You did?"

"Yes."

I tackled him, kissing him over and over again. Once I stopped, I said, "I knew you'd find a way." Jeremy got my letter. I could send another.

"I hope my dad never finds out."

"He won't," I said. "You're too clever. I'm sure they were thrilled. Did you see them get it?"

"I didn't. I didn't dare chance them seeing me."

"Thank you so much." I hugged and kissed him. My tablet beeped. Time to go.

"I still have tomorrow night. Let's meet out by the range around seven."

"All right."

***

Back in my room, I wrote my next letter. It included the information about Sterling, the assassination of the president, and that the location for the assassination was somewhere in DC. I slept well.

The next day, I was starting my day like I always did, on my knees in prayer, when Zoey walked in.

"You okay?"

"Yep," I said, standing up. "Just praying."

"Are you kidding me? I gave up on that crap a long time ago. How could a god allow this place to exist? No real god would allow such suffering. There is no god."

"You know Zoey, God doesn't control you. Aren't you glad about that? How would you like to be forced to do everything?"

She looked thoughtful.

"You'd hate it. You and I have our own free agency to choose what we do, just as Sterling does. You don't want to lose that agency. The other good thing is that while we get to choose how to live, we can't choose the consequences. What Sterling makes us do here, the killing, the horror, we won't be held accountable for it. He, on the other hand, will be. I would hate to be him when he dies. His judgment will be awful."

She seemed to understand where I was coming from and nodded. "You know, there's a group that meets early Sunday morning out in the English garden for church. You could go if you wanted."

I wasn't sure I would need that, but I nodded and said, "Maybe I will. Maybe I will."

A sporting tournament was being held today. It was like intramurals at school. You could sign up for whatever events you wanted to do and as long as you kept winning, you'd keep playing. A lot of the popular girls rolled up their sleeves and pant legs and sunned themselves the whole day near where the jocks played.

I played in the volleyball and basketball tournaments. My teams were okay, and I made it to the third round on both teams. It was a lot of fun. Over dinner, Frankie told me about a guy she'd just discovered, Rakon, who she thought was "interesting." This was usually the word she used to describe the next boy she would be crushing on.

After retrieving the letter I'd written, I jogged out to the firing range where Dakota was waiting for me.

We touched our foreheads together and held each other tight for several minutes. He felt warm and solid. I said, "You are going to help me get out of here, right?"

"Believe me, it kills me to see you in that jumpsuit. That you're here. But I can't do anything. If Sterling found out–it would be bad. Really bad. You have no clue how evil he can be."

"But I do know. I lived through the Circus of Feats. That's why you have to get me out of here so we can stop him. He's one man."

"One man with his own army. This isn't his only facility. He has people all over. He has everything. We have zilch." He turned away, stood up and started pacing. "I can't right now. I might be able to help your time here be better. But until you've succeeded with a couple of kills, Sterling can't know about us. Besides, don't you want to be with me? If you're gone, I'm nowhere. I need you. You are the sanity in my insane world. I love you and want to be with you forever."

"If you love me," I said, kissing him. "You'll get me out of here. I'll come back for you. I promise. I'll save you. Someone will help me. We can put an end to all of this."

"No," he said, still kissing me. "He would find out. He always does. He would find you before you could ever turn on him. He has judges, prosecutors, defense attorneys, police departments, jailers, politicians, and others paying him for his work. How do you think all this is possible? He's the biggest giant David has ever had to kill."

If what he was saying was true, this was bigger than I'd imagined. Maybe Sterling *was* untouchable and unstoppable. Jeremy would be able to figure it out though. I slid the letter I'd written last night into Dakota's hand and smiled.

He shook his head slowly, then put it in his pocket.

I told Dakota stories of my childhood, trying to get him to relax and fall asleep. He finally did. I made sure my hand was on his other pocket when he fell asleep. I kept talking even after his breathing evened out, and I slipped my other hand under the one on his pocket and pulled out the phone. With one hand, and still telling stories, I texted a coded message to Jeremy.

PROSECUTORS, JUDGES, JAILERS, DEFENDERS, POLICE DEPARTMENTS, POLITICIANS HIRE HIM. BE CAREFUL WHOM YOU TELL. FORT KNOX.

Dakota sighed, so I hit send. I got into his phone memory and deleted my text before putting it carefully back into his pocket.

Chapter 24

Heading off to bed, I felt jubilant. Everything was going great. Things were in motion to get us out of here. I'd be out of here before I knew it. I was nervous, wanting everything to go smoothly. The text would help them locate us. It would hit a cell tower nearby. It would also give Jeremy Dakota's number. Maybe they could hack his phone somehow. I could only hope Sterling wasn't monitoring his texts.

After classes, I played with Frankie and Zoey, who had both broken up with their boyfriends, in the lunchroom. I wondered if Frankie had been paying too much attention to that boy, Rakon. We would play video games and then discuss my findings and some of the things the subversives sent me. I had to be careful what I told Frankie. I didn't completely trust her anymore. She vacillated between loving Sterling and hating him so often that I worried about her ability to keep secrets. I had to be careful with Duncan, too. I told Zoey everything. She seemed impervious to Sterling's conditioning. I ran and lifted weights every day.

While out and about on a weekend evening, I noticed a group of kids sitting in the middle of the baseball field. I could see them because of the faint light emanating from their tablets. They sat in a circle. I made my way out to them, pretending I knew what I was doing. I didn't feel a spike in my spidey senses, so I knew I was safe.

One of the boys facing me stood when I got within ten yards and said, "Stop right there." Several boys came and frisked me from my shoes to the collar of my jumpsuit.

I laughed. "Why did you guys frisk me?"

"What do you want?" a boy asked, his back to me, still seated. "If you want TV, we've run into a snag. You can only get channel two. We're trying to fix the problem. But you still have to pay the entire fee because once we figure it out, you'll get all the stations and you won't have to come back to us." He said everything in rapid-fire sentences. He twisted his body to look at me.

"Wait. You don't even have your tablet with you. How do you expect to get TV without it?"

"I don't want TV," I said.

"Whoa!" he said and stood up. "You weren't referred?"

"No."

They all shuffled a bit away from me.

"Look. I'm just looking for a way to get on the Internet. I figured you guys were the ones to come to."

The same boy who'd been the spokesperson the whole time continued. "Sorry. No can do. It's impossible. We've tried and tried. It's not happening."

"You're kidding. I was told you guys are the bomb when it comes to technology."

"We are. In fact, Rakon here," he gestured to a boy sitting on the other side of the circle, "he got in, but only for about two seconds and it was gone. *He* was onto us. We stayed off for quite a while. We didn't want to get busted, ya know? But if anyone can do it, it'll be Rakon"

I nodded, forcing myself not to smirk at Rakon thinking about how Frankie liked him.

"We've been trying to build on his success but have nothing, yet."

"I bet it won't be long now," I said with a cheeriness in my voice.

Rakon said, "You got it man. He can't run from me forever."

"If I left you with some information to send, when you do break in, would you send it for me?"

"Sure, after the other thousand messages we already have waiting in line."

At that comment, all ten of them looked at me and grinned.

"What if what I had you send got us out of here?"

"Oh, well now that's another story," he said, sarcasm dripping from his every word. "We'll move your message to the number one slot. Let me guess, is it to the FBI. CIA. NSA?"

They all laughed. Several snorted.

I took a deep breath, suppressing my rising anger. Why *would* they send my message first? Everyone probably claimed to know someone that could help or knew just who to email to get us saved. I had to remember that they didn't know I was with Division and to them, I was just another assassin in training hoping to escape.

"What would it take to get to the top of the pile?" I asked.

"Something pretty darn big, that's what."

"Well, when you figure it out. Let me know." I turned and walked away leaving them in silence. If I got them out, that would be payment enough. I'm sure they'd figure that one out.

When I was about five yards away, I turned back to them and said, "By the way, which one of you opened the door for the scholars?"

"None of us would ever do something like that. No way," the leader said.

"Come on, who was responsible for that genius?" I persisted, making my way back to them.

The boy who'd cracked the Internet shifted slightly. I thought he was going to confess, but then the leader said, "No one here did that." His voice was firm. He was scared. "In any case, I heard that it was an isolated event. It hasn't been able to be duplicated."

"So this person has given up on opening doors at any price?"

"No more doors can be opened. Don't ask."

"Boy, you guys are touchy." I wondered why they were so afraid of opening doors. Had they been caught?

"Well, when you get asked a million times to do something you can't do, it gets a bit irritating."

"Did you happen to hear what made that particular door so special?" I asked.

"We heard there's this unique mis-feed around it. It's a mystery. But I heard it only took one ingenious line of code to break the lock."

"So, everyone worships you guys?"

"Worships and hates us because we have all the power."

"That I understand," I gave them a quick nod and wave. "Don't forget to discuss the price," I called back to them.

Programmers amazed me. I'd learned about hacking and using computers to my best advantage, but I had yet to take a programming class. If only I had all the time in the world to learn everything that interested me.

When I got back to my room, after pondering what price I could possibly pay to the programmers to get my note to the top of the pile, it hit me. I might have something that would accomplish it.

I got on my hands and knees and felt around under my bed. At first, I didn't find what I was looking for, then I felt around the far bed leg and my hand landed on something hard. I snatched it out from under the bed and held it up to the light. My index finger caressed the coded message Jeremy had left me. How could I have forgotten about the lip balm? It could have been a comfort to me so many times. Just knowing that Jeremy had cared enough for me to have it made for me sent a hopeful zing to my heart. I kissed the top before opening it and slathering my lips with its contents. I had my payment. But, for whom? The techies or the TV signal guys?

Over the next three weeks, Sterling was gone three Fridays in a row, so we only met on Mondays. We discussed a lot during those three hours, though.

"We need to cover the transportation of the president," Sterling said. "We need access to his travel route. At the same time, it's important that we take care of the guards and security." Sterling's cronies were making headway on picking a drug for the president. There were so many bad drugs, it was hard to choose.

It killed me that almost nothing happened during the week, but everything happened on weekends here. Occasionally, on my recon missions, I'd run into people making out or getting high, but a lot of the time, I was alone. I liked that. Zoey and Frankie hung out together when I was gone.

We came up with a few plans, carefully laying out everything, considering every contingency. While I was supplying Sterling with plans and ideas, my mind was going crazy trying to come up with counterplans and loopholes that might help me save the president. It was exhausting.

On Friday, my tablet beeped, showing I had a message. I groaned, thinking I must be in for another grueling planning session with Sterling, but to my delight the message wasn't from Sterling at all. It was from Dakota. He was back earlier than expected.

I met him that evening, deep in the woods, past the firing range.

"I have something for you. It's the reason I asked my dad to let me come back for a week."

"You do?" I said.

"Yes. I've been carrying it around for the last few days looking for a chance to give it to you."

He pulled a piece of paper out of his pants. I guess he saw the alarm on my face as I watched him pull it out. "Sorry," he said. "I didn't want to chance my dad getting a hold of it somehow." The paper was folded and wrinkled and a bit damp, but I didn't care. A heart sticker sealed the tri-fold together, and I carefully pried it open without tearing the heart. The letter was signed, Love Mom and Dad, but I'd know Jeremy's handwriting anywhere. Even though my mind captured it instantly, I read the letter over and over again, tears falling freely onto the paper, making the black ink run.

Dear Misha,

We can't tell you how comforting it was to get your letter. We are sorry for making you feel like you needed to run away from us to find happiness. We want you to know that we love you no matter what and we can't wait for you to come back home. It's not the same here without you. Stay safe. Do you need any money?

Please write us back as soon as possible. We miss you.

Love,

Mom and Dad

The coded text said,

Can't locate you. Will find you. Be strong.

"I saw it taped to the door jamb of your front door. When I saw it had your name on it, I snatched it up. Your parents must have hoped that whoever was bringing the notes to them would take one back to you. I couldn't resist. I knew you'd love it."

"Thank you!" I said, jumping into his arms. He hugged me tight. It felt good. I imagined the hug was from Jeremy. He would be coming. I would send more clues as to our whereabouts in the next letter. I screamed out in joy. "I won't forget this, Dakota. Never. I can't tell you how much this means to me. You put yourself in danger for me. You put me first."

"I've always put you first. You just couldn't see it."

"I was blind. I'm sorry." I squeezed his hand.

"My dad does that to people. Don't worry."

"Are you sure he isn't tracking you?"

"Yes."

"How do you know?"

"I have people check me for bugs before and after I come here. I'm clean."

"How are my parents?" I asked. I thought that would be a question I should ask.

"Their lives used to seem to revolve around finding you. Now they seem okay. I think your letter really helped."

"Then you won't mind taking them another one?" I'd been worried about giving him another letter, but it just seemed natural that I would after he brought one back to me. I had coded the same message I'd sent by text in the letter I pulled it out to give to him just in case the text didn't go through for whatever reason. I'd also added that the president was a target and named several insects, trees, and bushes on the compound. He took it from me without hesitation this time.

When I met with Sterling that week, he said, "You seem a bit giddier than usual. Why?"

"No reason." Really, I was feeling pretty good that my plans for escaping this place were looking better and better. I had found the techies, and they could maybe get a message out to Jeremy. I might be able to talk the tunnelers into digging a separate tunnel somewhere to escape. And, I could get to the hospital, save the president, and then flee with Jeremy. Yes, things were looking up.

"I know there's a reason, Misha. You can tell me."

"It's nothing really."

"It couldn't have anything to do with you finding the techies the other day, could it?"

My face flushed, and I was glad I was sitting down. My legs might have gone out from under me. He knew about the groups. I knew he knew about the main tunnelers, but everyone else?

"Certainly you're not naïve enough to think I didn't know about them. I welcome them. When they first started popping up years ago, I quashed them. But I've discovered that they give kids a way to blow off steam. It's amazing what happiness it brings to kids when they think they are getting away with something. Of course, I monitor them closely, and if they get close to doing something they shouldn't, I put an end to it."

I tried not to look too crestfallen, but wasn't sure if I'd managed it. He couldn't know about all of them, could he?

"I let them go wild for a day and a half so that I have a captive audience for five and a half. It's a good trade-off don't you think?"

I was struggling to pull all the hope I'd felt earlier from off the floor, but I squeaked out a yep, before it got too awkward.

"Yes. I give them everything they need to feel like they are pushing the limits so they keep working. It helps keep their creative juices flowing. It's great. They know to report to me. It all works out nicely. There is no way any of them can escape."

He looked me square in the eyes, unflinching. A warning. I must heed it, or die.

He turned the conversation back to planning the president's poetic death.

We'd figured out how to get the slow-acting drug on the podium and microphone. We made doubly sure his personal physician wouldn't help him once at the hospital and that the roads would be sufficiently blocked.

The days we discussed the assassination, he seemed remarkably lucid, but other times, I really wondered. Half of the time I was with Sterling, we watched TV encircled by the elements, which was still just completely bizarre. One day he took me into his *special* room. When he opened the door, he took in a deep breath through his nose and then let it out through his mouth. He raised his arms in the air like a conductor and then stepped in. The room was a large square with a bunch of rainbows all over. On the rainbows were animals, people, and buildings but the colors of those things were way off. The dogs were green, the cats purple, the people all different colors, as well as the buildings. Everything had its own distinct color.

His mind was so different from Dakota's. I couldn't help but admire Dakota for keeping his wits about him. I couldn't imagine how it must have been to live your whole life with a madman. How could you stop yourself from going mad?

"Isn't it beautiful? It's my little color world. If I'd have been God, I would have colored everything like this." As I moved closer to the walls, I noticed everything that was the same had the same color. All horses were gold, all lizards were yellow, and so on. I tried to look amazed and delighted because I knew that's what he wanted.

At our next meeting, he was back to business. We went over the plans about the president that we'd already made. Sterling went over the president's schedule for a typical day during the week and one when he was scheduled to speak.

We discussed security on the routes he'd taken and how to thwart those plans. He pulled up diagrams of the area where the hospital was located, but no street signs or real buildings were shown. Boxes were marked "building" and streets were labeled with the alphabet.

All our talk about power failures for the mission got me to thinking about how handy they were and really, how easy it was to cause one.

After waiting patiently for a long time, I finally met with the TV guys again and watched a fun show. I pulled who I'd figured was the leader to the side as everyone was leaving. "Have you ever tried to get a radio signal?" I whispered.

"Of course. I've been here for four years."

"So you weren't able to get a signal?"

"We got signals all right, all kinds of signals coming in, but we couldn't transmit out."

"Is it because of faulty equipment or lack of the right equipment?" I shifted my weight.

"I think it was lack of the right equipment. Something messes with outgoing signals here. If we could find a way to disrupt that, we could get a signal out." He rubbed his five o'clock shadow.

"Could a power failure cause that?"

"Sure. If electronics can't disrupt the signal, we might have a shot at getting a signal out."

"How long would we have?" I asked.

"It depends on how fast the electricity came back on, but I'll estimate about twenty seconds." He frowned.

"If I provided you with a power failure, would you send my twenty second Morse code message?"

"Now you're talking," he said, whistling. "I'd have to know exactly when this power outage would be occurring. You better pare that message down to fifteen seconds to compensate for human error."

"No problem. And how long do you think we'd have if you had this and a power failure?" I held up the lip balm.

"Chapstick? What do you think Chapstick is going to do?"

"That's the best part. It isn't Chapstick. It's an amplifier/blocker."

"Huh?"

"If you press the bottom, it blocks signals from being intercepted. It was coded to a tracker in my arm, but I'm sure you can recode it and use it to get a longer, completely secure signal out."

He reached for it. I pulled it back.

"My message goes out first."

His eyes shifted to mine. "Fine." He raised his eyebrows.

I handed it to him. "I'll let you know when we're going to have the power down."

I had Zoey sold on the idea of getting a radio signal out, and we brainstormed how to do it.

I asked the subversives to please give me any information they had on the power in this place. I wasn't hopeful. I was getting less and less information from them as time went on. I figured they didn't know whether to trust me or not. It was just like Duncan and Frankie. I wasn't sure what side they were on. Two days later, I got detailed drawings and specs on the power to this place.

When I saw Zoey next, I hugged her hard.

"I guess you got it?" She smiled.

"Yes. Thank you. I'm sure they wouldn't have sent it if you hadn't intervened."

"You got that right. They are so suspicious. And it cost me."

"Whatever chores you have to do, I'll do them for you," I said.

"It's not chores. Adam wants three dates with me." She frowned.

I laughed out loud then covered my mouth and giggled. "He totally likes you. How cute."

"It's not cute."

"Come on," I said. "He's not that bad."

"I know. I just hate to be forced into it."

"Just keep in mind that you are forging the way for us to escape, and the cost will be small."

"You better get us out of here. Could you hurry up?" She giggled and slapped me lightly in the arm. I laughed.

In the diagrams, I'd noticed some important connections, like cable and Internet. I sauntered out to the middle of the baseball diamond. The techies searched me and demanded I tell them what I needed quickly because they were busy.

"I need to talk to Rakon," I said. "Alone."

"Ooooh!" came out of almost all the other techies' mouths. Rakon gaped at me.

"You can't," the leader said. But Rakon was already standing, heading my way. The leader tried to get in his way, but he pushed past him.

We walked around the circle of techies and about half way to the far side of the diamond.

"If I knew where the Internet and cable lines came into this place, could you attach directly to them and have Internet and cable?"

"Of course."

"Would you be detected?"

"It's hard to say. The shorter the amount of time I was in, the smaller the possibility. That would mean I'd need the password. It usually takes me three to five minutes to get past that stuff. We'd probably have three minutes total before we were detected. Of course, if we used the line while a bunch of other stuff was traveling the same lines, it might give us another two minutes."

I thought about this.

"Are you saying you know where the cables are?" he asked, eyes wide, sparkling in the moonlight.

"I might. And if I did, I'd need you to send my message first."

"Is it long or would I have a chance of sending one, too?"

"Mine isn't long or complex. I'm sure you could send yours, too." I shifted my weight to my right foot. "I need to look into a few things. This is between you and me, you hear?"

"Sure. No worries. I stuffed this conversation in my vault, and no one's gonna get to it."

"Thanks, Rakon. By the way, do you know Frankie?" I tilted my head to the side and raised my eyebrows.

"Who doesn't? She's a babe." He snorted and chuckled.

"Well, she thinks you're a babe," I said, smiling brightly.

"No way," he said.

"Yes way," I said. "Just some food for thought. I better scram. I'll be in touch."

"I'll be waiting."

I met with Zoey and filled her in on the developments of our escape plan. Things were really looking great. If I could get to the Internet cables and have Rakon send out an email then immediately cut the power to the compound, making sure the generators couldn't kick in for at least four minutes and with the aid of the lip balm, I might be able to get a radio transmission and an email out to Division.

Tomorrow, I would physically locate the cables with Zoey and see if the gardeners had some tools that might cut through wire. The gardeners might end up being a very important part of my plan. I was up most of the night going through every possible problem we might run into and making sure there was no way the TV guy or Rakon would be discovered.

I woke to a message beeping on my tablet. It was ten. I shot up. Had I missed class? I tried to rub the sleep from my eyes as my mind focused. It was Sunday. It was okay to sleep in. I let out a deep breath and looked at my tablet. Why had it beeped?

Dakota wanted to meet me in an alcove on the north side of the main building. While I'd missed him, I'd been so busy, his absence wasn't painful this time. I had started reckoning my time with Dakota's absence and presence. That meant I'd been here almost five months. I hadn't given up on the idea that Jeremy would be saving me. He simply couldn't find me yet. I had to save myself, and I would. I hoped it would be Dakota that gave me my break.

When I got to the alcove, he handed me a letter, but I didn't get to read it. I had to slide it behind some bushes behind us because someone approached.

It was Sterling. When he saw us together, he said, "Son, what is this?"

Without even a second's hesitation, he said, "Father, we just ran into each other, and she wanted to see if I would help her escape since I wasn't wearing the neckband."

A ball of fire tried to annihilate my insides, but I forced myself to stay calm.

"Did she?" he said, walking around me like he was assessing his prey.

"She thought I would help her."

"Is that true?"

The word *true* hit me hard, and I knew that if I told the truth, I wouldn't live. I had to go along with his story, as stupid as it was. "Of course," I said, pushing my hip out in defense of myself. What else could I do?

He pushed something on his wrist, but he wasn't wearing a watch or anything that I could see. "Well, I thought we were coming along, but apparently, we weren't. I thought you understood the importance of our mission."

"Maybe I wanted to do it on my own." I was faking the attitude and it got harder to do as time went on. I knew I was in deep trouble.

A couple guards came and took me into custody, holding my arms tight. I struggled but I knew I stood no chance against Sterling and his army. I would have to endure whatever punishment he was about to give. My insides seemed to be filled with scaly worms, cutting into my gut.

"No. That's just not possible," Sterling said. "You work as part of this team or not at all. I think what you have done shows me that you are not. It hurts me, really." His voice was devoid of feeling, and the guards took me into the building.

Chapter 25

"Admit it," I said as the guards dragged me down the hallway toward Sterling's dining hall. Both Sterling and Dakota walked in front of us. "If you were in my position, you'd be doing the same thing." I had to keep playing up this angle hoping he would show some mercy. He would do just as I was doing.

He didn't answer until we were in his dining hall, and the wait made me wonder if I'd misjudged him. Ice seemed to form on my spine. We stopped by the table, Sterling and Dakota stood to our left.

"It's true. It's hard to work together on something like this. I think I better make my position abundantly clear. It would do you well to remember who your master is. Do you understand?"

I nodded. Then something crushed my neck. An invisible hand? No. It was the neckband. I leaned forward, gasping for air, but unable to get a breath. Nothing would come into my lungs and nothing would come out. I would die of suffocation. The guards held my arms tight–I couldn't even reach for the offending band.

"This little act of insubordination requires a bit of swift justice I'm afraid." His tone was icy cold and flat.

Then the pressure on my neck subsided, and I coughed and pulled hard on the air around me to fill my aching lungs. “Please,” I croaked. “I’m sorry. I just wanted to be in control. Under the same circumstances, you’d have done the same thing.” I looked at him, forcing a look of pleading to take over the look of hatred in my eyes.

“But I’m not in the same position, am I? I don’t have time to worry about your loyalty to me and our cause. I truly believed we could work together, you and I, but no, we are no longer a team.” He looked off into some unknown section of the ceiling, a look of despondence and betrayal on his face, as if he’d just lost his best friend.

Dakota looked pale and stood there beside Sterling, unmoving.

“I am your master, your King, and you do as I decree. Misha Roberts. You have been charged and found guilty of disloyalty. You shall be punished in a manner that ensures the infraction will never again occur. The severity of the punishment will match that of the crime. You will remember to treat me as your King. Who is your King, girl?”

“You are, sire,” I said, figuring humility was in order, and bowed. In truth, I wanted to send a crushing blow to his larynx.

“I am. Who is your King?” This time he said it louder, with more force.

“You, your Majesty,” I said, bowing once more. My anger had turned into a lance in my chest. It begged to be released.

“I think ten stripes should do it,” Sterling declared.

What were stripes? Did I want to know? Could he mean ten tigers? I was so wound up, I could feel the tension in my ears.

"Take her to punishment alley, please," he said, waving his hand toward me. "Room fourteen."

"Your Majesty," I said. "Should I be punished for not wanting to be tethered to another human being? I made a mistake. Forgive me, please. Aren't I allowed one mistake?"

"Don't beg, Misha. It doesn't become you."

Dakota had once used almost those exact same words with me. It made me sick.

"You are going to learn that you will always be tethered to me. Learn to like it. Crave it or you won't *be*." They grabbed me and brought me to a door on the left side of the room.

He then pushed his wrist again and said, "Please bring Yellow, Frankie to punishment alley room fourteen."

I craned my neck back to see him and he said to the men taking me, "She goes in the middle of the room."

"Yes, sir."

The hallway we entered was all white and plain. At the end, they opened a door that led into another corridor. The walls, ceiling, and floor were made of stones. We had reached punishment alley. The numbers were made of wood and hung above each door. I counted down the numbers until we hit fourteen. Near each of the four walls and in the center of the room were sets of hand and foot manacles. They took me to the ones in the middle of the room and had me facing away from the door. The manacles clanged into place around my ankles, and after they stretched my arms high above my head, the hand manacles clanged into place on my wrists. I was not stretched to the intolerable level, but I wasn't comfortable.

I heard someone coming so I twisted my body to see. Sterling and Dakota came in followed by Frankie, who walked in willingly, without force. Guards were on her back, however. Upon seeing me, she gasped and said, "Oh my gosh! What did you do? What did you do?"

"I didn't do anything," I said.

"The truth, girl. Give her the truth." Sterling walked in a slow circle around me while saying, "She was trying to plot an escape with this young man." He pointed to Dakota. I saw Frankie's eyes fall on him and show recognition, but she didn't say anything about it. I thought she'd yell at him, accuse him, something.

"It's true," Sterling said, "and it was foolishness, I tell you. Foolishness. And I'm sorry to tell you that her foolishness has caused us to have to include you."

Realization dawned on her and her eyes grew wide. She turned to leave, but the guards grabbed her. She screamed and pulled, but they were easily able to lock her hands and feet into the manacles on the wall in front of me, her face turned to the wall.

My whole body shook. "Let her go!" I screamed. I was cold to the bone.

"I knew this would be an effective punishment for you," Sterling said. "I'm truly sorry about that, but the punishment has to fit the crime. Only hurting you wouldn't be half as effective as hurting your friend."

I had played into his hands. I should have been impassive, pretending it didn't bother me that he was planning to hurt her. It made him even more excited about his chosen punishment. I had been a fool. If only I could have pretended she meant nothing to me.

"You will feel the depth and breadth of what you've done," he cooed. "Emotions are so powerful. It's simply your bad luck, Frankie, that she likes you. It's not a good position to be in right now."

Frankie's eyes were bulging, and a myriad of emotions flashed across her face as she twisted and stretched to look back at us. What had I done?

"You know," Sterling said. "I use this room so infrequently I was thinking of turning it into something different or at least using it for Halloween. I guess that would have been a premature move. I will always need it. Yes, I will need it for people like you."

I couldn't help myself. I had to plead for her. I couldn't stand to see her in pain because of me. "Please, whip me 50,000 times. Leave her out of it. She's innocent. She doesn't deserve it. She's done everything you've asked of her since she arrived."

"Yes. And that's what makes this all the more powerful and meaningful. It's quite poetic, don't you think?"

"Just shut up, Misha," Frankie raved. "Shut up! You're making it worse."

A man stepped into the room. He was tall and muscled. He held a whip in his hand. The whip had several leather strands hanging from the one handle. I counted five. My organs seemed to seize.

"Give the one in the middle three before her friend receives ten. I want Misha to know what her friend feels."

I heard the man snap the whip in the air behind me. It made a loud crack. This was going to hurt. I stared at a spot on the wall, praying for the strength to endure. He let it rip against my back. I clenched my teeth. I did not scream. Yet. The second stripe knocked the wind out of me, and I gasped.

A traitorous tear fell down my cheek. I clenched my teeth readying myself for the next blow. When the third blow hit, I screamed, long and loud. I was certain my jumpsuit had been penetrated.

I prayed for Frankie, that she would have strength and that extra angels would be sent to watch over her and bless her. She screamed with the first crack of the whip. I threw my head back, looking for Dakota. His body was turned away. I wanted to scratch his eyes out. He had betrayed me twice, now. How dare he? He did cringe with the next crack of the whip. After the fourth blow, Frankie's body went limp and the screaming stopped, but they didn't. She received all ten lashes. I had to look at the torn up flesh on her back as he finished the final two strikes. I was numb. Beyond feeling. I watched them carry her limp body away.

"Please, let her be alive," I whispered. "Let me die instead." It was hard to breathe or think.

Over the next two days, we were in the doc's office together. No matter what I said or did, she wouldn't acknowledge my existence.

We were tied to the beds on our stomachs and someone came every four hours to wash our wounds. They also put antiseptic on them and then covered them. The doctor said it was important that they not scab over. This would minimize scarring. Most of my time there was spent trying to win Frankie back over. It didn't work. The rest of my time was spent cursing Dakota.

We weren't allowed painkillers because Sterling wanted me never to forget my indiscretion. I was in excruciating pain most of the time. Especially when my wounds were being cleaned. When the doc came to check on us after four hours, I begged him to give Frankie some pain medication. She had been hurt because of me. It shocked me when he did. Was there a bit of the subversive in the good doctor? Frankie was finally able to sleep. I cried.

I was moved out of the doc's office and into my room on the evening of the second day. Frankie stayed there. Her injuries were much more severe than mine. I could sit, but with difficulty. Most of the time, I was either on my stomach, on my bed, or standing. The nurses continued to fix me up every four hours. Sleep rarely came.

My mind was one big jumble of despair. I would die here. We would all die here.

Chapter 26

I couldn't see my way out of the fix I now found myself in. I stood completely alone. Frankie would never speak to me again. Dakota had betrayed me again, and Sterling no longer trusted me. Jeremy would never come because he had no way of finding me. Even the subversives didn't really believe in me.

I was in jail, *in jail*. It seemed impossible, but it wasn't. I resigned myself to being here forever. My only hope was to win Sterling's favor once more, and I had no idea how to do that. I couldn't even find the strength to pray. How could God allow this to happen? He had deserted me in my greatest time of need. I would not be saving anyone. I couldn't even save myself. Guilt swept over me. I had become Zoey, unfaithful and unbelieving. Hours passed with me constantly railing on my beliefs and God.

Darkness shrouded me. I went to bed, depression taking me over. I was vaguely aware of the nurses and someone else tending to my wounds. It could have been Zoey, or anyone for that matter. It probably wasn't Zoey, I thought glumly. I'm sure she was roaring mad at me too. She really loved Frankie, and I'd almost killed her. I fell deeper into the darkness and shadows, as faceless bodies and faraway voices streamed in and out of my consciousness. I thought I heard someone reading to me, but then the voice moved away. Familiar smells filled the air. Was that Zoey's voice? Had Frankie spoken? Was Dakota near?

"Get up," a faraway voice said. "Get up, right now." Was that Zoey? "You are not going to wallow in your tears for one more minute." She was insistent. I didn't want to move. "I'm going to roll you out of that bed if you don't get moving right now." I didn't, and she did.

I felt the hard, tiled floor reach up and smack me awake. I shook my head and said, "Leave me alone. I'm a horrible person. Let me die here."

"Not on your life! A lot of people are depending on you. Now stand up!" When I didn't, she grabbed my hands and pulled me up. I would have let myself fall back to the floor, but she kicked my shin and it hurt. I hopped around on one foot, holding the injured leg in my hand and crying out in pain.

Zoey shoved me into the bathroom.

"Hey! Stop it!" I yelled.

She turned on the shower and shoved me in, shift and all. When I let my legs buckle, she climbed in with me, holding me under the freezing cold stream of water. I shivered and shook.

"Look at me!" Zoey said. "Look at me!"

I finally did.

"I need you," she said in a voice just loud enough for me to hear. "You can't give me such hope and then check out!" Tears were streaming down her face. "You have to come back. Now. You've wallowed long enough. No more self-pity for you."

I found my feet and stood strong, cold water numbing my back. The abyss lightened.

She grabbed my face. "I will help you pull it together. Then you will lead us out of here. You hear me?"

I nodded, slowly.

"Good," she said, climbing out. "Now, wash yourself and get out. I'll put clean clothes on the counter for you. Make yourself pretty and we'll go to class together. Don't dawdle. We only have twenty minutes to get there."

A tiny spark of hope rose in my chest as I washed. I fought the urge to fall back into the hole I'd been in. I made myself turn off the water and dry off. True to her word, Zoey had put clean clothes out for me. I couldn't help myself, and I turned my back to the mirror to look at my back. Pink lines raced across it. They looked almost completely healed. How long had I been in my dark hole?

I finished getting ready and noticed that my hair was longer by about half an inch. I couldn't wait for it to hit my shoulders. I also couldn't wait for it not to be yellow. It felt good to brush my teeth.

Zoey met me with bagels smeared with cream cheese and some orange juice. I felt like I hadn't eaten in weeks. I could only eat a few bites before I felt full.

"How long have I been 'gone'?" I asked, leaning back to stretch my stomach.

"You don't want to know," she said. "It was as long as you needed."

"Come on. I can't lose time and not know how much."

She cocked her head to the side, pressed her lips together and said, "Are you really ready for this?"

"Yes!" I said, opening my eyes wide and looking at her sideways.

"I'm not sure you are. I want to get you out of here and be well on our way to class before I tell you. I can't have you retreating back into your hole."

"Oh my gosh!" I said. "Just tell me."

She stood up and grabbed my hands. "Come on. Let's go. I'll tell you once we hit the green halls." I played along. It felt funny to walk, and I got a bit winded.

"Spill it!"

She kept walking and grabbed my hand. "You've been out for an entire month."

I stopped in my tracks. "What are you saying?"

"You've been in bed for a month. They were feeding you through an IV until yesterday. Sterling had them remove the IV early this morning."

I rubbed my arm where I'm sure the IV had been. It was still tender.

"I had been keeping in contact with the nurses," she continued. "And they told me Sterling was going to let you wither away and die if that's what you wanted."

"And I would have, had you not saved me just now."

"And don't you forget it." She smiled her big smile.

"Did I get you in trouble, Zoey?"

"No."

"I'm so glad. What happened with Frankie?" A chill swept over me.

"She's okay, but don't expect her to welcome you back. She's changed."

"I don't think she'll ever forgive me." A fierce pain shot up my back remembering what Sterling had done to her because of me. "How has she changed?"

"She totally loves Sterling. She's with this new guy, Rakon, though. I'm hoping he turns her around. He's a subversive."

Rakon. My Internet genius.

"She just needs time. And if she'd open her eyes, she'd realize it was Sterling who did that to her, not you."

We arrived at the poisons classroom and walked in. She went to be with the Blackies, and I moved hesitantly toward my group. It was as if I wasn't even present. No one made eye contact with me. From the things they said, I could tell they all were fully on board the Sterling train. I became a distant observer. One month of my absence, and Sterling had changed them. Without my constant reminders to stand strong against him, they'd embraced him.

I sat alone at lunch. No one wanted to be anywhere near me, and Zoey wasn't allowed to be. It was okay. I was plotting. The small dot of hope that had popped up this morning grew into a quarter-sized ball. I would please the heck out of Sterling and win him over so that I could get the heck out of here.

The weekend rolled around, and I was lonely. Zoey was the only person who would talk to me, and she was busy helping with the activity this week, the play *Seven Brides for Seven Brothers.* Though I didn't feel much like going, I went to the play to be supportive. I couldn't believe my eyes when I saw both Payden and Anna in the play. Payden was one of the brothers and Anna was an extra. I stared at them, unable to believe any of it.

They were in the hallway lined up for all of us to talk to them. I found Anna first and grabbed her up into a hug. We couldn't even talk. It felt like a knotted cloth was blocking my windpipe. Payden tumbled his way over to us and joined the hug. They looked exhausted, dark lines were visible in the hall light. The joy I felt bubbled over, and I tried to ask them a million questions at once.

"Are you happy with your assignments? What do you do all day? Have you seen Lunden or Maddie?"

They answered as best they could, but the crowds wanting to see the tumbling master forced me to leave them.

I decided to go for a long run and start getting my muscles back up to par, but first, I went back to an alcove where Sterling had found Dakota and me together. I retrieved the letter I'd left there. I glanced at it and then tore it into tiny pieces and divided the pieces between three trash cans and a drain. As I stretched and warmed up, I analyzed the letter in my mind. They were still looking. I wasn't to lose faith. I let a few tears drop, allowing a moment of weakness before wiping them away and setting my jaw firm. They would find me, or I would escape and go to them.

I was so weak; I was winded before running a few yards, but I pushed through the pain and kept running. While I was at it, I looked for weaknesses in Sterling's security that I might have missed. Someone was shooting on the range. I thought it was probably that Whitie that threatened me that one day. As I ran closer, I realized it wasn't him. It was Dakota. The moment I saw him, he turned quickly and pointed the rifle at me. I flinched back to hide in the trees.

"Misha," he called after me. I ran. My legs didn't want to work right. Push. Push. Escape. Away.

He caught up with me. It was easier these days. I didn't stop, though. I continued to run.

"Misha, stop," he said. "Please stop."

I guess he got the message that I wouldn't be stopping because he tackled me instead. We toppled over and over down a small hill. He was out of breath and so was I. I was tired. I hit at him, trying to get out from under him. His knees pushed on my arms and pinched my skin. His butt sat on my pelvis so I couldn't kick at him. I probably didn't have the strength anyway. I needed to work hard and build it up again. I couldn't stand that I had become so physically weak. I felt vulnerable not being able to shove him off me. It had been a long time since I truly couldn't hold my own. I hated this feeling. He shook his head from side to side as he held my shoulders to the ground. He was heavy and strong. I had no body strength left so I hit him with my words.

"Let me go, you backstabbing traitor."

"I know you think I made things bad for you, but I actually made them better."

"You did? You did?" I screamed. "You lied to your dad to save your butt. You sent Frankie to be whipped, and I've lost her forever. I got *whipped.* You watched. You effectively turned Sterling and everyone against me. You led me on. You betrayed me."

"Listen. The most important thing is that my dad doesn't suspect us. We have a chance now. He trusts me and knows that we've met. He believes there couldn't have ever been anything between us because I turned you in. Now we can move forward with our relationship as you work with him on your first assassination. He won't be looking for anything between us. He'll trust us to be together. That's huge."

"You left me to die in my room. Zoey had to save me. You think I want to be anywhere *near* you now?" Unwelcome tears fell to the ground.

He grabbed my hands and kissed them. "I read to you every night. I got the techies to disable your feed while I was in your room. I hated watching you waste away. You wouldn't even acknowledge me."

I vaguely remembered someone reading to me. That was Dakota?

"I didn't know what to do. It was so hard. I figured it was God's way of punishing me, making me pay for my many mistakes. I've been lost without you. I'm so happy you're back."

He believed in God? Guilt washed over me remembering how I had lost my faith after seeing Frankie whipped. I shook my head and said a silent prayer for forgiveness. I needed faith and belief more now than ever.

I knew he hurt, but I had too, so I kept punching with my words. "Why don't you take all that happiness you have and watch your best friend get whipped into unconsciousness? Then see how bright your happiness is."

"I'm so sorry about that," he said through clenched teeth. "I had no idea he would pull Frankie into this. All I could think about was saving you."

"Oh, you saved me? The scars on my back might disagree."

I saw anger and an old sadness rise in his eyes. "It killed me to see that happen to you. But, you don't know my dad. This really was the best thing for the long-term."

He truly believed what he was saying. I scowled at him and yelled, "Get off me."

He rolled off. "Sorry. I had to talk to you." Sincerity pulsed from him. "I'm sorry I had to throw you under the bus like that, but if I hadn't, it would have been a lot worse. If my dad even suspected there was anything going on between us, he would have truly made your life miserable. We just need to wait a little longer. My dad doesn't want me with anyone. Especially someone he sees as his prized protégé."

"If he once thought that, he no longer does. He doesn't even trust me."

"Besides his upcoming assassinations, you are the only thing he talks about. You should hear him. He talks constantly of his prized Blondie."

"I need to get back," I said.

"I was so worried you wouldn't make it. Rest a little while longer."

I looked at the forest I would have to trudge back through and said, "This compound is huge. Why hasn't anyone ever found it?"

"It's in a no-fly zone."

"No-fly zone?"

"Yep," Dakota picked at some twigs. "My dad used environmentalists to help push his request through. By making it a no-fly zone, he's supposedly saving fragile plant and animal life that could be drastically hurt by plane noise and exhaust."

"That's ridiculous." A new sense of foreboding and helplessness washed over me. No wonder Jeremy hadn't been able to find us.

"I know, but my dad has a way of getting what he wants. I wish I could get you out. I can't tell you how much I wish I could. Why did you do it? Why did you go with the Avengers?" Dakota threw his hands out, palms up.

"Why do you keep asking me that?" I asked.

"You're so stubborn. I wish you would have listened to me. I thought I'd be able to help you after your first kill, but I'll probably have to wait until after the second, now. Things really start relaxing after that. My dad is watching your every move right now. He got up and danced when he saw your 'dot' leave your room. He's probably looking at your 'dot' right now, wondering what you're doing and hoping you will go visit him of your own accord."

"I know he is," I said, picking at tiny strands of grass. "But I also know that if I didn't go explore, he'd know I wasn't being true to myself or that I was hiding something. He has me raw and exposed, and I'm showing him that. Help me get out of here, Dakota." I grabbed his hands.

"He has his claws in me just like he has his claws in you. I'm as much a servant of his will as you are."

"Turn away from him. Break free. Find a way to help me."

"You act as if I've just laid down my whole life and easily given in to everything he's asked. I've learned the hard way, just as you have. I tried to run away, and he found me and put me in solitary for a whole month after putting me through the dunking machine. I almost starved to death. And he killed my best friend, Sean, because he was the one who had encouraged me to run away."

"Oh my gosh!" I said. I felt my heart soften. He had reason to act the way he had. He did want to protect me. "I'm sorry. I had no idea."

"I didn't want to tell you," he said. "But you're so stubborn. I should have known I'd end up telling you sooner or later. I can't seem to keep anything from you." The look on his face tore at my insides. He was a pawn as much as I was. The horror of it all was compounded by the fact that it was Dakota's flesh and blood doing this to him. I had been blinded by anger. Stupid. Stupid.

"Play along, Misha, and after your first few kills, I'll start talking about you to my dad and see if he won't let me have you eventually. It's going to take time, though, Misha. Please be patient."

"I'll try," I said. I didn't want to be his possession. And it bothered me a lot that he wanted me to kill someone before we could even talk about an escape. "You know I won't be satisfied just getting us out. We'll have to find a way to save the others."

"Let's focus on ourselves, first."

"But you will help me, won't you? You'll help me get everyone out, eventually?" There had to be a way. I would find it.

"Yes. Bide your time. Get a couple assassinations under your belt, and then we'll let my dad start seeing us together more, and slowly, I'll let him know I think you're awesome. Hopefully, he'll bless the relationship, and we'll all stay alive."

There was some movement in how he felt about helping me. I would keep working and digging and let Dakota's subconscious mind look for a way to help. The truth was, if I wasn't able to get out by the time Dakota's plan was put into place, I would escape with him. Then I would leave him, free everyone, and kill Sterling.

Chapter 27

Somehow, bizarrely, life at the compound slipped back into old rhythms. I worked out every day really hard, and I began to regain my muscle mass. Classes continued on. I still worked with the chemicals instructor, and the other kids stopped avoiding me. I still couldn't get anyone in my group to talk to me, but I could tell Frankie was softening. She wanted to forgive me but wasn't sure how.

On Sunday that same week, I ran into something else that interested me a great deal. Some kids were meandering in the woods after the production and had been for a solid hour. Slowly, one by one, all but two disappeared without me seeing where they went. I moved in closer, going into stealth mode and watched one disappear after going in a particular area. I staked it out. Ten minutes later, the last wandering girl disappeared, too. But I had seen where she'd gone. I made my way over, and after pushing my way behind a big group of bushes, I found a hole in the bottom of a hill. Tunnelers?

I decided to be brazen about my discovery of them and slid on my belly through the small opening. Once through it, the tunnel widened so that I could sit and had three feet on all sides of me. Four of the kids I'd watched disappear were a few yards in front of me widening the tunnel walls. "Hey," I called out.

The four screamed, jumped, and grabbed at each other. Their reaction startled me a bit, and I took a step back. The tallest girl put her hands on her chest and gasped before crying out, "We're busted!" All digging sounds stopped and six, dusty, dirty kids emerged from the tunnel beyond the four I could see.

"Busted for what?" I asked.

"This tunnel," the tall girl said, looking completely annoyed. "It's top secret. No one knows about it but the ten of us, and now, you. You've ruined it."

"I don't see how I've ruined it," I said. "I'm not going to tell anyone."

"You've contaminated the site by following us in. Now others will find us."

"I doubt that very much," I said. "I'm great at stealth. You guys did everything right in trying to lose a tail. I've just had a lot of experience in this arena. And in truth, I almost didn't find the entrance you guys were so good, and I'm a pro. Besides, Sterling already knows where you are." I tugged at the neckband I wore. That's when I noticed none of them were wearing neckbands. How was that possible? "Wait a minute. Sterling doesn't know where you are."

They all looked at their feet.

"*How* did you manage that? You've got to tell me."

Several nodded with a bit of hesitancy. "Wait a minute. You're that girl that Sterling had to discipline for trying to escape," a girl with gold hair said.

My face felt hot, but I could tell she was trying to decide if that was a good thing or a bad one. I had to make her believe it was a good thing, that she could trust me.

"Yeah, and he whipped my best friend for my indiscretion. I intend to pay him back for that."

They all stared with wide eyes, so I forged on. "How did you get those removed and how close are you to getting past the barrier?" I asked.

"A guy in our group worked with a techie to figure it out. It's not easy. Today, Sterling thinks we're with some kids in the cafeteria," a short, tiny boned girl said.

I guessed they figured I was trustworthy.

"We think we've got about 500 feet," a tall, lanky guy said.

"Are you serious? How long will that take to go that far? And how can I get your guy to remove my neckband."

"About a month. We get about 500 feet every month," the tall guy said. "But we can't remove your tracker. You're too hot right now. You'll have to leave the escape up to us. We'll come back for everyone."

"Fair enough. But when you get within ten feet will you let me know, and I'll give you a note to take to a buddy of mine that can help spring the rest of us?"

"Hold on," the tiny girl said. "We're not trying to really escape." I could hear the false note in her tone. "We're just testing Sterling's security for him. He thinks all the tunnelers are working on the obvious tunnel, and we wanted to throw him a curve ball."

I laughed. "I totally understand. That letter I'm sending to my friend. It's just a test, too. For Sterling, I mean." I rolled my eyes, and they chuckled. "After you get it out, I'll let him know I breached it." We all laughed out loud now. Comic relief in a deadly serious situation.

"Any way you might speed it up and halve your time on this last 500 feet?"

"We might be able to do that with some extra workers."

"Don't do anything that would give yourselves away. I just figure, if we can get out of here, sooner is better than later."

"Amen," a black-haired girl said then smiled.

"I'll get you the coded letter ASAP. Thanks guys."

I figured I better hurry out of there and never return. They were right. I was too hot. Anywhere I went, Sterling was sure to take notice. As I left the cave, I took heart. More of the kids here were working to escape than I'd thought. I would have to rally the forces and get several groups heading for the exit with earnest. One was bound to succeed. If only I knew if Sterling was still going to let me assassinate the president and when it was going to be. I needed to go see Sterling. He would like that.

On Monday morning, I gathered my courage and walked purposefully to Sterling's dining hall. As I neared the door, fear almost made me turn back. Memories of the pain he could inflict were still very raw, but I pushed through it. I was a spy, and I was trained to fake it. I would fake it. I squared my shoulders, took a deep breath, and walked forward. I raised my hand to knock, but instead I got a shock as the door opened of its own accord. Was he actually expecting me?

Sterling sat at his usual place at the head of the table, and the familiar sight of him in a garish tie and boxer shorts nauseated me, but I let no hint of it show on my face. Instead,

I let my eyes fill with tears, and my expression showed nothing but hopeful admiration.

"You welcome me back?" I whispered, letting hope, disbelief, and gratitude mingle subtly in my tone.

"Misha, my dearest queen to be, I have waited here every Monday for your return. I knew that my patience would be rewarded. You see now that I am not only just, but merciful and forgiving. Where the colorless world would reject you, I am here to welcome you back with open arms. I knew you would recognize your rightful place is here beside me, if you were given the proper guidance. My faith in you has been confirmed, for here you are, ready to join me once again." He beamed at me. He had no doubt that his conditioning had been completely effective. He gestured to my usual place at the table.

I crossed the floor eagerly and sat next to him. He held out his hand to me, and I took it without hesitation. I had to play my part perfectly.

"Thank you, thank you, sire," I murmured. "This is all I've wanted."

He smiled blissfully, "Of course, dearest."

He let go of my hand, then pushed a button in his drawer and our meals rose out of the table.

After breakfast, our conversation turned seamlessly back to planning the president's demise. It was as if nothing had changed.

After we discussed some hiccups with the drug we'd chosen, we moved on to dissecting all the plans, trying to find faults, no matter how picky. My mind wandered. Did he know about the second group of tunnelers? They were so close to escaping. He must not know. How could I find out without giving them away?

I got my opportunity to ask him when he brought up using manholes to get his team around.

"I couldn't help but notice how close the tunnelers were getting to their escape."

"Oh, that silly group. Insane isn't it? They'll make it to the border in about six months, they'll come tell me about it and we'll fill the tunnel in. It may seem like a waste of our time, but this group provides us with valuable information about our weaknesses and the strengths of the kids. You know, things like how long someone will persist at something that is futile. We also gain insight into the process of tunneling and what it would take for someone to really escape this way and what the signs might be."

He didn't know about the second group! I rejoiced inwardly. He was talking about the first group, the one that operated more openly. I smiled at Sterling. Let him think I was admiring his methods; inwardly I was celebrating. The pieces were coming together.

"Time for your classes, Misha dear," Sterling said. I got up to leave, and he gripped my hand tightly. The strength of his grasp reminded me–I was playing a dangerous game. "It's good to have you back."

"It's good to be back," I said as I gently pulled my hand from his and began backing toward the door. "Thank you, for my second chance."

I tried to meet his eyes to show my sincerity, but he was once again staring off in the distance. I slipped out unhindered.

After a hard day of hands-on training classes, it felt good to be in Dakota's arms again even if we always had to sneak around. I wondered if he knew some of the kids had figured a way to unhook their neckbands. If he knew about the techies and got them to help him, what other resources did he have access to? I bet he could spring me tonight if I could find a way to convince him to do it.

Dakota brought me out of my reverie. "I've been thinking of places we could go hide after we escape. Places that my dad doesn't know about, of course. I've been researching to see if there is a way. I think it would be possible if you completed the kill first."

"I don't understand why we can't just go tonight. It would be like we were eloping."

He shook his head. "Tonight is no good. I'm getting it all arranged. Everything has to be planned out seamlessly if we can have any hope of escaping permanently. Have faith in me, Misha."

"If I agree to this, you have to tell me where this compound is so that I can send people to dismantle it."

"The truth is, I don't know."

"What?" I couldn't help but let shock hit my face.

"I was afraid to tell you before," Dakota said. "It makes me look really stupid, but my dad has me blindfolded every time I come here."

"You're kidding. His own son? You must have an idea, though. How many hours did it take you to get here from Oregon?"

"I've never really paid attention."

"Start paying attention," I said. "Let's do this. I wish we could do it before I have to kill someone, though. But, I'll do it if I have to. I knew you'd find a way." I actually planned to escape during the assassination attempt, which would make this option moot, but I needed a backup plan.

I could tell he was getting excited. "I can't believe I found a way."

"I knew you would," I repeated.

"I've been getting the passports, documents, and disguises all together. I can't believe I will get to be with you forever."

"It's wonderful," I said. "It's going to be great." Dakota was only my backup plan. I was counting on getting my messages out to Jeremy. He would pull through and meet me at the hospital.

I sent Dakota away with another letter that said I felt the president's assassination would be happening this month. Sterling and I had exhausted every possibility for failure and had a foolproof plan. I told him the assassination would occur at a little known hospital after a press conference. And that the president would insist on going there and it was a trap. He could save me at the hospital, and I would bring him back to save everyone else, even Dakota.

Dakota told me he only had a quick trip this time and would only be gone two weeks. I hoped to get a letter back in that short time. It would probably be info about my previous letter, but I didn't care.

I continued to work out every day, building up my strength to an even higher degree than a month and a half ago when I'd been whipped. I pushed myself hard, never wanting Sterling, or anyone else for that matter, to be able to overpower me.

I got the coded message to Rakon and the coded letter to the tunnelers. They had doubled their manpower and their efforts to get done in the two-week period of time I gave them. I collected tools from the gardeners. The tunnelers sharpened them for me, and I figured they'd have to do. I planned out every last detail of the mission. It took a lot of coordination. Zoey would play an integral role in making it all happen.

She had recruited Adam to help, too. Rakon filled in a few of his comrades, and we were set to go. The excitement inside me threatened to burst over during the four meetings I had with Sterling during those two weeks. We were about to save everyone. I couldn't wait.

The last piece of the plan fell together only a few days before I was to put everything in motion. On a trip to the bathroom, I discovered ten students in the biology lab working on something. I tried the door. It was open. The smell assaulted me immediately. It was dead-body smell. I covered my nose with my arm and made my way over to the kids. A corpse was on the table, and they were dissecting it.

I dry heaved. I couldn't help it. A boy about six feet tall with glasses and black hair came over to me. The rest continued to work.

"Never seen a cadaver before?"

"Not like that."

"It can be a bit disconcerting at first. Did you need something?"

"I was just wondering what you guys were doing." I dry heaved again.

"Here, let's talk in the hall." He led me out. "I'm Greg, by the way."

I had him follow me to a water fountain. I breathed deeply several times before taking a drink. "Misha. So what are you guys doing in there?"

"We all love medicine and want to be doctors, so Sterling gets us cadavers once a month to learn from."

"Oooh!" I said, lifting my chin high. "I don't think I'll be joining you, but thanks." I held out my hand and shook his, hoping I'd found the right guy. I wiggled my pinkie finger across the palm of his hand three times. His eyes went wide and he gave me the secret handshake back. He grabbed my elbow and led me out into the gardens.

"What do you need? This better be good."

"I need someone to remove my tracker tomorrow morning. I'd rather not have to do it to myself and risk bleeding to death."

Greg stared hard at me then said, "Meet me here at nine. I'll remove it and stitch you up."

"Thank you," I called after him as he disappeared behind the door. A little after nine tomorrow, I would be free.

Chapter 28

I woke early, excited that the escape plans were going to go into effect today. The tunnelers were only five feet from freedom and getting to a post office to mail my letter to Jeremy, the radio guy was sure he could get a message out to Division if I was able to cause the power outage, and Rakon was ready to hack into the main server of the compound and send out an email to Jeremy. One of those things was bound to give us results.

It was also the day Dakota was supposed to return. My tablet beeped and I snatched it up, thinking he was setting up a meet with me. But it was something altogether different.

Today's your day. Rise and shine. Meet me in my dining room in half an hour. Sterling

How could that be? I didn't even know he'd told the president he was going to leak the story. Why hadn't he told me when he had? My heart pounded in anticipation and sadness. I might not be able to cause the power outage we needed now. I had planned to do that part of the mission on my own. I couldn't explain it all to someone in less than thirty minutes. Zoey might have a clue; I'd talked it all out with her over and over. It was a long shot, but maybe it could still work.

Regardless, today was the day I had to escape. Today was the day Jeremy would save me. I smiled, thinking Sterling was about to go down. After six long, tiring, horrible months, not only would I be free, but so would everyone at Sterling's compound whether they wanted it or not.

Nervousness crept in as I showered and dressed. What if something unexpected happened? What if things went wrong like they had early on in this mission? I shoved my doubts and fears away with a prayer. I fell to my knees and begged God to make the right outcome occur. That his favor would shine on me today. I felt the burning in my chest and felt peace. The right thing would happen.

I smiled as I walked to meet up with Sterling. I sat in the seat right next to him at his oval table, and we discussed the mission as we ate bacon and eggs.

"I can't wait to see you in all white, pure and clean." There was a funny tone to his comment.

I hoped he would be having a lucid day. I couldn't have anything go wrong. I smiled at him then continued to eat. I couldn't say anything. My tongue seemed to be caught in my throat. The idea of coming back to this place after the assassination made me sick.

"We'll come back here and have a juicy steak dinner and watch your performance on my many screens. It will be so much fun." He laughed.

I lost my appetite, but forced myself to continue eating. Once we finished, he leaned back in his chair and wove his fingers behind his head.

"I'm assuming you set the trap. I mean you did inform the president that you were going to release the information about the bribes and the testing facility, last week, right?"

"Oh, yes," he said. "Did I not tell you about it? It went exactly as we'd planned it. He acted that same day, sending workers to the testing facility to hide what was really going on there. I'm sure he's trying to tidy up his records and make sure no mention of Harward Pharmaceuticals can be found in any of his paperwork. The thing is, I made copies of the originals. He can run, but he can't hide."

"It would have been nice to have had a heads up," I said, screwing my face up into a scowl.

"Well, Misha, I think I forgot, because plans have changed a little, and I've been busy getting that all set up. Are you ready for the twist?"

"The twist?" My gut tightened. This couldn't be good. He was going to do something crazy.

"Well, Misha, we've discovered that the vice president obtained his post through blackmail. Apparently, he's been hiding another of the President's follies. We can't let someone like that take over for the president, now can we?" He spoke with a condescending tone.

I looked at my hands to hide my mounting terror. Jeremy would most likely be in place to save the president. Who would save the VP?

"In fact, I have you to thank for digging up that dirt on the vice president and the action I took to alleviate the problem."

"Really? Why?" I said, regaining my composure.

"That first day you went to classes and I visited you, you said you wouldn't kill me because there were others that would gladly take my place. I can tell you are just itching to find out what I'm going to do about it."

"Of course I am."

"I'm glad you feel that way. You will be heading up his execution, after all."

"Really?" I said, putting on an excited air while my stomach churned. "Are we making both of them sick at the same time or something?"

"Oh, no," he said. "If the vice president's crime was only greed, we might give him a quick and easy death like the president's, but he has more serious judgment to face. You see, the vice president has secrets of his own. In his public life, he is a glowing example of the noble statesmen, while behind closed doors he beats his wife and children.

"Circumstances could not have been more perfect for orchestrating his own poetic death. He will be speaking at a women's rights banquet in DC, and should be done twenty minutes before the president's scheduled assassination. I took it as a sign. He speaks uplifting words to the public, but beats his own faithful wife in private. The end I have planned for him is fitting: you will catch him in a back room in the hotel and beat him as he has beaten others. Then you will quickly snap his neck."

A terrible, desperate thought took hold of me. I would never get out of here. Jeremy would never be able to find me. I had to focus to keep my shoulders from slumping.

"It's all been arranged. You don't have anything to worry about. Be excited. You look a little glum." He put his hand on my shoulder and squeezed. I was dying to shrug it off, but resisted.

"I'm not glum. Maybe a bit disappointed simply because I had my heart set on being a part of killing the president. But I'll get over it. I guess with the VP I would be the true catalyst for his death. With the president, it would be the chemical that did the killing."

"There you go. I knew you'd make sunshine out of rain once you'd thought it through."

"You're a genius," I said, leaning back in my chair and chuckling. I wanted to throw up.

"He will discover how it feels to be hurt by someone simply because they're stronger and faster."

I clasped my hands together and looked at my firm, strong arms. I had told myself after he whipped me that I would never be in a position to let Sterling get the best of me physically. I had forgotten that he owned me and would use my strength for his purposes, not mine. He had effectively beaten me.

"Then he will die in his despair," Sterling continued. "There will be plenty of witnesses planted who will tell the story to the press when they arrive directly after you leave. Everyone will know that he beat those he should have protected, his wife and children."

"Have you ever ridden a Harley?" he asked.

"Yes," I said.

"Great," he said. "That makes our job easier. We would have gone with plan B if you hadn't. We wouldn't have time today to teach you all you needed to know."

I smiled. "I'm a girl of many talents."

"Indeed you are." A wicked smile spread across his lips.

"You will be replacing the secret service agent who will be at the venue where the VP will be speaking. She is part of the escape plan should something happen to his guards in the southwest corridor that leads to the parking garage.

"Something will happen in that corridor and the VP will run to his agent, you, to save him. In case of danger, the agent is supposed to disguise him as a biker in two minutes, take him down a secret elevator to the bottom level of the parking garage, and ride to safety with him." He chuckled. "In reality, you will have exactly four minutes to beat him up and kill him."

He shook his head, "I know, I know. It's not a lot of time to make this death perfectly poetic, but it will be poetic, nonetheless. At the six-minute mark, every last one of his protection detail will converge on you. That means you need to be out of your disguise as a secret service agent and into a hotel worker's uniform and in the parking garage level one before the six-minute mark. I suggest you kill the VP in less than four minutes. We couldn't seem to extend the time. I sure wish we could have." He tilted his head to the side.

I had dug my fingernails into the back of my hand and it started to sting. I tried to relax and look at the positive. The good thing about the mission was that it was in DC. It was one place I knew like the back of my hand. That was the place where it all had started. It was where I'd witnessed the murder that brought Jeremy and me together and threw me on the path to becoming a spy. The bad thing was that part of my plan involved Jeremy, and I didn't know how far from him I would be.

"How good is the VP at fighting?" I asked. It was the question I should be asking.

"He's good, but not as good as you are. You can watch some video footage of him fighting as we fly to DC. I would like you to snap his neck in the end. That's what he threatens his family with when he hits them."

"How do you know?"

"Spies, girl. Spies."

"Shouldn't we give him a chance to repent?"

"No. He has been judged and sentenced, and now you will execute that sentence, death."

"Alright," I said. "I'm ready."

"Meet back here in three hours. Don't tell anyone of our plans. Not even Zoey."

"No problem." I hated that he knew how close I was to Zoey.

Walking out of the room and down the hall, my mind was whirling. How could I fake breaking someone's neck? Sterling was sure to verify the kill. He videotaped every killing. The VP couldn't have a pulse. That meant he couldn't have a heartbeat. That normally equaled death. What could I do? On TV and in famous plays, the characters were given chemical or natural concoctions that stopped the heart, but didn't kill. Was that available in real life?

I had two choices now. I could go to Greg and have him remove my tracker, or I could get straight to work figuring out how to save the VP. Removing my tracker would certainly make an escape easier. I knew what I had to do. I had to save the VP. I went straight to the chemistry lab and sat at a desk and searched all the information in my brain. I would not be getting my tracker removed. I didn't have time.

My heart burned right after I made the decision, and I knew I was on the right track.

There was nothing that could do both things I needed it to do at once. I needed a chemical or natural substance that number one, paralyzed the person ingesting it, and number two, made their heart stop without killing them. I knew one existed that paralyzed a person. Sterling had used it in the Circus of Feats during the fighting. I'd already asked my chemistry teacher about it a long time ago.

It was number two, stopping the heart without killing, that escaped me. I went to the supply cupboard to look for inspiration.

In my peripheral vision, I saw Mr. Kine enter the room. He walked straight for me. I had to act totally normal and natural when he reached me. I used biofeedback to settle my overactive nerves. When he touched my shoulder and peered down at me, I turned calmly and said, "Hi, Mr. Kine."

"I'm surprised to see you in here right now, Misha. Aren't you supposed to be having breakfast?"

"I ate with Sterling already this morning. I was just trying to figure out a puzzle that's been bugging me forever."

"Do you care to share?"

"Sure," I said, acting like it was nothing. "I was thinking about some of the most famous poisons ever and was wondering if they were real. Take the fairytale, *Sleeping Beauty*, for example. The witch poisons the apple, and the princess sleeps until the prince kisses her awake. I figured if you used hamaliel root, you could induce the sleep and if the prince ate cortiar flower before kissing her, he could wake her."

"Very well done. I haven't thought of that tale in a long time."

"But what about a story like Romeo and Juliette? I can put Juliette to sleep by paralyzing her, but I can't seem to get her heart stopped and keep her alive at the same time."

"This is an interesting concept, isn't it?"

"I'm going to keep searching until I find an answer."

"I don't know that there is an answer to that. I had another student work on this very dilemma last year. He got a chemical to stop the heart, but it was very short lived. The frog's heart started to beat again after only one minute, not long enough to fool anyone."

"How did he make this chemical? Maybe I can improve upon it and make the effects last longer."

"I can't remember. Let me go look it up. I'm sure I have it documented somewhere."

This could be my answer. Was one minute long enough, and did I have time to create the chemical? I only had two hours until we left. Trepidation boiled inside me.

Mr. Kine came back over with a printout only a few minutes later, and I looked it over. It wasn't an extremely difficult concoction, but it was still beyond me.

"Do you feel like helping me with this before class starts?" I smiled really big at him.

"Do you think working on this would be the best use of your time? I mean if you can't even make the initial chemical, how do you expect to improve upon it?"

"The scientific method. That's how."

He grinned and shook his head. "Go get the ingredients from the cupboard, and we can work together until class starts, then you're on your own."

"Great!" I said, standing to go get the stuff.

"Take copious notes if you intend to succeed."

"I will," I called back to him.

We started working at a station that nobody would be using during class.

We were able to finish putting everything together before class started. Now I just had to cook it at the right temperature for the right amount of time. I couldn't let anything distract me. I was in a world all my own. When the bell rang to go to our next class, I had two vials of substance #4bc. I slipped one into the pocket of my jumpsuit and after cleaning everything up, took the other to Mr. Kine and asked him to keep it safe for our next class when I'd try it out on some frogs. I had to hope he didn't know I was leaving on a mission in less than an hour.

"I'm excited to see if you were able to duplicate his experiment," he said. "Tomorrow will be fun."

I sighed loudly. "Yes, it will!" I didn't plan on returning tomorrow, so it would definitely be fun. I just hoped this concoction along with the gh#45 I'd snagged from the cupboard would do the trick with the VP and keep him alive for another day. I wouldn't get the chance to make sure it worked.

As I left, class ended, and I remembered everyone was planning on executing our three-fold mission tonight. I grabbed Zoey by the arm and pulled her out into the hall and then to the girls' bathroom.

"You're going to make me late, Misha. Hurry up, tell me what you need to tell me."

I turned all the water in the sinks on and made sure no one was in the bathroom. "My assassination is today."

She put her hand up to her mouth.

"I need you to make sure all three attempts at getting information out of this place succeed." It dawned on me that I needed to update the messages. I wouldn't bother with the letter, it'd never arrive on time, but the radio transmission and the email could be altered. I pulled out some paper towels. "Do you have a pen?"

"Of course." Zoey always had a pen.

I carefully wrote some coded information onto the paper towel and handed it to Zoey.

"Add this one," I pointed to the words at the top of the paper, "to the email. Then add this one," I pointed to the words at the bottom of the paper, "to the Morse code message. Make sure they do this, or none of our efforts will have mattered."

"Misha, I'm afraid," Zoey said, eyes wild. "I'm not you. I don't know if I can do this."

It was normal to get scared before a mission, especially your first one. I had to reassure her. "Zoey, you are amazing. You made this all possible, not me. You. You can do this. It's like the universe knew you were the one who needed to do it and put everything in place to make that happen. I'm so excited for you. You deserve this."

She nodded her head. "I can do this."

"Yes you can. One more thing. It needs to be done during lunch. It can't wait for tonight."

She stopped nodding.

"You *can* do this. You will be saving so many people. Now, you've got to run to class or you'll be late. Hurry and good luck."

She shoved the paper down the front of her jumpsuit, hugged me hard and then ran out.

I wanted to find Dakota to see if there was any way I could steal his phone really fast and use it just in case Zoey wasn't able to pull through. I searched everywhere I could think of. I couldn't find him.

I finally found him in the east gardens behind some tall hedges. "Oh Dakota," I said, running to him. "I'm leaving in a few minutes for my first mission. I'm so scared. I don't want this man's death on my conscience for the rest of my life."

He stroked my hair and said, "It'll be alright. My dad wants me to go with. He doesn't want me to miss this one. I don't know why, but I'm so glad I'll be there for you."

My heart leapt. Maybe we could get out together.

"You can pull on my strength. I know you can do this. You'll be okay. Just think about me and how we'll be together after this. I've worked everything out. We'll be free in less than a week."

"What if he's not guilty, and I kill him? I won't be able to live with myself."

"Remember," he said. "This will bring us one step closer to being together. You only need to be successful with this."

I could feel the cell phone in his pocket. How could I get my hands on it? Before I could even plan to steal it, the phone vibrated. He took it out and answered it. "Yes, sir. I'm on my way now."

My tablet beeped. It was time. I wouldn't be able to get a message out to Jeremy. I said a fervent prayer that Zoey and the gang would be successful.

Chapter 29

In Sterling's dining hall, I found hotel worker clothes laid out for me. I took them to the bathroom off the side of the room and changed. It felt good to be in something other than the jumpsuit. My heart was pounding so hard, I thought it might break my ribs.

I hoped I wouldn't be blindfolded when we left the compound, but I was. Sterling also put headphones on me that made it impossible to hear a word anyone said in the helicopter. This helicopter was different from the ones I'd been in before. The rotors were already moving when we got in, but I could barely hear them, they were so quiet. I inhaled deeply, willing my heart to slow. I would have to settle for keeping the time it took us to travel to DC as my clue to where the compound was.

After about half an hour, Sterling took off my blindfold and gave me a tablet to watch the VP fight in various dojos. He was good, but not nearly as good as I was. He was slower than I, age and weight taking their toll, but it was easy to see he loved it. It had been a good hobby for him.

Sterling put a dagger in a sheath and strapped it to my leg. He lifted my silencing earphones and said, "I'm sure you won't need this, but just in case he gets the better of you, slit his throat."

"If you're so sure, why give it to me?"

"That's assassination 101, Misha, always have at least one backup plan, preferably two. If I'd have doubted you, I'd have provided two backups." He let the earphones flop back against my ears. The knife at my ankle called to me, but I would be patient.

Before I knew it, we'd landed on a professional building. It had taken us exactly two hours to get there. Apparently, Sterling owned the building because everyone treated him with the utmost courtesy and respect as we exited through the lobby. Six of us made our way to a building three blocks away. We all climbed into a big van in front of it. A com was placed in my ear. I would be able to hear them, but they wouldn't be able to hear me until I was in the room the VP would be heading for. Sterling showed me the section of the hotel I'd be in on a TV monitor. It was real time. I watched as the woman I'd be impersonating suddenly fell to the floor. He must have gassed her.

"It's time for you to go."

Security had blocked off all the entrances and locked the doors leading from the building to the garage and disabled all the elevators except the ones the VP would be using.

I entered from the hotel garage. The fake ID Sterling had given me got me through the first checkpoint as I passed into the garage. It also got me up a service elevator that led to the room with the gassed secret service agent. Once on the right floor and out of the elevator, I was home free. The agent outside the elevator was owned by Sterling, and he led me to the correct room. It was eerily quiet. I quickly peeled the clothes from the agent and put them on. I hid her behind a desk in the small room.

Just as predicted, a few minutes later, the VP came running into the room I was in, hysterical.

"Help me. They've killed the others. Get me out of here."

"Stay calm, Mr. Vice President," I said in a soothing tone. "You need to remove your clothes as quickly as possible and put these on." I pointed to some biker clothes hanging from a hook on the wall. "Be quick, we've only got four minutes."

Just as he started to undress, I took him out with a swift kick to his calves. He hit the floor hard. I pounced on him, putting him in a headlock and whispering in his ear so that the cameras and mics couldn't hear me. "If you want to live, take this, it will save you." I shoved the liquids far back in his mouth, and he gagged. He didn't want to listen. I held his mouth shut until I felt him swallow. My body was arched over his head so that the cameras couldn't see.

"Fight me now." I whispered. I'm sure he didn't need me to tell him that; he didn't trust me, but I couldn't risk him saying anything about the chemical I'd just given him. I let him push me off of him, and we both stood and fought. I hit him hard in the mouth when he started to speak, and I spoke over him. "Mr. Vice President, you have been found guilty of lawlessness. You have repeatedly beaten your wife and children, and for that you receive the death penalty." Fear flashed in his eyes. I wasn't sure if it was from knowing he'd been found out or if it was because he thought he was about to die.

From the notes I'd read from the student who had created the chemical, it took a little over one minute to stop the heart. The gh#45 induced paralysis around one and a half minutes. I hope my modifications had been effective. They had to coincide today.

He had a hard punch, but I had a harder one. One minute doesn't seem like a long time until you have to count it down. Since I was being filmed, I'd have to make his death look completely real. He hit me firm in the kidney, and I returned the favor. He stumbled back, leaning stiff to the side. Forty-five seconds left. I kicked him hard several times. He gasped and sputtered each time my kicks and punches hit their mark, blood dripped down his face and off his chin. Twenty seconds.

"Please. Please," he pleaded. "I'll give you anything you want."

I would play this up for Sterling. "You have nothing I want. Prepare to die."

Then I heard Sterling's voice over my com, "Take him. Stop playing."

I needed to *play* for another fifteen seconds, so after a few well placed punches, I brought him to the ground with a roundhouse kick and put him in a headlock, his face kissing the cement floor. I whispered in his ear, "I'm sorry about this, but I hope I'm saving your life."

As soon as I felt his body go limp, I pretended to break his neck with a sudden, quick, fake jerk. By moving my arms wildly it would appear I had jerked hard enough to break his neck. I stood and looked down at him, hoping I hadn't just killed him with my chemical concoction, but hoping his heart had stopped all the same.

"Check him," Sterling said over the com. As I bent to do just that, two men appeared, one of them was the guard that had led me here. They checked the Vice President's pulse. Our small window of opportunity had played to my advantage. Since I had to hurry and get out of there, Sterling would never know he wasn't actually dead.

"No pulse, sir," one said.

"Good job, everyone," Sterling said. "Get out here, Misha. We have a date with the president." I could imagine the wicked smile on his lips.

In record speed, I changed into a new disguise I found hanging in the room and went back out the way I'd come. When I reached the garage, the agent checked my ID with an electronic scanner and then sent me to the next checkpoint. Once again, they checked me, but quickly this time. They seemed rushed, like they were expecting someone. Could it have been the VP? They wanted me out of there and quick. I obliged.

There was a heightened sense of alarm outside. Cars trapped in traffic were honking and people on the sidewalks were yelling at the cars to stop honking. Some of Sterling's cronies and I pushed our way through the crowds back to the building where we'd landed the helicopter. My spidey senses were out of control. Danger surrounded me. I heard whispers that the president was sick from several people we passed. We used the elevators to climb to the top of Sterling's building, where Sterling and Dakota waited. Once I got there, Sterling grabbed some binoculars from inside the helicopter and handed a pair each to Dakota and me. The pilot and a guard stood near the helicopter.

All the buildings in the area went dark, and chaos reigned. What was Sterling doing? Weren't we going to the assassination point? If we didn't, I wouldn't be able to escape as I'd planned. Sterling walked right up to the edge of the building, a three-foot-high wall protecting us from falling off, and we looked out over total mayhem in the streets. For miles and miles in all directions, no car moved. Streetlights and buildings were mostly dark.

"The hospital you are looking for is to our right and down five blocks." He giggled with glee.

Heat raced through my body. I heard one solitary beep, and I started.

"A bit jumpy are we, Misha?" Sterling said.

"I guess I am a bit," I said, trying to sound totally calm.

"Have you found it yet?"

"Not yet." I couldn't tear my eyes away from the massive confusion below us. I forced myself to look beyond the five blocks to the hospital where the president was supposed to be having a futile fight for his life. Had Jeremy or Division received my messages? Were they in the hospital saving the president right then? They had to be. They just had to.

The squat hospital building stood on a corner. Cars lined the streets around it, unmoving, a new parking lot created. People seemed to all be out of their cars. General looks of confusion, anger, and worry sat on the people's faces. No smiles could be found. More and more people flooded into the area, and the white limos parked just outside the hospital blazed in the sun and stuck out like a sore thumb. The president's conveyance was made unusable by the man standing next to me. No chauffeurs sat in the driver's seats. The plan—my plan—was working perfectly. Had Sterling won?

I could imagine the terror the physician must have felt as options for finding help for the president fell by the wayside, one by one, and the utter frustration that must have covered him when unable to go to another hospital. He must have felt horror when he discovered that this hospital absolutely did not have the means to help him save the president.

I imagined the chaos that must have filled the minds of the president's body guards as their escape routes came up blocked at every turn and the despair they must have felt in knowing they couldn't get him where he needed to go, nor could they inform headquarters because they had no ability to communicate. All communications for blocks were down. Not even cell phones worked. How their minds must have churned, looking for a solution.

"What room is he in?" I asked, in a calm voice. "Is the window open so we can witness it or something?"

"No, no, my dear. The president is already dead. That's what the beep you just heard signaled. We're waiting for the fireworks."

"He's already dead?" I whispered. A shiver started in my spine and fanned out. Division was supposed to save him. Had they failed?

"I think we're already witnessing those right now," I said, looking at the general bedlam outside the hospital. I imagined the faces of the physician as the president flat-lined. I imagined the hungry photographers, press, and public all clamoring for pictures and information.

"Just wait. It seems the 'hospital' was doing some illegal human testing of a drug that was unstable. They got a large shipment of it yesterday. Unfortunately, the system that makes it stable just lost power."

Time seemed to stop. My heart fell out of my chest, and a scream I couldn't voice blocked my throat.

"Yes," he said. "The hospital is about to go up in a huge ball of fire."

"I thought these were targeted hits," I croaked out.

"They were. But you know how much I like a good show of color. Just look at that building, Misha. It's grey. I couldn't leave it there. Besides, I love the bright colors of a great explosion. Of course, the media will try to blame the explosion on terrorists. I can't wait to hear the shocking news that no terrorism was involved, that it was simply unstable, illegal drugs that caused the explosion. The news flash will be that a double whammy has hit the *now dead* president's plan for re-election. It received its death blow, just like the president." He laughed loud and long.

"Don't say that," I screamed, my body hot with anxiety. "You can't be serious. They will all die if you blow up that building. Innocents along with the guilty. You have to stop this." I could hardly breathe.

"They don't know they're about to die. It will be quick, painless, I think. Besides, we really needed to drive home the fact that the good ole president was on the take for dangerous drugs. That way, the pharmaceutical company will also be destroyed. We will have gone a long way to combat man's greed and lawlessness today."

"But the innocents," I cried.

"We have a righteous cause here. If they're truly innocent they will find themselves with God, will they not?"

With that, the building blew. I screamed a scream no one could hear. Dakota pushed the side of his body to mine, and his hand quickly pressed mine and let go.

Sterling leaned over to me and whispered in my ear, "I'm really sorry about Jeremy." An awful smile twisted his face.

My whole body shook. My heart all but stopped.

"You–you knew about Jeremy?" I gasped out. He continued to smile, self-satisfied. This man was pure and total evil. Something clicked in my brain. "This isn't about the president or the pharmaceutical company at all!" I shouted at him. "You *planned* this all to kill Jeremy, and you killed thousands of people all to have the satisfaction of beating me. You are just as bad as any of your targets–you're a liar and a coward."

Sterling threw his head back and laughed a maniacal, crowing laugh that chilled me to the bone. I had to stop him. Without a moment's hesitation or any further thought, I reached for the unused dagger he placed on my ankle. It felt cold to the touch, my hand hot with rage. I lifted to strike, but Dakota caught my hand. I whirled to face him, my mouth hanging open in shock as he freed me of the dagger. He moved to stand beside his father, a resigned look on his face. I threw my arms out to my sides and screamed. I wanted to punch his lights out, but my body wouldn't work the way I wanted it to.

Sterling put his arm around his son. "I warned Dakota to be on the lookout for you. He's a good little soldier, isn't he? I'm sorry you couldn't save your little FBI friend. You did this to yourself. You need to take responsibility for your actions. Stealing Dakota's phone to give away our plan? That disloyalty had to be punished, and your punishment hasn't come to an end. You will never experience peace in your life again. You will be my very own little soldier. But you know what? I'm sure you will love it. I'll fill your life with one adrenaline rush after the other. One interesting kill after ano–"

Sterling lurched forward and gasped.

I looked at Dakota: he held the dagger, dripping with blood now, in front of him, staring at it. Sterling fell to his knees, blood poured out of a wound to his chest.

"Dakota," his father said. "A sword, boy. A sword. You should have used a sword. Then they could say, *He lived by the sword and died by the sword.* It's all about poetry, son." Blood gushed from his mouth now. "Don't let my legacy die with me," he sputtered. "A world without smut. A world without lawlessness. A world without indecision. A world without greed." He said no more, neither did he move again.

The dagger fell from Dakota's hand and clattered on the cement rooftop. Our eyes met, and sorrow and relief engulfed me. His whole body sagged, an indication that he'd felt it too. I moved to him and took his hand.

Chapter 30

Not a second later, my neck hair stood on end, my spidey senses raging. I tucked what had just happened away and focused on my surroundings. Two people were almost upon us. It had to be the guard and the pilot. I adjusted my stance and before finally letting go of Dakota's hand, I threw a kick behind me and struck the guard hard on the chest. While he stumbled back, I let go of a shocked Dakota and slugged the pilot, a sweet uppercut to the front of his chin and then threw a smashing jab to his kidneys as he flew back, turning as he went. The disoriented guard staggered toward me. I hit him hard in the face, and then swept his feet out from under him. I jumped on him, grabbing the handcuffs at his side and locking one on his left wrist.

The pilot sailed toward me and after a back kick to his groin; I cuffed him to the guard. After relieving them of their cells, radios and other paraphernalia, which I threw off the back of the building, I took a rope from the chopper and tied them to the metal landing gear. To slow them down even more, I elbowed each in the face, knocking them out.

"Come on, Dakota," I said, holding out my hand. "Let's go." He obeyed numbly.

Turning our backs on Sterling, we walked silently to the elevator, probably the only one working in a five-mile radius. Sterling had protected his own building from the blackout with a generator, of course.

Once out on the street, we smashed into the chaos. There was no way around it. We'd have to go through it. Dakota acted as my personal security guard the first three blocks, having to get very physical when creating a path for us, which I thought was touching, considering what he'd just seen me do. It was slow and very claustrophobic. He finally opted to take me through the streets. No cars were moving any time soon anyway. The closer we got to the scene of the crime, the quieter it became. I thought it would be the opposite.

It had been almost an hour since the building exploded, and I couldn't believe my eyes and ears. There was a palpable almost silence. The silence that you often feel walking into a church. People whispered and moved about carefully, quietly. I wondered if the solemnity was because the president had died or if it would have been the same if it had blown with only everyday people in it. Every person deserved such reverence. Maybe the feeling was more like a funeral or graveyard. The respect was incredible. I'd never seen anything like it.

Every building within one block of the explosion had damage. Windows blown out, jagged pieces of cement and wood strewn all over the place, cars tipped over, and glass and debris blanketing the streets, but people were calm, helpful. Injured people lay on blankets in rows on the street. A police perimeter had been set around the area, but volunteers freely moved in and around it.

From what I could tell, each person had someone next to him or her offering comfort. I watched a woman come out of her apartment carrying blankets and adding them to the stack that was already there. A pile of first aid kits sat next to the blankets, and water bottles were stacked next to them. The people who lived in the neighborhood had stepped up and made the best of a terrible situation. Decent human beings.

A man walked in front of the crowd and said, "We still need more men to carry the wounded to the hospital." A murmur rose in the crowd; it steadily grew the further away into the crowd it went and several people came forward.

Despite the fact that I wanted to sit down and bawl my eyes out, looking at the gaping hole in the ground that was once the hospital, I stepped forward. "I can help."

Dakota stepped forward, too. "So can I. We'll work together."

We were directed to a Red Cross worker. The Red Cross had tagged the people according to severity of injury. Because of the complete inability for traffic to move, people had to carry the injured five blocks to a line of ambulances waiting to transport them to the next closest hospital. As we carried a lady who had a jagged piece of wood sticking out of her leg, I noticed lights started to pop up in buildings and electric signs flashed on. The traffic lights started working again, too. The power company must have figured out a way to restore power. That was good news. I hoped communication was also working.

I pushed myself forward, believing completely and totally that by serving others our own problems and despair would disappear. When we arrived at the ambulance, and after we delivered our cargo, some nice volunteers with the Red Cross handed us water bottles. The first swallow burned as it went down, my throat was so dry. I finished the bottle on the next swallow.

"Let's go back," I said to Dakota. "They need more help." I knew if I stopped, grief and pain would overtake me, and I'd be completely useless.

"Sounds good," he said. "Just give me a minute." He bent over to tie his shoe and when he did, I couldn't believe what I saw. It was Jeremy–coming out from behind an ambulance. His arm was bound in a sling, and he was limping. He was alive. Fireworks exploded in my gut.

I thought my heart would burst on seeing him, but I was frozen in fear that he wasn't real, an apparition, a ghost come to haunt me. He was dead, and it was my fault. He blew up in that hospital because I told him I'd be there, and he went there to save me.

He turned just right and our eyes met. Apparently he was real because he screamed, "Christy!"

I tried to shout back, but it came out as a croak. All my doubts, all my concerns flew out the window. Jeremy was alive.

He came to me because I was frozen to the spot. I felt Dakota move off to the side, giving us room. After Jeremy hugged me soundly, he whispered in my ear, "How? Why?" He pushed back, his hands held my upper arms searching my face. My tears wouldn't stop falling, and I noticed his face was wet with tears, too.

"I thought you blew up in that building," I cried.

"I thought you were gone, back with that madman," he whispered.

My eyes searched every inch of his face.

"Not here," he said, looking around us and then guiding me to a large white van and helping me in. "How are you here?" he asked once we were inside the van. "What happened?"

"Sterling changed the plan on me this morning, and—"

"I know. I got the messages."

"They worked? Both of them?" I gaped.

"I don't know how you did it, but because of you, the president and most of the workers in that hospital are safe."

"What? But how—?"

"We got your messages in time, and I just had this feeling it wouldn't be enough just to get the president and his entourage out of there. So I started an evacuation. The president didn't know what was going on, but he was shuttled out of the hospital shortly after arriving and taken to a helicopter landing pad and flown to Maryland to Walter Reed for treatment. He's not out of the woods, yet, but the doctors are optimistic. We easily discovered the agent who was the traitor and forced him to signal Sterling that the assassination was successful. And here you are."

"Sterling had me kill the vice president—"

"You killed the vice president?" He gasped, reaching for his phone.

I reached out to stop him from calling whomever it was he thought he was going to call.

"Hear me out first. I tried to get Dakota's phone to tell you, but I couldn't. I was supposed to kill the VP—"

"You had access to Dakota's phone?"

"Didn't you get a text from me?"

"Never."

"That's probably how Sterling found out about you."

"He knew about me?"

"He knew I was talking to someone on the outside named Jeremy, and I think, no I'm sure, he orchestrated me being with the VP so that you would all die. He thought you worked for the FBI." I sucked in a deep breath.

"But you didn't kill the VP?"

"No. I poisoned him instead, making him appear dead. At least, I hope the poisons didn't kill him. I didn't get to test them before I gave them to him. Theoretically, he should still be alive. Sterling engineered it so that a ton of press would be on hand to get the story, so it's probably already all over the news."

He moved up to the front of the van and switched on the radio. The news of the attempted assassinations of the president and the vice president was all over the radio. He had lived. I sighed deeply. All sorts of speculation whizzed around. Everyone wanted to guess at what was going on, including the idea that terrorists had done it.

"I looked everywhere for you, but you weren't there." He moved next to me again. "You're real. I can't believe it. When I couldn't find you in the hospital, I figured he was making you watch from a different location, and I left the hospital to find you. That's what saved me. When the hospital blew, I thought I'd lost you forever, that I'd been wrong and you were somewhere inside." He touched my face.

I felt a pull, a draw, to move toward him. I wanted to feel his lips on mine and let him comfort me. For an instant, I thought he felt the same pull. The moment passed as quickly as it had come. I was letting my emotions run away from me. I had to take control or I'd do something I regretted. *I'm a spy. He's my handler.* I had to be professional. I let the flush that had overtaken me rush away. Jeremy seemed to feel the moment disappear, too, and sat up straight. He punched some things into his phone and then said, "Division's on their way for Dakota."

"Dakota is Sterling's son." I looked out the window in Dakota's direction. He stood on the sidewalk looking around like a lost puppy dog.

"What?" Jeremy looked, too.

"Dakota is Sterling's son. He killed his dad to save me. You've got to protect him."

"Christy, he's done horrible things. We can't just let him off the hook. He's going to prison. I'll put in a good word for him and do everything I can to make his sentence lighter, but he will spend time in jail."

"But he saved me. His dad forced him to do everything. He put himself in total danger for me. I'm here because of him. I owe my freedom and my life to him."

"I understand that. But you have to understand that he must be turned over to the authorities. He has to pay for his crimes." He pulled out his cell phone and texted. A few seconds later, he looked back at his phone and said, "We need the intel on the compound that he can give us. What I really want to know is how he was able to disappear when we were tailing him. We even bugged him, and he'd slip through our fingers. It was the craziest thing. We couldn't track him. He seriously disappeared into thin air.

"We couldn't believe it when you got that first letter to us. We figured if we couldn't get him to take us to you, we'd try and get him to take information to you. As you know, he took the bait."

"I cried and cried when I got that first letter from you." I shifted in my seat.

"You did a great job in persuading him to do that. I'm sure it was at great peril to both of you." He nodded his head.

"It was awful having to pretend with him." It felt even more awful knowing my feelings for him were partially real.

"You are a great spy. You do what you have to do and more."

"Are Agents Wood and Penrod here?"

"Yes. Well, not here, but at the building Dakota will be going to." He frowned. "They were supposed to go with you to the Callahan Mountains. They said you left before they were ready. Is that true? And why didn't you get your tracker replaced?"

I shook my head. "I was going to do it at lunch, but that's when Frankie got me and we headed for the mountains. I texted Wood and Penrod, but figured they'd have a hard time catching up with us. Did they ever make it?"

"Yes. But, they said they had no clue where you would be climbing, and your tracker wasn't working. They found the van, only after you'd been taken. They're lucky you corroborated the story. I was going to get them fired. You'll have to write up a report."

"No problem."

He looked at his phone. He must've received a text. "Division is ten minutes off. Let's go talk to Dakota."

I grabbed his arm as he reached for the door handle. "Those kids, in the compound, they need major help."

"About how many are there?"

"A good 200 in the training center and maybe the same amount in another building. About half of those have Stockholm syndrome. They love Sterling and won't go without a fight. Don't underestimate them because they're young. They're trained assassins, and they're well trained at that. They all need major counseling."

"We'll see to it. That's a lot of kids."

"I know. It was scary. And he has other facilities somewhere."

"Are you kidding me? Hopefully, this facility will lead us to his others." He texted someone.

"We should go out to Dakota and let him know they're coming for him," I said. "He's going to have a hard time."

"Yes he will. How's this going to end with Dakota?" Jeremy kept his eyes trained on me.

"I don't know. Help me."

"You are going to go out there and say goodbye." Jeremy looked at me, a deep sympathy in his eyes.

I sighed. "I hate this."

"I know. But I have faith in you that you will find a way to separate your feelings from your missions."

"You have to admit, I did better this time."

"That's true. But you can do better still." Did I detect a hint of jealousy in his tone?

We climbed out of the van and made our way to Dakota. He watched us walk up. Jeremy stopped walking with me when we got within about ten feet.

"Dakota," I said as I reached him. "They're coming to take you into custody."

"I had a feeling." He ran his fingers through his hair.

"Jeremy and I are going to speak for you so that you get a lighter sentence. It wasn't all your fault."

"No, but when I got old enough, I should have turned him in. It was wrong of me to do what I did. I never should have helped him. I deserve to be punished."

"But you've been punished your whole life. You need to fight to get your life back and then do good once you get it."

"I don't even know who I want to be anymore. I'm lost."

Dakota leaned into me, his chin resting on my shoulder, his face nestled in my hair. "I'm lost without you." I held him tight.

He pulled back. "Are you a spy then, sent to bring my dad down?" Resignation filled his voice. His shoulders slumped.

I wanted to die rather than tell him what I had to tell him, but I had to make sure he understood where I stood. "Yes," I said, looking at him straight in the eye.

"It was all an act then?" His chin was angled down, his eyes at me.

"Not all of it, but most." I shifted my weight from one foot to the other, heat rushing through me. In his case, most of it was real, but I couldn't tell him that.

"I should have known. You were too perfect."

"Don't become jaded toward love because of me. You're easy to love. After you get out of prison, you'll find love again. Be open to it. You'll find someone better than me."

Division agents arrived, and following Jeremy's directions, they handcuffed Dakota. I grabbed him into a big hug. I wanted to rip his handcuffs off him so that he could hug me properly. Then he sobbed. His chest heaved, rocking us gently. There was nothing worse than seeing a grown man cry from sadness. He had lost everything. The only family he had, me, and all his connections.

They pulled us apart, and after we took one last long look at each other, they led him away to the car that would take him to jail.

Chapter 31

Jeremy stood with a group of three others, throwing his hands out while he spoke. I walked cautiously in his direction, not wanting to interfere. When he saw me out of the corner of his eye, he waved me over, still talking to the others. I took that as a green light. Once I reached him, he said, “Well, I’ll catch you all later.” He turned from them and led me back to the van.

“Division is setting up the mission to free the compound early in the morning. We need your take on the area. Dakota is telling them everything he knows, too. You’re coming along. You need to see these kids go free.”

My heart burned with excitement. To see that compound fall would be the best thing to ever happen.

We climbed into the van and drove away.

“You know some won’t want to be freed.” My insides twisted.

“That’s how it often is in cases with kidnappings.”

“At least half really love him. You’ll need an army of restraints to hold them back. They are trained assassins, vicious, brutal killers with skills. Don’t underestimate them because they’re young.

"Three Avengers are at the training school, and four are wherever they keep the support staff. It's made up of kids who didn't make the cut to be assassins.

"Houston will be your hardest to subdue of the three Avengers at the training school. Frankie and Duncan are just confused.

"I'm sure Dakota knows more about the compound than I do, but I'll tell you everything I know."

As we drove, I told him all about the security of the compound and the layout and how important I figured it would be to cut the power, including the generators. Just outside the city, he pulled into a docking station at a big warehouse. Men opened the back doors, and then we climbed through them into what turned out to be a satellite building for Division.

We went into a big room with about fifty agents, and we all created a plan for ambushing Sterling's compound with the least amount of casualties. Dakota was conferenced in. He couldn't hear us, but we could hear him. A man sat next to him with a headset and when we needed some info, he would ask Dakota.

It shocked me to find that Dakota had lied. He hadn't been blindfolded when he came to the compound. He knew exactly where it was.

He told the man who asked him the questions, "Tell Misha I'm sorry I lied. I just didn't want her escaping without me."

A bit of anger fired in me. Jeremy could have found me several months earlier had Dakota not lied. The people who died in that explosion would also be alive, but then I remembered Dakota's hug, his sobbing, and I let it go.

He gave them a detailed survey of the compound. He didn't know about the guards, but I did. Between what I had found out myself and what the subversives had given me, we were able to knock out a pretty accurate picture of the compound and the security that was involved. I made sure they knew about the neckbands and re-voiced the concern that a majority of the kids would be protective of the compound and Sterling. They would need to be prepared to fight.

The plan shaped itself beautifully as the team discussed possibilities. We were going to go in like a SWAT team and take out all the outer security first. Next, using stealth, we would use Dakota's codes to get into the computer control room and take over that part of the operation. From there, at four in the morning, the agents would cuff the hands and feet of every person in the compound and gag them, leaving them in their own rooms. After that half hour, the captives would be taken out to the baseball field in two to three waves. Once they were all out on the baseball field, they would be sorted. I would help with the sorting. The Blackie compound would then be raided, and those kids would also be cuffed and gagged.

At that point, medical personnel would be on hand to evaluate the kids and sort them again according to how much help they needed. I wondered if some would ever recover.

The plan went down smoothly. Snipers took out all the guards in the towers and the ones roaming about the compound. A team of eight men then raided the control center and opened several gates that were built into the walls. Jeremy and I arrived with a helicopter just as the prisoners were being taken out to the field.

I helped sort those I knew would be problems from those I knew would not. As I walked down the rows, several boys and girls called me traitor while others yelled, "Thank you, God bless you, you saved us." They cried, sobbed, and ached to escape this place. My heart hurt looking out over the several hundred kids on the field. Their families would finally find out what happened to them. I imagined some reunions would be joyful, while others wouldn't. For some of these kids, this had been the one place they had felt acceptance and love. Most of these kids would be in therapy their whole lives and many would never get to leave government custody because their brainwashing was too complete. There were many that I didn't know where their allegiance lay. Frankie and Duncan were two of those people.

When I came upon Zoey, my heart about jumped out of my chest. I swept her up into a hug, holding her tight. She couldn't hug me back, but I didn't care.

"I knew you were the one to save us," she choked out. "I just knew it."

"I don't know how you managed it, but both the email and the radio transmission met their mark. Hundreds, including the president, were saved because of you. You were incredible."

"So, you really didn't believe I could do it?"

"Let's just say I hoped above all hope you would." I looked at her for approval.

She laughed. "I know what you're saying. I was so worried about you. I'm so glad you're safe."

"I'm so glad *you're* safe."

I called a guard over. "She's safe. You can uncuff her."

"Sorry. No one from those buildings that are on this field can be trusted, no matter what you think."

"Can I at least help her to the subversive section."

"Sure," he said, moving on.

We ran into Frankie on our way. I looked at her, pain filling me.

"You were the one, all along."

I gave her a half smile and shifted my weight.

"I'm sorry I believed anything Sterling said. I'm an idiot."

"No you're not," I said. "Sterling was a genius. He had you where he wanted you."

"I'm sorry I was so cruel to you after...you know." Her face screwed up in pain.

"You had every right to be. I'm sorry that happened to you." I meant it, too.

"I know now it was Sterling that did it, not you."

I hugged her and then got a guard to help me move both of them to the subversives' area. I was pleased to see Duncan, Lunden, Maddie, and Anna already there. I smiled at them and they smiled back.

I watched as the three distinct groups took shape: the subversives–those against Sterling, the advocates–those who were for Sterling, and those that were hard to classify, like the Blackies.

I found Jeremy, standing at the edge of the diamond, his arms crossed looking over the field of Sterling's madness.

"Look at what you've done," he said as I approached. "You saved all these people." His head swayed side to side then looked at me. "We've done all we can here. It's time to go. The chopper is waiting for us."

My whole body ached with sadness for Sterling's kids. I asked God to send them a million blessings so they could heal.

The sun shone hard on the baseball field now and the agents had started leading groups of kids to waiting busses to be transported somewhere they could be thoroughly evaluated and hopefully helped.

"It's unbelievable, isn't it?" I said, looking at the many faces on the field. "That one man could ruin so many lives."

"Isn't it unbelievable," Jeremy said, "That one girl could save so many lives?"

I turned to look at him. The smile on his face was somewhat grim.

"What we have to do as spies seems so horrible until you see something like this." I frowned. "I didn't think I'd ever come out of there, Jeremy. To my shame, I had given up. I even gave up on God for a while."

"That's understandable. You just experienced something no one should ever experience."

"I lost my faith, something I thought I would never do."

"But you found it again," he said. "We all struggle at times in our lives. It's good that you rallied. As long as you always rally, you'll be fine. Just don't accept such dangerous missions from now on. Take it easy. You've shown everyone you're worthy—now you can let others take missions like these."

I looked back over the field. "You know I can't promise that. It seems the scarier the case, the greater the impact I can have. I know I'm supposed to be a spy. I don't want to be any ordinary spy. I want to be the best. While my mind is telling me to quit, my heart, soul, and spirit are telling me I'm doing exactly what I should be doing."

He nodded, his mouth forming a smile. I had a hard time looking away from his lips. I wanted mine to be pressed to his, but that couldn't be. He was my handler.

"Someone told me once I was destined to save the world. And while I don't know I believe that, I do know the only way it might happen is one mission at a time."

Jeremy put his arm around my shoulders, and I closed my eyes, enjoying the tingle it sent through my body. I put my arm around his waist, pulling him in tight, and we headed for the chopper to get ready for our next mission together. I was the luckiest girl alive.

Acknowledgements

When people say it takes an army to get a book published, they aren't kidding. Every one of the people listed below played a role in making this book amazing.

A huge thanks to you all!

Jenny, Angela, Susan, and Cindy for loving my wacko villain. Shelly, Rebecca, Karyn, and Kathleen for keeping me on track.

My sniper information guru–Keltsey Waire. My good friend, Kirk Godfrey for the information about trains and train yards.

My FBI agent friends for keeping me on track with spy stuff. Bill, for making sure police procedure is accurate.

My editor–Charity West for keeping everything straight. My formatter–Heather Justesen for making the book look awesome.

My model–Madeline Coombs and her fabulous grandparents who introduced us. My cover designer, Steven Novak for making my covers irresistible, and Rachel Hert for her great advice on blurbs. And most of all to my fans who keep me excited to get out the next book. Thanks for all the emails.

Visit Cindy on her blog:
cindymhogan.com

For series trivia, sneak peeks, events in your area, contests, fun fan interaction, like the Watched Facebook Page:
Watched-the book

Follow Cindy M. Hogan on twitter:
Watched1

If you loved this book,
Jump into the exciting adventures of the *Watched* trilogy: *Watched, Protected, Created.*
Immerse yourself in a great mystery with *Gravediggers.*
Laugh and cry with Brooklyn in *Confessions of a 16-Year-Old Virgin Lips.*

ABOUT THE AUTHOR

Cindy M. Hogan is the author of the best-selling Watched trilogy. She graduated in secondary education at BYU and enjoys spending time with unpredictable teenagers. More than anything, she loves the time she has with her own teenager daughters and wishes she could freeze them at this fun age. If she's not reading or writing, you'll find her snuggled up to her awesome husband watching a great movie or planning their next party.

To learn more about the author and the books she has written, visit her at cindymhogan.com or on Facebook at watched-the book.